I0555561

Finding Lucas

A NOVEL

Samantha Stroh Bailey

Copyright Page

For my family

CHAPTER ONE

"Uh, ooh, hhh, uhhh, I'm going to come!"

I'm not, but really, that's great for you. I want to ask him what about me, but Derek, my boyfriend and live-in-lover of the past five years, has already jumped off me and headed straight for the shower. Like he always does as if being inside me has somehow dirtied him. But there was a time, so many years ago now, when Derek used to make me come just by sucking on my bottom lip, and I touch my finger to the mouth he didn't even kiss today.

I hear the whoosh of the water spraying, and I stand up to smush my face against the window of our hotel room in Montreal, where we're celebrating (I use that word loosely) our fifth anniversary. Instead of roaring fireplaces and dimly lit romance, we ate our dinners at expensive fishbowl-style restaurants, where being seen is more important than the meal itself, and every patron is illuminated by the glare of fluorescent lights bouncing off snow white walls just to get the best exposure. Anniversary, my ass.

Mont-Royal rises majestically towards the brilliant blue summer sky, and I see a crowd of people lazing around on the dewy morning grass, holding bongos, blankets and picnic baskets and wish I were there instead of here. Here being a five star, luxurious palace, $400.00 a night for the sole pleasure of three hundred thread count sheets, fresh-cut flowers in our room every day and crystal glasses to rinse out our designer toothpaste. I'd be happy on an air mattress under the stars. Well okay, not directly under them, but maybe looking at them from a cottage window. But suggesting a weekend at a cottage to Derek would be like asking him to swim in pee.

I turn away from the window, crawl back into bed (after

5

jumping up and hopping on because the bed is a foot off the floor as they usually are in the top hotels) and pull the crisp white sheet over my breasts. I burrow under the covers and wonder how the chain-smoking man I met at a seedy Chicago bar, who wanted to travel the world with just his passport and a pair of jeans, turned into the quintessential metrosexual.

Five years is a lot of relationship for a woman who isn't exactly the kind of person men chase after. I do the best with what I've got: average height (5'4), average weight (well, some parts are average, and others, are well, a tad round or a tad flat) and average hair (requiring some maintenance, like washing and combing). And I'm willing to put in a little work, but I've never been one to spend all day preening in front of the mirror or prancing around for a simpering salesperson to tell me I look fantastic when I know I don't. I'd rather be watching television.

And Derek used to like that I was natural, that I wasn't like the snooty, prissy things he used to date in high school (private school, naturally) or the polished "It" girls his mother encouraged him to date during and after college. The girls from "good families," ones to establish "relationships" with, whose main goal in life was to land a rich husband so they could vomit up their meals in marble toilets. I was just me, a middle-class Jewish girl from the North Shore, a suburb of Chicago, but my family is anything but average. And Derek loved me for all of it. But now, well, now I don't know what's happened to us. I love him. Of course, I love him. But are we in love? I'm not sure anymore, but God, at one time, we couldn't keep our hands off each other.

And though I ask myself how it happened, how everything changed, I know the reason for the Metamorphosis of Derek, and her name is Jeanette. Derek's nagging, overbearing, smothering mother, who hates my family, me and my bargain basement sense of style, crawled back into his life with the cunning stealth of a snake. Now everything about me that was once endearing to him, like my serious television addiction (so intense that I actually work as an associate television producer for the sleaziest daytime talk show in Chicago, aptly named 'Tell It Like It Is'), penchant for four letter words, the odd cigarette and complete ignorance of high quality hair products just seems to irritate him.

This was before the guy happily working at Starbucks became a top executive at a computer sales company, the Yamaha motorcycle became a BMW coupe, the threadbare furniture became an iPod, iPhone and iPad, and the Nietzsche and Kierkegaard (which for a girl with a shiny new Master's in philosophy was pretty damn perfect) became books with ridiculous titles like "Who Moved My Cheese?"

"Jamie! Answer my question! I hate when you disappear into your head like that!" Derek snaps.

I pull the sheet closer to me and shake my head to clear away the horrible sinking feeling that's been moving around my chest for awhile now. That feeling of being utterly lost that, for me, comes at the most inopportune times, like now on our anniversary and the last Sunday Snooze Fest, I mean charity dinner, that Jeanette hosted.

"Sorry. I was just thinking. What did you ask me?"

He exhales a noisy breath and runs his long, manicured fingers though the artfully gelled spikes and tufts of his damp brown hair. "When are you getting dressed? I wanted to do some shopping before our flight home."

"I don't need anything. I thought maybe we could go to the mountain," I say, wrapping the sheet around me again and walking towards the window. "Look how gorgeous it is outside, and there are already tons of people in the park. The websites I looked at before we left said that hundreds of people play bongos on Sundays, and it's supposed to be really cool. We could take a picnic and do it French style, baguettes, olives, some cheese, maybe a little wine."

"I'm not eating carbs right now, you know that, and cheese is so fattening. And I already booked you in for a makeover on St. Denis."

A makeover from what?

"You know I hate people monkeying with me."

I leave the window and wander over to where Derek is standing, a disapproving scowl on his freshly shaven face, and I curl one arm around his trim waist. He relaxes slightly and touches my face with his index finger. "Your pores are really visible, and I have that dinner coming up. I thought it would be nice if someone taught you how to put on makeup. You could be really beautiful if you tried."

Ouch. Stifling a retort because I really don't want to fight today, I grab a ponytail holder from my nightstand and pull back my thin, shoulder length dishwater blonde hair. Putting the end of the ponytail in my mouth, I know that he's probably right, and I could do with a makeover.

"I'll just jump in the shower and then we can go. Let's get outside, okay? It's such a gorgeous day, and we'll be spending most of it on an airplane. Hey, maybe we can go the mountain after the makeover?"

"Sure, dear, if there's time."

I stiffen because "dear" to me sounds like I'm some 1950s housefrau holding a turkey baster in one hand and feeding the five children stuffed in the pockets of my gingham apron with the other, and he knows I hate it. I quietly seethe (by scraping my teeth together: a childhood stress reliever that I've used for many, many years) that it's always got to be his way. I'm concentrating so much on internalizing my stress that I trip over the footrest next to the television and go flying face first onto the floor. "Fuck!"

"Jamie, you know I hate when you use that word. Is it really necessary?"

Okay, enough!

"Yes! Fuck, fuck, fuck! I just crashed into the floor, and it'd be really nice if you asked if I was okay instead of berating my language choice. Jesus, Derek," I bite down hard on his name. "Give me a break, okay?" I say as I get up off the floor.

By myself.

He rolls his eyes and opens the closet to take out his perfectly pressed dress shirts and pants. I go to the bathroom, slam the door, turn on the water and splash my face with cold water. Ah, that feels better. I look in the mirror, and my brown eyes, sad and hurt, stare back at me. I am one of the only blondes with brown eyes. Leah, as my mom insists on being called, and my sister, Rachel (luckily I escaped the biblical naming frenzy) both have big, bright blue eyes framed by thick, lush lashes. Why didn't I luck out in the gene pool?

I let out a frustrated breath and try not to scream. Why is he so angry with me all the time? And why don't I leave? Because I have nowhere to go, except home, and that's just not an option at thirty-two. And I can't throw away five years just because we've been fighting lately. That's why everyone gets divorced, isn't it? Because they don't try to work it out and leave at the first sign of trouble? Because they're not willing to take the good with the bad. And so humming the theme song to "The Facts of Life," I hop in the glass-enclosed shower and let the super spray do its magic on my hair.

After shampooing, shaving and all the rest, I grab the gold handle, push open the door and peek my head out to make sure Derek is still in the other room. Good, I'm alone. I stand on my tiptoes to reach for the shower head and pull it down. Setting it to "massage," I grip it hard and lower it. Derek had his turn this morning, and it's only fair that I get mine. And even though it's with the throbbing vibrations of the shower head, hell, at least it happened.

CHAPTER TWO

Derek and I spend most of the beautiful morning and sunny afternoon shopping around downtown Montreal on St. Denis and Ste. Catherines, and we never do go to the mountain to hear the bongos. He just "needed" a new suit. And socks. And tweezers. Oh, and a microdermabrasion kit. All of which he could have gotten at home. But don't think I got left out. Oh no, lucky me, I got a brand new mascara, eyeliner, lipstick and concealer. Half of which I'll rarely wear.

But after attempting a mad dash out of the garishly lit makeup emporium, a razor sharp claw attached to a bony skeleton in a white lab coat gripped my shoulder in a vice, waved a mascara wand in my face and dragged me away for my "lecon." Now I look like Tara Reid in drag, minus the boobs. My boobs are little and perky and barely fill a bra. When I remember to wear one. The plus side to all of this is Derek has been all over me since I was slathered in enough makeup to add ten pounds to my usual 130. Okay fine, 140.

"You look gorgeous, Jamie. You really should wear makeup more often. Look how it brings out your features."

To prove it, he pulls out a small compact from his brown leather Louis Vuitton satchel (I wouldn't actually know that it's Louis Vuitton except that Derek mentions the label every time he talks about his all important stuff, as in, "Could you pick up my Armani suit from the dry cleaners?" or "Have you seen my Dolce and Gabbana scarf?") and holds it up to my face.

I think I look absolutely ridiculous. Brown shimmery eyeshadow is gunked on my eyelids, obscuring my vision, and there is so much blush on my face, I look like I have a rash. I don't

11

look like me at all. Perhaps that's the point.

"My eyes itch." I complain and rub my eyes. "That damn woman stuck the eyeliner right in my eyeball."

"Well, she knew what she was doing. You look so...sleek," he tells me while stroking my face.

I'm surprised the orange foundation doesn't smear all over his hand. And I bite my lip to stop all my complaining. He did tell me that I looked good, and he did book the "lecon" for me, which was a sweet gesture. Derek just wants to take care of me, and though it's sometimes misplaced, I can't fault him for trying to make me better. Isn't that what couples do? Bring out the best in each other?

I reach out to hold his hand, and when he entwines his fingers with mine, I feel that great tingle I get on the odd occasion when Derek gently touches me the way he used to. We walk towards the hotel parking lot to get our rental car.

We'd checked out this morning because Derek gets a bit antsy when we're leaving to catch a flight, and he was worried we'd be late if we didn't do it before going shopping. I'm more spontaneous, well, a procrastinator really, and it drives him nuts to do things at the last minute. He's a neurotic list maker, and he practically has an orgasm every time he takes out his Mont Blanc pen and jots down his errands for the day.

Once we're on the highway heading for the airport, I take a deep breath, mash my back teeth together and just say it, hoping that this time, it won't start an argument.

"Remember we have to stop by Leah's on the way home. I promised Rachel I'd look over her summer school essay for her."

Derek's hand stiffens on the steering wheel. Well, it's always nice to have hope.

"Why don't we go home first, and you can take the car over?"

I bite the inside of my lip to stop myself from getting angry. "Because, as you well know, I don't drive stick."

He looks over at me and smirks. "Maybe you should learn."

"Maybe I don't want to. Anyway, it'll only take a second. Besides, you haven't seen Leah in ages."

He says nothing, but tightens his lips and stares straight ahead. He knows full well he can't tell me how he really feels about my family and their "alternative" lifestyle. But he doesn't have to say anything. I know the reaction well enough. I should after dealing with it for almost twenty years. And though she'd never admit it, it's the real reason that Jeanette hates me and probably the real reason why Derek asked me to move in with him one month after we met. It was his rebellious stage, and I was his "fuck you" to his mother.

Okay, so my not so average family. Really, that's quite the understatement. Leah and my dad, David (unbelievably, more biblical references) were married for twelve years. Growing up, I thought they were happy. I thought they'd stay married forever. What kid doesn't?

The day of the big bombshell, I had come home from camp to an empty house. I'd knocked and knocked and finally had to let myself in using the emergency key hidden under the potted plant on the porch. I couldn't figure out where Leah could possibly be because she worked from home and was always, always there when I arrived. She's a crystal healer and colonic herbalist (don't get me started) with an office in the basement where she cleanses and drains her clients. Every day, she'd fix me some nutritional snack like organic apple butter and spelt bread, and a cold glass of viscous soy milk to wash it all down.

Since no one was home, and the sun was burning hot, I snuck a drink from my dad's Diet Coke stash hidden in the back of the fridge. My father has always been Dad and never David to me. Anyway, I was drinking straight from the bottle, the fizzy liquid burning my lips and tickling my throat when Leah and my dad stormed into the house. I quickly sealed the bottle and stuffed it back in the fridge, not knowing that my safe, boring existence was about to forever change.

They walked into the kitchen and seemed surprised to find me there, which should have alerted me to a problem since they both knew when I would be home, which was the same time I came home every day. But, my deductive reasoning skills were just starting to form, and I thought they were pissed off about the Coke.

"I'm sorry. I was just really thirsty, and Leah wasn't home so I had a sip. But it was only a tiny sip..."

And then I'd stopped because they were crying. I'd seen Leah cry countless times (part of her emotional release and journal writing regimen), but my dad? I didn't even know that dads could cry.

"Your mother and I have something to tell you," my father said, his voice breaking.

I started to cry then too. I was really scared.

"Jamie, baby, sit down," Leah gently said and pulled out a kitchen chair for me.

No way was I going to sit. I couldn't. My feet were rooted to the kitchen floor in terror. Instead, Leah came over to me and put her hands on my face, but I angrily swatted them away because I knew I didn't want to hear what they were about to tell me. And even then I didn't really like people fawning all over me. She glanced at my dad for support, but he couldn't look either of us in the eye.

"Jamie, sometimes people, parents realize that they can't live together anymore. Your dad and I love you so, so much, more than anything, and we will always be there for you. But just not together. Do you understand what I'm trying to say?"

I was twelve, not stupid.

"Are you getting a divorce?" I asked in a small voice, looking at my dad and studiously avoiding Leah's penetrating gaze.

"Tell her everything, Leah. It's better she hears it from you than one of the neighbors."

Leah took a deep breath and told me. Everything.

"Honey, there are all different kinds of love. There's love between friends, a man and a woman, a man and a man, and a woman and a woman. Right?"

I nodded, wondering why she was repeating my sex education class.

"And you know Miss Dillon? Katie Dillon?"

"The weird woman down the street with all the cats?" I asked.

And then, my mom got this dreamy, faraway look in her eyes, which confused me even more. Why was the cat lady's name making Leah's face go all soft and stupid-looking?

"When I married your father, I truly loved him. Loved men. Sure, I experimented-"

My dad cut her off. "Jesus, Leah! She's only twelve. She doesn't need the sordid details. Just give it to her straight."

"Katie and I have fallen in love. Your dad is going to find another place to live, and Katie's moving in here with us."

And then I passed out. When I woke up (with both Leah and my dad hovering worriedly over me), I was filled with a hatred I couldn't deal with. Hatred for my strange mother with her musk-scented everything, cleansing rituals and creepy friends. She was tearing our little family apart because she loved Katie? Grosser, did she kiss Katie?

All I wanted to do was crawl into my dad's lap, like I'd done as a little girl and take him away from our horrible house. Then I threw up. Another reaction to stress that I've carried with me to this day. I'm sure it'd be easier to talk about the things that bother me, but, well, that's not me.

You'd think the story would end there. But, it doesn't. Katie did move in (without the cats, thank God, because I'm allergic), and my dad moved to the Loop. He's a philosophy professor (you don't need a psychology degree to decipher my educational choices) at the University of Chicago, and eventually he married Maureen, the dean of the drama department. But not before Rachel, my sister, came along.

We lived in anger and rebellion, Katie, Leah and I. All I wanted was to move in with my dad, but he wasn't really prepared to take care of a burgeoning teenage girl. And I guess he thought that if I left, Leah and I would never repair the already tenuous relationship that we already had. Of course, I never had friends over to the house. Not that I had many, and the few I did have weren't allowed to come to my place for fear they would catch "it."

A lot of the kids at school called me a dyke, played keep away with my hat, bag, whatever they could get their hands on and throw around. The popular girls, the tall, thin, smooth-haired, pointy-nosed ones that Jeanette would rather were with her precious son, would shudder in feigned fear that I would try to kiss them. Remember that this was in the early nineties: a time of "family values."

All of that and the disgusted sniffing of the neighbors caused me to learn self-protection pretty quickly. I ignored Katie a lot for the first few years, and slowly, I withdrew into myself. And into the television. Every day, I'd patiently circle the shows I wanted to watch in red pen and would sit for hours watching other people live their lives. I pretended I was a Cosby kid (I even fantasized about waking up black) living in their normal, heterosexual family.

Eventually, Ellen DeGeneres came out, and just like that, Leah and Katie were the belles of the North Shore. The disgust turned into curiosity, but my years of isolation were already set in me. I got through high school with a handful of like-minded misfits who were united in dysfunction, and I have no clue where any of them

16

are now.

It wasn't all terrible. Once I came to better terms with it and quietly admired them for their conviction (although I've never really told them that), I grew to love Katie. She is fierce in her beliefs and generous with her love. To see her and Leah together is a beautiful thing. No two people could adore each other as much. Or so openly. Mouths, tongues and hands flying, I've seen it all. Katie's a massage therapist, and between she and Leah, their business thrived with the Birkenstock-wearing new age hippies. And then really took off with the aerobicized lunching set.

When I was fifteen (expecting breasts to grow that never did) and just starting to like boys (much to my utter relief), my dad, Leah and Katie sat me down for a chat.

Not one to say more than is necessary, Leah beamed at me and asked, "How would you feel about a little brother or sister?"

Huh? How? Was my dad married and nobody had told me?

"Well, Jamie, your dad and I always wanted more kids, but the timing was never right. We never meant for you to be an only child," Leah told me while stroking Katie's frizzy mass of nut brown curls. I was always afraid a lost kitten would leap out of that wild mess and hurl itself at me.

I liked being alone. No one to share my stuff with; no one to bother me.

"No thank you. I don't want a brother or sister," I said with finality, assuming that that was the end of the discussion. But I should have known better. Leah never seemed to get that I wasn't as excited as she was at finding herself and "following her bliss." She really believed that I would want this.

"Jamie, honey, we know how hard the last few years have been for you. We never wanted to hurt you. So, we want to make sure that your brother or sister comes from the same mother and father."

Had they somehow spirited me away to Utah in the middle of

17

the night and were all going to share each other? Didn't they realize the damage they were doing to my poor adolescent mind?

"Here's the deal, Jamie. Leah is pregnant," Katie, not one to mince words, announced, her eyes shining with unshed tears. Tears that, at any moment, would begin to drip off her face and into her tea with no embarrassment or shame.

"What?! How could you do this without telling me? Nobody cares about me! What I want never matters! I could run away and no one would even notice!" I'd yelled.

And less than nine months later, my sister Rachel was born. The most perfect, beautiful child you've ever seen. How did they do it? To keep our family intact, Leah was impregnated with my dad's sperm in vitro, Katie massaged every swollen part of Leah (in open view), and I had a sister.

I wanted to despise her. But when I saw her big, blue eyes, tiny fingers and head full of golden curls, I fell instantly in love. Rachel is now eighteen, 5'6, slender, stunning, and the only person I'd lay down and die for. So to be fair, my messed up family does give people pause, but I'm used to it. They're all I have. And at first, Derek was enthralled. He'd never met anyone who lived life the way they wanted to, not caring what other people thought and doing what made them happy, even if it meant being different.

But, slowly, subtly, his mother's disdain and worry about what her friends would think crept into Derek's view of the world until it completely took over, and he changed. He became a male carbon copy of Her, and the complete opposite of me.

I stare out the window and watch the world go by. With a heavy heart, I say, "Fine, I'll take the 'L.' Let's just go home."

CHAPTER THREE

"Leah? Katie? Rach?" I call after opening the front door that my trusting family never locks. Wait until their precious crystals and enema paraphernalia get swiped.

"Jamie? Is that you?" Leah trills from upstairs.

"Yeah, I'm home."

Leah glides downstairs with the same grace and elegance she's always had. My mom is ethereal. There's no other word more precise. Tall and willowy, her once blonde hair is now silver and tied in a long braid that falls to the middle of her back. She's wearing her favorite pale blue gauzy skirt (the one with the tiny mirrors all over it, of course), a hemp tank top, and naturally, no bra. I've gotten used to seeing a lot of nipples around this house.

She pulls me close and kisses my hair, which I shrug off. Not giving up, she puts her hands on my shoulders and says, "Let me look at the gorgeous you. Hmmm, have you been taking your vitamins?"

"Yup. I guess they just don't work for me."

I *never* take vitamins, but it's a losing battle to tell her that because she'll inundate me with pamphlets about how flax seed oil will improve my mood. Trust me, it won't.

"Oh, wait! I'll get you some new powder I've been trying. It'll regulate your hormones. You just put it in hot water, let it thicken and drink it down. It works like a dream. Hey, where's Derek?" she asks, peering over my shoulder to see if he's crouching behind me.

I lower my eyes and inspect the navy blue front hall carpet decorated, naturally, with moons and stars. "Um, he had to work. We just got back."

I can feel her silently examining me from head to foot. "Did he ask you to marry him?" she asks warily, and when I look up, I see the worry in her eyes.

Obviously, Leah's not Derek's biggest fan at the moment. "No, of course not. Is that what you thought he was going to do?" I ask, surprised, because Derek and I never talk about marriage.

"I never know what Derek is going to do, Jamie," Leah replies cryptically and shakes her head from side to side, making the turquoise and silver earrings Katie made for her tinkle musically.

Now, any other mother would expand on that, but Leah speaks more with her eyes and her tone, without judgment, without doing the normal mother nagging or clucking. But the result is the same. Anxiety.

"We had a good time!" I throw up my hands in exasperation because I want to prove to her that everything is okay. I don't want Leah to think I'm not happy. Her whole existence is about being happy.

But Leah just smiles serenely. "Okay."

Can't she tell me that she hates him? Can't she tell me I'm making a mistake by staying with him? Why does she need to be so easy and relaxed when she knows it makes me so tense?

I sigh. "Where's Rachel?"

"On the phone. Where else? I'm glad you had a good time." She locks eyes with me, says nothing, and I want to scream.

"We did."

"Hmmm." And that one word says everything. "Do you want something to drink? I just brewed a pot of dandelion tea," she asks, walking towards the kitchen at the back of the house.

I follow her lavender-scented trail and say, "No thanks. I just want to grab Rachel's essay and go. I have some work to do before tomorrow."

She turns on the stove and puts the silver tea kettle on the range. "Oh, what are you working on now?"

"People who look like their pets."

She giggles. "I'll have to make sure to tape that one."

Leah loves my show. Of course she does. She supports everything I do. If I told her I was running off to become a fire-eater at the circus, she'd buy tickets for every city and show up to watch me. She'd probably even light the stick.

I know that sounds fantastic, having a mother who supports and understands everything you do without placing her own expectations on you. But, sometimes, I'd really just like a mother.

I leave her to brew her tea and run up the spiral staircase, past the oil lamps and incense burners to Rachel's room at the top of the house. Rachel and I are total opposites. Where I'm reserved and aloof, she's warm, outgoing, and bubbling with infectious energy. I rap my knuckles on her door."Rach?"

She flings open the door and hurls herself into my arms. "Jamie! I missed you. I have so much to tell you. Steve emailed me and wants me to go out with him, but I know that Becky likes him. But it's not like they've hooked up or anything..."

And she's off for about fifteen minutes about school, her teachers, friends, new clothes. I can't help but smile. Rachel's the only person I'll let paw me. I couldn't stop her if I wanted to. It's been a long time since we've lived in the same house so I no longer have to witness massage trains and hair braiding sessions with her equally affectionate friends.

"How was your hot weekend?" she finally asks, her blue eyes huge, searching my face for any vestiges of excitement.

"Not so hot, really. We fought a lot."

Rachel takes a deep breath to fill her lungs with enough air to respond to this. In a second, I'll be bombarded with all of the questions she can get out in one breath. "You fought? Again? About what? How was the hotel, though? And Montreal? Did you learn any French?"

I can tell Rachel about the problems with me and Derek, because at eighteen, she doesn't take them so seriously, and she can jump from one topic to the next faster than I can think.

"We just fought about stupid stuff, and no, I didn't learn any French. But, yeah, the hotel was really nice. You would have loved it." I sit on the edge of her bed, avoiding the twenty or so pairs of tiny thongs she's scattered everywhere. "And he took me shopping."

Her eyes light up and she plops down next to me. "Shopping? Did you get a lot of stuff? Did he buy stuff?"

"He got tons, and I got makeup. See the rash on my face?" I say and smile.

Rachel's soothing laughter makes me feel better. She tosses her shiny hair over her shoulder, grabs my hand and pulls me towards her hot pink computer. "Do you wanna see the email Steve sent me? I can't tell what it means. I'm not sure if he likes me likes me or just likes me."

I'm sure that makes perfect sense in the hormonally-charged brain of an eighteen year old who can't focus on anything or any guy for too long.

I read the email, take Rachel's essay and say my goodbyes. Katie's with a client (I can tell from the sound of rain and wind coming from the stereo system in the basement) so I don't have a chance to say hello. I don't leave empty-handed, however. Leah presses two bottles of garlic and fish oil pills into my palm before I leave. How revolting. To be tossed in the trash with all the other supplements Leah's given me over the years.

***

In the television studio, a cat is trying to climb on top of a llama, so I leave them to it and head towards my desk. I stayed up late last night putting together the interview questions for Mitzy, the dumb as a brick, gorgeous, straw-shaped host of our show.

Mitzy can't read very well so the questions are always whispered in her ear through a tiny earpiece speaker. I still have trouble believing they couldn't find a talk show host who's both telegenic and brighter than a burned out bulb.

I know that my boss, Sue, the executive producer, wants to find someone to replace her, but she's too terrified to do it. Most people have a boss they're intimidated of. Mine is so fragile that if you speak above a whisper, she faints in fear.

Sue is definitely not producer material. She holds a PhD in Media Communications, and with her stringy brown hair (always, always in a bun), wire-rimmed glasses perched on her nose (or on her head which invariably makes her look desperately for them) and timid voice, she's better suited to being a researcher.

I have no idea how she ended up at a cheesy talk show, but I know why she can't leave. Her mom is ill with some disease that is so rare only two people in the world have it (and why I can never remember its name) so Sue needs money to have at home care. Poor Sue.

She tiptoes around everyone, hates the spotlight and uses words like "pernicious" which not many people at this show can even spell much less understand. I can though because I do have that Master's degree, and I might as well put it to good use understanding Sue since I haven't done much else with it. Besides wave at it whenever I go to Leah and Katie's.

As her associate producer, one of my responsibilities is finding and meeting the psycho guests (like the girl whose husband slept with her brother), and I positively adore it. Probably because they make my family seem normal by comparison. I also have to go through the myriad of calls that come at the end of every show. Have you ever wondered who actually answers the questions like:

"If you or anyone you know is an obese transsexual, please call 'Tell It Like It Is'"? I'm absolutely floored by the flood of calls from desperate people who either really do need help or crave being on television once in their pathetic lives.

"Jamie? Could you come to the green room and get the guy who looks like a rat to zip up his fly?" Sue whispers from the intercom on the wall above my desk right as I'm sitting down.

After three years, I can finally decipher her hushed, mumbled sentences because that actually sounds like, "Hhhhhhhhhhhhh."

"Hey, Jamie, how was your weekend?" Lucy, the show's assistant director, and my closest friend at work, yells from her desk across the room from mine after I come back from dealing with Rat Man.

Decked out today in a thigh-high black leather mini, knee-high black boots, an orange leather vest and jet-black bob, Lucy is one of the reasons I love where I work. She can beat my potty mouth hands down, especially after a bit of vodka, which I think she has hooked up to an IV next to her bed. As drunk as Lucy gets on her off hours, at work, she's a consummate professional.

"It was okay."

"How are things with big, manly Derek?" she asks with a wink.

"I got well acquainted with the shower head."

"Babe, you don't need a shower head. I'll give you something good if you're hard up," Carl, the cameraman, pipes in.

"Mind your own business and stop listening to my conversation, Carl, you idiot. And keep your pepper in its shaker because I don't want it anywhere near me."

"Too bad. You don't know what you're missing," he responds, hikes his pants up over his hairy belly that's sticking out of his sweat-stained shirt and goes back to fondling his camera.

I roll my eyes at Lucy, and she makes the universal drinking gesture (one hand forming a cup and lifting it towards her mouth) from across the room.

"I can't today. I'm supposed to go to Hanna's for dinner," I tell her.

"Hanna's cooking?" Lucy's brow knots in bewilderment. Hanna, my best friend, wouldn't know a blender from a microwave.

"Pizza."

"Ah. Okay, another time. Alright everyone, time to roll. Carl, you ready? Jamie, are the questions ready for her Royal Vapidness?" Lucy shoots the usual barrage of questions before a show.

I must admit it was a bit difficult writing some intriguing questions for this elite group of guests. After the usual "Did you notice you and the hairy llama resembled each other immediately or was it more of a gradual thing?," that's pretty much it. So, we have a pet and owner parade of sorts, and the audience will vote for the best pair.

Besides the dog that used a guest as a fire hydrant, the show was a success. Breathe a huge sigh of relief. Thank God we're not live. We tape at 10:00 a.m., and the first show airs at 3:00 p.m. and again the next morning at 9:00 a.m. That gives us a few good hours to brighten the vacant look in Mitzy's eyes, bleep the crass and offensive language and make sure we're not breaking too many FCC guidelines.

"Hhh, shh, mmm, blah," Sue calls from the intercom.

Everyone in the room swivels their heads to look at me.

"Meeting in an hour," I translate.

I should so get paid more for interpretation. I have a few minutes so in a burst of sudden affection for Derek, I phone him at work.

"Derek Leeds the Third speaking."

Is it really necessary to tell everyone that your family had zero originality when naming you? And he only started using "The Third" when he got this job.

"Hi, hon, it's me."

"Jamie, you know I can't take personal calls at work."

Can't, Mr. Executive? Won't is more like it.

"You won't believe the show we did at work today," I say, completely ignoring his rudeness.

"I'm sure I would. What was it? Teen mothers knocked up by their teachers?"

"No, that's tomorrow."

"Jamie, we'll talk when I get home. Did you pay the credit card bill I left on the table this morning?"

I slap my hand against my head. "Shit! I totally forgot. I'll do it tomorrow."

"How could you forget something like that? I'm not paying the interest when the bill is overdue."

"It's not due for another two weeks. I know when to pay my own credit card, and I don't need you to remind me."

"No, but you need my money to pay it."

I clench my jaw and breathe through my nose. "It's all your stuff! I didn't want the damn $400.00 water purifier, I told you I'm fine with the tap, but you insisted. I only wanted the miles so we could go somewhere hot this winter. Look, I just called to tell you that I won't be home for dinner. You'll need to make yourself something. There're some perogies in the freezer."

"Isn't there anything healthy? Perogies are really fattening, you know."

I drum my fingers on my desk in impatience. "And delicious. Okay, there are some green beans, meatless hamburgers, an oxymoron if I've ever heard one, and portabella mushrooms in the fridge. Aren't you going to ask me where I'm going for dinner?" I ask, rubbing my neck in the sore spot I always get when I'm stressed.

"Fine. Where are you going?"

"Hanna's."

"Okay, have a nice day. I'll see you later."

"Yeah. Whatever."

"Don't get defensive, Jamie. I'll see you tonight. Have a good time. I hope she's paying for dinner."

"What does that mean?"

"Nothing. But she has more money than God. Have fun."

Click. I didn't know that God had money. Grind, mash, grit. Ahhh. Now, I feel like shit, my neck and jaw hurt, and the phone's still in my hand so I call Hanna at her shop.

Hanna owns an exclusive lingerie boutique on North Michigan Avenue. Known as Magnificent Mile, it's Chicago's version of glitz and glamour. Ornate street lamps light the wide cobblestone walkway leading to the most expensive and intimidating of stores, and Hanna's boutique is strategically located right next to the swanky hotels where the stars stay when they're visiting.

She snags some very famous clients and closes the store when they come in. Every once in awhile, she lets me pretend I'm her assistant so I can gawk over Kim Kardashian choosing bras (in huge sizes, but it would be indiscreet to reveal the actual size), and George Clooney fingering the crotches of tiny thongs.

Hanna's got everything delicious in her store from tasteful teddies to raunchy leather panties lined with fur. There's a secret room in the back for the more risque items, like crotchless panties and those naughty bras with the nipples cut out. Her store is one of the most popular in Chicago, regularly featured in New York Magazine in their "Where to Shop in Chicago" section.

I will always have a fond feeling for the DMV, which is where we met twelve years ago. We were standing in different lines at the counter, both screaming and cursing because we'd forgotten something and wanted to blame it on someone else. Hanna had forgotten her money, while I had left the bill with my proof of address on my desk at home.

In the midst of our tirade (when one of us finally got too hoarse to yell for a moment, we could hear the other), we looked at each other and both burst out laughing. It was like finding a long lost sister. We had that instant chemistry that doesn't need words. We just get each other and never have to explain ourselves or apologize for our faults.

"Creme de Soie," she answers the phone in her velvety, I can give you everything you desire voice.

"Hanna, you busy?" I ask, feeling anxious after my call to Derek.

"Never for you, babe. What's up? How was the anniversary weekend?"

"Fine. It was fine."

"Fine?"

"Good. Nice."

"Those aren't exactly the adjectives I'd expect after a romantic weekend in Montreal."

I sigh and bite my pinkie nail. "I don't want to get into this right now, Han."

Hanna, having known me long before Derek came into my life, and who has witnessed the many ups and downs of our relationship, has been after me for awhile now to leave Derek. But she doesn't know him like I do. And she knows when to let it go. For about an hour or so.

"Fine. When are you coming over?" she asks.

"Eightish."

"Sausage or healthy?"

"Oh, definitely sausage. Deep dish."

We hang up, and with the annoying phone call from Derek and

the words that Hanna wanted to say but didn't still on my mind, I do what I do best. Get to work and ignore the nagging voices in my head. Everything will get better. It has to.

CHAPTER FOUR

Hanna's spacious and immaculate loft, 1600 square feet, 12 foot high ceilings, bay windows, renovated to within an inch of its life, is in Streeterville, a chi-chi little area just walking distance from the Tribune Tower where the television studio is. When I get there, Hanna's not home so I let myself in with my key. Hanna and I have always had keys to each other's places just in case. This pisses Derek off to no end because he thinks Hanna will walk in on us right when we're having sex. I guess he doesn't realize that we actually have to have it for her to see it. Montreal was the first time we've had sex in a month. He's always too busy. Or so he says.

I throw off my shoes, temporarily blinded by the white on white decorating scheme she's got going on in here. I totally don't get the whole minimalistic look. Isn't white what's there before you move in? I wade through the plush, ivory carpeting in the living room and slide down the polished wood floor to the kitchen. Grabbing a cold beer, I settle myself on the couch to watch a "Friends" rerun.

I'm not one to cry often (and never in front of people), but when that show ended, I bawled like a baby. So sad, but true. At the commercial (even though I've seen this episode about ten times, I don't want to miss anything), I look around the place checking for new purchases.

Hanna's a huge shopper and not bargain basement buys, either. The store has made her incredibly wealthy. Not hoity-toity rich, but generously, comfortably, never worry again rich. I see a new marble candle holder on the mantel above the fireplace. I'm so proud of her and the fact that our friendship has stayed the same all these years despite our differences in lifestyles and bank accounts.

Hanna is a stunner. Six feet tall in flats, which she almost never wears, model thin (with very natural looking implants to help befuddled customers see how the bra is supposed to look) and a sleek cap of straight chestnut hair cut sharply around her angular face. All bones and angles, I could open an envelope on her cheekbones. Her emerald eyes are so piercing that sometimes I can't even look at her without going slightly catatonic.

It's surprising really that she and Derek don't get along better. They both chased the capitalist rainbow and grabbed the pot of cash at the end. I hear her key turn in the lock and the usual, "Oh, motherfucker," as everything she's carrying crashes to the floor.

"Hey, Jaim, what's up?" she calls from the floor, and when I look over at her, I see that she's awkwardly positioned on her hands and knees.

"Do you need some help or are you just waiting for the sexy neighbor to drop by?" I call out.

"I'm fine, smart ass."

She's crawling on the floor trying to gather her keys, papers, purse and assorted lingerie samples from the shop. I walk over to help her, and when she looks up at me, she stares as if I've grown two heads.

"What the hell happened to your face?"

I touch my hand to my cheek. "What do you mean?"

"Why in God's name are you orange?"

"Oh. That. Derek got me a makeup demo in Montreal, and he bought me foundation and all this other stuff. I thought I should wear a bit more makeup. Why? Did I do it wrong?"

I can see that she's trying not to laugh, but when she stands up and gets a closer look, sudden convulsions of giggles make her bony shoulders bob up and down, and she falls back on the floor laughing. Amazingly, her implants don't even move a fraction.

"Whew," she says wiping the tears from her eyes. "Sorry, Jaim,

I shouldn't laugh, but girl, you look like you poured half of the bottle on your face. Didn't they show you how much to use?"

"Yeah, but I wasn't really paying attention. The woman was huge and scary, and she just kept leaning in so close to me and slathering all of this stuff on my face."

She licks her finger and reaches up to wipe it across my face. There's an inch of orange on her finger, and looking from her finger back to my face, she snorts and breaks out into hysterical laughter again. I glower at her, and she covers her mouth with her hand.

I reach an arm down to pull her up off the floor and say, "Fuck off. I was trying to be a woman. Anyway, I'm starving. Let's order. I didn't have time for lunch because it was the pet parade, and a few of the animals hadn't practiced."

After washing my face, I sprawl myself on the cream-colored couch (I'm not allowed to eat on it) and stretch while Hanna orders our usual sausage and three cheese pizza. Four slices for me, two for her now, two for her later. Not because Hanna thinks she's fat and is on a diet, but because she has an Obsessive Compulsive Disorder. I'm the only person she'll eat in front of because she always thinks she has food in her teeth. Rather than making a face like a horse to all dinner companions (so they can check for her), she's a closet eater.

"Hey, what happened with that lawyer guy you've been seeing?" I ask as Hanna does some impossible yoga contortion on the other matching couch in the living room, spreading her legs wide apart and making her mini-skirt ride up so high I can see her garters. Peach today.

"And can you stop flashing your crotch at me?" I ask politely.

"Don't look. And don't put your face against the couch."

"Oh my God! Shut up already. I washed it, and it's gone. I will *never* wear it again."

32

"Do you promise?"

"If you can keep your skirt on. Or stop doing the splits over there."

"Wanna learn it?"

"Not in the least, and you didn't answer my question," I remind her.

"He's hot. And nice. And broke. He decided he didn't want to be a lawyer anymore. Now, he's an *artiste,*" she says, curling her four inch talons around a sweating beer. If I were a guy, I'd be terrified of castration from those finger knives.

"But if you like him, who cares? You have money. You don't need anyone else's."

"I'm not eating at Burger King on every date either."

"He took you to Burger King?" I ask, lifting my head off the couch in surprise.

"No, he actually took me to a very cool cafe. But still, he's broke." She puts down her beer, lifts her arms above her head and then plunges her head down to the floor.

"What the hell are you doing? Anyway, is he a good artist, at least?" I'm trying to focus on his good points. I know firsthand that the money doesn't make the man.

She lifts her head from her feet and says, "He paints beautifully, actually. I did some modeling for him after we slept together."

"How Titanic style of you and how cheesy. Are you going to see him again?" I sit up and peer closely at her lovely face to see how she really feels. Hanna lifts the upper half of her impossibly long body and pulls her knees into her chest.

"I *never* want to have to struggle like my dad did, and I never will."

I know that Hanna's adamant statement comes from the fact that she was single-handedly raised by a father who worked two, sometimes three jobs to give her everything she needed. She watched him not sleep, not eat, just so he could make enough money to take care of her. Her mother had been a high fashion French model who had met Hanna's dad when he was playing guitar in a Paris cafe. She fell in lust with him and wound up pregnant.

When Hanna was a year old, her mother disappeared, never to be heard from again. Hanna's dad was crushed and lost. He had no clue what to do with a little girl, but he gave her the best life he could. But it wasn't easy. Sadly, her dad died of prostate cancer a few years ago, before he could see the success she's become. But he always knew she would make it.

"He's a great fuck, but there's no future in it," Hanna continues, resting her chin on her hands, eyes downcast.

The pizza arrives so I don't press her on it because I know she'll tell me more about it when she's ready. I understand having to process something before you talk about it. Or wait years before doing anything about it. I gobble the spicy cheesy pizza in a nanosecond, but Hanna holds the slice inches from her mouth and tries to chew without using her teeth. "You know, Han, that looks even worse than food in your teeth."

"I know. Just let me be," she says, but she does start chewing more normally.

Three beers later, I'm falling asleep on my side, one leg curled under me, my hair plastered to the side of my face.

Hanna shakes my shoulder. "Okay, darling, you gotta go. Stop avoiding Derek."

"I'm not avoiding anyone," I say, spitting out sausage-scented hair and pulling myself up to a seated position.

"Sure you're not. You know, Jaim, there's nothing stopping you from leaving. You could always live with me. As long as you clean every now and then."

I nod glumly. "I know, Han. Things will get better. It's just a bit of a rough patch right now."

God, the words sound empty even to me, but when I think of the night Derek and I met, and I remember those heady feelings of lust and excitement, I have to believe I'll get them back somehow. And that he'll turn back into the man I met at Blackie's that fateful winter night five years ago.

Hanna and I were seated at a table near the door when it burst open, bringing in a blast of icy air and a tall, scruffy and oh so sexy man in torn jeans, a leather jacket and shaggy chocolate brown hair lightly dusted with snow. Hanna and I both noticed him, and even though I knew it wasn't a competition, if it were, she surely would have won.

As I said before, Hanna is stop-in-your-tracks-gorgeous, and I'm not just saying that because she's my best friend, but because she's one of those women who is undeniably beautiful and everyone's type. And normally, when a guy would practically sit on top of me (thinking I was part of the furniture) to get closer to Hanna, I really didn't mind (honestly) because I'm not so good at being the center of attention. It's probably why we're such good friends because most women hate her. But that night, and that guy, well, I wanted him.

He caught me gawking, ordered two beers from the bartender and wandered over to the table with the two beers in his hand. My heart sank because I just knew he was going straight for Hanna, and I was in utter shock when he put the beer next to me, leaned in close and in a husky whisper said, "Hi."

That's pretty much all it had taken for my hormones to go into overdrive and to follow him to a dark corner of the bar to furtively rub and grope. And I was going to get all I could because I knew I wouldn't get a second chance with a guy like that. And I'd never had a one night stand (more like a one night everything but), and that night it was a rite of passage I was about to check off. Lubricated with a large quantity of alcohol, we ended up back at his apartment, and I never left.

"There are so many guys who would love to go out with you. And nobody should date a man named Derek."

"What's wrong with his name?" I ask, standing up and knocking my fake Prada bag off the coffee table. It was a gift from Hanna on my 30th birthday. She tried to buy me a real one, but there was no way I was letting her spend that kind of money on me when I could care less what company makes what and when I am notorious for throwing all kinds of crap in my bag. Case in point, now strewn all over the floor are old receipts, pizza delivery pamphlets, cigarettes with the tobacco sprinkling everywhere and pennies stuck together with old pieces of gum.

"It's the name of a mama's boy," she says, handing me some of the crap that's dirtying her pristine carpet.

"So, what, I should only go after men with certain names? Like I've always had so many to choose from. Maybe that works for you, Han, but not for me."

"Why do you need a wool hat in the summer?" she asks, shaking her head and looking at my hot pink ski cap.

"I might have a bad hair day, you never know," I tell her, taking the hat and cramming it back in the purse. It's a big purse.

"I could set you up like that, you know," she says, snapping her fingers.

I smirk. "And what would be the name of this dream man?"

She closes her eyes for a moment. "Nick."

"Nick? That sounds like someone from the 'Young and the Restless.' Why Nick?" I know I shouldn't ask.

She flashes a lascivious smile. "Nick is a dirty, sexy, fuck you and leave you kind of name."

"And why is that possibly a good thing?" I ask and sit back

36

down on the floor to find the coins that have rolled under the couch. Hanna watches me press my face to the carpet and stick my hand under the couch. Anywhere else, I'd be worried about what little bugs I'd find under there, but Hanna's place is so impeccably clean that I could lick the floor, and it would taste good.

"Because, girl, you need to get laid so bad."

"I love Derek," I tell her, locating the pennies and curling my foot towards my face so I can use one to pick the skin off my feet.

She looks at me and shudders. "That's gross. Stop it. Loving and being in love are two very different things. Don't you want more?"

I look up from my feet and shrug. "Not really."

***

All the lights are off in the apartment when I get home. Even the dim hall light which Derek knows I need. So I trip over his shoes, bag and the coat rack. It crashes loudly to the floor and lands on my foot.

"Fuck!" I scream in pain.

Derek rushes out of our bedroom (wearing the ghastly royal blue and white pinstriped pajama set Jeanette had given him, all he's missing is the pipe and ascot) and frowns at me. "What's wrong with you? I just fell asleep. I have an early meeting tomorrow morning. Thanks for waking me up. Now I'll never get back to sleep," he says, glaring at me through slitted eyes.

"You didn't leave the light on for me. And don't you have mink earplugs or something?"

Ignoring my comment, he asks, "How's the rich witch?"

"Oh, shut up. You're just jealous because she makes more money than you do."

Oops. Did I just say that out loud?

"Thanks, Jamie. You really know how to make a guy feel

good. Sometimes, I think my mom's right."

My blood turns to ice. What was Jeanette saying about me this time?

"Forget it," he says and starts walking back to bed.

I follow him, hating myself for being drawn into his little game. "Not forget it. What did she say?"

"It doesn't matter. And maybe it's not your fault. Sins of the mother," he mutters under his breath.

I'm shaking with frustration, and all I want to do is punch the wall in front of me. Or his head. I can feel my heart thudding against my ribcage.

We've had this conversation countless times, and nothing ever changes. I blow out a noisy breath. "Derek, I'm so fucking tired of this. What are we doing? You're not happy. I'm not happy."

"Life isn't about fluffy pink clouds and flying elephants. Deal with it. I'm going to bed."

Slam!

I sit down heavily on our chenille couch and prop my bare feet on the glass and cherry wood coffee table. Good, smudges. I look around the home that's more to Derek's taste than mine. Three bedrooms (for the guests who are never asked to stay), rich, glossy wood everywhere—a condominium, of course. I'd wanted to move into a two bedroom apartment on the main floor of a house in the Loop near the University of Chicago and close to my dad and Maureen. A nice, laid back community with cozy cafes, funky restaurants and eclectic second hand bookstores dotting the cigarette and paper strewn streets.

It wasn't upscale (pretentious) enough for Derek so I conceded to living on the outskirts of the Gold Coast (which prides itself on its self-important, rich and smarmy scene). Designer shops, upscale clubs with strict no jeans, no running shoes dress codes, and not one woman with thin, dry hair. I hate it. But, Derek wanted an "image," and really, it didn't matter much to me. Then.

Sometimes I fantasize about what my life would be like without Derek. Packing my bags and just leaving a note on the $1000.00 coffee table. But even though I know Hanna would let me live with her, I need my own space, and I certainly can't afford to live alone because the associate producer's salary is nothing next to the paycheque that Derek gets from his Ken Dream job.

And if I lose Derek, what else do I have? My family, friends, job. No love. I might never be with anyone again. At thirty-two, it would be too hard to find someone else now, and I just can't trust that another man will fall in love with me because before Derek, it had never happened.

I know most women analyze every nuance and sentence spoken in relationships so when something just doesn't feel right, they tell all of their friends and break it down word by word. I love being the listener for these conversations, but I'm not so good at talking about the things that bother me. So, for me to talk to Derek about our problems, or try to, is a pretty huge deal. And obviously neither of us is happy.

This weight of discontent seems to fill the air around us. But every time I bring up our problems, he acts as if nothing's wrong. He won't even talk about it. Lately it seems like he's not thinking about me at all. I'd probably have to text him to break up with him.

Sighing audibly, I pad to the bathroom to wash up. My little bottle of no-name soap looks depressingly inconsequential next to Derek's wide array of cleansers. Hmmm, maybe I should try some of his apricot scrub. What does a scrub do? I try to tie my hair back, but the stupid ponytail holder keeps falling out. I twist my hair in a bun and open the bottle. Squeezing out a healthy amount (Wow, it's pink. Should it be pink?), I slather it all over my face. Ow, ow, ow! It's making my skin tight and itchy, and it hurts like a bitch. This cannot be good for me.

39

I read the back of the tube, which tells me I should leave this crap on my face for twenty minutes. After three, I'm impatient so I scrub it off and look in the mirror, and all I see is a blotchy mess of mottled pink skin. Gorgeous I am. And I finished the tube. Derek has so many products, I'm sure he won't even notice.

I shut the light, tiptoe into the bedroom, and change into my favorite over-sized red t-shirt from a consignment shop in Wicker Park. It's downy soft and comes to my knees. The sheets (Egyptian cotton, three hundred thread count, of course) are cool, and I slide under them, wiggling my fingers and toes. The room is pitch black, with only the moon illuminating the handmade bureau, giant black leather armchair and Tiffany lamps on each of our bedside tables. I throw my hands above my head and turn my face toward Derek. It's amazing how peaceful people look when they're sleeping. Derek's long, thick lashes are fluttering against his smooth skin, his strong jaw is relaxed, and a faint smattering of stubble gives him that sexy, mussed look I'd once loved so much.

I reach over to stroke his cheek, and Derek twitches in his sleep. Shockingly (because we just had sex the other day), his hand rests on my thigh and starts creeping upwards. I grimace slightly, wishing the next eight minutes (I've got it down to a science now) wouldn't be so predictable. Here it comes: left breast, right breast, quick stroke of my back, a spit of saliva around the clitoris, insert. Bang, bang, bang. Done.

Well, that was refreshing. Passion dies, friendship remains. Isn't that what they always say? And now I can't sleep because I'm annoyed. Annoyed that Derek didn't notice that I didn't come. Again. So while he's washing off, I go to the couch to finish what he started. Maybe I should call that hotel in Montreal and get the make and model of the shower head.

CHAPTER FIVE

"Jamie, what did you do with my apricot cleanser?" Derek bellows from the bathroom the next morning.

Shit.

"I thought I should try exfoliating," I call back from the bed.

"Buy your own cleanser. This one is for normal, not greasy skin."

Isn't that oily skin? Thanks a bunch, boyfriend o'mine. I sit up and prop my back against the pillow. "I'm going to my dad's with Rachel tonight. Are you coming?" I ask, already knowing the answer.

"I can't. Dinner meeting with Mr. Chipchuk. I think he might promote me," he tells me and hurries back into the bedroom to check out his suit in the mirror. Again.

Promote him to what? CEO? Mr. Chipchuk is a sleazy, grey-haired (plugs) man in his late fifties who believes women are best suited to being on their backs and in the kitchen. I don't wear thongs to corporate events anymore because the painful smack on my ass (and a little squeeze if he's particularly joyful) hurts less with granny panties on. Derek says he's harmless, but I sure wouldn't want to run into Mr. Cheesehead in a dark alley.

"Fine. I'll see you whenever," I say and crawl back under the covers to avoid talking to him.

"Don't get snippy, Jamie. I'm doing this for us."

I don't see how eating prime rib and drinking fine wine is for "us." I close my eyes, feigning sleep until I hear his key in the door. And then the hard push to make sure it's locked, the check through his bag to count his cell, necessary files, toiletry bag, compact and lipstick. Okay, I'm joking about the lipstick. I think.

41

Once he's gone, I reluctantly throw off the covers and head for the shower. The warm water sluices over me, and I raise my face to let it wash away all my problems. Just as I'm rinsing my hair (and watching enough of it swirl down the drain that I get worried, I don't have that much hair to lose) I hear the phone ring so I jump out, naked and dripping water all over the floor (uh oh, water marks) to answer it.

"Hello?" I pant.

"Ms. Jamie Ross?"

"Yes?"

A telemarketer? Publisher's Clearinghouse?

"This is your credit card company calling, Ms. Ross. We were wondering if you've been receiving your statements in the mail," the mechanical voice drones.

Jeez, they sure are thorough.

"Yes, I'm going to pay the balance today."

"This is the third month in a row that the payment has been late."

Okay, when I said that the bill was due in another two weeks, I lied. The thing is that I hate asking Derek for money. He always says that it doesn't bother him that he makes so much more than I do, but then he lords it over me with snippy comments and eye rolls. But, most of the stuff on my card are things that he wanted because he's on a self-improvement frenzy that includes $400.00 water purifiers, Egyptian cotton and a fine wine collection. So, I try to pay the bills, I really do, but I just don't have the money. I know ignoring them doesn't make them go away, but it's a hell of a lot easier than asking him to pay.

"I'm sorry. I'll pay it all today. I was away on a business trip."

"Ms. Ross, you should call us and let us know if you won't be able to pay the bill on time. The balance is at $3500.00. Can you pay that?"

If I don't eat. I furiously shake my head in anger, dripping water all over the receiver, because I can't believe Derek spends so much money on things to make his life "better" when it's our relationship that needs the most improvement.

"Yes, I'll pay it today."

"Thank you. We'll be waiting for the payment. And while I have you on the line, would you like to increase your limit?"

A stream of expletives bursts from my mouth, and I slam the phone down. I don't have time to think about the fact that I'm going to have to work overtime to pay that stupid bill because I'm now running late. I dress hurriedly in black pants ($20), white button down ($5, just a small stain on the collar, but my hair will cover it) and high-heeled shoes ($30). I slide a comb through my hair, slap on some mascara and lipstick, and I'm out the door.

Today's meeting day at work. The associates and higher ups get together in a stuffy room (no windows so we have no clue how much time has passed) and brainstorm ideas for the next few months of shows. This all comes after the taping. Our show this morning is makeovers for goth teens. The sullen, deathly pale, pierced little faces staring evilly at their parents for humiliating them are not my favorite. I don't blame them, but, boy, does it make for good television.

I wander into one of the "green rooms" (which is actually brown and the size of my underwear drawer) and find Sue, who's flustered and red-faced, arguing with a furious twelve year old. Even though Chicago's oppressively humid summers are best spent in an air-conditioned igloo (it's a hundred and ten degrees already, and it's only 8:00 a.m.), Sue is dressed in a thick black cardigan buttoned to her chin.

I can't hear what Sue is saying, and actually, the little girl monster probably can't either, but I do hear the so-called child's response.

"Fuck you!" Mini-Satan stands up and screams; her spittle landing on Sue's glasses.

Sue looks at me beseechingly, and I cooly wander over. "Hey," I say nonchalantly.

"Fuck you too!" Cruella screams at me in her girlish voice.

Unlike Sue, I don't back down. I set my mouth in a hard line, clench my jaw and coldly lock eyes with her until she has no choice but to look away.

"What are you looking at?" she says rudely. But she's a bit less confident now.

"Look, little girl, take out the ring. Do the show, and you'll have enough money to mutilate your nipples."

She glares at me, but does what I ask. What can I say? I have a gift. Because even though I never went for the goth look, I was once a very angry young girl myself.

"Hhhh," Sue whispers.

"No problem."

Show finished (barely, a teenage boy kicked his mother in the shin with a steel-toed boot, and Lucy had to restrain dear mom from throttling him), we all pile into the "Idea Room" where stale donuts and cheap coffee await us. See why I love this place? Nothing fancy, just the basics.

"Okay, everyone, have a seat. Put your thinking caps on," Stacey, the executive director, instructs us from the front of the room.

Stacey is like that favorite teacher: gentle, soft, always making you feel like the best thing since toast. To do her job well, she has to be able to charm and placate the fruitcake guests, but also be firm when necessary so no one gets hurt. Numerous instances of observing her calm the two wives of a very satisfied husband and talent contests that become more of a match of foul mouths and spitting ability than innate talent have shown me how to manage.

I love the control I have at the show. Getting the segments, creating a scenario and finding the guests willing to pour out their sordid tales for entertainment. Of course, it isn't the most meaningful and won't help attain world peace, but I work hard. And really, what else would I do with a Master's degree in philosophy? I don't want to teach, and I love television so this always seemed like the best fit. And it's heartening to realize that everyone has something they need to deal with. I, however, would never dream of announcing my dysfunctions to the world on national television.

Our shows are planned about one month in advance. This helps us to check the other talk shows so we don't have the same ideas at the same time. Each associate producer (there are five of us) gets one show at a time to work on, and these are first come, first serve. Most of the associates are really cool, and we're pretty good about giving each other the chance to do the shows we really want.

Adrienne, Jennifer and Horace are fun and totally willing to trade if the topic hits too close to home. Everyone understands I don't do the "My Mother is a Lesbian" stories. Everyone except the newest associate, "Eva the Embittered." She's been gunning for Sue's job since the day she arrived two months ago, always letting everyone know she's "taking the initiative" (blech) by effectively stealing the highest rated shows. She's already had "Have a Date with a Celebrity," "Producer Makeovers" and "$100,000 Shopping Sprees." The fact that she could model for Derek's hair products irritates the hell out of me.

She's constantly flipping her long, thick auburn hair in my face, muttering half-hearted apologies, a satisfied gleam in her cold, aqua eyes. What bugs me the most is that she's always asking about Derek. Not in an interested way, but in a "why is he with you?" kind of way. He'd actually taken me out for lunch a few weeks ago (trust me, that doesn't happen very often), and like a bee to shit, I mean honey, she came swanning over to introduce herself.

It didn't help that I could see his reaction immediately. Even $3000.00 suits can't hide the massive erection he was sporting. I placed a proprietorial hand on his arm before sticking my tongue in his mouth. "This is my boyfriend, Derek," I'd introduced him.

"Why hello," Eva said, kissing him on both cheeks like she was French or something. She's actually from some small town in hicksville Iowa.

At lunch, Derek had said, "That one is going places."

Yeah, straight to hell with my heel in her ass. Today, she's wearing what can only be described as a hot pink towel and skintight pink capris. Her tanned, toned abs are laughing at me.

"How's Derek, Jamie? We haven't seen him around here very much," she says bitchily and takes the seat right next to me.

There are about ten other chairs she could choose from, but no, she seems to get off on this conflict between us that she created the minute we were introduced. Not to disappoint her, I lie, "Oh, he's fantastic. We just celebrated our fifth anniversary and had the best time."

Lucy glances at me and smiles knowingly.

"Funny you're not engaged yet," Eva continues, sinister eyes boring directly at the stain on my shirt.

"Is it?"

Grind, mash, grit of the teeth. Ahhh.

"Okay guys, before we begin, I want to introduce our new executive producer. Sue will be going part time," a sad look for Sue, "and Andrew Harris will be coming on board. Andrew has worked in documentaries for the last five years and was excited by what we do here. Let's all give him a warm welcome," Stacey tells us.

Sue's going part time? Why didn't she tell me? Looking at Sue, who's blushing crimson to the roots of her hair, I'm not so sure this was her decision. Out of the corner of my eye, I sneak a quick peek at Andrew who's sitting next to Sue. Tall in his grey t-shirt and blue jeans, he looks nice. Messy brown hair, pert little nose and lean, lanky body. No suit, no mousse, no compact. Lucky girlfriend (or boyfriend) he must have.

He stands up and says, "Hi, everyone. I'm Andrew Harris. After working in documentary film making for five years and for the most part, travelling to war-torn countries, I wanted to do something that allows me to stay in one place for awhile. I'm looking forward to working with all of you."

Eva takes the opportunity to show him exactly how he can work with her. She slinks over to him, shaking her hips (looking positively ridiculous doing her catwalk strut) and presses her breasts into his arm. "Hello, Andrew. We want to give you a warm welcome. It's wonderful to have some fresh blood around here."

Her fangs jut out, and she sinks her pointy teeth into his neck drawing blood. Okay, she doesn't, but it seems like she's about to. Andrew looks a bit scared and not so subtly, he removes her massive globules of flesh from his arm. "Um, well, thanks ah..." he stutters.

"Eva."

"Thanks, Eva. Thanks everybody." And he sits down.

Handing each of us a thick marker and chart paper, Stacey splits us into groups of four to brainstorm ideas. I'm with Lucy, Adrienne and Horace. No more Evil for now. We head to the corner closest to the donuts and get to work. I'm the fastest writer so I'm put in charge of the jotting. After uncapping the marker and inhaling the noxious fumes, I'm good to go.

"Sex changes," Lucy calls out.

"Penis enlargement," Horace adds.

"Plastic surgery to look like a celebrity," says Adrienne, who already looks like Courtney Cox.

The brainstorming is always very telling because, of course, we mention what we'd like to do if we could go on the show. I steal a furtive glance at Horace's groin and see why he came up with his idea. Too bad for Horace.

"Boys raised as girls," I write.

"Cheating with your husband's sister," Lucy tells me.

"Sexy stalkers."

"Men who love fat women."

"Almost all of our ideas focus on sex," I tell my horny little group.

"Sex sells," Lucy answers, brushing donut sprinkles from her red leather pants.

"Time's up," Stacey says, clapping her hands together. "Group one, come to the front, please."

We send Horace to post the chart and explain our ideas. Here, everyone will either nix them or keep them. Stacey tells us that half of our ideas will appear on one of the other talk shows (probably because they're much better), but she likes "Men who Love Fat Women" and "Plastic Surgery to Look Like a Celebrity."

"Shh, hhh, blah, mmmm," Sue says.

I turn to her and argue, "Yes, some women might think the fat idea is degrading, but won't it also empower larger women? Present them as just as sexy as a skinny girl?"

"I agree with Sue," Eva interrupts and narrows her eyes at me.

Of course you do, you bitch.

"I like it. I'm fat, and I'd like to be seen as a sex object once in awhile," Jennifer says, patting her very round, fleshy tummy.

"Okay, it's in. Next group."

Most of the ideas are very similar until Andrew's group (which Eva's in) gets up. He walks with confidence to the front of the room, but I can see he's a bit nervous because the marker in his hand is doing a shaky little dance. I smile at him, and he grins back

48

gratefully.

"We have one idea, but we think it'll be different and interesting. Other shows have done it, but not for awhile. I did some research last night, and no other shows are doing it for the next six months. It's surprise reunions with high school crushes. We'll give the surprisers makeovers so they look and feel great. These shows generally go well, and our ratings will skyrocket if a couple or two actually go on a date after, which we'll pay for," Andrew finishes, puts the marker down and pushes his hair out of his eyes. It's then that I notice his jaw moving. A fellow grinder.

"I love that idea, Andrew," Eva simpers, running her finger down her throat to her breasts.

Does she think that's sexy? It probably is. To me, it just looks like she's wiping dirt off herself. Everyone seems to like the topic, and after the other groups have their turn, Stacey tells us to "talk amongst ourselves" while she compiles the topics we'll choose from. I decide to talk to Sue. I want to know what's going on so I wander over to the corner of the room where she's buried her nose in papers.

"Hey, Sue? Is everything okay?" I ask quietly.

She looks up at me, her sad brown eyes filling with tears and explains. Turns out her mom isn't doing well, and when Sue asked for some time off, the Powers-That-Be decided that cutting her hours and lowering her salary would help relieve her stress. But, she still needs the money. Lines of worry are etched in her pale forehead, and her hair is falling out of its neat bun because she's been nervously tugging on it.

I awkwardly pat her hand, not sure what else to do. Sue's a really wonderful person who's had some horrible luck. In the middle of our tete a tete, Andrew walks over. "Sue, can I speak to you for a minute?" he asks gently, placing a hand on her shoulder.

Sue flinches and looks unsure. After all, this guy just took her job. Although it's not his fault. She follows him to another corner of the room, and I watch them protectively. Sue is saying nothing, just listening and nodding. Then, the strangest thing happens. A huge smile breaks out on her face, and it makes her look...beautiful. She gratefully squeezes his shoulder, and it seems like she's thanking him profusely, which he shrugs off.

I wait until he walks away, cornered by Eva, and I head over to Sue, who's positively beaming. "What happened? You look so happy," I ask curiously and lean against the table.

Right into a chocolate donut which smears all over my hand, the table and my white shirt. This is why I never buy quality. Or wear white very often.

She hands me a napkin and explains. "Andrew feels terrible about taking my job. When he was interviewed, they told him the position was open, not that he'd be sharing it. He gave me some websites and companies that he does editing for. They apparently pay exorbitant amounts, better than what I'm making here, and I can work from home," she relates in a surprisingly clear voice.

And I know that Sue is leaving. I also know that my first impression of Andrew Harris was dead on. He *is* really nice. But what's someone with his experience doing working at our bottom of the barrel talk show? I don't have any time to mull that one over because Stacey assembles us for the topic selection. I've learned pretty quickly that whenever Eva notices I want something, she'll throw her body in front of mine and raise her hand so Stacey can't see me.

Today what I want is the reunion show. It sounds like it'll be fun to find the crushes and hear their stories. And there will probably be some travelling involved, and I could get away from Derek and really think about things. About us.

Andrew glances at me, his eyes knowing. He's a perceptive one this guy. When the topic is up for grabs, I try to insert myself in front of Eva, and at the same time, she's trying to push me back. Her shoulder cracks into my chest, and she slams me back in my chair.

"Ow! That hurt, Eva!" I yell.

"I bet. There's nothing to cushion the blow."

"I think Jamie's interested in the reunion show," Andrew points out.

How did he know my name?

"Jamie, you want it?" Stacey asks, holding the marker to write down my name.

"Absolutely," I tell her, giving Eva the hugest shit-eating grin.

"Bitch," Eva mutters under her breath.

"Yeah," I whisper back and smile again.

Nice.

CHAPTER SIX

Heeeyaaak. Heeeyaak. I hear a reverberating squawk that sounds embarrassingly like a sick goose with stomach problems. I push open the door of Randolph station (decorated in creative graffiti telling me to fuck myself, and believe me, I would if I could) and immediately, sweat is dripping down my face in the sticky heat.

Wiping my forehead, I look around the busy parking lot to find the clunky, rusted seven year old Honda that our stepmother Maureen, or Mo as everyone calls her, had given Rachel. Rachel's pressing the horn impatiently, causing everyone in the parking lot to stare at her. Which is probably exactly why she's doing it.

Mo didn't think it was safe for such a pretty girl to take the train alone at night so when she got a new car, she gave her old one to Rachel. Considering I've never owned a car, what does that say about me? But I'm not jealous. Who would be of a smelly, gas-guzzling eyesore like "Eleanor"? Yes, my darling sister named her car.

I hop in the front seat after throwing the shopping bags, Diet Coke cans and books haphazardly piled on it in the back. Kissing Rachel's smooth, tanned cheek, I settle myself in for what might be my last ride. With Rachel driving, you never quite know what will happen. True to form, she slams her sandaled foot down on the gas.

"Could you not get us killed?" I ask.

"I'll try," she says easily and grins.

"What's going on with Steve?" I ask, after checking her blind spot and both sides of the road.

"Well, he asked me to go to a movie this weekend, but I don't

52

know. There's this other guy, Jake, in my history class at summer school, and oh, Jaim, he's soooooo hot!" she exclaims and peels out of the parking lot, her old tires screaming their disapproval.

Oh, to be a teenager again. Although I didn't have as many or as varied romantic encounters as my beautiful sister.

"And that way Becky won't be angry with you for stealing her boyfriend."

"He's *not* her boyfriend," Rachel says hotly, two bright patches of color rising in her cheeks.

Oops.

"Sorry, you're right. But there's the golden rule of friendship, you know."

"Don't covet your friend's crushes," she says monotonously. "But, Becky likes everyone. So, if I stay away from every guy she likes, I'll never get any."

I shudder because I can't believe my little sister just said "getting any."

"I lost a friend like that."

"You stole her boyfriend?" Rachel is incredulous and turns to gawk at me.

Unfortunately, she's still driving.

"Rach! The road!"

"Oh yeah." She giggles.

"No, she stole mine. Anyway, it was a long time ago. Just decide who's more important, I guess. Guys come and go, but friends stay."

"Well, Becky can't have every guy she wants to herself. But, you're right that Steve isn't the guy for me. But Jake, oh, he's perfect."

I don't remember saying that about Steve, but Rachel hears what she wants to. "Anyway, what's Mo making for dinner?" I change the subject because I think Rach and I have totally different

53

opinions on this.

"Ribs," she answers and changes lanes, effectively cutting off the car next to her and ignoring the sharp blare of the horn.

We give each other a look. We both love Mo because she's mad for our dad, and she's so good to us. But, it's the grossest thing to watch her wrench the meat off anything with a bone in it. She says it's part of her Eastern European background. We think it's just disgusting to see her pearly little teeth rip the meat off and then practically swallow the bone to suck out the marrow.

We arrive alive, and Dad and Mo are sitting on the front porch holding hands. After Leah and Katie had shacked up, my dad was pretty destroyed. But, being the most incredible man alive, he sucked it up, moved out and actually came over for dinner once a week. He didn't want me to grow up in a house filled with hate.

Mo came to the university about five years after my parents' divorce. The second she laid eyes on my tall, lean, hunky dad, she fell hard. And Mo was patient. Instead of pouncing on an obviously deeply hurt man, she became his friend. Lunches became drinks and drinks became dinners. And Mo was smart. So was Leah.

When Leah found out about all the dinners, she called Mo and invited her to a spiritual renewal workshop. Leah wanted Mo to know that she wanted my dad to find someone else to love. Mo had her auras analyzed, her chakras aligned and lymph nodes drained. During this time, there was a lot of talking and female bonding. Leah convinced Mo to go after my dad, and the rest, as they say, is history.

This was about three years after Rachel was born. To this day, I still can't believe that Mo willingly walked into our deranged family. But, she had no problem with my mom being gay, with my being surly, and my dad being a sperm bank. Because naturally, she's a lot like Leah. They must have all dropped a hit from the same tab of acid.

Mo is earthy. No makeup, no bra, and she's one of Leah's best clients. She was an actress before she became the head of the drama department at the university. Over the years, I've had to endure impromptu trust exercises and family improv night. But I love her because she makes my dad happy. Plus, she always tells me how wonderful I am, and she eats meat. Unlike Katie and Leah who actually tear up when they see the steak at the supermarket.

"Jamie! Rachel! Come, come," she calls from the sun-drenched porch.

Rachel races over, and I meander. Throwing herself into Mo's arms, Rachel starts talking immediately. I kiss Mo on the cheek, and she turns away from Rachel's chatter. "You look beautiful, honey. Things must be going well for you."

Okay, obviously Mo's not the most astute. Or that expensive concealer really does work better than the cheap kind.

"Where's Derek?" my dad asks in his booming voice.

This is the voice that mesmerizes hordes of female students every year. My dad's one of the most popular professors but doesn't realize that it's probably more than his teaching ability that's the cause of the highest female enrolment ever in Introduction to Philosophy.

I stand on my tiptoes to give him a quick hug. "He has a dinner meeting. He's sorry that he couldn't make it."

"We haven't seen him in awhile. Is everything okay with you two?" he asks, rubbing his chin thoughtfully.

"Just peachy."

"Leah told us that you haven't been taking your vitamins. Your health is the most important, sweetie," my dad reminds me and chucks me under my chin.

Mo touches my dad's arm. "David, she just got here. Give her a break. Jamie, did you guys have a good time in Montreal?"

"Sure." No need to mention that the best part was the shower head. I have a bad feeling that my family has a cache of sex toys hidden in their houses and would have no problem giving me a detailed demonstration.

"Well, let's go sit until dinner's ready. I've made ribs, yum, lots of little bones, and we can eat in the backyard," Mo tells us as she leads the way through the messiest (I mean dishes, cookbooks and plants are piled onto every available surface) kitchen in existence.

Their hundred year old house is just a quick ride on the "L" to the university. It's situated in the middle of a winding street, three stories high (one which they use and the other two are rented out to whomever will pay), red brick with a lush, dense garden in front and an incredible backyard. Every spring, Mo has planting parties. Everyone invited has to bring anything that will grow so there's no rhyme or reason back there. Roses are mixed with apple trees, lilies and basil coexist and huge sunflowers spring up wherever they feel like. I love that there's no order to it. Derek thinks a garden needs a plan and design, and it drives him bonkers to wade through the weeds and knock his head on a tree that has suddenly arisen out of nowhere.

A massive picnic table rests on the cobblestone patio, chairs and tables are scattered in and around the garden, and a terra cotta chimera hovers next to the barbecue to warm up frigid nights. When I'm here, everything seems safe. I feel at peace in the chaos and mess.

My dad hands me a gin and tonic with a splash of lemon (I hate lime) and gives Rachel a Diet Coke.

"Why can't I have a gin and tonic?" she whines.

"Because you spit it back into the glass the last time, and you're driving," I remind her.

"Oh yeah, right."

Mo gets herself a beer, and we sit together in the garden.

Lifting the beer to her mouth, she glimpses at me from the corner of her eye and looks away.

"I'm worried about you, Jamie." She says this while not looking at me. She knows that if she looks at me, I'll clam up.

"I'm fine, Mo. Work's great, Derek's doing extremely well. Everything's fine."

"Fine isn't good enough. Did you know I was married before your dad?" she asks, now looking me straight in the eye. And, of course, I look away and fiddle with a new hole in my pants.

"I know something about it, but not the details."

"No? Well, listen to this story. We'd met at a theater company. He was the director."

"Svengali syndrome?" I ask, turning my body towards her.

She crosses her legs, making the bells on her skirt dance, and tucks her wavy brown hair behind one ear. "Pretty much. He was older and gorgeous. Not nearly as handsome as David," she tells me and looks over affectionately at my dad who's turning on the barbecue and wearing a red apron reading 'Kiss the Cook,' "but powerful. We fell in love, and six weeks later got married. For the first couple of years, we had a whirlwind, passionate relationship. That time when you can't get enough of each other. He was attentive, supportive, loved taking me places and showing me off. We lived in this great, rambling house, and everything was wonderful until he got the opportunity to direct a movie. All of a sudden, it was as if I wasn't there. And I certainly wasn't glamorous enough for the Hollywood film crowd. So, I changed. Cut my hair, went to the gym, wore whatever was 'in,' took roles I didn't want. And he left me anyway. For another actress."

"Wow, Mo, I had no idea. What an asshole."

She nods. "Well, yes he was, but people change. And you might think that a relationship is supposed to last forever, and you'll always be together. But sometimes you just grow apart. I was devastated after he left, but, and David helped me to understand this, I realized that for years, I was just going through the motions because being on my own seemed worse than being with someone who didn't really love me."

"I know what you're getting at, but Derek would never leave me for another woman. He has no time."

She puts her hand on my knee, and her eyes soften. "Selfish people don't do things for other people. They do it for themselves."

"I know, Mo. But it's just a rough patch. Derek is really good to me."

"How? How is he good to you, Jamie?"

I don't answer her. Instead, I look around the chaotic garden and inhale the fragrant scent of the flowers. The freshness and stillness of the plants only serves to show me how messed up my own life has become. I know that Derek wants me to be a better person, he tries to get me to be more ambitious, he buys me the nicest of everything. But, in fact, he's trying to change me instead of letting me be myself. The garden grows just as it wants to, but Derek doesn't nurture that in me.

Mo pats my knee and stands up to check on the ribs. And now my dad takes her seat to give me the extended version of her lecture. No one in my family believes in letting things lie. Everything has to be analyzed, chewed over and spit out in emotional catharsis. But whereas Leah just hmmms a lot, my dad goes straight to the heart of the problem and philosophizes about it.

"Jamie, honey, are you happy?" he asks.

"Define happy, Dad," I sigh and wonder how long this little talk is going to last. I need to refill my drink.

"Being where you want to be and doing what you want to be doing."

I sip the remnants of my deliciously cool gin and tonic. "Yup, right now, I'm enjoying the sunshine, sipping a great drink, and I'm relaxing."

"Oh, you are so much like your mother. Don't be flippant. This is your life you're talking about, and you don't have to stay with him."

"Dad, I love him, and things will get better." I grit my teeth in frustration. "Look, I'm getting really sick and tired of everyone analyzing me, okay? I'm fine."

"You know what love means? It means loving the person you are now and not the person you want someone to be or the person they will be. If you think about it that way, do you and Derek really love each other?"

I don't want to think about it anymore at all. I kiss my dad on his whiskery cheek and join Rachel at the picnic table where she's devouring a bag of sour cream and onion chips. While she's text messaging all her friends and downloading music at the same time. Oh, to be oblivious to the turmoil.

I grab a handful of chips and shove them in my mouth. I'd have to be a complete moron not to realize that Derek and I are in serious trouble, and I have to take action. But, I don't know if I'm ready to lose him.

"Dinner!" Mo singsongs and calls us over to the barbecue.

I hand her my plate, and she winks at me. "You'll figure it out," she tells me and gives me a steaming plate of ribs smothered in her special spicy sauce.

"You'll figure what out?" Rachel asks, suddenly behind me and elbowing me in the back.

"How to get you to stop texting boys all the time," Mo says and smiles.

"I don't text them, Mo. They text me."

Mo looks at me pointedly and says, "Rachel's on the right track."

Yes. She is.

CHAPTER SEVEN

A misspelled neon sign is screaming at me to buy "Budweezer," and I'm being attacked by a hungry swarm of buzzing mosquitos. I slap my arm to kill one, and it gets its revenge by sucking the last bit of blood out of my skin and then dies on me. Lucy and I are sitting outside (which is a bit chilly and nippy, but she's got the hots for the waitress who's serving the next table) on the terrace of a local watering hole near her apartment in Wicker Park, and we've been here for a few hours already.

I've been feeling pretty gloomy since dinner at Dad and Mo's, and I just needed to get out and not be preached at about Derek. And now that I've had a few days to think about what Mo said about her ex-husband, I've been trying to convince myself that there's no comparison between him and Derek. That guy left her for another woman, and from the sound of it, treated her like shit. Derek doesn't have time to treat me like shit. Or to treat me right. But, I really don't want to think about it. I just want to be out and have a good time. No stress.

"Eva's a real cunt, isn't she?" Lucy asks, breaking into my reverie, making the "c" sound extra harsh.

"Such a fitting word." I take a sip from my third lychee martini. I can't taste the alcohol, and it's going down real smoothly. "Did you see her try to steal the show I wanted?"

"Yeah, she hates you. So, what do you think of the new guy?" Lucy asks, raising her thinly arched eyebrows and sucking in smoke from what must be her tenth cigarette.

I can't take it anymore. I must have a cigarette. And if I'm going to be shivering and eaten alive all night, I might as well enjoy it.

60

"Give me a cigarette. You're driving me crazy."

"Derek'll kill you," she tells me and glances at her pack of cigarettes lying between us.

"My life, my choice." I grab her cigarette from her hand and take a drag, letting the instant gratification thrill me as the smoke fills my lungs. "Ah, that's better. Thanks. Andrew? He seems nice," I offer, blowing out the smoke.

"He's kind of hot in a bookish sort of way. One of those guys you just know harbors dirty little fantasies. Bending me over, taking me from behind..."

"You're gay, Luce," I remind her and point out that the reason I'm so fucking cold is because of the girl in the pleats.

"I'm bisexual, thanks."

"If you had to apportion your sexuality, how would you do it? 50% for men and 50% for women?" I ask, noticing that I've finished her cigarette so I reach for another one from her pack.

Might as well go all the way.

"99% for women, 1% for men. With women, it's like a song that has highs and lows." She dips her hand up and down in wave-like motions. "It builds, slows down, builds again. With men, it builds to a crescendo, and then, wham, it's over. For you?"

I smirk at her because she already knows the answer to that. Lucy is a strong believer in Kinseyism, the continuum of sexuality that determined most people have bisexual tendencies, just to varying degrees. Mind you, the only men I've ever seen Luce give a second glance to are firemen. She'll hop on any firetruck that's stopped at a red light, and by the next block, she'll be the one wearing the big boots.

"Well, not 100% anymore. More 99.9% now. Have you seen Angelina Jolie lately? I'd do her."

"Angelina Jolie would fuck Angelina Jolie."

"Mmm, that's lovely. Anyway, I'm not interested in anyone

else. I have Derek. He's just being a bit of a dick right now."

"Now? Jaim, you've been unhappy for ages. Why do you stay? What's the point?" Lucy lifts her shoulders in a question.

"Does there always need to be a point? Jesus, why is everyone bugging me? I can take care of myself, damn it! I'm so sick of talking about this. Why is everyone searching for some big meaning of life? Maybe there *is* no meaning. You feel happiness in the moment, but you can't look for it," I say, punctuating my point by waving my freshly lit cigarette in her face.

Lucy ducks left and right to avoid being burned. "Hey, don't take it out on me, okay? I'm not the enemy. If you want to talk, you can talk. If not, I can harass you about something totally different. Like the fact that you think it's great to just do the same things day after day, being satisfied in the brief moments of happiness that come when you're watching reruns of 'Sex and The City.' But, I know you must dream about things. You just don't talk about them."

I'm quiet. I hear smacking kissy sounds coming from the next table and a sickening pang of jealousy impales my stomach. "I've just never really had something I wanted enough, I guess. I'm pretty content with working at the show and stuff. You know me, I like things to be low-key, calm, and fairly stress free."

And as I explain it, something niggles at me. Why don't I dream? Why don't I want to find passion and happiness like everyone else? Maybe because I've never been like everyone else. I've always had this feeling, ever since I can remember, of not fitting in. I'm nothing like my family, obviously, and as close as I am to Hanna and Lucy, I'm also extremely different from them.

I've always felt like I'm on the periphery, observing from the outside and looking in at all of the people who seem to have some connection to life that I just don't. I think I haven't found my place yet. But, at thirty-two, I guess I kind of should.

"But it's really not that way, is it?" She holds up a hand to stop what she knows will be my barked retort. "I don't mean about Derek. I mean about you. You're not realizing your full potential."

I roll my eyes at her and take a sip of my martini (they keep showing up, and I don't think I've ordered them) before answering. "Oh, puleeze. My full potential? I know what I like, and I know what I'm good at. So, I shouldn't rock the boat too much. Why mess with a good thing?"

Lucy reaches out and holds my hand. Her eyes soften, she takes a deep breath and says, "Because sometimes the good thing isn't so good anymore."

I snatch my hand back. "What happened to this wasn't about Derek? Have you and Hanna been conspiring?"

"No, of course not. Okay, let's just drop it. I mean, in other ways, you aren't going after what you could have. Like Sue's job. It was posted, and you didn't apply."

"I thought we were dropping it. And I didn't notice the job was posted. Since when? I've been out of the office a lot recently."

"Three weeks ago."

Oh. I was there three weeks ago. And every day as I passed by the job board on the way to my desk. And probably got the email and promptly deleted it. Okay, that's a bit surprising because I actually would have loved Sue's job. To be honest, I've been doing Sue's job for three years. But, she has the education and experience, and I have a philosophy degree and great phone etiquette courtesy of a telemarketing stint after graduation.

Lucy is now getting worked up, and she slaps at the air with her hands. "That's what I mean, Jaim! You don't go after things. You let them come to you. There's that story from the Koran. Have you ever read it?"

"Why would I read the Koran? What the hell are you talking about?" I ask, knotting my brow in confusion.

63

"You studied philosophy. Didn't you read religious texts?"

"Parts. Not the whole Koran. Okay, fine, what's the story?"

"Well, in Islam, drinking alcohol is a huge taboo, right?"

I nod slowly, absolutely stupefied how this relates to me not noticing that Sue's job was up for grabs.

"There was this queen who loved to tempt the men to do her bidding. Anyway, one day she was out walking, and she found an extremely religious man. And, being the queen, she could order him to do what she wanted. So she gave the man three choices: kill a child, have a drink or sleep with her. The man figured that the least of the three evils would be to have a drink. So, he drank. And he got so drunk that he ended up killing the child and sleeping with the queen," Lucy finishes, butts out the cigarette and crosses her arms in front of her chest.

"What would have happened if he had chosen one of the other two?" I ask.

"You're missing the point." Lucy purses her lips in annoyance.

I glare at her for confusing me so much. "As much as I enjoyed the story, I have no clue what you're getting at."

She rolls her eyes as if to say that I'm not listening. "You stop yourself from taking chances, and one day, you'll do it. But to the extreme. And then who knows what will happen?"

I grin. "I'll sleep with the queen?"

"Maybe not such a bad idea," Lucy laughs and winks at the waitress who's dropping off drinks for the tongue wrestling couple. They must be parched.

"Who was your high school crush?" she asks me once she and the waitress stop ogling each other.

I smile because ever since the reunion segment came up at work, I've been thinking about him. About Lucas. With the long, lean biker's legs, tight little butt, messy black hair and sea green eyes. Lucas. The only person in my life who made me feel like I was normal.

"Earth to Jamie. Wow, you have the stupidest look on your face. There *is* someone."

I nod and grin. "Yeah, of course there is. But it was such a long time ago, God, ten years now since I've seen him."

"So tell me," Lucy leans over, resting her ample cleavage on the table.

"What's to tell? Well, okay, there's something to tell. When I was sixteen, this new guy started at Tecumseth, my high school. He'd moved here from Oregon with his mom. Anyway, on the first day of junior year, I saw this group of kids sitting and smoking on the grass. In the middle, wearing torn jean shorts and no shirt, I can't believe I remember this so well, was Lucas. The second I laid eyes on him, I wanted him."

"Your bad boy fetish."

"Exactly. He was sullen, moody, uncommunicative. I was so shy and insecure so I never said anything to show him I liked him. Finally, he noticed me at a party. And you know how you do when you're sixteen, and you talk for two seconds and then, awkwardly fool around? Well, there was nothing awkward about it. Now that I think about it, at sixteen, Lucas was more in tune with my body than, well, whatever, he was really good. For about two months, we went out. The problem was we had absolutely nothing to say to each other. So I did the 'maybe we should break up' thing. You know what I mean? You say it hoping the other person will fight for you?"

"Always backfires," Lucy interrupts and grins, a rosy blush making her normally pale face glow.

"Yup. So we broke up, and he went out with a friend of mine. The same friend who'd listened to me talk about him all the time and told me I was better off without him. See why I don't trust people?"

"What happened to her?"

"To Claire Howard? No idea. It's funny, I was just talking about her with Rachel the other day. No, I never really spoke to her again."

As I tell Lucy, something funny moves around my heart, and I think it's pain. There must be some reason that an ex-boyfriend or whatever from ten years ago makes me feel more than everything that's happening now. As the realization hits home more than I want to deal with, the waitress of Lucy's affection drops a napkin on our table, licks her lips and says to Lucy in a whiskey voice, "Call me."

I'm stunned, and I stare open-mouthed at the napkin that has a phone number on it. Under the name "Leticia." "How do you do that? With no effort."

"Are you kidding me? I've been checking her out for a few days now. I came here yesterday and the day before. She's cute, huh?"

"Very. Can I continue?" Now that I've started the story, I want to tell it all.

"Sorry. Go on."

"Well, we broke up, and we'd see each other every other weekend at these parties. There was this guy in our school, Jason, who had a huge field behind his house. There'd be a hundred of us crowded back there every Friday night, drinking, smoking, jumping off the roof, making bonfires. It was insane." I giggle at the memory that has long been buried in the years since then.

Lucy rests her elbows on the table and leans closer to me. "Where were his parents? Tied up in the closet?"

"Too drunk or too stoned to care."

"Suburban upbringing."

"Only the best for their kids. Anyway, Lucas and I would sit in front of the fire, weekend after weekend, smoking, not saying

66

much. But, God, I just wanted to be with him. He was the first guy who made me comfortable about my body, you know? I was not the least bit attractive and my hips were growing a hell of a lot faster than my chest. Mind you, I still look like that."

She blows out a heavy breath. "Would you stop putting yourself down? You're sexy. Not everyone's a breast man."

"Do you like big breasts?" I retort.

"Actually, yes, but I'm not everyone. And I like small ones too. Stop talking about your boobs and tell me the story already."

"Fine. After months of going to these parties, bored out of my skull and freezing cold, he finally kissed me. Somehow, we ended up fooling around in his car and at his house every Saturday night for the next three years."

"In his car? That's classy." She laughs, lights two cigarettes and hands one to me.

"Thanks," I say, taking the smoke. "You know what's funny? We probably could have been at my house. Leah and Katie would have rathered I be at home screwing around with some guy than in the backseat of a car. But there was no way I wanted them to know about any of this."

"You don't think they knew?"

I smile. "Oh, I know they did. But they also knew I would deny it if they had asked me. I was never really into sharing my personal life. Unlike Rachel, who tells them everything."

"She has a lot to tell. I can't believe you were with this guy for three years, and this is the first I'm hearing of it. Actually, no, scratch that. That's so you."

I make a face at her and say, "But he wasn't my boyfriend. We just had sex. I even lost my virginity to him. We almost never went out or talked on the phone. We just had this crazy sexual connection. And I guess since the stress of being in a relationship wasn't there, we could finally talk to each other, and we became

67

friends. Best friends."

"I lost my virginity to my driving instructor."

"That's gross. How old was he?"

She shakes her head, looking incredibly sexy as the cigarette dangles just so off the right corner of her lip. "She was twenty-one. I meant my lesbian virginity. And it was mind-blowing. I slept with my brother's best friend when I was fifteen. Useless."

"Because you're a lesbian?"

"Bisexual, but no. Because he was tiny. No bigger than my thumbnail." And she holds up her own burgundy painted nail to demonstrate.

"Ugh." I shudder.

"No kidding. There's more to your story. How did it end?"

"We both graduated, and he went to Colorado to study, um, something, and I went to the University of Chicago. So he left, and I guess we both thought that'd be it. We wrote letters, talked on the phone and stuff, but since we weren't living in the same city, we never had sex. And I had different boyfriends, but nobody who made me feel like that, though. Like I was alive."

"Because you go for the wrong guys?" she asks, smiling sardonically and pulling her glossy black hair back into a ponytail.

"Sometimes. Back to my story please. One day, he called me. He was home for the weekend and wanted to see me. It must have been six months or so since he'd left. And we started the whole thing again. For the next four years, every time he came home, we saw each other."

"How long did this whole thing go on for?"

"Seven years or so."

"Good God! And you were still just sleeping together? No commitment?"

I shake my head. "None. We never even talked about it."

"Was it just lust?"

Looking back now, I can answer that question. Then, I would have said yes, no way was it love, we were just having sex. I'm not a perfectly confident woman now, but I'm sure a lot more secure than I was in my teens and early twenties.

"No. I think it was love. We just didn't know what to do about it. We saw each other one last time. We had sex in his basement, rolling all over the scratchy carpet. I ended up with quite the burns, let me tell you. Anyway, just as I was leaving, I rolled down the window to say goodbye, and he handed me this letter and told me he loved me. Just like that and for the first time. I was so freaked out that I just drove away. But God, I read that letter so many times, it was falling apart," I say, that strange pain now sitting in my chest and pressing my lungs to my back.

"Do you still have the letter?"

I shrug. "Probably somewhere. At Leah's, I think. I haven't looked at it in years. I haven't thought about Lucas in years. I never saw or spoke to him again."

"He never called the next time he came in? You never called him?"

"No way. I wasn't about to make the first move. And I had no idea what was going on. I thought he just wanted me for sex."

"You're such a wimp," she says.

I grab another cigarette, light it and slap the mosquito that's just landed on my jean-clad (Salvation Army, $10) leg. "Yes. But then I don't get hurt."

"Don't you ever wonder what happened to him?"

"Sure, for awhile I did, and then it sort of faded away. I dated a few other guys, and then I met Derek, and that was that. But now that we're talking about it, yeah, I wonder where he's living, if he's married, or God, what if he has kids? I can totally picture him with kids."

Lucy's eyes widen, her chest rises, and I get a bad feeling.

"Why don't you find him?" she asks, her eyes lighting up.

I knew it. Lucy has some half-cocked idea that she wants me to jump all over. "Why? What would be the purpose almost ten years later?" I ask, getting more nervous by the second.

"Closure," she says, draining the last of her drink and motioning to the waitress for another one.

"There's no such thing. You just move on."

"Maybe now that you're both adults, presumably with more maturity, you might fall madly in love."

"I have Derek, Luce."

She grimaces and says nothing.

"What could I possibly gain from finding Lucas? Awkward silence after the initial 'What have you been doing for the last decade?'"

"You could find him for the reunion show. It's perfect! While you're searching for everyone else's lost loves, you can find your own. It's destiny. The universe is sending you a message here."

My eyes pop open at the lunacy of her suggestion. "Are you crazy? I'd never in a million years go on our show."

"No, no, not for television, just for you. You'll have all the resources."

I look at her shiny face flushed with excitement. And for a second, I get a taste of that excitement. And I like it. Time and time again, I somehow find myself jumping on the Zany Lucy Bandwagon, and every time, it's a disaster. Once she thought it'd be great if she, Hanna and I went to Las Vegas on a whim. I ended up with food poisoning, heatstroke and minus the $500.00 that was given to the blackjack dealer.

I try arguing with her. "But on their dollar. They'd kill me."

"Who'd know? You'll be using the phone and fax anyway. It's not really using their money. It could be an adventure." Lucy's eyes flutter up and down, creating spidery shadows on her cheekbones.

And now, thanks to Lucy, the idea sets in my head like a bad song, and I know full well that it's never going to leave. But this Lucas idea is just too ridiculous. Chasing down my high school fuck buddy. Please. But instead of just changing the subject, I hear myself ask, "What would happen if I found him?"

"You don't know. That's the whole point. What if he's the One? Not that you believe in the One, but what if you're wrong? What if this is your chance to find true happiness?"

"The 'Pursuit of Happiness' is a defunct Canadian band. But it might be fun to see him again, talk to him again. Just to find out what he's been up to, who he's become. Would he even want to hear from me?"

"You won't know until you try."

No, I can't do this. How would I feel if Derek went to find his ex-girlfriend? Although they all sound like frigid ice queens from what he's told me about them. The type of girls who "debut" and wouldn't stoop to sullying themselves in the backseats of rusted cars. But maybe it'll make me realize why I love Derek. Like comparison shopping. "Okay."

"Okay what?" she asks.

I take a deep breath and smile at her. "Okay, I'm going to find Lucas."

CHAPTER EIGHT

It's Saturday morning, and crap, it's sunny and gorgeous. A perfect summer day. Normally, this weather would have me donning a knee-skimming skirt and perhaps even going for a walk. But, today, I wish it were raining so I wouldn't be dragged out on one of Derek's extreme cycling days. When Derek turned twenty-nine, he decided it was time to take control of his health. He stopped smoking, eating junk food, drinking beer. Do you know how many calories beer has? No? Well, neither do I. But Derek has an electronic calorie counter that he carries with him everywhere. He also started this insane workout schedule that he never ever strays from. Even on vacation, he'll strap on running shoes or bring his hand weights.

A couple of years ago we went to one of those all-inclusive resorts in Mexico. The trip was not my idea because the idea of trading perfunctory smiles with the same people (and having to talk to some of them) and eating the same food every day in and out is not my idea of a good vacation. But Derek said we needed to relax. For me, that meant reading, watching television and sitting on my ass for seven days. For Derek, it meant windsurfing, sailing, and cave diving. He'd be up at sunrise, impatiently tapping his foot until I would wake up. It was the most exhausting trip of my life.

Not that his healthy attitude isn't admirable. It is. But like everything in his life lately, he needs absolute control and discipline and doesn't see the fun in anything. Life has stopped being fun for him; it's become a race. He stands naked every night in front of the bedroom mirror, examining himself from all angles and measuring his fat with calipers. Seriously. It's not me who asks, "Do I look fat in this?," it's Derek.

72

He even has this anal workout schedule taped to the fridge. Monday: triceps and biceps, Tuesday: quads and calves, Wednesday: lats, Thursday: abs and obliques, Friday is a miraculous day off, and Saturday, well, Saturday is Psycho Sports Day. I've claimed cramps many a time to avoid rock climbing, hiking, bungee jumping and rapelling. But, unfortunately, Derek knows full well I had my period just two weeks ago because I used it as an excuse to get out of a dinner with Mr. Cheesehead.

So, sadly, on this stunning, sun-filled day, we're going for a thirty mile bicycle ride from our apartment around the different neighborhoods in Chicago to a cool down at the Lakefront Trail. A cool down for me is an icy beer on a patio. It's infinitely better than a stationary bike that doesn't go anywhere, but still. Thirty miles! And it won't be a slow, leisurely cycle. It'll be lung-burning, heart racing and pedal pushing.

He's been clattering around the kitchen for the last hour in an obvious attempt at waking me up. It's 7:00 a.m., and I didn't get back from drinks with Lucy until about 2:00 a.m. I wonder if she's going to call that Leticia girl from last night. I yawn and stretch, dying to close my eyes and go back to sleep. I. Am. Not. A. Morning. Person. And I was having the most incredible dream. Actually, it was more of a night fantasy.

After that whole discussion with Lucy, of course I dreamed about Lucas. And Derek. Derek and I were at a party at someone's house. Whose house and why we were there I have no clue, but we were standing in the kitchen getting ourselves some drinks. At least, Derek was getting the drinks, and I was watching him when I felt someone (a man, I'm sure, because somehow my hand was rubbing against his crotch) run his hands up and down my body and slip one inside my pants. Suddenly, the most intense and tingling shiver zapped through me, and I didn't care that at any moment, Derek could turn around and catch some guy with his

73

hands wandering around in my underwear.

About two seconds from orgasm, I turned around and there he was. Lucas. Looking twenty years old, wearing frayed jeans, and oddly, because everyone else was fully dressed, no shirt and grinning. I melted, just about to kiss him. Crash! I *never* get to have an orgasm when Derek's around.

"Jamie, are you up yet? I want to go before it gets too hot to cycle. It's ninety degrees already!" he yells from the kitchen.

Isn't ninety degrees too hot to cycle at any time? Reluctantly, I throw off the covers and raise myself to a seated position. "Derek, could I have a cup of coffee, please?" I croak. God, I must have smoked half a pack of cigarettes last night.

He stomps into the bedroom and stares at me defiantly. "I can smell the smoke from here," he says disapprovingly, wiping dust from the bureau.

Invisible dust because Trina, our cleaning lady, was here just yesterday. I hate having a cleaning lady. I used to follow her around offering her drinks and snacks to assuage my guilt that this girl was cleaning my house. My toilet. It's just not right. Derek finally got fed up that I was bothering the "help." His mother had a talking to with me to explain the intricacies of having "assistance," as she called it. So now he only schedules her to come when he knows I won't be home.

"So move back. Did you bring my coffee?" I ask, crawling back under the covers.

"No. I didn't make any. You'll have a caffeine crash and won't last a mile."

That's the idea. "Fine. I'll make it myself. I'm not cycling for twenty hours on no coffee," I say and get up to go to the kitchen.

He follows on my heels, coughing and holding his nose. "Why did you smoke last night? I told you how I feel about that. Don't you have any self-control?"

74

When I get to the kitchen, I see a sparkling coffeepot awaiting me. Empty. I groan and fill it to capacity with water and beans. While the smooth, rich liquid prepares itself for the magic rush down my throat, I reach into the dishwasher for a clean mug.

Placing it next to the pot, I say, "Considering I'm not beating you senseless right now, I have a wealth of self-control. Leave me alone about the smoking. I only had a couple. I was with Lucy, and the conversation was so great, and we had a few drinks. You know how it is."

"Can't you find some healthy friends?" He's frowning at me as I put my huge mug under the filter to catch the nasty caffeine that's dripping from the pot.

Taking a much needed sip, I ask, "Like Chad and Brad? The Oh So Dynamic Duo?"

Chad and Brad are "new friends": executives and golf buddies. Derek used to think that golf was for people who didn't want to sweat. Now it's his favorite sport after driving me crazy. They met at the "club" (which doesn't allow women and I'm sure not Jews either, of which I am both, isn't that lovely?)

They all go there together once a week to discuss stocks and stroke each other's egos. Chad and Brad own a financial investment company (huge yawn) and both have wives named Patsy. I'd never known anyone named Patsy before, and now, lucky me, I know two. Small, blonde and bouncy wives who don't do work, they do lunch.

Until I smartened up, I'd go to their matching, indent-a-kit Gold Coast homes (the fact that they're actually in it and not hovering around it like a gate crasher at a cool party is the current bane of Derek's life), eat their catered dinners and express absolute delight over their newest china patterns, jewels and cars. And every time, they'd ask me the same question and give me the same mechanical response.

"What do you do, Jamie?" Patsy #1 would ask.

"Oh, that must be...interesting," Patsy#2 would answer after I'd told her. Yet again.

I might be a touch sensitive, but I just know they wipe down all the Chippendale furniture after my second hand ass has sat on it. Or Trina does it. Yes, surprise, surprise, she's their cleaning lady too.

"At least they have some ambition," he says and takes a drink from something yellow and thick. Protein shake. Blech.

I try not to gag as he swallows his steroids. "Hanna and Lucy have a lot of ambition. It's just not attached to a pole up their ass."

"Nice, Jamie."

I sigh. I know the constant bickering is my fault too, but I just can't help myself. Though, trust me, I do let a lot of stuff go. "Look, Derek, I'm sorry. Can we try not to fight today? It's a beautiful day, and we'll go out and enjoy ourselves." I put the coffee down to show him that I'm trying.

"Okay." And he kisses the top of my head. "But I'm not the one who's fighting."

Grind, mash, grit. Ahhh. Twenty minutes later, my body is encased in electric blue spandex (which looked much better in the store than in the bright light of day), and my butt is resting on my gel bike seat. Made for comfort. Not for thirty miles.

"Okay, let's go. Drink lots of water," Derek instructs before happily speeding off.

I pick bits of dust off my tongue and set off behind him. He does look awfully good in his black shorts and sleeveless white shirt. I can see his leg muscles straining, and I wonder, for the umpteenth time, whether we can work things out. Surely it's not good if I have to keep convincing myself. But the alternative's certainly no better. Being alone again with only the TV for comfort. I don't want that either.

I cycle past laughing truckers and children in backseats of cars sticking their tongues out at me. We stay on the main roads until we hit the ravine that cuts through the North Shore. Thickly wooded, steep and gravelly, the embankment is so uneven that I wobble precariously through the woods to the bottom of a huge hill I know I'll never make to the top.

"Derek, there's no way. What if we stop for brunch and head home? It's really hot," I complain and swoon for emphasis. It really is boiling hot, my water's gone, and black dots are dancing in front of my eyes.

"We just started. We can't give up. We need to do thirty miles."

"Why?" I ask, wiping sweat from my neck. A small pond is also pooling uncomfortably in my built-in bra. I pull it away from my chest and a gush of water spills to my feet.

"Because it's the plan."

Right, Igor. The Plan. Derek races up the mountain (okay, steep incline), and panting and pushing, I get my bike to the top. There's a fairly level clearing so I release the kickstand and flop to the ground. "I can't."

"You're in really bad shape, Jamie. We haven't even gone halfway."

"I don't care!"

"You don't care about anything," he says, hands on lean hips, not a drop of sweat on him. "Not your financial situation, your health, me."

Ouch. I bolt up from the ground. "That's so fucking unfair! I love you, you prick. I've been trying to make this work. I fight and I fight with you to pay attention to me. To notice how bad things have gotten. I try to do everything you want. What about what *I* want? What *I* need?"

"What do you want?"

I don't know so I don't answer. We get back on our bikes and cycle wordlessly back to the road and to the grocery store. I guess we're not going out for brunch. We lock up our bikes, and Derek walks ahead of me to get a cart. A hard lump of anger is stuck in my throat, and I want to scream. But I don't.

I plod behind him, tossing all sorts of junk in the cart while he keeps putting in uber-expensive, brand name items, like a $20.00 case of bottled water. He isn't saying a word about the chocolate and microwave dinners, and this is a very bad sign. Derek's pretty anal about what he eats. I'm reaching for a bag of salt and vinegar chips when I hear, "Jamie Ross? That *is* you!"

No. Please no. Not when I'm red-faced, sweaty and looking like an electric blue sausage. I recognize that husky, snide voice instantly, and I slowly turn around. Yup, it's Claire Howard. The high school nemesis I was just talking about last night. The one who stole Lucas right out from under me. Who was it who said that when you talk about someone you see them?

And she's breathtaking. Still. Long, shiny, strawberry blonde hair, startling grey eyes and porcelain skin. Not the pasty, dehydrated kind, but the creamy, smooth kind. Diamonds drip from the sparkling studs in her perfectly adorable earlobes to her little toe ring.

I look at Derek. He's staring; his mouth, hanging open slightly. I want to smack him. She kisses my clammy, crimson cheek with cinnamon lipstick. Just to leave a mark, I'm sure.

"God, Jamie, how long has it been?"

"Fifteen years, Claire."

Like you don't know, you man-stealing slut. I probably wouldn't be so angry if Lucy hadn't dredged up all that stuff about Lucas last night. But now it feels like it just happened yesterday.

"You look exactly the same," she tells me, moving her left hand in front of my face just so I can catch the massive rock on her finger.

She is not giving me a compliment. I've already mentioned my unfortunate awkward years, and to add to the pear-shaped body, I also had glasses and braces. But I was smart and funny, and that's what got me Lucas. I'm sure the adoring gazes I'd constantly shot in his direction didn't hurt any. But, Claire had the Southern Belle accent (her family had moved to Chicago from Savannah) and the DD chest.

Looking at her now, the chest looks suspiciously higher and firmer than it should be after all of these years. With small boobs, you never really worry about sagging and future nips and tucks.

"Jamie, introduce me," Derek says, scowling.

"Oh goodness, how rude of me. Derek, this is Claire, a, um, girl from high school. Claire, this is my boyfriend, Derek."

Her eyes are huge with amazement that I could have a boyfriend who looks like Derek. Clanging warning bells go off in my head. What if she does it again? Steals him too? If I turn my back for a second, she might toss him over her satiny shoulder and walk right out. Maybe that's not such a bad idea. They're both looking at me strangely. Perhaps because I'm grinning like an idiot and laughing to myself.

"Do you live around here, Claire?" Derek asks, slipping an arm around my waist.

Considering we weren't even speaking two seconds ago, I know this means he wants me to invite her over. I know that he doesn't know who she is to me, but can't he see how stiff and uncomfortable I am? After five years, you'd think he'd be able to read my body language.

"Oh no, not down here," she says, eyeing me up and down and smoothing her yellow wrap dress so it hugs her curves even more tightly. "I was at a breakfast meeting for my new marketing campaign. I'm the advertising director at Goldman Sachs. We live in the Gold Coast. Do you know the new gated community?"

I wish I had a sweatshirt to cover my huge butt.

"Oh, so you've just moved then?" Derek asks, mesmerized by the words 'gated community.'

I realize that this is the most he's talked to a friend of mine in years. I feel like I'm watching a tennis match, and I'm the ball boy.

"Yes, and we just adore it. We entertain a lot, and it's so important to keep a nice home."

"I couldn't agree more," Derek simpers.

Why don't they just fuck right here?

"So, Claire, you're married?" I ask, feigning interest.

I would also like to be part of this super fun catching up. She looks me up and down again, slower this time, and doesn't answer. Instead, she peers at her French manicure. A snub. An obvious, cold, arrogant snub. Why that little bitch! Surely Derek noticed that. I look at him, waiting for him to tell her off. He can be very biting when he wants to be. But no, that's not at all what he does.

"So, Claire, you're married?" He repeats my question.

She just snubbed me, and he actually repeated my question! All of a sudden, a surge of adrenaline takes over, and I lose total control. "Oh, looky there! Apples are on sale. Must go!" I squeal in a high-pitched, squeaky voice and swing the cart around so quickly it knocks Claire in the backs of her knees. What a shame.

"Jamie!" Derek calls after me.

Not worried. Angry. In front of her. I walk faster until I'm all the way out the door. Unfortunately, I still have the cart, and the alarms screech their warning.

While security stops me from the grand theft of bottled water, I see Claire and Derek. I think they're laughing at me. I have never wished so much for a cellphone (mine wouldn't fit anywhere in my supertight spandex) so I could call Hanna. Because I am leaving.

CHAPTER NINE

I shove away the cart with all the food in it (wishing I'd grabbed an apple or something, I'm starving) and sprint down the street until I find a payphone. I end up running for quite a few blocks because there are no working payphones left in this damn city. Strangely, I'm not crying. Even over this, I can't shed one measly tear.

"Hanna, pick up, it's me. I'll call you right back!" I yell into her call answer.

I count to a hundred and call again. This time she picks up. "Jamie? What's wrong?" Hanna croaks.

"Oh shit, I woke you. I'm sorry," I apologize.

"Whatever. What's wrong?"

I tell her the whole awful story (of course she remembers who Claire is), and she doesn't hesitate to console me.

"That motherfucking prick! I'll stuff his small penis so far up his ass!" she screams.

"Why would you think his penis is small?" I ask, not focusing on the problem at hand.

"No man needs to prove who he is as much as Derek if his dick can do it for him."

"Actually, it's a very nice size." And now I start crying. About his penis. I have serious issues.

"Oh, hon, I know. You told me. I was just trying to make you feel better. Are you crying? Where are you?"

"I'm at the grocery store, just near the ravine. Can I come over? N-now?" I sob.

"Of course. I'll send Jack home."

"Oh, fuck, I'm sorry. You have a guy there?"

81

"It's okay, we're done. Jump in a taxi, and I'll meet you outside."

"I have no money!" I cry and catch the attention of the homeless guy lying next to the phone booth. He looks at me and shrugs.

"I'll pay for it. Just get here. Okay?"

I nod, but of course, she can't see it. I don't care that I've left my bicycle outside the grocery store, and anyway, I'm sure Derek will take it home. He paid for it.

So I hail a taxi (the entire ride is a blur), and when I get upstairs to Hanna's place, I collapse in a greasy, limp heap on her white couch. She grabs me a cup of coffee, and the scalding burn down my throat is exactly what I need.

"Thanks, Han." I gulp down another mouthful. "This is really good coffee." I look at her in surprise.

"Jack made it."

"I like him already."

"Whatever. You're staying here," she commands.

"I know," I say and swallow another mouthful.

"It's over."

"I know."

"He's not the man for you."

I look at her and exhale a painful sigh. "Yeah, Han, I know."

I feel empty. The intellectual side of me knows this is the right thing to do, and it was a long time coming. Obviously, I wasn't happy anymore, and I couldn't go on like that. Seeing how he treated me when Claire was around was the final shovel of dirt on the casket. But I think I have to admit that I'm slightly terrified. I'm alone. I'm penniless. I'm homeless. And I've just walked out on five years of my life. Holy shit.

Hanna gets up and starts walking away. "Do I smell?" I whine.

"A bit. But that's not why I'm moving. I'm going out."

"You're leaving me? Don't leave me." I'm so pitiful.

She grins and shakes her head. "I'm getting you a breakup kit. I won't be long."

I forgot about our breakup kits. I haven't needed one in years. Between us, Hanna and I have had about fifteen or so failed relationships. Sadly, in mine, I was generally the "dumpee" (like with Matthew, the guy I was seeing before Derek, who told me we had to break up because he was moving away. Which I believed until I saw him with a tall redhead at a blues club a week later) while Hanna has always been the "dumper." So, we'd created the kit. Cigarettes, bubble bath, vodka, cranberry juice, ice cream, chocolate and trashy Hollywood gossip magazines.

"Okay. Thanks. You go out, and I'll wallow. I'll sit here and think about how shitty my life is, how I can't keep a relationship. I can't do anything right."

She stops walking and swings around to face me. "I am not going to tell you all of the amazing things about you right now because you won't listen. But I do want to say one thing. When you started going out with Derek, I was jealous."

"Jealous of me?" I interrupt. "With your ten foot tall body, perfect hair and men tossing themselves at you constantly? Please, I snort. "And you hate Derek."

"What I was trying to say, if you'll listen for a minute, is that I thought Derek was perfect. He had all of those qualities we were looking for. Smart, funny, didn't give a shit what people thought of him. But he changed, Jaim. He became his mother. And it wasn't what you signed on for. In a sense, he tricked you into believing he was someone he wasn't. But you were always yourself. He never really was that rebellious guy from the bar. He was always a snob. Total misrepresentation."

I let all that sink in while I trudge after Hanna to her bedroom. I flop down on the king-sized, wrought iron masterpiece she calls a bed and close my eyes. I see Derek. The ponytail, leather jacket, gentle fingers. The money clip, gel and three piece suit.

"So why haven't I changed? Why haven't I grown up? I'm thirty-two, and I still have no fucking idea what I want. I don't even think about it. Derek hates that. He thinks I have no ambitions, no goals. And maybe he's right."

"Don't you dare let him do this to you. You're determined to do things your way. I promise you that when Derek has the house, the CEO job and the best of everything money can buy, he'll look around and wonder why he's so miserable. He'll realize that none of it matters. Because none of it will ever be good enough for Jeanette," she says, her voice muffled because she's now inside her cavernous walk-in closet.

I say nothing. I simply watch her come out of the closet, shuck off her red silk robe and change into dark low-rise jeans, a pink camisole laced with white trim and pink stilettos. Her phenomenal breasts spill over the top, and I squeeze my tiny ones together to see if I can get a quarter of her cleavage. My boobs look like a double pancake.

"You think Derek stopped loving me because I have no breasts? How will I find a new boyfriend if he has nothing to hold on to?"

"He can squeeze your ass."

"Thanks, Han, that helps."

My ass, though firm, is round, like a grapefruit and usually referred to as my "booty" because it'd be better suited to a curvy black woman. When I was in high school, my few friends called me "Sweater Girl" because I always wore a sweater tied around my waist to ward off the cries of "Shake it and bake it, baby." I have learned to embrace (somewhat) my voluptuous rear. The rest of me is just fine, but my ass is special.

Hanna leaves, and I stay on the bed, staring at the eggshell-colored wall in front of me. I should call Derek. I owe him that at least. He must be worrying about me. I blush, thinking of the little exchange at the grocery store. Claire must think I'm a total freak. Well, screw her. I reach over to pick up the cordless phone lying on the bedside table next to about five torn condom wrappers. I really had interrupted something. Five? Jesus. Is that what I'm in for? I don't think I want to have sex five times in a row. Once would suit me just fine right about now.

I hold the phone in my hand, my heart pounding wildly. If I call, it's over. If I don't call, it's over. Either way, I can't go back. I dial our number. Derek picks up on the first ring.

"Hi, it's me," I say in a small, shaky voice.

"Where the hell are you? What's wrong with you?!" Derek yells into my eardrum.

Where's the worry? "I'm at Hanna's. Look, Derek, I'm, um, I'm, I think I'm going to stay here for awhile."

"Fine, when will you be home?"

How does he not get it? Is he really this obtuse? "You don't understand. I'm not coming home."

"What?! Because you saw a girl you don't like? Because I asked you to get some exercise and take care of yourself? Grow up, Jamie."

I take a deep breath and start furiously grinding. I won't scream. I won't swear. I'll do this maturely.

"Derek, wake the fuck up! We're not happy. We used to be so good together, but lately, for months, years, actually, we've only brought out the worst in each other. We fight all the time, we never have sex, why should we keep doing this? I don't want us to hate each other."

"You have to have some emotional depth for hate, Jamie. You're a shell. You never want anything but to watch stupid television shows. You'd be happy living in a crappy basement apartment with second hand furniture. You're thirty-two and going nowhere. With me, you'd have some promise. Without me, you're nothing."

A huge shard of pain slices through my stomach. But I will have the last word. "*With* you, I'm nobody. You want a little carbon copy of your mother in the shape of a trophy wife to feed you, coddle you and show up to business dinners wearing pearls and knocking back Prozac while sucking your cock. Without you, I'm everything. It's over, Derek. Go to hell!"

And I slam the phone down on the bed. It bounces up and knocks me hard in the chin. Super. A bruise. I can't believe that five years has just been reduced to a screaming argument. It's true that you never know when it's over. I mean, sure you see the signs, and you know the end is near, but not when it's the last time. Last fuck, last kiss, last fight.

And I realize that I feel good. Like I'm a thousand times lighter and airier. Okay, now I sound like Leah, and I'm scaring myself. I crawl under the soft covers and curl up on my side. All of a sudden, I'm completely exhausted, and I think we only got through five miles of that bike ride today. Bloody Derek. I've fallen dead asleep by the time Hanna gets back.

"Hey, Sleeping Beauty, your medication is here," she says, while giving me a not so gentle shake.

"Mmm, fff," I think I grumble. I open my left eye and try to focus. I am so tired. My bones ache, my chin is sore, but I'm hungry. Mmm. Chocolate.

"Chocolate, please," I whisper.

Hanna inserts a hazelnut cream into my mouth, and I'm on the sugary road to recovery.

CHAPTER TEN

"There's no coffee," I say, scrunching up my face in disbelief and severe disappointment when I stumble bleary-eyed into the kitchen the next morning. Even though he never drank it, Derek always made coffee for me in the mornings. Well, except for yesterday. Was it only yesterday?

"Not unless you make it," Hanna says, sipping what looks suspiciously like Chai tea and sitting at the kitchen table.

"Did Leah give you that?" I ask, pointing at her mug.

"Yeah. When I was at the house. Your sister's such a little tart. I was a lot like her, actually."

"Great. I'm sure you're a wonderful role model." I sit with her at the table and ask, "When were you at the house?"

"I had a massage. Like I always do." She's looking at me strangely over the rim of her mug.

"I know. I just didn't realize you'd been there recently."

"Have you talked to them lately?" she asks, cocking her head to the side.

Oh no, here comes the therapist. One course at the Learning Annex does not a healer make. But, Hanna does have this uncanny ability to see right through people's covers. And she knows I'm miffed. And she also knows why. "You're feeling guilty for not being in touch with them."

And this is why she's so successful. She knows what people want (hot sex) and provides how to get it (slutty lingerie).

"Maybe. I haven't really called anyone lately. I just felt so down. I thought that if I didn't talk about it, the problems, they weren't happening. I feel like a failure."

She smacks her hand on the table. "A failure? Why? You did a

87

great thing walking away. It's not easy after five years to finally leave. Even though he was a prick for a long, long, long-"

"Okay, Han! I get it, and you're right. I just thought things could go back to the way they were. But you can never go back. So, I'm moving on. I'm finding Lucas."

"Pardon?" She puts her mug down and asks.

"I'm moving on."

She rolls her eyes. "No, the next part."

"Lucy wants me to find Lucas. She thinks I need an adventure and that I don't go after things. So, anyway, our show is doing a high school reunion segment. You know those humiliating crush ones? It's an idea my new boss, Andrew, came up with."

"New boss? What happened to Sue? It's like you've disappeared in the last while. I know *nothing* that's going on with you."

"Sue is going 'part-time,' euphemism for fired," I tell her and rub my still crusty eyes, "and there's a new producer, Andrew. Nice guy. Anyway, Lucy thought I could find Lucas while I'm doing my other searches. What do you think?"

"Why would you want to find Lucas? You haven't seen him, or mentioned him, mind you, in like ten years." She crosses her slim legs and leans back in her chair.

I shrug, not sure of the answer to that myself. "I don't know. I guess because he was my first love, my first real sexual experience, and I have no idea what happened to him. We had this intense chemistry that I never really felt again."

Her lips curl up in a smile. "Everyone has chemistry at eighteen. It's called hormones."

"Well, it'd be good for me to have a goal, something I need to get."

"This is your goal? Finding your high school fuck buddy?"

"And college," I remind her, pulling a cigarette from the open pack on the kitchen table.

Hanna looks at me and smirks. She must have had a high school booty call situation too. She lights a cigarette and blows out the smoke in a sexy ring. "Yeah, I can see how that might be fun."

"Well, we'll see. I've never had much luck with guys, and Lucas made me feel things I'd never felt before. And in years, if I'm being totally honest with myself about Derek. You know how I almost never cry? Well, with Lucas, I had no problem crying, and he let me. He used to sit there and just watch the tears rolling down my cheeks, and then he would wipe them away. And he didn't say much, but whatever he did say was always the right thing. And he's *nothing* like Derek, you know? Lucas was so cool, into nature, animals, the outdoors. He didn't give a shit about what other people thought of him. Plus, since I started thinking about Lucas, I've felt light, free, no jaw pain."

"It's been less than twenty-four hours, and Lucas was young. He might not be the same guy anymore. Seriously, though, I'm proud of you, Jaim," she says, getting up.

I watch her walk to the sink, fill the coffee pot and scoop out the beans. Aw, she's making me coffee. I love this girl. In a fit of manic affection, I race over and kiss her on the cheek.

"Down, girl!" But she's laughing.

"Thanks, Han. Really. I appreciate all of this. I wouldn't know what to do without you." I stand next to the machine, watching the liquid gold drip, drip, dripping slowly into the pot. Could I just take some now? It'll take two seconds to pull out the pot and splash some into a cup. Just a sip.

"Jamie, did you hear me?"

"Huh?" I tear my eyes away from the coffee and look at her.

"I said you can stay forever if you want. I've never had a roomie."

"And if you say 'roomie' again, you never will."

I spend the day lounging in silk pajamas. Hanna had picked up this soft, aqua treat when she went out to get me my breakup kit. The loose pants swish against my legs, and I keep rubbing the whispery fabric of the camisole against my face.

Hanna and I sit on her couch, watching movies on her 60 inch flatscreen TV. I am never leaving. I feel like I'm inside the television. Perhaps it's the seven vodka cranberry cocktails I've been guzzling, but I feel just fine. A little dizzy, but otherwise great.

Eventually though, Hanna makes me call my family. I'd rather just sit in front of the screen for the next few days, but she's right that I haven't been very open with them recently. I wait to call until she's gone to work.

"Katie? It's Jamie," I announce when I finally get the energy to tell the story again.

"Hi, Jaim, how are you sweetheart?"

"I left Derek."

"Sorry, what? Leah's turning on the air purifier, and I can't hear you. Hold on."

I wait while Katie says something to Leah, and I hear someone pick up another phone. "Jaim, it's me. What's up?"

"I left Derek."

Silence. I can't even hear them breathing. "Where are you?" they ask in unison.

"I'm staying at Hanna's. Did you know she has a 60 inch TV? And coffee. So, I'll be okay. I feel like I'm inside the television. Have you ever seen one?" I think I'm a little drunk.

"Have you been drinking? You sound like you've been drinking. Are you drinking water? You don't want to get dehydrated. Did you take your milk thistle? You must protect your liver."

"Does milk thistle have alcohol 'cause I want to get falling over, stinking drunk."

"We're coming over."

"No! I mean, no, thanks, I'm fine. I just realized that I can't do it anymore. He let Claire snub me."

"Who's Claire? He's seeing someone else?" Katie growls. She may look all nice and flaky, but she would beat the crap out of anyone who hurt me or Rachel.

"No, no. It was at the grocery store. Claire, you remember Claire. She went out with Lucas."

"Lucas? What are you talking about? We're leaving now."

And then the dial tone. Shit, they're coming over. Not that I don't want to see them, but my head is spinning, I'm giggling for no reason, and there's a "Big Brother" marathon starting in five minutes. And I don't want to see them.

Bzzz. That was fast. How did they get here so quickly? Am I so drunk that twenty minutes felt like two seconds? I press the buzzer on the phone to let them in. There's a loud knock at the door.

"Come in," I whisper from my half-sitting, half-lying position on the couch. Nothing happens.

"Come in!" I yell this time.

The door opens, and standing there is Derek. And Jeanette. Holy fuck, why is he here? And a better question is why did he bring his mother? I look down at myself, and even though I'm lounging in the chicest of pajamas, there's a cranberry stain on the chest and the black lacquer coffee table is littered with half-smoked cigarettes, chocolate wrappers and coffee mugs.

I touch my hand to my hair, which is half up (the other half, sticky with vodka and cranberry juice, is mashed against the side of my face), and I scrape it all back into a bun. Why do I even care what they think? Derek struts over and sits on the couch while Jeanette makes herself comfortable in the armchair. And glares at

91

me. Why is she here?

"Hello, Jamie. I wanted to see for myself that you'd really left. I couldn't believe that a girl like you would walk out on my Derek. After all he's done for you," she says in her nasal tone (as if she's pinching her nostrils together), clutching her Fendi bag to her skinny chest and primly crossing her spray-tanned legs.

Today Jeanette has dressed down in a pink tweed Chanel suit, pink chiffon scarf, pink heels and pink nails. I've always hated pink.

"After all he's done for me, Jeanette? I don't mean to be rude, but why are you here?"

"You broke my boy's heart. I thought we could talk. You and I have always had a good relationship."

I snort. She ignores it and surges ahead with her pile of shit. "I understand, dear, that you have many family issues to work through. I know it hasn't been easy for you, what with your mother being that way."

I cringe and mash my teeth together to calm myself down. "What way is that, Jeanette? A dyke? Yes, my mom is a lesbian. So what? Why do you even care who she loves?"

I can't believe I just spoke to her like that. I want to slap my hand over my mouth, but I restrain myself. Though built like a skeleton on the Zone, Jeanette has always scared the hell out of me because she is the coldest person I've ever met. I mean, I'm not exactly warm and fuzzy, but next to her, I'm like a big, cuddly teddy bear on E.

The first time she met me, and Derek had crowed about Leah and Katie (he was fun then), she rushed over to me, patted my hand and whispered, "You poor dear. How difficult and unfair."

By that time, I was long since over the embarrassment and full more of admiration than resentment for Leah and Katie. Katie makes my mom so happy, and when you see them, you know it couldn't be any other way. Really, I should have more faith in relationships and trust that real love, crazy, intense love, does exist.

Anyway, I told her right then and there that I love Katie and Leah, they love each other, I am perfectly well-adjusted (not entirely true, obviously, but that's my issue) and to back off. She stared at me for I think two straight minutes, with her blue eyes, devoid of any warmth, trained on me. I stared back, and we were at war. Of course, Jeanette, being a member of the Chicago Debutante Society, and the fact that I'd also never seen her in anything but a twinset or suit, made it a silent war. But deadly.

She has always made me feel like everything I do is wrong or inappropriate, and though I didn't show it, I did always want her to like me. I desperately wanted to be part of Derek's family. But she never made it easy, and I was never good enough. So I'm not sure if it's the adrenalin pumping, hot and thick, through my veins giving me this surge of bravery (or stupidity) or that I've finally had enough.

Jeanette smiles condescendingly, and her eyes fill with pity. And, oh, what is that? Ah, yes, the cold gleam of satisfaction. She knows she's rattled me, and she likes it.

Derek sits down on the couch next to me. "Jamie, dear, I know it's been hard watching all of my success the last couple of years while you aren't progressing. I didn't realize you were so jealous. Mummy made me see how your job, your lifestyle, it isn't your choice. It's how you were raised. But, I'll help you sweetheart," he says, pressing his body against me and repeatedly stroking his thumb back and forth over mine. "We'll go home, I'll run you a nice hot bath, and we'll start working on your resume. We'll get you a real job, a good one, and not that silly thing you do now."

His touch just irritates me. Each stroke is making me wince with annoyance, and I want to smash my cocktail glass on his manicured hand. Really crush it into his over-inflated ego.

"Stop grinding your teeth, Jamie. It's not becoming," Jeanette tells me.

Is this for real? Are they really here treating me like this is an intervention? My drug of choice? Obviously failure. I turn to face Derek, who is still sitting uncomfortably close to me.

"Derek, since you need backup to face me, I have no choice but to say this in front of your mother. I'd much rather do this in private, but there are some things I'd like to tell you. You used to care about enjoying life, living it to its fullest, not only about your expense account. But you've changed. Instead of appreciating the simple pleasures, it's all about the fancy condo, designer clothes, promotions, golf buddies. Who are you? You're certainly not the guy I fell in love with."

He sneers at me (I should tell him that that will cause unflattering frown lines), moves over a bit and strokes his gold Rolex instead of me. I have a feeling it's more important to him anyway.

"You're right. I've changed. I grew up, took responsibility for my life. I've thought about what I want it to be like and how hard I have to work to get there. I can't just hang out all day with my friends watching demoralizing television. And making it. I can't drink until I'm stinking drunk and reeking of cigarettes and fall home at two o'clock in the morning-"

"Excuse me? You make it sound like all I do is drink and smoke and screw around. I work all day as a television producer, I take care of you. I cook and do almost all of the cleaning-"

"That was the deal. I make the money! I have a real job! You do the same thing, watch the same shows, wear the same clothes, that's living life to the fullest? Don't give me that crap. You don't do anything to better yourself. And I want to be successful, I want to have the good things in life."

I stand up and stab my chest with my index finger. "*I* used to be one of those good things. I'm not who you think I am. I'm not that insecure woman you met at the bar, Derek. I'm smart and -"

"And people like you?" he says sarcastically.

He just totally mocked me. No way is he getting away with that. Amazingly, Jeanette is just sitting there watching all of this, and staring back and forth from Derek to me, she's too stunned to interrupt with her always unwelcome directives.

"Don't you dare talk to me like that! No, I am not driven by the Almighty Buck, but I have passion, which I think you had removed when you first had your back waxed."

His face flushes furiously red. Eeeexcellent. I continue, now waving my finger in his scarlet face.

"And, Derek, I live in the present, not twenty years in the future. You live on the edge of the elite, and you're never going to get in. You'll hover over the Gold Coast until you're too old to walk there. I want you to go. I'd hoped we could be friends after all these years, but now I know what you really think of me."

Go, go, go before Katie and Leah get here. Pleeeeze.

"Fine. Then, we have one more thing to discuss," Jeanette says and opens her purse. Her gnarled fingers reach into the bag, and she pulls out a crisp sheet of pink paper. With numbers on it.

"What's that?" I ask.

"If you can't be responsible, and see that I'm trying to help you, you leave me with no choice," Derek says to me and takes the mystery paper from Mummy and places it on the table. He couldn't just hand it to me? Even when we're breaking up, he can't escape the buttoned up and repressed business persona that has infiltrated every area of his life. I roll my eyes and pick up the paper.

As I scan the sheet, I feel both amazement and anger as my brain (befuddled with alcohol as it is) slowly registers the series of numbers. In front of me is an itemized list of all our expenses over the last three years. Rent, holidays, groceries, clothes, phone bills, cable bills. Neatly divided into two—with a grand total of $30,000. My name (full name, Jamie Ellen Ross) is at the bottom next to a figure of $15,000. What the hell is this?

"What the hell is this?" I demand.

"That language is so uncouth, Jamie dear. Derek and I wanted to help you. But you can't get help until you see you have a problem. So, obviously, coming here was a waste of time because you won't listen to reason. If you insist on leaving, you're going to have to pay Derek what you owe him. For three years, he has effectively paid your way. You could never afford that beautiful condo, all your holidays. And if you're not staying together, he deserves financial restitution for a bad investment."

"Bad investment? Is this a joke? C'mon, where's the camera?" I look around for the hidden photographer who must be behind the couch or something. No one's there. This is not a joke.

"Jamie, I shared my money under the assumption that we would one day get married, and everything would be equal. I thought..." He looks down at his feet for a second. "I thought that once we had children that you'd quit your job and stay home. But now that you're leaving, you owe me that money. I worked hard for it."

I hear everything they're saying, but it's coming through foggily. My mind can't make sense of this craziness, and I furiously suck on my pinkie in shock. After all of the nights awake laughing and having sex, the camping trips, tooling around on his 1984 Yamaha Virago motorcycle, this is what I'm left to remember. A bill.

And at once, I feel incredibly sad and run out of energy. But I have enough juice in me to say one last thing.

"You know, Derek, and Jeanette, since you're here for this whole disgusting conversation, I do make money. I buy my own clothes, I paid a lot of the bills. I never wanted all the furniture,

96

toys, useless stuff you bought. Those were yours. I don't need the best of everything."

"That's very obvious. And you barely make anything. I don't recall hearing you complain so much."

"Because you weren't listening," I whisper. And wish my voice could be strong and clear, but I feel completely beaten up.

"You don't exactly say much, Jamie. Look, I don't expect it all in a lump sum. Installments are acceptable," he tells me, as if I should be agreeing to his very reasonable terms.

My voice cracks as I bark, "You want me to give you $15,000 because I'm breaking up with you?! How old are you? That's the least creative revenge tactic I've ever heard of. You could at least put itching powder in my underwear or crazy glue on my coffee mug."

"You don't own your own coffee mug. I do."

And just as I'm about to start seriously flipping out (which I'm sure would be taken more seriously were I not drunk and in silk pajamas), there's a knock at the door. Jeanette actually has the gall to get up and answer it. "Leah, why hello, it's a pleasure to see you," Jeanette says and leans over to give her an air kiss. And totally ignores Katie.

"What's going on?" Leah asks suspiciously, trying to see past Jeanette to where I'm standing near the television.

"Maybe you can talk some sense into your daughter."

"My daughter has her own sense," Leah says and walks over to where I'm standing, shell-shocked.

She puts her hand on my hair and pulls me close. She rubs my back (I let her), and wordlessly, I hand over the bill. Services rendered. Leah and Katie scan it and both burst out laughing. Fat tears stream down their faces from the amusement of it all; Derek and Jeanette stare at them open-mouthed, helplessly at a loss with almost half of the Ross clan. For once, the pair of them aren't getting the kowtowing they're so used to.

"You can't be serious. You want Jamie, sorry, Jamie Ellen, to pay for the breakup? After Derek let Claire snub her?" Katie asks, winking at me. Clearly, they've finally remembered Claire.

"Who's Claire?" Jeanette asks, nervously wringing her hands, clearly worried that Derek has followed in his illustrious father's footsteps.

"My nemesis. It's not important now. Look, I think we should just stop this. Let's agree to end this, and we'll both just..." Just what? I have no idea what comes next.

Derek's facade doesn't break for a second, and for the first time, I truly understand that this is the real Derek now, and the cool, funky guy I knew has gotten lost in designer suits and the promise of wealth and success.

"Jamie, if you want this to be over, fine. You're right. We're not suited for each other's lifestyles anymore. But I really do think that I deserve some monetary compensation for the things you had because of me." He says this while trying to avoid Leah and Katie's beady-eyed stares.

The womb crew is here, though, and Derek does look a little pale. Truth be told, Derek is afraid of women. Especially confident ones. It's why he really doesn't like Hanna and Lucy. When he can't control the situation and have the upper hand, he's stumped as to how to act, an unfortunate genetic casualty of being his mother's son.

"Monetary compensation? You want my daughter to pay for being with you? She's not a client, Derek, she's a person. Something you've obviously forgotten. She's strong, smart and beautiful. Don't you dare make her feel worthless because she doesn't measure up to your standard of perfection and success. She doesn't care what purse she's carrying, she cares about people. You used to be like that. I'm extremely disappointed in you."

Derek has the grace to look abashed, but Jeanette's squinty little eyes are popping out of her Botox shrunken head. She's about to spew out every nasty little thought she's ever had about me and my family, and I better stop this before it gets very ugly. And dangerous.

I'm not drunk anymore, which is a shame, because if I were, this might seem more comical. But it's not funny, and I've had enough. I bite my lip, willing myself to remain calm. My jaw is moving a mile a minute. "Look, if you want money, fine, I'll get you the damn money. If you want to reduce five years to this, do it. Just know that I did love you, and we did have something really good once, and you're tainting every good memory and moment that we shared. If that's what you want, I don't care anymore. Just leave, okay?"

My hands are shaking, fear is licking at my spine, and my heart is an ear-shattering cacophony of drums. Derek walks over to Jeanette, takes her hand and leads her out. But he leaves the bill on the table.

CHAPTER ELEVEN

"My God, that woman has the darkest aura," Leah says.

"Black. Like her heart," I say and sprawl my exhausted body across the couch while Katie goes to the kitchen to make tea. I'd much prefer more vodka, but I don't think either of them will let me anywhere near the bottle. Maybe I'll just splash a little in my tea.

Leah sits down next to me, takes in the garbage on the coffee table and smiles. "Breakup kit?" she asks, pointing at the cigarettes.

I can't believe that the breakup kit is for me this time. I never thought this would happen. I nod at Leah. "Yeah. I can't believe it's over. It's like all the good years never happened. We were really happy, you know that, you saw us. And I know I should cry. I just feel so empty."

"I wish you wouldn't smoke cigarettes. You know what horrible damage that wreaks on your system. Not to mention your psyche. Maybe you should take some Vitamin C. And Jamie, honey, crying might help some people, but my love, you can't be someone you're not."

The phone rings, and I check the call display. "Hi, Dad," I answer.

"Baby, are you okay? I'm so sorry."

"How did you know? It just happened," I say bewildered.

"Leah called me earlier. Do you want us to come over? Mo can cook you a nice, fat steak, we can watch some movies, whatever you want," he offers.

"Good news travels fast, huh? Thanks, Dad, but I think I need some time on my own. Leah and Katie are here, anyway."

"I'm really proud of you, honey. I know it hurts right now, but Derek wasn't good enough for you. Who needs him, right?"

"Right," I whisper. "Do you want to talk to Leah?"

I pass her the phone, and as she's telling him about the payoff, I go to the bathroom. When I see Hanna's cleansers lined up on the counter, a huge rush of sadness overtakes me. I sit down on the toilet seat. And I cry. Wet, fat, uncomfortable tears slide down my face and drip onto the pajamas.

Moaning, I let them fall, my shoulders trembling as I cry for a good five minutes. But it doesn't make me feel any better. I feel worse. And now, my eyes are rimmed with red, my nose is dripping, and my skin is blotchy.

Knock, knock. Leah and Katie must have heard me. I grab a wad of toilet paper and furiously rub my eyes. Leah gently opens the door. "Oh, baby, I'm so sorry. I know this hurts like hell, but you did the right thing."

I know she wants to touch me, but she knows me well enough to just crouch beside me next to the toilet. I grab some more toilet paper because I have a feeling the waterworks aren't finished flowing yet.

"Is it? What if they're right? I'm not successful. I'm thirty-two and going nowhere. I don't have money or a place to live. I can't stay here forever." I sniffle.

"You can always come home," Katie says, coming up behind Leah and playfully pinching her stomach.

It's really not helping to see how in love they are. The physical affection has always made me uncomfortable. Now it's making me mad.

"Stop that! No touchy feely stuff right now. I can't come home. I need my own life. For five years, everything has been about me and Derek. And Derek's right about the money. Not the $15,000, that's just stupid. But about the fact that he did pay for everything,

101

and I usually let him or I was completely irresponsible and didn't pay the bills on time because I didn't want to ask him for the money. You guys always taught me to be self-sufficient and not to rely on any man, but I did just the opposite."

"Jamie, there's nothing wrong with sharing what you have. It's not like you're unemployed. You make enough money to take care of yourself. It was Derek's decision to get all the rich, fancy stuff. And you have the spark. You showed him what fun life could be."

I wipe another tear from my cheek. "How does someone change so much? He used to have so much passion. He loved travelling, learning, not just being at the top of the pay scale. It's Jeanette's fault. She's so mad at his dad for leaving that she punishes him, and he doesn't even see it. He tries so desperately to make her proud, and she doesn't realize that he has no sense of who he is. Everything he does, he does to please her. The funny thing is I know he's not happy. He's always under so much stress. And she's made him so closed-minded."

"You mean about us?" Katie asks, handing me the mug of hot, milky tea that she blew on to cool down for me.

Vodka and milk? Not a good combination. I should probably sober up anyway. I take a sip of the scalding liquid and enjoy the searing heat in my chest. Swallowing another burning gulp, I say, "About everything, but yeah, also about you."

"You want to know something? The people who are most afraid of homosexuality are the ones who fear that they are gay. Every time I see that scrawny, pinched, unhappy woman, I sense a lot of pent-up lust."

I shudder. I think Jeanette is asexual. Since Derek Senior left, she's never had a date, much less sex.

"Did I waste my time? Have I lost my chance at happiness now?" I ask in a small voice.

Leah swings her silver braid over one shoulder and inspects its

102

ends. Resting her chin in her hand, she looks at me carefully. "Jamie, you have never believed that people find happiness. So don't start changing who you are now. This is a fresh start for you. And you will be happy again like you were before. Forget everything they said about us, your job, yourself. You are a rare gem, my darling girl," she says and lightly touches my knee. "And just like it always happens, someone will come along who loves you for you. And you need to see that age doesn't matter."

"I didn't fall in love with Leah until my mid-thirties, and I'll never think I wasted my time before that. Think about what you've learned from this," Katie chimes in.

"Never date a man with a mother," I say, laughing. Snot flies out of my nose, and I brush it away with my sleeve. Another pretty stain on my pajamas. Whatever. They're already beyond ruined.

"Okay, I know exactly what you need. I'm giving you a massage," Katie tells me, hoisting herself up from where she was squatting, and I can hear her knees creak. It makes her vulnerable, and my heart tugs that Katie, really my second mother, is getting older.

I vehemently shake my head in refusal. "No way, Katie. I hate massages."

"You've never had one. Live a little."

They leave the bathroom so I can clean up in private. I take off the pajamas and stand naked on the cold ivory tiles. I look in the mirror that takes up the three walls surrounding the white ceramic sink and see how ridiculous my hair looks. Greasy strands hang down from the haphazard bun, my skin is pasty and uneven (my nose, forehead and chin are shiny, the rest is dry and flaky), and my body is doughy.

I hold up one arm and flap the skin under it back and forth. I've never even been inside a gym, and it shows. I'm built like a Weeble. Skinny upper body and round bottom.

I turn around to see the back view and there are my bone-sharp shoulder blades sticking out next to my knobby spine, and if I stand on my tiptoes (which I do), I can see the little dimples of cellulite that start at the top of my ass and don't finish until my thighs. I don't need a massage, I need a huge overhaul. Especially if I'm going to find Lucas.

Maybe Lucy is right. I don't really think you get spiritual messages, but, obviously, my belief that life is how you live it got me here. It's time to take a chance. And part of that is changing how I take care of myself.

I see how Lucy and Hanna spend time on themselves. And it works. So, I'll devote more time to all that silly girlie stuff. What man wants a fleshy, complacent, dimply woman who doesn't even know how to put on eyeliner? Not that Lucas ever cared about makeup, and he certainly didn't like me for my looks way back in the day. But, Hanna's right that people change, and he's older now. So am I.

We'll race across a field of sunflowers, our hats will fly into the heady, spring air (I'd never actually wear a hat if it weren't winter, but it fits this scenario), and we'll fall into each other's outstretched arms. We'll run to the nearest judge to get married, live in the mountains (forget my paralyzing fear of heights, this is, after all, a fantasy) and raise sullen little children. Yes!

I wrap myself in the fluffiest, softest towel and walk into the living room. Wearing just the towel and a huge smile, I say to Katie, "Rub me."

Katie is stunned and leaping up from the couch, she races to the front door to get her supplies. Well, more like plods. She's put on a few pounds in the last couple of years. I actually have her body type more than Leah, my dad, and Rachel's. We've all had a laugh about how Katie and I look more like family than my actual blood relatives. Although I never find it quite as amusing as they

104

do.

I guess she brought her massage table in case Hanna was here. Or maybe to see if I'd actually give in this time. She's been after me to get a massage for years now. She carries it under one arm through the living room and says, "Let's go to your room, sweetie."

My room is the guest bedroom/office. A massive mahogany desk sits under a large window, the top covered with papers, bras, and the same pink computer Rachel has. There's a double bed pushed against the wall under the window, a pure white duvet, lacy white pillow shams and a mint green throw resting on top.

Katie sets up the table opposite the bed, pops a classical CD into the portable stereo and lines up her oils and lotions. I bite my lip nervously. Maybe this isn't such a good idea. I'll never relax if she's got her hands all over me.

"Hop up, Jaim. I promise I'll be gentle, and I won't touch you where you don't want me to."

She turns around while I slide naked under the soft, cool sheet. This is very weird. I've never been naked around Katie before. Nor Leah since I was thirteen. "I can't see anything, Jamie, and I'm not looking. But you have to take your hands off your butt if I'm going to do this."

She takes my hands and places them above my head. I stiffen when I hear the squelch of the oil between her hands. "What are you doing?" I ask suspiciously.

"I'm oiling up the dildo."

I bolt up, and she laughs. "I'm kidding. I'm just warming up the oil. Close your eyes and think about nothing."

How does one think about nothing? With the lightest touch, Katie puts her hands on my back and starts kneading. After the initial creepiness, I start relaxing as knots of tension unravel; I stop tightening my muscles (the few that I have) and let her do her magic.

Oh my God, it feels so good. It seems like Katie has five hands as they move over my lower back, legs and feet. Oh, the feet! Everything is melting away with each touch, and I'm slipping into a state of relaxation and pleasure like I've never felt before. "Harder!" I demand.

She chuckles and digs her elbow into my shoulder blade. She turns me over, puts a hot towel over my face and massages my fingers. Bliss! Now I know why Katie makes a bundle. She's a goddess. I don't even know how much time has passed because apparently, I've fallen asleep. Her cool lips kiss my lemon-scented forehead (she'd never try that were I not boneless and motionless) and says, "Wake up, Jaim. You're done."

I open my eyes and look at her. "That was unbelievable. Oh my God, you're amazing. I feel like a new woman."

"I still like the old one."

Well, she's got to go. Operation Rebirth has begun.

***

Katie and Leah leave me with a yellow silk sachet filled with healing crystals to rub away my pain and oils mixed with lavender and chamomile to massage myself out of stress and tension. Luckily, they understand my need for some space and time to myself, and after years of living with me know that it's easier for me to wallow when no one else is around.

A quiver of excitement and naughtiness urges me to begin the reinvention of Jamie in Hanna's closet. She's still at the shop so I wander into her bedroom and play dress up in her skinny person wardrobe which requires me to be at least six inches taller than I actually am. In hindsight, this is a ridiculous idea.

I'm swimming in red stilettos and a sparkly black cocktail dress so I bunch up some Kleenex to fill out the top. For a split second, I consider getting implants, but no, that's going too far. Twirling in a frantic circle in front of her full-length mirror, I trip and stumble over the toe of one shoe and hear the resounding crack of my head against the edge of the bed going down. Oh God, that hurt! If I did have implants, I'd probably burst them with my supreme lack of coordination.

Rubbing the egg on the top of my head, I sit up, lean back against the wall and stretch my legs out in front of me. My head is throbbing, and the stark realization that I am on my own now sends a sharp jolt through my skull. But it's not painful. It's just...strange. I'm single. I broke up with Derek. I press my hand against my mouth in awe. I really did it.

And now I can actually do what I told Lucy I would. I'm ready to move on. To be honest, I moved on a long time ago. I just didn't have the guts to admit it. The questions "Have you been looking for your high school crush? Do you think there's a second chance at love?" have been out there for a few days, and Cindy, the receptionist, has been logging them for me. If they're somewhat sane (always questionable in my business), we'll communicate by email and phone until I have all the necessary information to hook them up.

But I don't know where to find these people. Or Lucas. How do I find a bunch of people who went to high school together decades ago? Wait a minute. There's Facebook! God, this will be so easy. I've never wanted to join because I'm already in touch with everyone I want to be, and I feel no need to reconnect with the people who made my school years a living hell. But since everyone and their dog is on Facebook (Hanna and Lucy are constantly "friending" weirdos from their past), maybe Lucas is on there, too.

I heave myself up off the floor and put the glittery dress back on its padded peach hanger (I swear Hanna's hangers cost more than all my clothes combined). In her drawer, I find a lycra t-shirt

107

and a pair of white drawstring sweatpants that just about fit me if I roll up the legs twelve times. Back in my bedroom, I turn on Hanna's computer and am greeted with a color picture of Gisele Bundchen in a barely there scrap of ice blue silk. One of Hanna's ads. Well, what a great start to the day that is, with a jab of envy in the gut.

After one search, I find exactly what I'm looking for, but to find someone from Tecumseth, I need to become a member. Even though it's free, there is no way I want anyone from high school (crusty Claire, especially) to see my name on this reunion website. So I use her name instead. I type in Claire Howard, list her job as a stripper, and explain that she's recently gotten out of prison after a prostitution arrest. Hee hee, this is fun. I add that she has four children from different fathers and is living in a rent by the minute hotel in Crack Town.

Then I type in Lucas. And realize that I've forgotten his last name. Did I ever know his last name? I must have. How can I not remember the love of my life's last name? Think, Jamie. I squint, hoping that wrinkling up my face will jog my memory. I wish I had my yearbooks with me. Leah will be able to find them so I dial their number.

"Hello?" Katie answers breathlessly.

"Are you okay?" I ask.

"Oh, um, yeah. We were, um, hi."

"I really don't want to know. I just need a favor."

"Sure, anything. You want to book another massage?"

"That's not why I called, but actually, yeah that would be great. Thanks so much, Katie. I know I was totally against massages, and I certainly don't want some stranger touching me, but I never knew that you were so good at it. I need to come by and pick up some old letters anyway. How about next week sometime?"

She laughs. "Nice to see you've changed your tune. Call me

later and let me know when you're free. What's the favor then?"

"Could you run up to my room and grab a high school yearbook for me?"

"Okay, why?"

I bite my lip, not used to lying to Katie. "Um, I need some last names. It's for work."

"You certainly recover quickly. What are you working on?"

Hanna and Lucy are enough informants for my mission. If nothing comes of it, I won't want to talk about it, and my family's all about the sharing.

"Changing embarrassing names. I have to find people with humiliating names, like Seymour Butts," I lie smoothly. I'm getting better at this.

"Hang on."

She drops the phone, and I wait. I'm going to need to ask for a whole bunch of names so she doesn't get suspicious. "Okay, where should I look?" Katie asks.

"Check the class of 1998. Just read off the names."

"Jaim, there's over two hundred people on the list."

"How about just the guys?"

"You're lucky you're in an emotional crisis right now. Gotta pen?"

"Shoot."

"Should I just find the funny ones?"

"Um, no, all of them."

"You're very thorough. Okay, Jim Applebaum, Steven Astor, Michael Axelrod." The list goes on and on, and I'm tuning out. "Lucas Simpson."

Yes! Now I remember. Lucas Simpson. "Thanks, Katie. That's perfect," I interrupt.

"I'm not done yet."

"I have everything I need."

"They're not particularly funny names. You've got your work cut out for you."

"Yeah, I always come out on top."

"Best place to be."

"Don't go there," I warn her.

Why must they be so open all the time? Is nothing sacred?

"Sorry. Call back if you need anything else. Didn't you date that Lucas guy?"

"Mmmm. Thanks, Katie," I mutter.

We hang up, and I roll the name "Lucas Simpson" around my tongue. Jamie Simpson. Jamie Ross Simpson. No hyphen. Back on the computer, I enter his name. Nothing comes up. Of course it doesn't. Lucas was never a reunion type of guy. He didn't even come to our graduation. He was at the prom, though. But not as my date.

Unfortunately, my date was our overweight, nasally-challenged next door neighbour, Drippy Daniel. He carried Kleenex in his shirt pocket (next to the pens, of course) to blow his perpetually running nose. He was the only guy in our school who had started balding at the age of sixteen.

Neither Lucas nor I had the guts to ask each other (and didn't want anyone to know we were together at all), and I refused to go stag. I waited for Lucas to ask me until the day before prom. Realizing that he wasn't going to ask, I was left with Drippy. He stepped on my toes, tried to feel me up by kneading my breasts like they were dough balls and got a swift kick in the groin for his effort. I wonder what happened to Drippy?

Lucas and I did dance. To Madonna's "Crazy for You." And I still love that song. I close my eyes for a moment. There is Lucas in his rented black tux, the tie stuffed in his pocket and the shirt unbuttoned enough for me to see his golden throat and smooth, hard chest. I was wearing a black halter dress with colorful flowers splashed all over it, my hair up (and staying up for once because it had been professionally done), and I felt beautiful.

But, it didn't matter what I wore because Lucas always made me feel beautiful. He used to stroke my tiny breasts and giant bottom and tell me how spectacular they were. I hear the scuffling of our shoes on the just waxed floor and feel his hands gripping my waist, and remember how I wished the song would never end. Where did those feelings of giddy anticipation go?

Okay, the next thing to do is an email search. Again, I don't have enough information. If I can't even do this for my own trivial search, how will I do it for the show? I'm used to doing most of the legwork myself, but for this segment, it seems I'm a bit stuck, and I think I'm going to need Andrew's help. But I don't even know him, and the whole idea of getting to know someone new stresses me out. I don't love putting myself out there and being asked a whole bunch of personal questions about things that are nobody's business.

It's easier for me to work with the same people for years because it takes me a long time to feel really comfortable. Lucy asked me out for drinks for weeks before I finally said yes. It's a bit of social anxiety, but it's never really been a problem. I have my family, Hanna and Lucy, and I used to have Derek, and that was enough for me. But, I see that the number of intimate relationships I have is dwindling. So, really, by finding Lucas, I'm coming out of my shell a bit.

I lean back in the desk chair and smell something bad. Oh God, it's me. How is that possible after a patchouli-scented massage? Maybe because I haven't showered or been outside since yesterday afternoon, and I really need to get some air. Or be aired out myself.

I stand up, fully intending to go outside for a walk, but luckily, I catch a glimpse of myself in the mirror first. I'm dressed in sweats that don't even fit, and I don't have any clothes here. I'll have to go back home, I mean to Derek's, to pick up my stuff.

He's probably at the club today. I could call, and if he answers, I'll hang up. Nope, can't do that. Call display. I could block the number. But what if I go there, and he comes home while I'm packing up? The last thing I want or need right now is to see him. When Hanna gets back, I'll beg her to go for me. I just can't face him. I don't want to fight anymore. And what if Jeanette is there? Ugh, I'd rather tweeze my eyebrows.

I know what I'll do instead since going home isn't a possibility. I'll have a beauty day. And eat. I'm starving. I root around in Hanna's fridge for something remotely edible, but all I find is champagne, caviar, capers, and a crusty jar of Dijon mustard. Maybe the freezer has something better. Stuffed in the very back (next to her eye pack) is a frozen box of Lousiana chicken wings. Hanna's comfort food and something she'd never eat in front of another person. Not even me. I'm sure she sits in front of the mirror examining her teeth after every little bite.

Once the wings are spitting and sizzling in the microwave, I pour myself a vodka/cranberry cocktail. Yes, it's only noon, but I'm in crisis mode here. This is a great kitchen. Sunny, warm and open, with plants everywhere, high quality stainless steel appliances and green granite counter tops. It's all sparkling clean because Hanna's never cooked a meal in her life. The most useful tool in her kitchen is the phone.

As I chew on the hot wings, I realize that if I'm really going to find Lucas, I want him to see that I've changed. No more glasses (contacts), perfect teeth now (braces), and I do have some style. Hanna's naturally beautiful, but she does get some help along the way.

After I finish eating, I check around her bathroom to see what she's got that will help me be beautiful. And, whew, to take the smell of ripe cheese off of me. Under the sink, I find a plastic

112

basket brimming over with hot wax, scrubs, scrapers, masks, and something that looks like an iron. I could spend all day in here just trying to figure out what everything's for.

I run a bath and once I'm immersed in the scented, bubbly water, I furiously scrape the heels and soles of my feet. I'm beautifying from the bottom up. Moving the pumice stone back and forth over the broken, cracked skin of my feet, I see little flakes fly on the walls and vow to stop picking at them. It really is a disgusting habit.

And today, I am not going to shave. No, today, I'm going to wax. Derek always wanted me to wax everything, I mean everything, off. Isn't that a little sick? Aren't women supposed to look like women and not pre-pubescent twelve year olds? But, I know that Hanna does it, so what can it hurt?

Well, it hurts like a bitch. After towelling off, I heated the wax and started on my left leg. I didn't have the courage to go for the gold yet. I followed the instructions, but nowhere on that innocent looking box (a smooth, happy looking blonde is reassuring me that this won't hurt a bit) did it say that this is akin to childbirth. Of a twenty pound baby!

Once the wax was slathered on, I pressed down the cloth that is supposed to "cleanly and easily" remove the hair. False advertising! Yanking the cloth hard, I tore off layers of both hair and skin and emitted a scream of pure agony. When I looked down, I was shocked to see that there was no blood. There must be blood. And when I looked at my leg, I saw that most of the hair was still there. What kind of masochistic torture is this?

How do women do this all the time? My pubic hair? It's staying, in all its lush glory. There's no way I'm ripping another hair from my delicate body. I'll shave instead. If Lucas wants me, he'll have to deal with my stubble, as well. A few hours later, I've exfoliated, moisturized and loofahed myself as much as I can. By the time Hanna gets home, I look exactly the same.

CHAPTER TWELVE

Last night, while Hanna went to Derek's to get my stuff, I sat comatose in front of the television for hours. I watched re-runs of "American Idol," "Celebrity Rehab" (we should get some of those sad losers on our show) and three "Sex and the City" episodes without moving once. My eyes were glazed over, stomach filled with the sumptuous and calorie-laden meal I'd cooked (honey garlic ribs from Hanna's secret stash, which I forced her to eat in front of me), and I slept well for the first time in months.

What saddened me the most was not sleeping alone, but the fact that Hanna could barely fill two boxes and a duffel bag with my stuff. Five years, and it took her less than an hour to pack it all up. Yet another glaring sign that my life with Derek was never really mine.

Now I'm at my desk, waiting for Lucy to show up to work. I've been dying to tell her about me and Derek, but I just didn't have the energy to call last night. Unfortunately, Eva arrives first.

"Good morning, Jamie. Rough night?" she asks snidely as she sidles up to my desk and perches her snooty little ass on the edge of it.

"Oh yes, fucking like maniacs. You look like you've gained some weight over the weekend."

She sneers and walks away. Well, that was fun. Finally, Lucy waltzes over to me in her red PVC catsuit, not an ounce of body fat anywhere. She's streaked red dye through her black hair to match her outfit. Only Lucy could pull off the Dominatrix At The Office look.

"What's up? You look different," she tells me, looking me up and down suspiciously.

115

I nod. "Because I'm free."

"How much do you usually charge?"

I give her a withering look. "I left Derek."

She opens her mouth. Then closes it. And opens it again. "Oh my God! You didn't? You did! Oh, Jaim, I'm so proud of you! Why now?"

"Everything really. But then on Saturday, I just had it."

"Saturday? Why didn't you call me?" Her mouth turns down in a look of hurt.

"I'm sorry. It's just that I didn't much feel like talking to anyone."

She sits on my desk where Eva had just been and crosses her legs. "Yeah, I know you. So what happened?"

I tell her the snubbing story, and she jiggles on my desk excitedly, tapping her foot up and down.

"You know what that is? Serendipity. We were just talking about Claire and Lucas, and all of a sudden, you run into her. The universe is trying to tell you something."

I don't necessarily agree. I tuck my hair behind my ears and say, "Well, whatever made it happen, I feel great. And I *am* going to find Lucas."

"He's your destiny. I feel it."

"How do you feel anything in that outfit?" I grin.

"You want to touch it?"

"Um, no. Anyway, I'm staying at Hanna's. I think the three of us should go out tonight."

"Dancing?" she asks, hopping off my desk and slapping her ass. I knew the Carmen Electra strip videos would be a great birthday present for her.

I want to say no because I so rarely go out to dance clubs. Hanna and Lucy are always trying to drag me, but the people there just annoy me. Everyone dressed in the sluttiest of clothes, grinding with strangers, trying to show why they're better than the person dancing next to them. And that's just my friends. But a tush like mine is a bit of a waste if I don't shake it once in awhile.

"I'm not wearing leather, I'm not going to a gay bar and I'm not dancing with a bunch of desperate men," I tell her as I turn on my computer.

"Anything you *will* do?"

I look up from my email that I just opened. "Drink."

"Okay, I'll meet you at Hanna's at nine. Any luck on the Lucas front?" she asks. Loudly.

I shove a finger against my lips. "Shhh! I don't want anyone to know. No, none. I can't find anything. I have to log the calls today so maybe they'll inspire me. I think I'll have to get Andrew to help me."

"With Lucas?" she mouths.

"No, you idiot. With the other ones."

And then the phone rings. Lucy goes back to her desk, every eye in the room on her shiny, pert butt. I forgot to ask her about the waitress she'd picked up on Friday night.

"Jamie Ross," I answer the phone.

"Ms. Ross, this is your credit card company calling."

Of course it is. You're stalking me. I'm not going to get anything done today. "Yes?" I ask wearily and cradle the phone against my head so I can click through my emails.

"We haven't received your payment yet."

I spin in my rolling chair so I'm facing away from the screen. And just as I'm about to come up with yet another pathetic excuse, I have a brainstorm.

"You know what? I'm going to take out an advance on my other credit card to pay this one."

"This would be the corporate card registered to you and Derek Leeds the Third?"

"Yes."

Look, all of that stuff that sent my bill sky high wasn't for me anyway. I really don't think I should be the one to pay for Derek's high class lifestyle. And considering that shit with his mom and the bill, I think we're even now.

"That's fine. We'll take the advance from the corporate card and your account will be clear. But, Ms. Ross, could you please pay the minimum by the due date the next time?"

"Of course."

And I will because I'll actually be able to afford it.

"Thank you for your time. Now, would you like to increase your limit?"

"You betcha!" After hanging up, a huge smile spreads across my face. If Derek wants to play, I'll show him that I'm not some loser who can't do anything for herself. And it's not like I've done anything wrong. He asked me to pay the bill, but he also asked me to dress up like a schoolgirl, and I didn't do that either.

But, enough about Derek. I really have to work or there won't be any show at all so I listen to the messages the love seekers have left me.

"Hi, I'm an eighty year old woman who's been searching for my high school boyfriend for years. His name is-"

I skip the rest of the message. Too old for TV.

"Hello, um, I'm looking for Harry, my invisible boyfriend from eighth grade. Nobody else could see him, but I know he's real."

Skip.

"Um, hi, um, I'm l-l-looking f-for m-my l-l-love."

Skip. Stutterers don't do well on television.

"Hello, my name is Ray Smith, and I haven't seen my ex-girlfriend for twenty years. When I went to college, we lost touch, but I'm ready to see Lisa again."

Hmmm, that's a possibility. He sounds relatively sane, which won't be the average caller. I listen to fifty-one messages, and out of those, only five are callbacks.

To show Andrew I'm a team player, I go to his office to discuss the candidates with him. He's in faded jeans and a white t-shirt, reading something intently with his feet propped up on the desk. I knock on the open door, and he smiles when he sees me.

"Jamie, how are you?" he asks, peering at me in an oddly concerned way and taking his feet off the desk.

"Why?" I ask defensively, leaning against the door frame.

"Eva told me you don't seem like yourself today. Is everything okay?" He pushes his papers to the side in a show of "I'm a listening kind of boss."

"That little...I'm fine. I just wanted to show you the people I'd like to contact for the reunion show." I walk over to his desk to hand him the list, and he takes it from me.

"Great. You work quickly. Sue told me she could never have survived here without you."

I blush. Not so good at taking compliments. "Well, anyway, these are the most normal people who called. I thought I'd check the Internet, do an email search and then a cross-country phone search."

"You know you'll have to go and meet these people. There'll be some travel required. I hope that won't interfere with anything."

"Oh, it won't," I mutter under my breath.

"Pardon?"

"That won't be a problem. My boyfriend works a lot."

First rule of boss-employee relationships: don't unload personal problems at the workplace. Andrew doesn't need (or I'm sure, care) to know about my weekend.

"Why don't we split up the list?" he suggests.

"Oh," I say, slightly taken aback. "I usually do all of the research on my own. Sue really didn't have the time for-"

119

"I know," he interrupts me. "But I like to be involved in all of the projects. I'll do a bit for every show. But this one's my personal favorite," he says and grins.

He really has the sweetest smile. Straight, white teeth (except for a slightly crooked one at the bottom in the front), and a dimple in his left cheek. And I like the way he looks at me when he talks to me. He really listens. Poor guy. Eva will have her hooks in him before he knows what hit him.

"Okay, thanks. Do you want to hear about the callers? Some of them seem pretty interesting."

"Sure. Do you want to get a cup of coffee?" he asks.

"Coffee? I never say no to that."

He stands up and opens his desk drawer to get his wallet. While he's busying himself with that, I glance around the office. He's put up posters of all the requisite revolutionaries: Che Guevara, Martin Luther King and their ilk. There are hundreds of books and magazines crammed on the bookshelves, and I peek at a few titles. "Human Rights as Politics and Idolatry," "No Logo," "Downsize This." No question where his politics lean.

On his messy desk, there are a couple of framed pictures. One is of an older couple holding hands on a boat; the other, a beautiful brunette, tall, slim, laughing gaily at the camera. My amateur detective skills deduce that the first is of his parents, and the second, his girlfriend. He's not wearing a wedding ring. He catches me looking.

"That's my mom and dad on their thirtieth wedding anniversary. They went on a cruise of South America. The other one is Kelly, my girlfriend."

Forget talk shows, I could consult for "Criminal Minds." We leave the building and head to the Starbucks on the corner because I'm the only person who'll drink the sludge masquerading as office coffee. "So, um, how are you enjoying working here?"

He pushes his hair out of his eyes (he really needs a haircut, it keeps flopping back in his face) and says, "I like it. It's very different from my work before. I've seen things I'll never forget. I just got back from the Middle East, actually, and that's what made me stop. We were supposed to be shooting a documentary of the citizens' reactions to all of the changes over the years, and then everything went completely out of control, and we got the hell out."

"You seem disappointed."

"It's the first time I've walked away from a project. I usually follow through, and I'm not so good at walking away."

Neither am I. "This must be a step down for you. Producing a sleazy talk show," I say after we get our ultra-expensive coffees and take a seat at the back of the cafe.

He pours three sugars into his coffee and stirs it. "Well, it's certainly not blood and guts."

"You ain't seen nothing yet. You haven't seen a scorned wife."

He laughs loudly, and the amusement reaches all the way to his eyes lighting them up with pleasure.

"So, Jamie, what's your story? How'd you end up here with a Master's in Philosophy?" he asks.

Surprised, I blink and take a sip of coffee (grande, of course). "How did you know I have a philosophy degree?" I ask suspiciously.

What else do you know about me that I don't know?

"I make it a point to know who I'm working with."

"What's Eva's degree in?" I ask.

A smile plays at the corner of Andrew's mouth, and his eyes twinkle. "What's the deal with you two anyway? She studied economics."

That prompts me to roar with laughter, which is never a good idea with a mouthful of coffee. The coffee splurts out of my mouth

121

and splashes on the table.

"Sorry," I say, mopping up the table and my nose, where the coffee has also shot out from (kill me now). "I didn't know that."

"She's as jealous of you as you are of her."

I wipe the last bit of coffee from under my nose and say, "Listen, Dr. Doolittle, I'm not jealous of anyone. I was just curious and surprised. I thought she studied basket weaving or something."

He raises an eyebrow skeptically and takes a sip of coffee. "So who was your high school crush?" he asks, leaping from one dangerous topic to the next.

I almost snort my coffee again. Does he know? Did he bring me here to wheedle information out of me and then fire me? No, that's impossible. I haven't even really started looking. "Why?" I ask harshly.

"You're very suspicious, you know that? I'm just curious. I've never worked with topics like this, and it fascinates me. Finding someone you used to love."

"Whose yours?"

It's always better to get information before giving it.

"Well, I've had the same girlfriend since I was eighteen, so I guess she was my crush."

"You've been with your girlfriend since you were eighteen? Holy crap! Sorry, I mean, that's a long time. How old are you now?"

Shit. That was rude. He *is* my boss.

"I'm thirty-six. I know. It is kind of crazy. Eighteen years."

"Why aren't you married?"

Shut up, Jamie. I don't usually ask inappropriate questions. What's wrong with me? Andrew doesn't say anything, but his eyes darken, and the twinkle disappears.

"I'm sorry. That's none of my business. I don't even know you," I apologize and abashed, look down at the table.

122

"No, no, it's okay. It's just complicated. Because I travelled so much, the years just flew by, and we live together, but, I'm not, uh, I'm not...You know what? I didn't mean to get into this."

He stops talking, and instead, unfolds the rim of his coffee cup. Then his jaw starts moving.

"The grinding feels good, doesn't it?" I point to his jaw and ask.

He rubs his hand along his jawline and says, "Oh fuck, I'm doing it again? I don't even notice anymore."

"I do it too. I think my back teeth are all worn down."

"So, tell me about our callers," he says.

The last part of our conversation is forgotten. I think we're both embarrassed to have gotten onto a topic that neither of us wants to talk about. He keeps his eyes on the list I'd given him and starts jotting notes on the paper. Not looking at me, he says, "These look great. I like that it's more men than women doing most of the calling. Okay, so what's our first step?"

Our? I don't know if I'll get used to that. "Well, I'll get the Internet stuff done, and then, I'll make the calls to get more information and set up appointments. It depends on how far the budget extends."

Andrew lifts his head and spreads his lips in a slow smile. "Not very far, as you know. We'll probably have to do a lot of driving."

There's that ubiquitous "we" again. "We?"

"Of course. I'll come with you."

"Can't stop travelling?" I ask, grinning back at him.

"Partly. But I think it looks more professional for the producer to go as well."

My grin disappears. "And not just the lowly assistant?"

"You really like to put yourself down, don't you? You're an associate, not an assistant. And it's not that I don't think you'll do a bang up job, but I like working in a team."

"Oh. Right." I'm embarrassed at my childish retort, and I

quickly change the subject back to the segment. "Well, the show's going to air in a few weeks, so hopefully, I'll get as much information as I need this week."

And as I'm talking, what I'm really thinking is how I'm going to find Lucas if Andrew is with me the whole time. And how much of a bad first impression I'm making on my new boss. I'm coming off like an angry and invasive gossiper and that's the total opposite of me.

"Sounds good. Ready to go back?"

We head back to the office, and when we get to my desk, I feel Eva's unnaturally turquoise eyes (contacts, I'm sure) shooting daggers at me from across the room. She heads over to us and looks pointedly at me. "Hey Jamie, there was a phone call for you while you were out. It was Derek, and boy, is he pissed off at you."

"Why did you answer my phone?" I spit out.

"Since you're not doing your work, someone has to do it for you," she answers as her beady eyes sweep over my desk trying to find something juicy to incriminate me with.

"Answer your own damn phone, Eva. I was in a meeting with Andrew."

I see a quick flash of annoyance cross her face, and her eyes glint sadistically. Uh oh. "So you and Derek broke up, huh? I understand why. I always wondered how you and he stayed together. You're sooo different."

I am not letting her get to me. So what if she knows we broke up? So what if Andrew is still standing there giving me a surprised look? I'm the one who left.

"I give fantastic blow jobs," I answer, sit in my chair and click on the computer.

Eva stalks away. One for Jamie, zero for Evil. Unfortunately, Andrew is still standing there, and the twinkle is back in his eyes.

124

CHAPTER THIRTEEN

Instead of calling Derek back because I have absolutely nothing to say to him (and it makes me angry just thinking about him and why it took me so long to leave), I spend the rest of my day trying to find five very different and very mysterious people. Four of them are for the show, and one, of course, is Lucas. Feeling bad that I'm looking for Lucas when I should be working, I search for the work-related people first.

I hit the jackpot with Facebook for two of them. The nice man's ex-girlfriend lives in Indianapolis, and the other guy, with a very gravelly and pompous sounding voice, wants to be reunited with a girl in Milwaukee. I easily get email addresses and phone numbers for both of them.

Lucas is the most challenging. He's obviously too cool to be on a reunion website. After googling Lucas Simpson, I get one thousand, three hundred and forty-eight hits. I can cross off the men over forty (ten!), but knowing nothing about his life now, I'm not sure if he's the marathon runner, AIDS activist (I hope he's not because that makes me a little nervous considering how many times we slept together), author, forest ranger or billionaire. The easiest thing to do would be to call his mom, but then she'll call him, and the jig will be up.

I lean back in my chair, put the ends of my hair in my mouth and sigh. Is this really a good idea? I have so many other things to worry about. I can't stay at Hanna's forever, I don't have enough money to live alone, I'll never have sex again. Not that I was getting much of it lately, but something's better than nothing, right?

For the first time in years, I am independent, single and free.

125

The problem is I don't know if I can take care of myself. I don't even make good coffee. The phone rings. The credit card company definitely.

"Jamie Ross."

"You bitch! What are you trying to do?"

"Lovely to hear from you, Derek. To what do I owe this call? During work hours no less. You're not slacking off, are you?"

"You have serious problems! How dare you take out an advance on my corporate card! You said that you were going to pay it and what? Since you've lived off me for years, you thought you'd just let me continue doing everything for you? And I know you don't have the brains to do that. Maybe it was Hanna or Lucy. I'm not paying it, you fucking-"

I lower my voice (Eva does not need to hear this) and say, "Is that language necessary? It's really not becoming of you."

I can hear him spluttering and banging his fist on his desk. Goody.

"I'm sorry we ever met," he tells me.

Okay, that hurt.

"You're sorry? I'll accept that as a long overdue apology for constantly putting me and my family and my job down. For making me feel worthless. For bringing your mother over with a bill! Like I'm some fucking client, and not the person you lived with for five years. You're an asshole!"

Slam! Now I'm angry all over again. The second the phone hits the cradle, it rings. I glance at my watch. 6:00 p.m. Quitting time. Ignoring the incessant ringing (I'm sure Eva'll pick it up anyway), I get my bag, turn off my computer and go to Hanna's.

When I get there, she's not home yet because she's at some glitzy perfume launch or something so I pore through the two boxes of my things she'd picked up for me. The condo had always seemed filled with books, CDs and knickknacks. But not mine. I've

126

got a few CDs, a couple of books, a snow globe (of Disney World, I think this is actually Rachel's), some costume jewellery, a lot of candles and my movies. Those I have a lot of. Oh, here's "Pretty Woman," "Bridget Jones's Diary," and all of the "Lethal Weapon" films (so what if I like a little action now and then?)

From the bottom of one of the boxes, I unearth an awesome pair of black pants. Hip-hugging, form-fitting and oh so slimming, these pants make me look lean and mean. I haven't worn them in years. They are my dancing pants, so obviously, I also haven't gone dancing in a couple of years. Is that true? Has it really been years? When did I last go dancing? And then I remember. And know exactly why it's been so long.

Derek and I had gone clubbing with Hanna and some guy (there have been quite a few so I don't even bother remembering most of their names), and it was a total disaster. At least the tunes were retro 90s so I knew how to move my body, but Derek showed up in a suit. A suit! To a funky club. He was just in the first year of his new job and "image is everything" phase (which at the time I thought would be short-lived).

Everyone snickered when we walked by, and when people would spot him, they'd purposely bump into him and yell, "Excuse me, sir!" very loudly. I was mortified, but Derek didn't get it at all. He wouldn't dance or play pool, and he sipped Perrier with lime while scowling at everyone. Hanna and her guy went at it all night while I flailed about by myself. And when we'd gotten home, Derek told me I'd embarrassed him. "You represent us as a couple, and when you dance like you're looking for sex, it makes me look bad," he had said.

Why oh why did it take me so long to leave? There must be a support group I can join for losers like me. "Hangers-On Unite," "Fear Change? Join Pathetic Souls Are Us."

I slip off my shoes and put some hiphop CD into the stereo.

127

The beat pulsates through the speakers, and after cranking up the volume, I shimmy to Hanna's bedroom. Before I get my ass on the dance floor (as the song is instructing me to do), I want to see what my ass looks like. I haven't done this in awhile.

Standing in front of her full-length mirror, I try to catch the beat. I twist my hips, raise my hands above my head, do a little booty shake. I don't look too bad. I dance into the kitchen, open a bottle of champagne (I know Hanna won't mind because she buys a bottle practically every week) and slosh some into a beer mug. I take a huge swig, letting the bubbles pop and fizz in my mouth before swallowing.

Back in front of the mirror, I pretend I'm dancing with a man. We're grinding, lowering ourselves to the floor, I curl my body around his-

"What the fuck are you doing?" Hanna is standing in the bedroom, wide-eyed.

I jump in surprise, and the champagne spills all over the carpet. "Oh shit! You scared me, Han. Sorry about the mess, I'll clean it up."

"It doesn't stain. Don't worry about it. What are you doing?"

"Dancing with Mr. Whomever. You scared him off."

"I think your dancing scared him off, Madonna. We need a little lesson. You have to learn to move the lower part of your body while the upper half stays still. Like this."

Hanna's nonexistent ass (besides her massive boobs, she's a rail) does a very Beyonce-like shake while her other parts stay still. God, even I want her. "I can't do that. When my ass moves so do my boobs."

She puts her hand on my waist and moves my butt back and forth.

"Do you know this is the most action I've had in ages?" I look over my shoulder and say.

She laughs. "Not if you learn how to dance."

I stop dancing and catch her eye in the mirror. "I'm not having a one night stand."

"Never say never."

After two hours, I think I've almost got it. Lucy shows up in her catsuit, Hanna's wearing a very revealing halter top and flirty little skirt. I'm in my pants and a bra. "I have nothing to wear!" I whine, standing in the middle of Hanna's bedroom.

They look at my outfit and start throwing things out of Hanna's closet into my arms. Finally, they find something I'm almost willing to wear. Everything she has is either meant to show way too much midriff or too much cleavage, and neither of those are my best assets.

Lucy gives me a black, filmy shirt that has no back, with only flimsy strings that tie at the bottom to keep it on. I hold it up in the air, inspect it and hand it back to Lucy. "I can't wear this. Where does the bra go?"

She hands it back to me and says, "No bra, lucky girl."

The wonders of an A cup. Okay, AA.

"What about her hair?" Lucy asks, picking up a limp wet strand off my head.

I've been sucking on my hair a lot lately, and since it's already so fine, ends dripping with saliva certainly don't give it any more body and shine.

Hanna runs to the bathroom and returns with her laundry basket of supplies: gel, shiner, straightener, volumizer. She's also got an eyelash curler (or portable torture machine it looks more like), blush, foundation, lipstick, lip gloss, mascara, eyeliner and something she calls a "contourer." I rummage through the basket realizing that I don't even know what most of this stuff is for.

They pull, iron, slather, pluck, and an hour later, let me look in the mirror. Who is this gorgeous woman? Not Jamie Ross certainly. This woman has cheekbones, full lips and thick, shiny hair.

"How? What? Is this? Am I?" I stutter.

"You're beautiful. Let's go," Hanna says.

"We'll do this for you when you find Lucas," Lucy says and drapes an arm around my shoulders. "You have to arm yourself with everything you can."

"If it's destiny, she doesn't need any help," Hanna says, smirking.

"Even destiny needs a little lipstick," Lucy retorts.

Hanna rolls her eyes at me. She's supportive of my search, but is also not a believer that your life's path is set out for you. She'd rather think you realize what you want as you live through things rather than living for them.

The taxi drops us off at "Boom," a huge, dark hall, illuminated only by cleverly placed candles for the best lighting effect (everyone looks better by candlelight), black suede couches (the dark also helps hide cigarette burns and other interesting stains) sit in four corners, and the bar is teeming with Beautiful People. At least I think they're beautiful. It's kind of hard to tell when they're shrouded in complete darkness.

Okay, first things first. Inhibition lowering alcohol. Despite my new ego that has formed in the last half hour, I'm still nervous being here. I'm not so great at making the first move with people, especially male people. To cover my discomfort, I get bitchy. Or quiet. We stand at the bar, and I can't even get to the counter because there are so many people clamoring to get a drink. All I can see are women's midriffs (many with less than perfect abs are braving it, but I'm still never showing off my white, jiggly tummy) because the average height must be 5'10. And that's just the women.

Hanna stretches out a long, slender arm and motions to the

bartender. Once he sees Hanna, everyone else disappears. It's those damn eyes of hers. And her spectacular heaving breasts. She returns carrying a tray bearing nine shots of different fluorescent colors. I think the pink ones are Sex On The Beach, the blue, Blue Lagoon, and the green, well, I don't know any green drinks.

"Alright, girls, down 'em!" Lucy shouts to be heard.

"Shouldn't we toast to something?" I ask. I'm really just putting off drinking these nuclear shots.

Remember what happened the last time I was so drunk in a bar? Yup, Derek.

"To Lucas!" Lucy yells.

One down.

"To freedom!" Hanna screams.

Two down.

"To me!" I shriek.

Three down.

Uh oh. My chest is warming up, my head is spinning, and my body is moving to the music. But I can't feel a thing. "I'm really drunk," I tell the girls, grabbing their arms and grinning.

"Already? Jeez, you're a cheap date. Let's dance!" Hanna says.

We go to the dance floor, and when Beyonce's "Crazy in Love" comes on, I shake my ass like I'm trying to get something off of it.

"Having fun?" Lucy asks, while eyeing a svelte brunette standing next to us.

I nod, and dance, dance, dance. I've forgotten Hanna's lesson, and I don't care. My butt and my boobs are all wobbling, and my arms are waving hello above my head. I have got my groove on.

Instantly, a trio of silly men try to join us. Just to entice them further, Lucy grabs me from behind and slithers her body up and down my back. The men (wearing pants that are too short, and much, much too tight, basically banana hammocks with legs) are wide-eyed as their every sordid fantasy appears live.

131

And even though I'm so drunk that they are slightly appealing to me, I do not want to be a later jerk-off image or accused of causing a heart attack because the way they're breathing, labored and panting, is scaring me a little.

And then I see him. No, no, not Lucas. But a man who fits my very short list of necessary masculine attributes. Tall, check. Stubble, check. Tattered jeans, check. Hair that needs a cut, check. Mustering up my liquid courage, I gaze right at him with what I think is a sexy, intense stare. Unfortunately, the air in the club is so dry that my contacts are glued to my eyeballs, and it hurts to keep both of them open at the same time. So it looks like I'm playing some strange winking game. He winks back.

Hanna notices me noticing and whispers in my ear, "Go get him and bring him home."

I gape at her. "No way. I can't. What if he turns me down? And anyway, I'm not sleeping with a stranger. But it would be fun to flirt."

"So, go talk to him," she says and pushes me forward.

I look around for Lucy to ask her what I should do, and I find her in a corner making out with the brunette. I wonder what happened to the waitress? I also wonder if it's easier for lesbians to pick up because Lucy finds a woman wherever we go. Or maybe it's just easy when you're gorgeous.

Rather than interrupt the tongue wrestling (which I got enough of watching growing up), I make up my own mind. Why shouldn't I go talk to him? I've never picked up a guy before, but come on, I'm a mature, confident woman. I can take rejection. And I'm wasted.

I shove aside the sweaty bodies, step gingerly over dropped drinks and broken glass and get to the other side. I think we talked, I'm almost sure we danced, and I'm positive we drank. Because that's the last thing I remember.

CHAPTER FOURTEEN

Bang, bang, bang! A jackhammer is pounding away somewhere outside, and I'm going to kill the person who's responsible. I try to lift my head off the pillow to yell at the construction workers. Fuuuuuck! That's no jackhammer; it's my head, which I can't lift or it'll explode. My brain rattles around, soaked in alcohol, and needles of pain puncture my forehead.

What the hell did I do last night? I hear a groan. It's not me. Oh my God, *who* did I do last night? I open one eye and see a naked back and a naked arm. I take a quick peek under the covers. A totally naked man is in my bed!

I leap out of bed, taking the comforter with me, and race to the other side of the room. Sliding down the wall to the floor, I hit my head against my hand. Ow! How much did I drink? I think I've had a one night stand, but I'm not really sure. I have never, never done this before. Did we have sex? I'm pretty sure I wouldn't do that.

There's a torn condom wrapper on the floor. Well, I guess I have done that. I hear a toilet flush outside the bedroom, and I look wildly around the room for a way to get him out of here before Hanna wakes up. Mind you, she won't care who's in my bed. She'll be thrilled that I'm finally getting nailed.

So, maybe *I* should leave. Or maybe I'm dreaming. Yes, that must be it. I'd never pick up a strange guy in a bar and bring him home. Okay, that's not totally true, but I was younger then, and we actually went to his place.

Naked Stranger stirs. No dream. I back myself further in the corner hoping the wall will swallow me whole. My thick tongue and dry mouth are screaming for a glass of water, but I can't move. If I move, he'll wake up. But if I just reach for that doorknob above

133

my head and turn it gently, I can-

"Good morning," Naked Stranger says and smiles at me.

Do nothing. Or say anything. Because he has an accent. South African? I don't remember talking to anyone with an accent.

"Cat got your tongue, girl?"

Irish?

"You have to leave," I tell him.

"What? Why? We had an incredible time last night."

We did?

"You're amazing, Jamie."

I am? And how do you know my name? Although he pronounced it "Yamie." Mexican?

"Can I at least get your number? I'd love to be part of the adventure you kept talking about last night."

"No, you have to go. There's no adventure."

"But I want to help you find luck."

Luck? What the hell is Naked Stranger prattling on about? "I don't need luck. I need you to leave. Now," I say curtly, really just masking my shock that I don't remember one thing from last night.

"You're sure different in the morning. Don't you want to do it before I go?" he asks, allowing the sheet to fall away and revealing a very happy (and large) morning erection.

Considering I don't remember doing it the first time, not really, no. But at least (even in my drunken state), I have good taste. He's very lean, dark, smooth and hairless. He's kind of sexy. Maybe I could? Oh God, no. Then I hear someone cough outside the door. A male cough. Are there two of them? I am *never* drinking again.

"Look guy," I say, trying to push myself further into the wall to keep him from coming any closer. "I'm sure we had a great time, and you're a wonderful person. But I just got out of a very serious and long relationship-"

"With Derek, I know," he interrupts me. And scratches his

balls. Charming.

"But I was really drunk, and that's no excuse, but I don't feel like doing anything right now. I just think it'd be better if you go."

"So you don't want me to help you find-"

"No!"

I bury my head under the comforter. Like a baby, perhaps if I can't see him, he's not here. I hear Naked Stranger get dressed, and I don't raise my head from the comforter until I hear the door click closed. I pull the blanket away from my crusty eyes (shit, contacts still in) and breathe a huge sigh of relief.

I desperately want coffee (oh, and to change the sheets so I can fall back into bed and never wake up), but I'm terrified there's another man out there who wants to help me find luck. Then it hits me. I must have talked about Lucas. And Derek. And everything. Oh God. Knock, knock. "Go away. No more sex, please."

The door creaks open, and Hanna is standing there, gorgeous and rumpled in a black camisole and panties, holding a steaming cup of coffee.

"Quick! Get in here!" I snap, grabbing the mug and the two aspirin she's also brought me.

"Well, someone got laid," she says.

"You?"

"Well, yeah, but you, too. What a Spanish stud!" she exclaims, sitting on the bed of sin.

Ah, Spanish. "Han, I don't remember a thing. Not him, his name, the sex. What did I do?"

"You took a chance."

I groan and fall face first into the carpet, hoping it will smother and kill me. Asphyxiation By Rug.

"Stop it! It's okay," Hanna says, standing up and pulling me up off the floor.

"It's so not okay! I just slept with someone I can't remember.

135

At least we used a condom." I sit up and look at the wrapper. Next to a few other wrappers.

"Four or five by the looks of things. I can't talk now. There's someone in my room."

"Oh thank God! I thought I slept with both of them," I say and cradle my sore head in my hands.

Hanna giggles. "Yeah, sure, Jaim. No, it's Jack. The lawyer cum artiste I was telling you about. He was at 'Boom' too. You met him."

"Before or after the shots?" I ask, my voice muffled because my head is now hanging down in shame.

"After."

"Then we've never met. And we won't because I'm going to kill myself now."

And just so I can get as far away from the bed as possible, I curl up in a heap on the floor. But not before my eye catches a black pubic hair resting on my pillow. I don't even want to know how it got there.

Hanna looks disgusted with me. "Well, I'm sorry you can't remember because it sounded like you were having fun."

"You heard me?" I raise my head and wince.

"Hard not to. This is good for you, Jaim. Don't be so uptight. You let loose, forgot about Derek, picked up a guy, didn't get rejected. Nothing terrible happened."

"Hanna, I don't even know the name of the second guy I've slept with in five years!"

"Mathias."

"Mathias? *You* know his name?"

"You were screaming it all night long. Drink your coffee, sleep and you'll remember later. Adventure is good, huh?"

I stumble back to bed. Alone.

Five hours later, I remember. Mathias, a musician, guitar

player, I think, living downtown. Works at "Subway" when not strumming. Young. Twenty-two. Fuck me, he's twenty-two. Ten years younger than me.

Is that even legal? A master at oral sex. And though recalling the quick strokes of his velvety tongue, and the words he whispered in Spanish is making me slightly hot, I am so not proud right at this moment. Isn't a one night stand supposed to be liberating? I feel like shit.

This is not how I behave. I barely enjoy dancing with strangers. This one was inside me. Shit! I sit up with a jolt not because of the Naked Stranger, I mean Mathias, but because my eyes have just caught the day on the calendar above Hanna's computer. It's Tuesday! And it's 2:00 p.m. Fuck, fuck, fuck! I have to go to work. And I didn't call in sick.

I throw off the covers and almost scamper out the door, but luckily I catch a glimpse of myself in the mirror first. I am totally naked. I find my ratty sweat suit (the one I've worn so many times the knees and butt are practically rubbed out), run into the hall, skid down to the kitchen and reach for the phone. There's a hot pink Post-It note stuck to it.

Jamie, you slut,

I phoned Lucy and told her you wouldn't be at work today. The "flu." She said Andrew wants you to call him before 4:00 p.m. Take it easy. No guilt.

Hanna

I'm glad she had the foresight to think about my job. Not only have I screwed a stranger, but I put my only source of income at risk. I'm a horrible, irresponsible, useless person. I really wish I could enjoy the after sex body buzz: bruised thighs, achy muscles, exhaustion. I'm sure Derek's not sleeping with strangers. Derek would never forget to go to work. And then I smile because I am nothing like Derek, and that's a very good thing.

CHAPTER FIFTEEN

To alleviate my mounting guilt, I boot up Hanna's computer (after dry swallowing two more aspirin) and resume my searches. I have email addresses for everyone now, except, of course, Lucas. If it's this hard to find him, maybe he doesn't want to be found. If he wanted to see me all of these years, he could have. He's the one who said he loved me, and then, he disappeared.

It's funny that I've stored all of these memories and haven't thought about them in so long. Someone who was so important to me just vanished from my life and my mind, and he was such a huge reason I made it through my high school years without therapy.

I didn't have a lot of friends like other teenage girls did. I didn't often go to the mall, movies or friends' houses to hang out. I was either alone or with Lucas, and even though my entire high school knew about Katie and Leah (how could that not be great gossip?), with everyone else, I pretended that it was all cool.

Lucas and I would sit in his car, summer or winter, my feet up on the dashboard and whatever "in" music of the moment playing on the radio. Usually it was something hard and angry, like The Red Hot Chili Peppers or Ice-T, and he would tell me about his alcoholic father (long gone) and ask me if I thought Leah had ever loved my father or whether I worried that I might also like women.

Lucas was great at touch. Every part of my body fascinated him, and just the scratching of his fingers down my arm could send me into a shaking frenzy of longing. But he's probably married by now, and I'll just humiliate myself by trying to surprise him. I'm sure I barely cross his mind because until Lucy started all of this, he had barely crossed mine.

139

And anyway, I have other things to take care of right now. And trying to find my old fuck buddy isn't going to make those other things go away. I need to find a home. So, I stop looking for Lucas (just for a bit, I do have to find him now that I've begun this whole thing) and start looking for an apartment. I love Hanna, but I can't stay here forever. I could never afford to pay half her rent, and I know she loves living alone.

On the kitchen table is today's "Tribune" so I open it and scan furnished one bedroom apartments. I might not have the most elegant of taste, but there's no way I'm living in someone's dank, moldy basement. Also, every piece of furniture in that mausoleum is Derek's. Bought and paid for by him. That's perhaps the most humiliating of all.

I just let him take over because I didn't want to make waves. And whenever I'd suggested something for the apartment, Derek would always say that it wasn't the "look" we were going for. We. It was never really "we," was it? So, now, I find myself with nothing. I came to him with nothing, and I'm leaving with nothing. Except a jaw that feels a hell of a lot better now that I'm not ferociously grinding it anymore. Oh, and my pride, of course. Can't forget that.

Who knew apartments were so expensive? To live alone, I might have to pay at least $1500.00 a month. I barely make $2500.00. I'll have to cover phone, groceries, cable (there is no way I'm living without cable), insurance. How do other single women do this? I'm going to need a sugar daddy. Or a roommate. I lay my head on the table and press my cheek to the cool wood. I am so, so tired.

I am the last person to live with a stranger. It's hard enough for me to be close to people I've known for years. Sleep with a stranger? Clearly, not a problem for me. But live with one? Yuck. Stumbling through stilted conversations, waiting for them to leave in the morning (so I won't have to chatter cheerily with no coffee in my system), arguing over the television. Who needs it? I'd never lived with anyone until Derek. Through college, I lived with Leah, Katie and Rachel. And sometimes I stayed at my dad and Mo's. Home was safe. Home was comfortable. Most importantly, home was free.

But I have no other choice. Lucy has a one bedroom (no room for me), and I am not moving home at the age of thirty-two. I'd be taking vitamins all day and listening to Rachel's romantic woes all night. No thank you.

I raise my head, take a swig of coffee and look through "Shared Apartments." Because of my severe cat allergy, half of the ads are moot. Why do so many single women have cats? It's just not normal. There are three possibilities. One is a three bedroom, with a front garden, $1200.00 in Greek Town. I've always liked souvlaki. Mmm, and gyros, tzatziki. I'm hungry.

Another is a two bedroom, $1500.00 in Wicker Park, which is very artsy and eclectic and close to Lucy's. The third is another two bedroom, the main floor of a house, $2000.00, in the Loop, backyard, washer and dryer. Washer and dryer? I hadn't even thought about that.

Before Derek, Katie did my laundry for me, and then Derek got everything dry-cleaned or had Trina do it. I've never had to lug huge bags of dirty clothes to a decrepit laundromat. Number one looks the most promising, and it's the cheapest. I have to call Andrew so I leave making appointments for later.

"Andrew Harris."

"Hi, Andrew, it's Jamie," I say and launch into a round of spastic coughing to show him just how sick I am.

"Jamie, are you okay? You don't sound too good."

"Just the flu. Fever, body aches, sore throat. Sorry I missed work. But I have contact information for everyone."

"Don't worry about it now. You shouldn't work when you don't feel well, and it's better that you're not here spreading whatever it is you have. Just concentrate on making yourself better, and we'll see you soon."

Now I feel guilty. He's being so understanding. But I am sick. Sick in the head. "Thanks, I'll be back tomorrow. I'll start getting in touch and making plans to meet everyone."

"No problem. We'll need to match our schedules and find a good time to go. By the way, your boyfriend was here earlier. I guess he didn't know you were sick."

Was he not paying attention when Eva blurted out we had broken up? She *was* wearing a very low-cut top that day. And anyway, what was Derek doing there? He barely came to visit me when we were together. He probably wanted to scream his head off about the credit card bill. Or the $15,000 ridiculousness I'm completely and forever ignoring.

"He was? He probably wanted to take me out for lunch."

"Probably. He left with Eva."

I drop the phone, and it crashes to the floor with a loud bang.

"Jamie? Hello?" I can hear him calling my name, but I don't move.

Motionless, I stare at the phone. Steam is coming out of my nose. I'm furious. Derek and Eva? If that little bitch is moving in on my territory... He's not really mine anymore, is he? And yes, I'm pissed off, but, oddly, I'm not jealous. What are they talking about? Me probably. I'm sure they're sitting in a sparse, overpriced cafe sipping Chardonnay and laughing gaily about my ass.

"Jamie? Are you there?" I hear a voice call me from the floor.

Shit, Andrew's still on the phone. I reach down and pick it up. "Sorry, I just dropped the phone. I'll see you tomorrow."

"Okay. Um, Jamie, did I upset you? About your boyfriend? Did I say the wrong thing?"

142

"No, no. I was trying to blow my nose and hold the phone at the same time. I'm fine. I'll be back to my old self tomorrow."

"Eat some chicken soup or something and sleep."

"I will. Thanks."

And I hang up. My old self? She's out with last week's milk. How can Derek already be after Eva? We haven't even been broken up for a week. I at least have the decency to wait before I- Oh, right. Mathias, the Spanish babe. My luck seeker.

It doesn't matter. Derek can go out with any slut he likes. But why Eva? Oh, Jeanette will loooove her. Desperate to bag a rich husband, all trim and taut (not everywhere, I'm positive, because you just know that girl's been around the street a few times), and eager to get on her knees for a pair of Jimmy Choos.

Adrenalin fuels my energy, and I call each place to make an appointment—Wednesday, Thursday and Friday. Now, I have something to do. No more prim and pretentious for me. For fuck sakes, I have a plan.

***

I'm either still drunk or very bored because I actually spend the rest of the day making lists. Never before have I made a list for anything. Not even groceries. I go to the store hungry and choose what appeals to me at the moment. How do I know on Monday what I'll want to eat on Thursday? And my do as I please attitude towards errands and weekends used to drive Derek crazy. He would even write the brand (and if I didn't pick up that specific make, well, what a travesty for King Anal) and on which shelf it was located. None of that no-name cold cream, Q-tips, gauze. It had to be the best of the best. Why am I even thinking about Derek? I'm a busy woman.

TO DO:

1. Get a haircut

143

2. Find an apartment

3. Find Lucas

Okay, three things to do. Not bad. First things first. Haircut. "Han? Where do you get your hair cut?" I ask after calling her store.

"Why? You want to sleep with my hairstylist?"

"You crack me up. No, I want to get my hair cut."

"In a style?"

"Yes."

"Oh my God! On Magnificent Mile, between Chanel and Armani at 'David's.' Down the street from my shop. It'll cost you more than Super Cuts, you know."

"I don't go to Super Cuts. I go to the place in Little Italy. Twenty dollars for a nice, simple cut. But I think I need a bit of, um, pizazz. Can you make an appointment for me?" I look at myself in Hanna's gleaming stainless steel toaster. This is more than Luigi can handle.

"Sure. What time?"

I check the clock on the stove. It's 3:30 p.m. now.

"4:30 p.m. today?"

"Jamie, you can't get an appointment in an hour."

"No, but you can. And you made me sleep with Naked Stranger."

"Mathias! Oh, get over yourself. He's hot and Spanish. Bask in the afterglow and shut up."

Five minutes later, she calls back with an appointment for me. Most things, I like to do alone. But for this, I need backup. I need Rachel. So, I call my sister on her cell.

"Jaim! What's up? How are you? Are you feeling awful?"

I just slept with a twenty-two year old musician named Mathias. "Are you busy?" I ask instead.

"I'm going to the mall with J.P. Do you want to come?"

Not in the least. But I'll break her heart if I tell her that. My sister is a sensitive soul, and I tread gently because I love her more than anyone else in the world. "Actually, I was wondering if you could come with me to 'David's.'"

"Are you meeting Hanna?"

"Nope. I'm getting my hair cut."

"Get out of here! No way! *You're* going to 'David's'? For real?"

I hear the blatant shock in her voice. Poor Rachel has never had the type of sister to share clothes and makeup with and do each other's hair. But, I'm a great listener. It's a trade off, I guess. "This is the new me. And the new me wants a good haircut."

"Of course I'll meet you. Will you take me for a drink after?"

"No. But you can take me shopping."

"Ooh, even better!" she squeals.

We make arrangements to meet, and suddenly, I'm petrified. I've had the same haircut (parted on one side, shoulder-length, blondish, straightish) for ten years. What if I don't like it? What if I look exactly the same when it's done?

Outside the salon, Rachel rushes over to me and twirls me around in a tight hug. The pile of glossy hairstyle magazines she was holding tumbles to the ground, and she laughs. "Let's sit. We need to talk about this first."

I plunk my butt down on a bench while Rachel comes nose to nose with me and examines my bone structure. "Layers. You need layers. All one length just drags your hair down. And highlights," she tells me, flicking my hair around while her golden curls gleam in the sunlight.

"Rach?"

"Yeah?"

"I'm scared."

She reaches over and holds my icy hand, and she's still holding it when we enter the salon. A mix of spicy hiphop and mellow reggae battle it out on the speakers, and impossibly gorgeous women are sashaying around in short skirts, tight pants and sporting a variety of frighteningly asymmetrical and razor sharp, blunt bobs. Those are the stylists. The clientele are, well, perfect. I really don't belong here.

"I've changed my mind. Let's go," I say, turning around.

Rachel grabs my shoulders and steers me to the reception desk. With an air of authority (as if she comes to places like this all the time), she cocks her left hip and rests her hand on it. "Hi. This is Jamie Ross. She has an appointment with David."

The receptionist (blue hair! blue hair!) runs her black-rimmed eyes up and down my body and points me to the sinks. Once I'm smocked and washed, I sit in a chair facing a very well-lit mirror. I am tanned, skinnier and I think even taller. Nice effects.

"Helloooo," a high-pitched voice drawls.

A tiny man (shorter than Rachel, maybe even shorter than me) peeks around my shoulder and rests his head on it. This man is touching me, and I don't know him. Bad place to start. I cringe. He moves back and grins. "Nervous? Don't you worry. I have strict instructions from Hanna. We love your girl."

"What did she tell you?" I demand and narrow my eyes at him.

Of course I trust Hanna implicitly, but who knows what she'd do to my hair had she the chance.

"Relax, Jamie, love. She said you're not big on trends and like simple elegance."

"Oh. That sounds about right." I unfold my arms from my chest and uncross my legs. But before he can even tell me his ideas, my sister enthusiastically (embarrassingly) pipes in.

"My sister's beautiful. Isn't she beautiful?" Rachel waits for David to nod. When he does, she continues. "But, see, she doesn't know it. She just broke up with her boyfriend, and God, they were together forever, like years. So now she needs to get out there and attract some hot men. So, I was thinking highlights, layers, chin length."

I'm bright red that David (and the whole salon because Rachel doesn't talk, she shouts in case the people in the back can't hear her) now knows my whole depressing life. I glare at her and turn to David. "Sorry, David. She's eighteen."

He grins at Rachel, obviously taken with her youthful spirit and beauty. Like every man. How come Katie and Leah don't have her under lock and key? "Jamie, I agree with your sister on the layers. I'd also like to lighten the color, make it warmer and softer. A nice, buttery blonde. How does that sound?"

"How much?"

I'm sure that's not so classy (at least according to Rachel who looks horrified at my question), but I need to know before I find myself in debt for a haircut.

"Not to worry. This is Hanna's treat."

Maybe I *can* live with Hanna forever. "It is? Well, how much is it anyway?"

"Jamie! You are so uncool sometimes."

David smiles at Rachel again and reaches over to ruffle her hair. She coos at him. Hellooo, back to me here.

"It's $300.00," David says.

My face drains of color. This is the cost of beauty? This is what Hanna pays once a month? I now realize she has a lot more money than I originally thought.

"She knew you'd freak out. I wasn't supposed to tell you. But, you deserve to be pampered."

"Do you think Hanna would get me a haircut, too?" Rachel asks hopefully and bats her eyelashes at me.

I purse my lips and narrow my eyes at her. Her pouty siren look only works on men.

"Maybe Katie and Leah would-"

"No."

"Maybe Mo and Dad-"

"No."

"But-"

"No!"

This is not a word she hears very often, and she's confused. But she forgets her plea as David slops some purple, toxic goop on my hair and covers each chunk in tin foil.

This is what costs $300.00? Five dollar foil? Also, I look like I'm ready for takeoff. And my sister, bless her heart, pulls out her phone and aims it at me to document my transformation. Every time another silver chunk is piled on top of the last one, she snaps away until I grab the phone out of her hand.

"Hey!" she protests.

I glare at her, and pouting, she sits down and stares at me. "You look so funny," she says, still angry that she can't get a $300.00 haircut too.

My hair has been separated into foil-protected pieces about a foot tall, and when I look in the mirror, I recognize the look in my eyes. Fear. An hour and a half (and a lot of photo snapping, magazine flipping and heavy sighing) later, it's over.

"You are stunning. Now you need to believe it," David says after brushing stray bits of hair off my neck.

I stare at the woman in the mirror. And I don't recognize her. Actually, no, I still look like me, only better. I am really blonde, and not just in-between; I have cheekbones, a jawline and nice eyes. And my hair's not flat or limp. Thick, golden chunks of glossy hair fall in sleek sheets to my chin.

This guy is worth every penny. I stand up, hand David the robe and reach out my hand for a professional shake. He grabs me and kisses me on both cheeks. Amazingly, I don't even flinch.

CHAPTER SIXTEEN

After Rachel takes me and my hair shopping (at Banana Republic, I am a khaki dream), we sit on a patio at a nearby restaurant. I order a glass of wine for me; a Diet Coke, for her. She won't stop staring at me. The same goes for the two older (I mean at least fifty) men at the next table.

"Stop it! I hate being the center of attention." I put my menu in front of my face.

Rachel laughs and yanks the menu away. "Get used to it. You really look amazing. Imagine if you had done this years ago. Maybe you and Derek..." Her voice trails off wistfully.

Truth be told, Rachel's always been a little in love with Derek. It's understandable. She met him when she was only thirteen, and he'd listen to her chatter nonstop, let her do his hair (it was long then), put makeup all over his scratchy face. And Derek basked in the attention.

He'd bring her a present every time he saw her: magazines, lip gloss, sparkly barrettes. She would follow us around to the point that we had to lock her out of our bedroom while she whined and scratched outside. In the last few years, Derek spent less and less time with my family and a lot more with his party of one. But your first crush is hard to forget, and I know that as angry at him as she is, there is also a part of her that wishes we had stayed together.

Our drinks arrive, and after taking a well-deserved sip of the icy cold wine, I say, "Rach, Derek changed too much. To the point that he wasn't making me feel good about myself, and we were always fighting. And like I can't expect him to grow his hair back and toss out the club membership, he can't expect me to be a woman I'm not. A haircut is just a haircut. I'm still the same on the

149

inside."

"You're not going to go back to your old hair, are you?" Her face contorts in fear.

I laugh. "No, but I'm also not going to change myself for Derek or anyone else. This was for me. And I don't think I'll go back to that salon. It's not my kind of place. And I'm still shopping at 'The Salvation Army.'"

We finish our drinks, and I walk her to her car. Eleanor looks sad and insecure next to the Ferraris, Porsches and Lamborghinis crowding Michigan Avenue.

"Do you want a ride?" Rachel opens the car door, completely oblivious to the cyclist she nearly clipped.

"I'd like to live long enough to enjoy my hair."

Her face falls.

"I'm just kidding. I should get some exercise. I'll walk, but call me later."

I give her a tight hug and watch her sideswipe two cars on her way to meet her newest boy-toy. I walk back to Hanna's, which is only fifteen minutes from the restaurant, and today, is a strange parade of stares and leers from a variety of men and women. Is this how Hanna and Lucy feel? Usually, I'm like wallpaper; I just blend in.

But now, with my glossy bob, women are enviously checking me out, and men are whistling and sending appreciative glances my way. And instead of feeling uncomfortable, I add an extra bounce to my step and stick my chest out a little more (no shoulder hunching) than usual.

When I unlock the apartment door, it bangs into something hard. "Ow!"

The door swings open, and Hanna is there waiting, rubbing the foot I just smashed into. She must have seen me from the security video and run to the door to greet my new hair.

"Holy shit! Is this my best friend? You look stunning. Really, absolutely beautiful. And you're blonde! I can't believe you let David highlight your hair," she tells me, spinning me around and examining my hair from all sides.

I get serious and grab her arm. "Hanna, thank you. I can't believe you paid for this. You are the bestest, funnest friend in the whole world. Really, thank you."

"Blah, blah, blah. It's nothing. You'd do it for me. Hungry?" She deflects my gushing with my stomach.

"Starved."

"I think we should take your new hair out."

"And clothes."

"Clothes? Let me see."

I take out the new pants, shirts and skirts from their shiny bags and model them all for her. Slack-jawed, she inspects the price tags. "These pants are $100.00."

"I know," I say, smiling as I try them on for her.

"And new."

"Yup."

"What drugs have you taken? Do you need your stomach pumped?" she asks.

"No drugs. Rachel. She made me buy all this stuff, and to be honest, it was fun. These things fit a hell of a lot better than my other stuff. Look at my butt in these pants." I put my ass in her face.

Hanna nods her approval. "How did you pay for all of this?"

"Credit card. They keep increasing my limit."

"You'll eventually have to pay that back, you know," says the voice of reason.

I toss everything back in its bags and flop down on the couch. "I'll worry about it later."

"Thank God. You're still Jamie. Okay, let me change. I know

the perfect place to debut the new you. It's a bit expensive, but really cool. They have tapas, and they bring you little bits of everything. Lots of candles, dark."

Propping myself up on one elbow, I curl up my lip in distaste. "It sounds trendy."

"Interesting trendy, not pretentious trendy. And anyway, I hate to break it to you, but you're pretty trendy now yourself."

I grin at that. I've *never* been trendy. I haul myself up and follow Hanna to her bedroom and into the walk-in closet. She flips through racks of exquisite clothes until she finds a pair of Roberto Cavalli jeans (apparently the best, whatever) and what looks like a black bra, but I think it's supposed to be a shirt.

"Okay. I'm just going to put some makeup on," I tell her while she's getting dressed.

Hanna hobbles over to me with her jeans around her ankles and presses her hand to my forehead.

"No fever. Do a little dance for me."

I attempt a hiphop move (hand raised in the air, body lowered to the ground).

"Yeah, all Jamie." She grins and pulls up her jeans.

I go to my room and change into my new khaki drawstring pants and a beige backless halter top. No bra. My nipples are straining against the material, but I try not to cover my breasts with my hands. I apply eyeshadow, eyeliner, mascara, blush and lipstick and go back to Hanna's room for approval.

"Agh!" she screams when she sees me. "What happened to your face?"

"I put my makeup on."

"With a shovel? Come here, crazy girl. You're orange again. You need to do it subtly. It should look like you're not wearing makeup at all."

"That's stupid. I am wearing makeup."

She shakes her head and smiles. "No, you're wearing a mask."

Hanna sits me down on the edge of her bed, rubs off most of the makeup with cold cream and tissues and does it again. Then she hands me a mirror.

"Oh, I see what you mean. Thanks."

Hanna has made every feature on my face more pronounced, but it appears like I naturally look like this. I think because I have the earthiest mother and two step-mothers who don't ever wear makeup, I never really learned how to do this.

We call a cab, and when we step into the restaurant, I nearly trip over the hostess because it's so dark. Small, intimate tables adorned with those fabulous candles in little lamps that you see in the movies are set far enough apart to make the patrons feel alone, but not sequestered. We take the table closest to the bar and sit down. Within seconds, the waiter saunters over to hand us the menus, and Hanna orders us a bottle of red wine.

"A bottle? Han, I have to go to work tomorrow. And I told you I'm never drinking again," I protest weakly.

"The food will absorb the alcohol, and we need to celebrate. You, for your freedom and new hair, and me, for Jack."

I put down the menu (which I can't understand anyway. Why can't they just write lettuce instead of radicchio, and what the hell is reduction?) and gape at her. "What about Jack?" I ask.

Hanna toys with her napkin and ignores me. That's interesting. Hanna's never evasive about men.

"Han, I asked you a question."

She puts down the napkin and instead, starts fiddling with her nails. "Well, I've been thinking a lot lately about the men I date. Generally, they're wealthy, ambitious and successful, right?"

I nod.

"But they're so mind-numbingly dull. And they don't really care about me. Do you remember Grayson?"

"Yeah."

Grayson was an impossibly good-looking, richer than sin, owner of a big time New York modeling agency. They'd hooked up after one of his models had worn Hanna's "Luscious in Lace" line in Vogue. Strange life my best friend leads. Fascinating to observe, but I could never imagine living among such glamour and excess.

Anyway, Hanna had introduced me to Grayson at a party she had taken me to. He'd been quite surprised to see her there. As was his wife. The rest of that night was a blur of red wine being tossed in Grayson's face by his furious wife, Hanna's nonchalant nod in his direction as he cleaned his suit with a towel, and my shock as she grabbed my hand to lead me out. And I was the only one who knew how upset Hanna was because her hand was trembling and ice cold.

"Yes, I remember. What does he have to do with Jack?"

The waiter serves us our wine, and Hanna takes a long, slow sip. "Well, I don't know if forever exists or if monogamy's even possible, especially after my mother left without a backwards glance. But, I get lonely, you know? And thinking about guys like Grayson who only wanted me for sex, and watching you have the guts to walk away from Derek and find someone you used to love, well, it's made me take a hard look at myself."

"And?"

"And Jack's really wonderful. He's so smart and fucking kind. He always asks me if I'm hungry or cold or if I need something. He really cares about me. And not many people care about me."

"That's not true," I vehemently disagree.

"I don't mean my friends, of which I don't have many, you know how women feel about me. But my dad was everything to me, and when he died, I put up all sorts of walls around myself. I've been afraid. I always think I'm so tough, but I'm not. I'm so afraid to get hurt, afraid to get left."

I sip my own wine. Slowly. I am not getting drunk tonight because I'd probably take the waiter home.

"Has Leah been talking to you?"

She grins. "Yeah. Your mom is so awesome. We had a long talk about it, and she thinks that I'm afraid to let someone love me. And what's really fucked up is that Jack reminds me of my dad. But, he has no money, and he doesn't care about it. My dad had to work so hard to take care of us, and I promised him that I'd never let myself work like that. And if Jack is broke, I will have to work like that. If this thing continues. Not that it's serious or anything." She tucks a stray strand of hair behind her ear and avoids my gaze.

"No, of course it's not serious. You just see him all the time. Han, your dad was so proud of you. And he would have wanted you to find someone who truly loves you. You know, your mom didn't love him and that was probably way more painful than all the jobs he had to work at. And it sounds like Jack really cares about you. Not about your money or your body, but you."

"I know. That's what scares the shit out of me. He even understands my tooth thing. Will you meet him? For real this time?"

Hanna's eyes glisten with excitement, but they are also clouded with insecurity. I know she's scared shitless that she might have genuine feelings for this guy and that gives him the potential to hurt her. Really hurt her if she lets him in. But, for the first time since I've known her, I imagine that Jack is a guy I might even like.

"I'd love to meet him. Preferably when I'm not drunk or naked, though. He's in love with you, isn't he?"

"He tells me all the time. And he says he can wait until I feel the same way. But the thing is, well, I can't believe I'm going to say this, but I do feel the same. But he's not the guy I'm supposed to end up with."

It's good I didn't just take a sip of wine because the spluttering would have caused quite the stain on my new clothes. "What did you just say?"

"I'm in love with him."

Speechless, I stare at her, but I recover quickly enough to respond to that shocking statement. Hanna has *never* said the word "love." Not even to me. "You don't believe in destiny either. Who knows what 'supposed to' means? Was I supposed to end up with Derek? Was Leah supposed to marry my dad? It doesn't work like that. Things happen because they just happen."

"Aren't you supposed to find Lucas? Don't tell me you don't believe that there's something to what Lucy says."

The smooth wine glides warmly down my throat as I sip it, and I rub my hand on my hair (partly because it's so sleek, partly because it helps me think).

"I think Lucas and I never had a chance. We were so young and stupid. We were both afraid to admit our true feelings to each other, and then he left. If he'd gone to school here or lived here, things might have been different. I do know there was always something special that tied us together because even though we were never really a couple, we could never stay away from each other. And he was the only person I was ever truly honest with, ever really myself with, and I just have to find out if it's still there. But is he my destiny? Is anyone my destiny? I just think... Well, I just think I should be with him now. That feels right to me, but I don't know about the future."

Hanna looks thoughtful, and she twists her lips into a small smile. "Do you think my dad knows what I've done with my life? Would he be happy that I'm successful? Would he be happier if I were in love and poor?"

"Your dad would have been happy if you were happy. And

156

Han, c'mon, you could never be poor. I know it's your greatest fear, but look at the store, the lines in magazines, the stars. Do you even realize how good you are? No, of course you don't. Look, does Jack make you happy?"

She leers at me. I laugh, and we order dinner. There has been way too much sharing at this table for one night.

An array of tiny and succulent appetizers is set before us, and just as I'm popping a tiny quiche in my mouth, I feel a hand on my shoulder. With the quiche rolling around in my mouth (I must savor it, it's so good), I turn around to face whomever's behind me. Oh, fuck me. It's Andrew. And I'm out for dinner. With the flu.

The quiche lodges itself in my throat, cutting off my air, and I start choking. Great whooping coughs prompt Andrew to whack me on the back while tears stream down my face. There goes the makeup.

He hands me the closest liquid to wash down the quiche. I swallow a huge gulp of wine, and it makes me cough even harder. Hanna's watching this little exchange with interest. She doesn't seem to be worried that I can't breathe and I'm dying. She's wondering who Andrew is.

"Are you okay? You shouldn't be out with the flu although near death by quiche might make a good show," he tells me, a smile in his voice.

Luckily, Hanna's picked up enough clues to realize that Andrew is from work.

"Jamie was feeling better so I thought some dinner would be good for her," she says, leaning over so her creamy breasts are directly in Andrew's field of vision.

He doesn't notice. He's still worriedly rubbing my back and looking at my hair.

"Andrew, hi. What are you doing here?" Now. At the worst time. Aren't there any other restaurants in Chicago?

157

"Kelly and I come here all the time. The food's great. Well, maybe not the quiche you just swallowed whole. Small bites next time, okay? Your hair looks incredible, by the way."

I blush. "Thanks. I, um, like to go for a haircut when I'm sick. It makes me feel better."

"Hmmm. I've never heard that one before. I'm glad you're feeling better, though. It's not like you to miss work. At least that's what Sue told me."

I was fine until I saw you. Now, I'm definitely ill.

"Yeah, I must have caught one of those twenty-four hour flu bugs. Did I miss anything important?"

"No, the show went well. Makeovers for Moms. Eva asked about you."

"Did she? How kind."

He laughs. Hanna coughs, obviously tired of not knowing what's going on. "I'm Hanna, by the way," she introduces herself and sticks out her slender hand for him to shake.

He takes it and says, "Andrew. Nice to meet you. Oh, here's Kelly."

Striding purposefully towards our table is a naturally gorgeous woman (the type who looks much better without makeup than with it). I can see the lines of definition in her fit and toned arms and shoulders, and her face is flawless. But there's a distinct line of disapproval around her full, lipstick-free mouth. "Andrew, our food is here," she says, looking carefully at me and Hanna.

"Sorry, hon. This is Jamie, my associate, and her friend, Hanna." Niceties all around, and he follows her back to their table.

"Hmmm," Hanna says.

"What?" I ask.

"He's cute. You haven't mentioned him."

"He's my boss. I told you Sue left. I guess he's cute. He's been with her for almost twenty years, can you believe it?"

"From the looks of things, it's not going so well."

I furrow my brow. "Huh? Why do you say that?"

"She certainly didn't seem to appreciate his hand on your back."

"I was choking. You're analyzing too much. But he is a great guy. She's gorgeous, huh?" I glance at Kelly over Hanna's shoulder.

"A lot of makeup."

"What? What makeup? She wasn't wearing any," I argue.

"Sure she was. A ton of blush and foundation. You're way better looking."

I wave my hand in dismissal. "I am not, and I don't like him like that. For one, he's my boss, two, he's involved, and three, I'm not attracted to him. I want to find Lucas, and I want to do it without Andrew knowing because it's embarrassing."

"So what's so hard about that?"

"I usually take some time at work to look for him, and Andrew insists on working on this show together from beginning to end. And, there are over a thousand Lucas Simpsons on the Net, and I don't know what to do next."

"Does his family still live here?" she asks and inspects her teeth in her portable mirror. I think she should just have it permanently attached to a helmet, like a miner's light.

"I don't know. But I can't call them because he'll find out. And I want to be fully prepared before I see him. Also, I don't want him to think I'm stalking him."

"I'll call. I'll pretend I'm doing some high school alma mater thing, and I need a bio on him."

I stroke my chin with my index finger, purse my lips and think about it for half a second. It's brilliant! "Han, you are a life saver. That's perfect! How did you get so smart?"

"It's the implants."

159

CHAPTER SEVENTEEN

"Hello, is this Ray Smith? This is Jamie Ross from 'Tell It Like It Is.' We'd like to set up a meeting to discuss your guest appearance on our show."

"Hello, is this Meghan Mullins? This is Jamie Ross, associate producer of the talk show 'Tell It Like It Is.' Someone from your past wants to see you again, and we were wondering if we could set up a time to meet?"

"Hi, is this Bubba Barkley? I'm Jamie Ross from the talk show. We've located your ex-girlfriend, and the executive producer and myself would like to arrange a time to meet with you."

It's Friday, and after a week of logging and making calls and finding people who are not easy to locate, I've drunk so much coffee that my skin has turned a strange milky color. That was my last call. By the end, I was ready to just say, "Bubba, Jamie here. Meeting?"

I've also been to see two apartments, and neither were at all what I want. I haven't been this productive in, well, I've never been this productive. Andrew and I have been working together all week, and between us, we've found everyone. I honestly couldn't have done it without him. We have two "couples" tentatively booked for the show, and we have four people to meet, greet, and analyze for any severe psychological problems that will get us into trouble with the FCC.

When I got back to the office from my "flu," he'd already made an electronic color-coded chart of the places we'll have to go (Milwaukee, Indianapolis—none too exciting), where we'll stay and the cost of it all. Usually, it'd be me doing all of that. Now I have more time to do the work I'm supposed to, oh, and find

Lucas. But Andrew doesn't know that.

We've been at work late every night, ordering in greasier and greasier food and laughing a lot. On Wednesday night, he brought a bottle of red wine, and after we had drunk it and scarfed down a mess of oily Chinese food, he started talking. A lot. He told me about Kelly, who's a CPA at one of the Fortune 500 companies. Apparently, she's always working, and when she's not, she rock climbs. Every weekend. It also sounds like she's really hard on him. He's never made a lot of money (although the executive producer's salary is nothing I would sneeze at), and she wants him to do an MBA. He doesn't want to, but he's considering it because it's something she wants.

And he also said a lot about his family (who it seems are also not thrilled by his line of work; they'd rather he had been a doctor or lawyer and tell him every chance they get), and I told him tidbits about mine. Not everything, certainly, I don't know him *that* well yet.

He's a great listener. Andrew asks all of the right questions and remembers the little details. Derek never really cared about my fears, sadness or family issues. He listened, sure, but the next day, he'd never ask if I was okay or try to talk more about something that I clearly needed to.

The thing that I don't understand is why Andrew stays with Kelly. I'm not one to talk really, but I did leave when I couldn't take it anymore. Andrew doesn't even see that as a possibility. But I guess after more than half his life with the same person, he can't imagine being on his own or starting again.

As much as I've been enjoying Andrew's company, foremost on my mind is finding Lucas. Every time I feel sad about Derek, I remember Lucas. It's an easy escape, and at the moment, it's just a sublime fantasy to hide in. And it's not like I'm wallowing over Derek. No, I know that I wasn't in love with him anymore, and there was no way we could have stayed together.

But I'm sad that all that time is gone, and I can't get it back. That's why I have to find Lucas. I'll feel like there's been a purpose for the recent chain of events in my life and a reason for me to have stayed unhappy for so long. It scares me that I let the relationship go on for so many years because I was too afraid to leave. And that I so easily let go of the one guy who truly got me.

One night, Lucas and I had been in his car fooling around, and I was really cold so we drove back to his place. It was after midnight, and we knew that his mom would already be fast asleep. Lucas laid some blankets down on the floor, lit a fire and slowly undressed me. Naked under the warm covers, with the flames licking our skin, I had decided that it was time to have sex with him. I was eighteen, and there was no one else I would have wanted my first time to be with.

"I want to do it," I'd said after he'd trailed his tongue across my stomach and made me so excited, I couldn't see straight. And I knew Lucas kept a box of condoms just in case.

"Are you sure, Jaim? We don't have to, you know. We can just do this. I like this."

"No, I really want to."

He raced upstairs to his bedroom to get the condoms and also brought back some massage oil. Lucas was also the only one to ever massage me because I was only able to completely relax with him. He squirted some oil in his hands and rolled me over onto my stomach. He spent almost an hour digging his long expert fingers into my skin, and gasping with pleasure, I pulled him on top of me.

"You're really sure?"

"Yes."

He hovered for a moment and then slowly started entering me, and I froze. I had already said I wanted to do it, and I didn't want to look like an idiot so I didn't say anything. But, I was terrified and not ready. He knew. Lucas stopped, kissed my forehead, pulled off the condom and just held me in his arms. And I laugh out loud as I remember that just at that moment, his mom came into the room because she'd smelled smoke. Lucas made sure I was fully covered, and I pretended to be asleep.

That was the kind of guy Lucas was. One month later, we did have sex, and he was so sweet and gentle, and it hurt like hell, but after that, oh, it was so good.

I'm glad I'm going tonight to Leah's to find the letter Lucas wrote me. Maybe the letter will tell me why I'm not with him now and haven't been all of these years. And while I'm gone, Hanna's going to call his mom. I might pass out if I can hear her talking to his mom. But first, I need to see the last apartment on my short list. I'm positive it will be smelly and run-down, numerous cats will have lived there in the last five years (causing loud and wet sneezes to occur every five seconds), and the people will most definitely be weird because that's been my experience so far.

The first apartment I saw was in Wicker Park, but the ad neglected to mention that it was above a bar (the type with poles and dirty old men), and "quaint" really means cracked walls and unidentifiable stains covering every surface. In every dusty corner, there were mouse and ant traps, and in the bathroom, I found a yellowing rickety toilet with holes in it. After years of what I've come to realize is pure decadence, a tiny bit has rubbed off on me. Creaky pipes and peeling walls I can deal with, but animal infestation and a broken toilet, no thanks.

The second was like stepping onto a B horror movie set. Outside the house, stuffed animals of all kinds were garroted with silver wire and tacked up to the brick walls at the side and front, making it look like the poor teddy bears and little dogs had been strangled and then crucified. When I opened the front door, I had to immediately adjust my eyes to see inside the tiny front room,

163

dark and ominously illuminated by a single red light burning over a huge painting of Jesus. Once I could see properly, I found the room stacked with hundreds of blonde Barbie dolls still in their packages and postcards upon postcards of famous musicians from the 50s and 60s covering every spare square of space.

Crosses of every color and style, wooden, gold-plated, bejewelled, hung on every wall, and, chilled to the core, I scurried out of there without a backwards glance. I didn't even wait to meet the landlord because I was afraid that this was some kind of eerie cult, and I'd never see my family and friends again. So, here I am, at number three. Not expecting much.

The apartment is on the top two floors of a house in Greek Town, just west of the Loop and an easy train ride from work on the blue line. A wild assortment of irises, lilies and roses crowd the front garden (much like Mo's), a small porch with dangling crystal ornaments and wind chimes leads to a heavy oak door. With a shaky hand, I knock lightly.

A wiry, tiny blonde with a mouth full of braces, who looks about fourteen in her short denim skirt and white t-shirt with yellow ducks all over it, whips open the door. "Hi, I'm Amy," she says and gives me a huge metallic grin.

"Uh, hi, I'm Jamie. I'm here to see the room."

She's so warm and buzzing with hyperactivity that I take a step back.

"Our names rhyme! How cool is that? Chris is on the computer. He's such a techno-geek." Amy rolls her sparkling blue eyes at me.

"Chris?" I ask.

"My boyfriend. He lives here too."

My heart sinks. "I didn't know two people were living here. The ad said one."

"Well, we are like one. Anyway, does it matter? Like, see the place and then decide."

My first instinct is to leave. I don't want to live with a couple who refers to themselves as "one." But, the neighborhood is exactly my style with its Greek restaurants, cool, dimly lit bars, relaxed attitude. Sambuca flows during street festivals, and the scent of souvlaki mingles with the sweat of hundreds of people milling around. Not one person has perfect hair around here.

I always let Derek make the decisions, and now that I don't have him anymore, I can do anything I want.

"Okay, why not?" I agree.

She leads me through a long, crimson hallway to the living room. It has high ceilings, windows edged with rustic wood, sponge-painted walls, and an attached dining room with a mess of Eastern art is resting on every surface. The kitchen is decent-sized with a huge counter for chopping, and a square opening between the kitchen and dining room makes it easier to pass food back and forth and gives the apartment an open, airy feel.

There's a bedroom off of the living room, and it would be mine. It's huge! A giant L, with one window overlooking the tree-lined street, a big closet, queen-sized bed (it has an ornate headboard, not that I'll be doing much head-banging in here for awhile) a desk, and a gorgeous oak wood chest.

But the thing is that I don't want to live with a happy, bouncy couple. I don't even like happy, bouncy people. They stress me out. How is it possible to smile all the time? But I also can't keep looking for places when I've got work to do. And will any other places be better? Really, the house is gorgeous. Run-down enough for me to be comfortable kicking off my shoes and relaxing, and there's not a sign of anything with more than two legs anywhere.

Chris joins us a moment later. Tall and skinny to the point of starvation (I hate to see men who are thinner than me, it's just not right), he's wearing wire-rimmed glasses that protect the most beautiful eyes I've ever seen. Liquid brown, radiating innocence, topped by long, thick, fluttering lashes that don't stop moving.

This couple is the poster child of young, naive love. His next words (given to me in the most maddening of fits and starts) clinch the deal. "We'll put, um, huh, a thirty-two, uh, inch television, er, huh, in here once you've, ahem, settled in."

One hour later, I'm their roommate. I tell them I'll call to arrange a time to move in, and I realize that I'm a bit excited. And with three people, I only need to pay $450.00 a month. I can definitely afford that.

I leave (after Amy has hugged me, I think we'll have to discuss the touching thing) and take the "L" and a bus to the North Shore for a scenic view of "Dynasty" worthy homes, endless golf courses, and long stretches of nothingness. I have mixed feelings about this place. Growing up, it was so boring to live out here and especially challenging when Katie moved in. There weren't a lot of hippie homosexuals living on our manicured, pristine block.

When I go home, I feel both physically repulsed and have trouble breathing (the further I am from the smog, the more my air passages constrict), but I also feel safe. Like nothing bad can happen out in the boondocks, because nothing much happens at all. I was always surprised that Katie and Leah didn't move near the university like my dad and Mo, but they love the peace and quiet, and I think they really like being the rebels of the neighborhood.

The house is dark, and shockingly, the door is locked. No one's home. That makes this easier because I don't want them asking me a bunch of questions when I'm tearing apart my old room trying to find the letter. I know Katie, Leah and Rach would fully support this scavenger hunt of mine, but before I know it, the whole family will be traipsing across the country to find Lucas. In a VW van.

My childhood bedroom is now everyone's storage space. Rachel's colorful and tiny clothes (even in the dead of winter, she proudly displays her washboard abs and silver navel ring) take up all the closet space, and boxes and boxes of files are pushed up against every wall. But some things haven't changed. My "Nirvana" and "Pearl Jam" posters are still taped to the walls, my high school math and biology textbooks peek out from the shelves (brand spanking new from lack of use, actually one still has the plastic cover on it), and my bed with the black comforter (I went through a phase, but Katie and Leah vetoed the black walls) is exactly how it was when I left. Except that it's now neatly made.

Okay, where could the letter be? I see my old yearbook, but neither of us is in any pictures. We both tended to fly under the radar. No clubs, no committees, no candid shots. I pore through the closets and have to crawl past a smushed up futon mattress, rusty hangers and bags of old clothes to find the box with my mementos in it. Presents from my bat mitzvah (on a rooftop, female lesbian Rabbi, drummers and tofu), old key chains, glittery erasers, fluorescent bangles, a silver glove from my Michael Jackson phase, but no letter. Where is the letter?

A ripped, very thin square of paper is tucked into the corner of the box. My heart starts pounding; my mouth goes dry. Is that it? Why is a simple piece of paper making me shake like this? I have to get a grip. I don't believe in destiny or soul mates. But why then is my stomach dropping out?

This is all Derek's fault. If he hadn't turned into an executive's wet dream, we'd still be together, and I'd have control. I wouldn't have turned into this flaky, flighty version of Leah that I don't recognize. I pull the paper from the box and hold it to my chest. Will everything make sense after I read it? I'll probably laugh at our childish attempts at cool nonchalance. God, it's been ten years, and it's just words.

I carefully unfold the yellowing paper that hasn't been touched in almost a decade, and it practically falls apart in my hands.

Dear Jamie,

Do you remember the night we danced at the prom years ago? I do. I felt so good. You made me feel alive, and for a moment, I forgot everything else. I swear I have never felt so connected to someone before. With passion and our soul mate, we can make one minute become a lifetime if we know how to use it. I will forever remember that night and you.

Lucas

Tears are blinding my vision, and the letter falls to the floor. I'm sitting cross-legged, staring at the fallen paper and sobbing. I read it again and again and again. How stupid and blind I was. How could I not have realized then that he really did love me? He thought we were soul mates. Maybe Lucy is right. Maybe he is my soul mate. And I let him go.

What nags at me the most is the fact that we never spoke again after he gave me this letter. Why didn't he ever call me? Or write again? I know why I didn't. I was too afraid of getting hurt, and I knew it would be so hard to see him with both of us living so far away from each other. We had never talked about love or even about being together. We just were. Together.

But Lucas was always stronger than me. He had to know I was wrapped around his finger and would do anything for him. Maybe he didn't know. Sure, I saw him whenever he wanted me to, I touched him with all the love I had in me, but was I warm and open? Definitely not. I've never been easy to read, and back when I was with Lucas, I'm certain I was so protective of myself that I barely let even him in.

The soft paper rubs against my cold hands, and I toy with it, trying to find the answers in the beauty of his words. Funny though, they're not exactly the words of a twenty-two year old man, but I guess Lucas was always a bit different.

My life with Derek is over. And Lucas knew me long before I

had a job, bank account (although it probably has the same balance as it did then) and my own place. He knew me when I lived with Katie, Leah and Rachel. He knew me when I was so angry and hurt that nothing but the television would make me happy. And he loved me anyway. How come I didn't know?

Something in me snaps. Clarity dries my tears, and I know that I'll find him. Lucas was my friend at a time I didn't trust anyone, and I can't let that slip away again. I don't know what I'll find when I see him, but I have this feeling that everything will make sense.

I stuff the letter in my bag and go back to Hanna's. She's not home yet, and I'm too antsy to even watch TV so I'm just sitting on the couch and digging my nails (stubs) into my palms to stop the nervous gurgle in my stomach. What if Lucas is in another country? What if he doesn't remember me?

And I can't go anywhere far with Andrew. God, if Sue were still my boss, this would be so much easier. She'd never ask what I'm doing or tag along. But I like Andrew. The nights spent working together were a lot of fun, but can't he be lazier?

"Jaim, I'm ho-"

I race to the front door and immediately barrage her with questions. "So, did you find him? Where is he? What did she say exactly? Word for word. Was she suspicious?"

"You sound like Rachel. Can I at least get a glass of wine first?" Hanna asks, walking around my twitching body.

"No! I mean, I'll get it for you, just keep talking."

She follows me into the kitchen where I snatch the bottle of red wine from the counter and pour as much as I can into a glass without spilling any. My hands are shaking uncontrollably as I hand it to her.

"Okay, he's in Detroit. He teaches biology at a college. Single, no kids, just ended a seven year relationship."

"Oh my God! He's a teacher? Lucas is a teacher? In Detroit?

169

He's so close. Did she say anything else?"

Hanna takes a sip of wine and settles herself on one end of the couch. "She said his research on stem cells are on the Net if the Alumni committee wants to take a look."

I sit across from her and gulp my own wine. "I can't believe he's a teacher. He hated school. Oh God, I almost forgot the letter. Han, he wrote me this beautiful letter before he left for school, and it says everything. Can I read it to you?"

"Sure." She nods and lightly touches my arm. "It's really good, Jaim, to see you so excited. You're sparkling. I missed your sparkle, you know."

"Me too. I didn't even notice it was gone until I got all excited about this. Okay, here it is." I pull the paper from the side protective pocket of my bag (maybe Derek's right about little compartments) and open it.

Tattered and yellowing, this letter is the first thing that's made me feel jumpy and tingly in years. How sad. Hanna sits silently, listening intently as I read, smiling and raising her eyebrows at the perfect moments.

"I've never felt so connected to someone before? We can make one minute become a lifetime? Wow," she says.

"Yeah, wow."

"How old was he when he wrote that?"

"Twenty-two or so."

"And you only realize now what it all meant?"

"I was so caught up in being tough and not getting hurt that I didn't see what he was trying to tell me."

"You were a moron. And he writes like a girl."

"Yes, I was a moron, and he was sensitive."

"For sure you're smarter now, but it's been ten years, Jaim. Do you think love can last that long? Can you really go back to where you started?"

I stretch out my legs and say, "Before this reunion show and before Derek, I would have said no. There's no going back. It's about the moment you're in. Like Lucas said. And, I still don't think you can search for what will make you happy. You get what you want by working for it. And I need something to work on right now."

"So when are you going to see him?" she asks.

My heart skips a beat, and suddenly, I'm very nervous. Chewing on my pinkie, I swallow the remaining sliver of nail and tell her, "God, even the thought of seeing him, just seeing him, scares me. Well, we're leaving for Indiana and Wisconsin in the next week or so. And Detroit's not too far so I guess I'll just have to find a way to get there. But the problem is that I have to figure out how to see him without Andrew."

"Andrew? Your boss? Why would he want to see Lucas?"

"He wants to meet all the guests. He doesn't know anything about Lucas, and he won't. I've been using company time and stuff to find him. But, I don't know how I'll get a minute without him."

"He likes you, you know."

"Who?" I wrinkle my forehead in confusion.

"Andrew."

"And I like him."

She shakes her head. "No, dummy, I mean he's attracted to you."

"No, he's not. We just get along well. He's got a girlfriend. You've seen her. I'm not his type. He likes tall and skinny. And if he's attracted to anyone at work, it's Eva."

"The skank with the silly clothes? No, she's too obvious for him."

I smirk. "You're wrong on this one, Mistress Seer. Oh, I almost forgot to tell you! I found an apartment."

"What?" Hanna looks completely taken aback and dejected.

"When?"

"Today. The other two places I looked at sucked. I told you that. But, today I went to the last one on my list, and I really liked it. It's in Greek Town, old, lots of character, and my room is massive. And they're even setting up a thirty-two inch TV for me."

"They?"

"Yeah, there's a couple living there. At first I almost ditched the idea because I don't want to live with a happy, kissy couple. And they're a bit weird, but nice. She looks twelve, she even has braces, and he's skinnier than you. But he seems to be on the computer all the time, and I think they work a lot. Anyway, I'm kind of excited."

Hanna pouts and pours herself another glass of wine. "I'll miss you," she says, running her fingers around the rim of the glass.

"Me too. But I have to do this. And I'm on a roll. You know, I'm actually taking care of all the stuff I let Derek do for me. And you'll come for dinner."

"So, when are you leaving?" she asks quietly.

"Hey, are you okay?" I ask.

"Yeah. It's just that it's been really nice having you around." She inhales an oddly shaky breath. "Look, I love living alone and being able to come and go as I please, I really do, but it'll be so lonely here without you."

Now I'm sad. We sit in abject silence, sipping our wine. At the same time, we look at each other and burst out laughing.

"What's happening to us? We're the tough ones," Hanna says and shakes her head. "I can't believe you found a place a week after you broke up with Derek. Who are you these days?"

"I'm not sure, but I think I like her," I say.

"Me too."

CHAPTER EIGHTEEN

Moving on the weekend will be the best time to do it because I won't have to take any more days off. Between placating Hanna and thinking about Lucas, I don't have that much time left to get everything organized for my trip with Andrew. We're leaving on Monday. Somehow, between us, we got all of the meetings booked and the route planned. So, instead of leaving in a week, we're leaving in a few days.

It's Saturday morning now, and Hanna has woken up before me. She's brewed the strongest, vilest coffee and has prepared the worst breakfast I've ever eaten. I choke down the raw potatoes, oily onions and burned omelet (at least I think it's an omelet, but I don't see any eggs) because I know what this means. I didn't even know Hanna could turn the stove on.

After breakfast, we throw all my stuff back in its two boxes and duffel bag, and she gives me two gorgeous camisole sets (one black, one fire-engine red) as a goodbye present. The taxi driver buzzes up just as she's putting the presents in my bag, and she clutches it tightly in her hand and won't give it to me.

"Hanna, I'm not even leaving the area code. This isn't like you," I say and try to wrestle the bag from her fingers.

"I know," she says, and giving a little laugh, lets go of the bag so she can swipe at the tears that have sprung to her eyes.

Why do her eyes look so bright and mesmerizing filled with tears while mine look puffy and runny?

"I think all the crazy things you're doing are affecting me too. I just feel like I'm also on the edge of something."

"This isn't about me. It's about Jack." I take her cold hands in mine and squeeze them. "Han, if you love him, tell him. Don't let

173

him walk away."

She nods and shoves my shoulder. Hard. Back to her old self. "Put the lingerie to good use, Jaim."

"I'll try. I'll call you later."

The driver comes up and takes my boxes, and I sling the duffel bag over my shoulder. Once inside the cab, tears prick at my eyes. I wipe them away before they can fall. I'm not sure why I'm crying because this is a good thing. Maybe it's just that everything's happening all at once. This is all new for me, and it's a bit overwhelming.

A funny flutter lands in my stomach and jumps around until we pull up outside the house. My house. Amy comes running out, wearing pink shorts and a lighter pink, midriff baring top, this one with a smiling pig over the chest. Seriously, what's with all the animals?

"J! Great! I'll help you carry your stuff. We're like so happy you're moving in. Is this all your stuff?" As she walks up the steps to the porch, she's still chattering away (to herself I guess because I can't hear her anymore), and I smirk.

We get inside, and Chris is sitting at the bottom of the oak stairs holding a screwdriver. His bony knees jut out of his shorts, and I'm afraid if he lifts my stuff, he might tear a nonexistent muscle.

"Hi, Jamie, um, er, mmm, welcome. Your, eh, room's all, um, ready, and the, mm, uh, TV's set up," he mumbles.

Thank God for my years with Sue; otherwise, we'd be doing the "Pardon?" "Sorry what?" dance every day.

"Thank you. I'll just put my stuff away." This is my hint that I want to do it alone.

But, as I walk towards my room, Amy follows closely on my heels.

"Can I help? I'm like so great at organizing. Although you don't seem to have a lot."

She's very sweet, but if I'm going to live here in relative peace, I need to set some ground rules. So I turn around, and in my nicest voice, say, "I appreciate the offer, Amy, but I kind of like to do things on my own. Why don't we have a coffee or something when I'm done?"

She looks crestfallen but recovers quickly. "Oh, sure. No prob. Just one thing. Always knock if the doors are closed, okay?"

Of course I'll knock. Do other people just barge right in?

"Sure. What do you guys do?"

"Oh, um, we run a web-based company."

She's being uncharacteristically vague (at least I think it's uncharacteristic considering how much she talks), but I don't really care what they do as long as they give me my space.

"So, I'll see you later, J."

"Jamie."

One more ten watt grin, and I'm finally alone. I pull out the set of sheets Hanna had bought me (part of the breakup kit, she couldn't resist the green and white stripes) and make the bed.

Climbing on top, I lean against the headboard and let out a deep breath. It doesn't feel real. I keep expecting to hear Derek snipe at me about something I haven't done or to have to pretend everything's okay when it's not. But this isn't my home. I've never really felt comfortable in any of the places I've lived. Even Leah and Katie's was always theirs, not mine. Sure my bedroom was the way I wanted it (well, except for the black walls I'd begged for), but the second I'd open that door, I'd be assaulted with the mingling scents of musk, incense and oh, the marijuana they used to grow in the sun room.

I listen to what's happening outside my room. It's eerily quiet. Whatever they're doing, I can't hear a thing, except for the sound of Amy's high-pitched laughter every now and then. The television is directly across from my bed, and I flick on the remote to see what channels I've got. Pressing the buttons, I realize that the numbers just keep going. I'm at two hundred already, and there's more. Oh yeah, I've made the best choice.

I should be doing some work or unpacking, but I don't feel like it. I want to get back in my pajamas, brew a pot of coffee and stay in bed. And I do because I can. No extreme sports, no Derek telling me I'm wasting my precious time, nobody wanting anything from me. Do all single women feel this free and elated? Probably not, because they're out searching for their One. I just know that when I see Lucas, I'll have found him.

At 5:00 p.m., Amy knocks on the door and peeks her head around it. "Hi, J. All settled in?" she asks, taking in the still packed boxes pushed up against the wall and three mugs of half-finished and now cold coffee cluttering the bedside table.

"Call me Jamie. I needed to relax first. Did you have a good day?" I ask politely. Small talk is not my forte.

"Super. Chris and I got a lot of work done so I'm free for the night. Do you want to do something?"

"Um..."

"C'mon, we'll make dinner, get to know each other. It'll be tons of fun!"

Will it?

"Okay, sure. I'm just going to take a shower first."

"Fantastic! I'll see you in a bit." And she hops out.

I would really rather lay in bed all night, but it wouldn't be a good start to my new living situation to have them thinking I'm a social recluse. But, I hope this won't be a nightly event. I rummage through my boxes for my no-name shampoo and conditioner, razor, and soap and change into my red, fluffy, three sizes too big for me robe. It's been a long time since I've needed a robe to take a shower.

The bathroom is small, decorated in pink and white (Amy's decision, I gather). Pink soap dish, pink toothbrush holder, pink shower curtain, and of course, every bath product and washing tool is pink. It's like being inside a Pepto Bismol bottle. But at least it's very clean. I wash my hair, feeling strange being in someone else's shower and knowing that eventually I'll think of it as mine. I shave (not sure why because no one's going to be offended by my stubble for at least another week until I go to Detroit) and do a few butt clenching exercises. Three to be exact.

After I've towelled off and changed into jeans and a black t-shirt, I head to the dining room for my chat with Miss Happy Pants. Amy's sitting alone at the mahogany table, sipping a beer and flipping through a magazine.

"Do you want a beer? Do you think this hairstyle would suit me?" she asks, pointing to a picture of Natalie Portman in a pixie cut.

"Um, it's kind of short."

"How about this one?" Now she's looking at Jennifer Aniston. "Or this one? Oh, what about this?"

Amy is so much like Rachel that I suddenly feel an overwhelming urge to call my sister. "I'll be back in a second," I tell her.

She nods, poring through the glossy pages for a new style. I quite like the hair she has now. Almost white, it falls, thick and impossibly shiny, to the middle of her back. I go to the kitchen, take a beer from the fridge and call Rachel.

"Hello," she answers in a higher voice than normal.

"Hey, Rach, it's me."

"Hey, Jaim. Where are you calling from? I don't recognize the number."

"My new apartment. I moved."

"What?! When?! Nobody tells me anything," she whines.

"I haven't told anyone yet. I wanted to wait until I've settled in. Are you busy now?"

"I'm at J.P.'s. We're watching a movie," she tells me and chuckles.

I remember what watching a movie meant when I was eighteen.

"Are you using a condom?"

I worry about my sister's sexcapades. Okay, and I'm a bit jealous since she gets way more action than I do. Probably than I ever have.

"I'm on the Pill."

"So?"

"So I can't get pregnant."

"No, but you can get some horribly disfiguring or deadly disease."

She exhales a breath filled with frustration. "Yes, I'm using a condom. God, you're worse than Leah. Did she give you a box of ribbed condoms for your sixteenth birthday too?" she whispers.

"Probably. Anyway, if you're busy, I can call you back later."

"No, I want to see you. Can I come over?"

"Yes. I think you'll love my new roommate."

"*You* have a roommate? No way. You don't like strangers."

"Not only do I have a roommate, I have two." I give her directions, and she tells me that she'll see me in half an hour.

"My sister Rachel's coming over," I tell Amy after I hang up.

"Cool! What's she like?"

I sit next to her at the table. "Like you. Friendly, outgoing." I want to say bouncy and annoying, but I don't.

"I like your hair," Amy says, touching a strand.

I stiffen, but she keeps touching. "My hair?" I ask, moving an inch to the left.

"It's so trendy and stylish. How old are you?"

178

"Thirty-two. You?"

"Twenty-five. Chris is thirty. Do you want to know how we met?" she asks and puts her pinkie in her mouth.

When she does it, it's sexy; when I do it, it's a bad habit.

Without waiting for me to answer, she continues. "I was working at a bar, and he came up to me and told me he had fallen in love with me the first time he saw me. He said he like just knew I was the woman he was meant to be with, and he'd do anything to be with me."

"Wow." Chris isn't the most manly or attractive of men, and Amy is gorgeous. I'm just surprised he had the courage to say that to her, and I have to give him credit.

"So, at first I thought he was just this skinny, geeky guy. But he came in every night for a month, and eventually, I knew he was like the bomb. All the other guys I've been with never stuck around for very long, but Chris immediately loved me for who I am."

"He fell in love with your personality at first sight?" I ask sarcastically.

She totally misses the tone in my voice and nods enthusiastically. "Exactly. He like made me feel so special. It's been one year, and I love him more every day."

I'm going to gag.

"Do you have a special person?"

"Sort of."

"Where did you live before here?" she asks.

Does she have a list of questions hiding somewhere or does she ask the same of everyone she meets? I'm more of the school of if someone wants me to know something, they'll tell me.

"With my friend Hanna."

Short, direct answers usually stop most people from asking more. Hop Along Amy, however, is clueless. "Oh, are you gay?" she asks, peering at me very closely, her eyes lighting up with anticipation.

I take a sip of my beer and smile to myself. Amy has no idea how many times I've been asked that same question. Finally, I answer her. "No, she's my best friend. I just left my boyfriend."

A look of pity crosses her face, and she says, "How horrible for you. Are you like totally devastated?"

"No, not really. It was over long before I left."

"Gawd, I'd like die if Chris ever left me."

I shake my head. "No you wouldn't. But you and Chris are happy. Derek and I weren't."

"How long were you together?" The magazine is forgotten as my little soap opera is far more entertaining for her.

"Five years."

She inhales a sharp breath and exclaims, "Five years! That's like forever. What happened?"

"We grew apart. So, what do you and Chris do exactly?"

If I spin the conversation back to her, it'll be a lot more comfortable. Because the tension in my neck and the death grip I have on the beer bottle are definite indications of my discomfort.

"Oh, um, we're in marketing," she says, lowering her eyes to the magazine.

There's that succinct vagueness again. For someone who will reveal all the other personal details of her life, I find this somewhat strange. But I don't care enough to pursue it.

"What about you, J? What do you do?"

"It's Jamie," I tell her for the umpteenth time. "I'm an associate producer for a television talk show. 'Tell It Like It Is.'"

Amy hits the table excitedly. "No way! That's like totally my favorite show. I watch it every day. So, do you get to meet famous people and everything? Can I get on the show?"

I grin. Whenever someone finds out that I work for a television show, they always want to know if I can get them their fifteen minutes.

"Only if you have a deep dark secret you're dying to reveal."

She blushes a deep shade of red. "No, no secrets. I'm an open book. But it would be wicked to be on TV."

I shake my head in disagreement. "You really wouldn't want to be a guest. So, did you guys have another roommate before me?"

Another rush of bright color to her cheeks. "Yeah, but it didn't work out. Clash of personalities, I guess. But, Chris and I just know that we won't have that problem with you."

I squint at her, wondering how she could possibly think that when she doesn't even know me.

"Why?"

"Because you don't seem to care what other people do."

I take another long sip of beer and say nothing.

She looks nervous and flutters her hand up and down. "I don't mean that as an insult. You just seem to be cool. You know, you like take stuff in, but it doesn't seem to affect you."

"I guess I'm just easygoing." I shrug.

Her finger stabs the air, narrowly missing my right eye. "Yes! Exactly! But you seem shy."

"Shy? Not shy. Just careful."

Ding dong. Saved by Rachel. Thank God because this conversation was getting way too intimate for my liking. For fuck sakes, I just met her, and she's already analyzing me. "That must be my sister."

I run to the door, and there is Rachel, flushed, mussed and smelling like latex. "So you did use a condom?" I ask, sniffing her hair.

She pushes my face away. "You're gross. Listen, I had a small accident back there. I just dented the car a bit, but I left a note. Do you think that's okay?"

But before I can even think of an answer, she's thrown off her shoes and is running towards the living room. "Wow, Jaim. This place is great. I can totally see you living here," she says, touching everything until she sees Amy.

The two of them size each other up the way only stunning women do. Who's better looking? Has better hair? A better body? Not something I've ever had to deal with. Eva's the only woman who's ever had a problem with me, and I'm not even sure why she does.

"Hi!" Rachel says brightly to Amy.

"Hi!" Amy chirps at Rachel.

And suddenly, I disappear. It must be some blonde camaraderie thing because within seconds, Rachel is sitting next to Amy, and they're both flipping their hair and jabbering away about who knows what. I catch the words "hair," "ceramic iron" and "curls."

"She is, isn't she?" Rachel agrees, glancing at me.

"Totally."

"I'm what?" I ask, defensively and suspiciously.

"Hot," Amy answers.

Now it's my turn to blush. Can't we talk about something other than my physical appearance, oh, and my personal life?

"Show me your room!" Rachel exclaims.

I stand up and both of them follow me to my bedroom. Amy walks around my room, pointing out everything to Rachel. "We put in a TV for her, and she's got everything she needs."

"*She* is standing right here," I say.

"Oh, Jaim. She's a little sensitive sometimes," Rachel explains to Amy.

"Is she?"

Aaagh! I hold up my hands in frustration. "Okay, enough show and tell. Amy, why don't we make some dinner?" I turn to Rachel, who's bouncing up and down on my bed. "Rach, have you eaten?"

An hour later, I've whipped up Fettucine Alfredo, a Caesar

salad and garlic bread. I'm so happy to be on my own in the kitchen to breathe. I'm trying to come out of my shell, but this is like instant detox. The oddest part is Chris never ventures from his room the entire time. Amy brings him a plate of food and comes back with it empty. Whatever business they have, he's obviously the one in control. As Amy and Rachel fall in love, he never comes out.

***

After Rachel's left, and Chris has finally emerged for a few tense moments of muttering and nodding, I've had enough bonding. I need to call Hanna anyway.

"Mwah," I yawn loudly, "I'm exhausted. I think I'm going to go to bed."

I get up off the couch, and Amy, lying on her stomach on the floor, beams at me. "Sure, J. Have a good night. Sweet dreams."

I let the annoying nickname go. You have to choose your battles. "Yeah, 'night."

In my room, I get into my silk pajamas (well, I washed them so they're more crushed silk now) and crawl under the covers. I pull out my cellphone and call Hanna.

"Hello?" I can barely hear her over the noise of wherever she is.

"Han, it's me!"

"Jaim! How are you? How is it?"

"It's really strange. But good, I think. I don't know what I'm doing anymore."

"Jaim, I can hardly hear you. Hold on!" she yells.

"No, it's okay. Go have fun. I'll call you tomorrow."

"You sure?"

"Yeah. You with Jack?"

"Yes. We're having dinner, and then, he's taking me to see a play."

"So, he *is* a good date."

"He tries. Are you sure you're okay?"

"I'm fine. I'll talk to you tomorrow."

"Bye, Jaim."

"Bye."

I put the phone down and lean back against the pillow. One of the only things in this room that's mine. How did that happen again? And damn it, here come the tears. No holding back, huge drops of water stream from my eyes, and with my chest heaving, I sob. And it doesn't feel so bad. I press my hand to my mouth to muffle the noisy wailing, while years of compartmentalized pain pour onto my pajamas, sheets and pillow.

When I'm finally done, I use my sheets as a Kleenex and turn off the light. Crying may not solve my problems, but at least I can identify the major issue here. Everything I've done, everywhere I've gone, I've always felt like I'm in the wrong place at the wrong time.

And Amy's wrong. What other people do does affect me; I just don't show it. Showing it always meant weakness or conflict to me, and I hate both. Lucas is the only thing in my life that's all mine. Strangely content with this thought, I turn on the television, comforted by the shadowy images it splays on the walls, and I settle in for a couple of hours of late night talk shows and seedy phone sex ads.

It feels so bizarre to be in a bed by myself in a strange house. And I live here. I haven't slept alone this much in years, and I roll back and forth across the bed that's all mine now. I snuggle under the cool sheets, get lost in the flickering images on the screen, and go to bed in my new house for the first time.

184

CHAPTER NINETEEN

Sunlight streams in through the window, bathing me in warmth and waking me up. I squint at the clock (mercifully, it's plain white). 8:00 a.m. Sunday. I could go for a run. I move my hand across my stomach and jiggle the soft flesh. I definitely have to do something.

When I was in my twenties, even though I had zero muscle tone, everything was still pretty firm. And it's disheartening to realize that now it'll take some serious work (effort in general) on my part to firm up my more wobbly bits.

I get up and wander quietly into the kitchen. The house is silent, only the creaking of the floorboards making a sound. Chris and Amy must still be asleep. After brewing a pot of coffee (I'd better go shopping soon before they evict me for pilfering all of their food), I sit in the living room while it does its dripping. A soft blue blanket is laying on one of the two black leather couches, and I wrap it around myself.

It's so peaceful here. Normally, I hate mornings because Derek would bark at me to get moving, and that is the least relaxing thing. But here, I can do whatever I want and move as slowly as I want. This house and all of its furniture might not be mine, but those are just things. Why did I let Derek choose where and how we lived? Why didn't I leave sooner? If Lucas and I do get together, I am not letting him take over. I won't let-

"Oh, goody, you're up!" Amy screeches directly in my eardrum, showering me with cinnamon-scented breath.

Her long, blonde hair is tied up in a high, perky ponytail (the kind I stopped wearing when I was ten), and her impossibly slim body is encased in tiny orange silk shorts and a matching camisole.

185

"Ugh," I grunt and move my head away slightly.

I do not smell like cinnamon in the morning. More like roadkill. Also, no coffee, no talk. The coffee must be ready by now so I go to the kitchen, and there she is, right behind me.

"You're so sweet, J. You made coffee."

Well, okay.

"I'll go shopping today. I'm sorry I've been taking all your food and stuff. I can't survive without caffeine," I explain.

"Oh, sure. No prob. You can just pay us back. We trust you."

Why would she possibly trust me when she knows nothing about me? "Hey, Amy, I have a question."

Her eyes light up in excitement. This is the first overture I've made. "Sure, anything." She breathes heavily.

"Do you work out?" I ask.

She wrinkles her pert nose in confusion. Obviously, she was expecting a juicier (more personal) question. Nodding her head, her ponytail bobs up and down. "Of course. I have to."

"You have an unbelievable body. Why do you have to?"

The bobbing stops. "How do you think I got this body?"

"You were born that way?" I ask pouring myself a cup of steaming coffee and bringing it to my lips.

"No way. I used to be skinny and flabby. Before Chris, I didn't realize I needed to tone and firm up. But, because of Chris, I now have a body people want."

I find that comment odd. But, I guess it makes sense. I want a body that Lucas will want. Because he did go out with Claire right after me, and she had the best body in our high school. "So, um, how do you do it?" I ask, the coffee cup never leaving my mouth.

"The gym. Five times a week. Do you want to come with me? I have like tons of guest passes. We could go today."

The gym? Where people can see me? See my ass jiggling, arms shaking, red face sweating? "I've never been to a gym," I tell her.

Her mouth drops open and hits the floor with a thud. "Never? You've *never* been to a gym?"

"Nope."

"Well, then, that's it. We'll have breakfast and go to 'Beautiful Bodies,'" she says decisively as she takes a carton of orange juice out of the fridge.

"Oh, I don't know. Don't you have a DVD or something I can use here?"

"The best way to get into shape is to have an incentive. That's what Chris says. So if people see you, you'll work harder."

"Chris goes to the gym too then?" I can't imagine Chris bench pressing anything. Even Amy weighs more than he does. My ass is the size of his entire body.

"Oh no," she giggles, making the juice carton she's pouring from shake. "He doesn't have to."

"But, why do you?"

"Do you have gym clothes?"

Abrupt topic change. Interesting. I could manipulate the conversation to get some answers. That's what I do with the guests on our show. But, she obviously doesn't want to talk about it, and I'm certainly not going to push her. I'm all about privacy.

"Um, I should have a t-shirt and shorts somewhere," I say, pinching the roll of fat on my stomach. How great would it be to have abs like Rachel's?

I refill my (her) mug, add a healthy dollop of cream and almost spill it all over her when she grabs my hand.

"Show me!" she commands and plunks her orange juice down on the counter.

In my room, I dump the contents of both boxes on the bed. At least now I'll put them away. A pair of black spandex shorts and an extra large t-shirt are pretty much all I have. She tosses everything aside to get to the electric blue nightmare I'd worn on that fateful cycling trip last weekend. "What's this?" she asks, holding it in the air.

"No, not that. I'm burning that. It's what I was wearing when Derek and I broke up."

"Yeah, it's gotta go. But is that like the only thing you have?" she asks, pointing to another outfit I haven't worn since frosh week of college. Actually, the t-shirt *is* from frosh week, and there's a big beer mug on the front.

"I think so."

"We have to go shopping. You have a, um, curvy bottom, and we need to dress it appropriately."

Does curvy mean huge? "Cover it you mean?" I ask.

She frantically shakes her head. "Oh no, it's like super sexy. But, you need to dress for your shape. You've got a tiny upper body so you should wear tight, form-fitting shirts. The bottom is curvier so pants should rest on your hips to slim the more, ah, bodacious parts."

Bodacious? I wince at her description of me. Obviously though, this little goddess knows what she's talking about, and I could use some lessons.

So, after breakfast, I let her drag me to "Stretch It!," a luminous, airy shop filled with multi-colored workout clothes (so much pink!) at ridiculous prices.

"Um, Amy," I whisper after seeing a pair of shorts for $100.00, "I can't really afford anything in here."

"Just wait 'till you see this stuff on you. You have no idea how good you'll look."

She selects a pair of black yoga pants with a thick pink line of fabric circling the top. I pluck them out of her hand and exchange them for the green.

"Amy, if we're going to do this, you've got to know that I hate pink."

She cocks her head to the side as if I've just spoken in Chinese. "Nobody hates pink. Pink is a happy color," she argues, looking at the assortment of pink clothes slung over her arm.

"Yes, I hate pink. I'm not a happy color sort of girl."

"Yellow?" she asks.

"No. Green is good." I run my hand along the leg of the pants I'm holding. It's so soft. I've never felt anything so soft. Amy sees me lovingly caress the material and grins, her braces reflecting the fluorescent lights in the store.

"Okay, you need a shirt," she tells me and speed walks to the display of teeny weeny bra tops.

I put my hand on her arm to stop her. "Oh no. No way. I don't show my stomach."

"Have you always been like this?" she asks and turns around to face me.

"Like what?"

"Afraid of trying anything new. Covering yourself up so no one can get close to you."

Wow. I know she's talking about clothes, but her words slam me hard in the gut. She's just summed up my personality in two sentences. I narrow my eyes at her and cross my arms over my chest.

"Look, Amy, this is me so take me or leave me. I had a strange childhood and a bad breakup so I've done as much change as I'm going to right now, okay?" I say harshly, furiously grinding my teeth together.

Oy, where did that come from?

"I grew up with an abusive stepfather, a drunk mother and have been in more bad relationships than you can count. Life sucks. But if you let it beat you, then you let them win."

Guilt churns in my stomach. "I'm sorry. I didn't know. I, um, don't know where that came from. Did Chris give you that advice?"

Her lovely face shines at the mention of his name. God, will I ever feel that way about someone?

"Yes! Chris saved me. Now, I'll save you."

"Amy, I really appreciate what you're trying to do, but I don't need a 'Pay It Forward' kind of experience right now," I say, more gently this time.

She totally misses my point (again) because she says, "I'm happy to do it."

"Fine. Get me a variety of shirts. I'll be as open-minded as I can," I say to her retreating back.

"Hello! What's your name?" A small, fit brunette in head to toe yellow Lycra suddenly appears, grinning at me and clutching my hand.

"Pardon?" I ask, snatching my hand back.

"What's your name?" she asks again and reaches for my hand.

I hide it behind my back and ask, "Why?"

"So I can help you, silly. I'm Karen!"

I sigh. "Jamie."

"Jamie! Great! I'll grab you a change room, and if you need anything, just yell Karen!"

The tiny woman (she's maybe 4'11) races ahead of me, chattering non-stop. "Oh, you picked these pants? Awesome choice! They're fab with the half-halter! Did you see it?"

Every word out of her mouth is followed by an exclamation point of inexplicable excitement. I am in hell. It's too bright, too friendly and everyone keeps touching me. But, it is making me wonder what's wrong with me. No one else seems uncomfortable. Every other woman here is sporting a huge smile, they're affectionately rubbing each other and nicknames abound.

I go to my little change room and yank the curtain closed. Luckily, there's a small bench for me to sit on, and I sink onto it, grateful for a second to myself. With Hanna and Lucy, I'm one of the girls. We giggle, talk loudly. But I'm only like that with them. Derek accused me of being an emotionless shell, and maybe, there's something to that. The women in this store have never met before, and they have no problem fawning all over each other. But I do.

Even Amy and Rachel, who've only met once, know each other better than I know some of the people I've worked with for three years. Keeping people at a distance has done exactly that. I don't know how to get close to people.Amy hinted at some serious shit in her life, while I'm bemoaning a loving family who's always been there for me. For a long time, I blamed Leah for fucking me up. All she did was fall in love and follow her heart. If I'd paid closer attention, maybe I would've learned something.

Instead, here I am, huddled in a cubicle, too terrified to let go of my defences and looking for my high school fuck buddy.

"J? Where are you?"

"Here," I whisper.

"J?"

I fling open the curtain. "I'm here!" I exclaim.

"Ready to try on your stuff?" she asks tentatively.

And suddenly, I realize that she's intimidated by me because I'm older, and because I'm not so easy to talk to.

"I'm so excited!" I say, with forced enthusiasm. There must be something to all this happy-go-lucky stuff. Everyone deals with shit, and it's time I got over mine. Or until I do, I'm going to fake it. Just like everyone else.

CHAPTER TWENTY

We leave the store armed with an assortment of neon Lycra, and my face hurts from smiling so much. And while in the beginning, my grins were maniacal impressions of Julia Roberts, by the end, they were genuine. I've never had many girlfriends, and the pleasant intimacy of it surprises me. I touch Amy's shoulder lightly.

"Thank you."

"For what?"

"For everything. You don't even know me, and you're doing all these things for me."

"That's what friends do. And you're my roommate. C'mon, let's get you toned up."

The gym is huge, and the sound of loud clanging competes with grunts of pain or pleasure, I can't tell which. Amy leads me to the front desk and proffers a laminated guest pass. We walk past the cardio machines, and I'm stunned to see a wall of televisions mounted across from the treadmills, Stairmasters and stationary bikes. There are TVs here?

I follow her into the change room where loads of women are stripping off their clothes with no inhibitions whatsoever. A few are actually wandering around naked. I'm surprised to see that not everyone has a perfect hard body. Lots of fleshy bellies, sagging breasts, puckery cellulite. I've always thought that the women who go to the gym are already in perfect shape and just want to show it off. But, these women look like me. Actually, I look better than most of them.

Amy grabs a couple of lockers and starts taking off her clothes. I try not to stare, but I can't help it. She's exquisite: tanned, silky skin, not an ounce of body fat or cellulite anywhere. And then there are the lean, muscled legs, a tiny, curvy waist, toned stomach and two of the most spectacular breasts I've ever seen.

"Are those real?" I blurt out.

"What? My boobs?" she asks, pointing to her chest. "Yeah, all mine. Chris says they're magnificent."

"They are," I say without thinking.

She grins and pulls on the smallest pair of shorts (at first I thought they were a hat) and a tiny half-tank. "Thank you. You're like not so bad yourself," she says, pointing to my still fully-clothed figure.

How will I get out of my clothes while she's here? I'll look like a real idiot if I change in the bathroom. I take a deep breath, close my eyes and pull my shirt over my head. Then, the pants come off, and I'm standing in just a bra, underwear and socks. No one cares. I force myself to stand there for a moment in my underwear, pretending that I too don't care.

"Aren't you going to change?" Amy asks.

I put on my new pants and full-length sleeveless shirt, scrape my thin hair into a ponytail and lace up my ten-year old sneakers.

"Ready."

I'm really not, but I shyly follow Amy's very practised workout routine: stretching, running, lifting. After an hour, sweat is pouring down my red face, and I can barely breathe.

"Do you want to do a kickboxing class or stomach work?" Amy asks, not a hair out of place or a discernible pant.

"Ugh," I answer, not able to speak anymore. A hundred sit ups later, we're done. I lie flat on my back, listening to my thudding heart and massaging the muscles that have already started to ache. I did it. I really did it. And to be honest, it felt so good to release all those years of toxins. But I'm done now. A good body isn't made in a day unfortunately.

Back at "our" place, I head immediately for a long, hot bath. Every bone in my body hurts, but it's a good kind of pain. I feel alive. I'll never be an adrenalin junkie like Derek, but I will go again. I might even join if I can find the $200.00 registration fee. I actually think we have a corporate gym rate at work. I'd ask Eva (I'm sure she's at the gym every day, strengthening muscles to whack me around with), but I can't give her the satisfaction of knowing that I don't belong to a gym already.

Amy and Chris are huddled in their "office" doing God knows what, but I have a new appreciation for her. I've always hated people making first impressions about me, but then I went and did the exact same thing to her. I'd written her off as a total ditz, but really, she's very kind and has made me feel better about myself than most people can.

Lying in the tub, my tiny breasts bobbing on the surface, I check out my body. I swear I can see some muscle tone already. If this is what happens after one time, I'm definitely going back. If I work out every day this week, then by the time I see Lucas, I'll be five times more toned and five times better.

The phone rings, and since Chris and Amy are working, I know they won't answer it. I let the machine pick up because it's probably not for me anyway. Wrong. When I get out of the bath, there's a message from Andrew who's left his home number and asked me to call him back. So, I make myself comfortable on my bed and dial his number.

"Hello?" he answers on the first ring.

I never noticed what a soothing voice he has. Smooth and masculine, like a radio announcer. I wonder if he's ever done voice overs.

"Hello?" he asks again.

"Andrew? Hi, it's Jamie."

"Oh, hi, Jamie. Thanks for getting back to me so quickly. I'm sorry to call you at home. I guess you've moved?"

"Yeah, yesterday. Although it feels like ages already. What's up?"

"I wanted to go over our travel schedule. I thought we'd leave tomorrow so we can get a good start on the meetings."

Well, there goes my hard body. Maybe I can do some leg lifts in the backseat.

"Okay. We have to go to Milwaukee and Indianapolis, right?"

"Yup, that sounds about right."

And I *need* to go to Detroit. How the hell will I get to Detroit? Think, Jamie, think.

"Jamie, are you there?"

"Sorry, I was thinking. I actually have to go to Detroit when we're finished in Milwaukee, and I was just trying to figure out how to get there."

"Why do you need to go to Detroit?"

"Um, I have a friend there I want to visit."

That's pretty much true, right?

"I could call Cindy and have her book a couple of hotel rooms, and we could go together. I love Detroit. I was born there, you know."

"Really? So was my mom."

"Small world. So, where does your friend live?"

Fuck. I have no idea.

"Downtown."

"Great. Maybe we can get some time to walk around. I haven't been back in so long because it's not really Kelly's favorite place. She thinks it's got a little too much crime. But I keep telling her that every city has crime. Detroit's got a great edge."

"I used to go with Leah, my mom, when I was younger. And Derek and I went a couple of times."

I never even thought about being there with Derek the whole

195

time I thought about Detroit. Lucas was the only thing that figured in. But now that I recall that horrible bill, and Jeanette and well, everything, I'm mad all over again.

"Well, this should be fun. How about I pick you up at noon? We'll go to Indianapolis first, and then loop back to Milwaukee and Detroit, and save the best for last. Maybe there's a festival or something we can see."

This all sounds great, but there are two problems. I really don't want Andrew to know about my hunt for Lucas because he'll think I'm a total loser, and I don't have the money for a hotel. Obviously, the show won't be paying if this is just for fun and not work. I don't want to tell Andrew I can't afford to do it, but it's better than telling him the real reason I'm going to Detroit is to surprise my fuck buddy from ten years ago.

"Yeah, that sounds great, but even though I really want to go to Detroit, I don't think I can."

"Why not?"

I bite my lip and twist my mouth into a grimace. "I can't afford it. It's not part of our trip so I'd have to pay for it myself, and now that I'm living on my own and everything, well, I just can't."

"Jamie, if you want to see your friend, you should see...him or her?"

"Him." Silence. "Andrew?"

"Sorry, now it was my turn to think. Look, I'll cover it. It's only a hotel room and the gas, and I'd love to go back to my hometown. I would have gone soon anyway, and this way, I'll have company."

"I can't ask you to do that."

Is this guy for real?

"You didn't ask; I offered. No more discussion. I'll pick you up at noon, okay?"

Forget being mad, I'm going to see Lucas! I know Andrew's still talking, and since he's my boss, I really should listen, but what the hell. Lucas!

"Okay?"

"I'm paying for dinner, and Andrew, I'll pay you back."

I can't believe I've just agreed to letting Andrew pay for me, especially since I hated that about myself with Derek, but there is no way I'm not going to Detroit. And he said he'd go anyway, and I will pay him back after I'm a bit more settled.

I'd better get off the phone and schedule an emergency meeting with Hanna and Lucy. I need to know what to pack, how to do my hair, what to say.

"Whatever. It's not a problem, okay? We'll spend the night in Indianapolis and head to Milwaukee early on Tuesday."

"Sounds good."

"What kind of music do you like?"

"Huh? Why?" I ask.

I really have to call Hanna. I'm about to burst.

"So I know what CDs to bring. Or you can bring yours."

"I don't have any CDs. Well, I have the soundtrack for 'Dirty Dancing,' but I don't think you want to hear that."

"How can you have no CDs? Don't you like music?"

"Of course. But, Derek owned all the CDs, and in our breakup, I kind of just left everything there. He bought them anyway."

"I guess that's a true fresh start. We're going to have to get you some music. Maybe we can go check some out while we're gone. Anyway, I'll bring some, and we'll just find out what kind of music you like."

"Sure."

I don't really care about the drive at all at the moment. There's always the radio, and anyway, I'm planning to sleep.

"Thanks, Jamie, for all your hard work. You're very easy to work with."

A bubble of unexpected pride warms my chest. "Thanks. Um,

so are you. I'll see you tomorrow. And Andrew?"

"Yeah?"

"Thanks. Really."

"No problem."

No sooner do I hang up than I call Hanna at the store. The downside to being your own boss is that you have to work all the time. Even on weekends.

"Hanna, guess what?"

"Jamie, what's up? How was your first night?"

"I'll tell you in a second. I'm going to see Lucas!"

"You spoke to him? You actually called him?" Hanna sounds shocked at my supposed initiative.

"Of course not. I'm going to Detroit, and I'll find him at the college. Which college does he work at anyway?"

"Wayne County. How are you getting there?"

"Andrew and I are leaving for the meetings tomorrow, and after Indianapolis and Milwaukee, we're going to Detroit."

"That's amazing. But how did you convince Andrew to go to Detroit?"

"I didn't have to convince him at all. Actually, it's really weird. I told him that I had to see a friend in Detroit, but I couldn't really afford to go, and he offered to come with me and offered to pay."

"Your boss is going to pay for you?"

"Um, yeah."

"And he doesn't like you?"

"No, I told him I'd buy him dinner and pay him back. He's just a really nice guy."

"Nobody's that nice, Jaim."

"Aren't you cynical? Okay, forget that. I have other things to think about. I need to see you tonight. I have no idea what to wear!" I whine.

"Okay, come to my place at nine, and I'll coach you."

"Can Lucy come?"

"The more the merrier. Can Jack come?"

"Jack? Oh, I thought it would just be us girls. He might think I'm a total loser. Unless he knows already."

"Um..."

"Han!"

"I know. But, he's just easy to talk to, and he wants to know all these things about my life, my friends. It just came out."

"Oh, what the hell. It's time I got to know him anyway. Maybe he can give me the male perspective."

"Exactly. See you tonight."

***

"You know, if it weren't for me, you'd never be doing this," Lucy tells me, as she finishes her second vodka tonic.

We're sprawled on Hanna's floor, surrounded by pieces of crumpled paper, empty glasses, and pizza boxes. Jack is writing something down. For the last hour, we've been brainstorming what I'll say to Lucas when I see him. I've vetoed every suggestion. Jack has been an enormous help. And it doesn't hurt that he's gorgeous and totally devoted to my best friend. He refills her glass whenever it's empty and even checks her teeth for her. And she lets him. Also, he's really into this Lucas thing. He thinks it's amazing that I've decided to take this chance at love again.

"If it weren't for Jamie's guts, this wouldn't happen," Jack argues.

Lucy grins at him; she's also enamored with his charms. She whispered as much to me and Hanna when Jack left to get more wine.

"Maybe what I say should just be spontaneous. I'll probably forget everything anyway when I see him. Agh! There's that pain

199

again. Whenever I think about seeing him, I feel like I'm having a heart attack," I say and press my hand to my heart.

"Love hurts," Lucy tells me.

"It doesn't have to," Jack answers, staring at Hanna.

Instead of retching (like she normally would after a comment like that), Hanna's eyes soften, and she reaches over to stroke Jack's cheek. I've never seen her like this. There's hope for me yet.

"Wouldn't you think I was a stalker if you were Lucas?" I ask Jack.

He grins and shakes his head, causing a hunk of inky black hair to obscure his piercing blue eyes.

"Not at all. It's not like you two don't know each other. I'm sure I'd be surprised and shocked, but once he sees you, he'll be so impressed."

"What should I wear? I don't have anything."

"Something low-cut and that shows off your ass," Hanna says and gets up to grab another bottle of wine.

"No, no. Something casual. It's a college, Hanna, and Jamie's a more laid back kind of girl. And that's how he knows her," Jack calls to Hanna, who's now in the kitchen.

"How he knew her," Lucy corrects.

Jack tears himself away from Hanna and looks at Lucy. "Yes, but that's how he liked her."

"I don't even know what to say to him. I'm sure the fantasy won't measure up to the reality. It never does." I tear the remaining bit of nail off my pinkie and frown. "And what if he doesn't remember me? That's my worst fear."

Hanna comes back into the living room and plops down on Jack's lap. This is not the Hanna I know. I have never once, in all the years I've known her, seen her be physically affectionate with anyone unless it was going to lead directly to sex. Usually, the guy is draped all over her, and she's itching to get away.

She buries her nose in his shoulder and says, "Jaim, it's not like you've changed *that* much in ten years. He'll remember you. That's the least of your worries."

"What's the worst of my worries then?" I ask, sitting up and hugging my knees.

"There are no worries," Lucy assures me and glares at Hanna. "Everything will be fine. You have to promise to call after you see him."

"Oh God, of course. Do you think this is really stupid? I've been known to do stupid things."

"The only stupid thing you did was to stay with Derek for so long," Hanna says.

"Thanks. That helps," I say and slap the leg that's dangling over Jack's.

"Jamie, this will be amazing, you'll see what it is when you see him, and then, go from there," Jack says, nuzzling Hanna's ear.

God, this is like being with Leah and Katie.

"Right. That used to be my motto. Okay, I gotta get some sleep, and you guys should get a room. I'll see you in a few days." I get up off the floor and grab my heavy bag from the armchair.

Hanna holds up a finger to stop me. "Just one more thing. Are you going to wear makeup?"

"I guess so, why?"

She cringes. "Just remember—you want to look like you're not wearing any."

Jack shoots her a strange look. "I will never understand women."

"You're not supposed to. You just need to love us," she says.

And I nearly pass out from shock.

201

CHAPTER TWENTY-ONE

Ding dong. I so don't feel like getting up to answer that because I only have a couple of hours before Andrew picks me up. I place a vibrating hand over my heart. It doesn't just quicken when I think of Lucas, it races full speed ahead to ear-shattering proportions. How am I going to get through four days of this? I can't wait. I certainly don't plan anticipatory events. There's no delicious excitement in this. It's just the sheer, endless torture of waiting.

Lucas might be the man I'm going to marry. His parents got divorced before he was one. Lucas told me that after bailing his dad out of jail for drunk driving one too many times, his mom finally kicked him out. And his dad would visit him a bit when he was younger, taking the bus in (eventually he lost his license) from whatever city he was living in at the time, but after awhile, the visits stopped, the letters became sporadic, and all Lucas had left were wrinkled pictures and memories.

In his wallet, he carried a picture of his dad, ruggedly handsome with the same clear green eyes and jet black hair, holding him as a baby in his arms. And he clung to twisted memories of a man who abandoned him and didn't care enough about him to even call on his birthday. But he always believed he would. A sadness fills me, for Lucas, who never really knew his father, and for Leah, who married my dad because she felt she had to. Not that I'd really know how she felt about it because I never asked her. I didn't want to know. I only saw the pain she was causing me and my dad. I never thought she might be hurting too.

I'm sure when Leah married my dad, she had serious doubts, but, she succumbed to the pressure to repress who she was and married the wrong person. Until she found Katie and couldn't resist any longer. That's why we don't talk to or even see my grandparents. They were around when I was little, but once Leah and my dad were divorced, we never saw them again. They've never even met Rachel. Leah grew up in a fairly religious and strict household in which she was expected to graduate from high school and marry the man who would support her. And Leah did marry him to please them.

I stayed with Derek for much too long (three years too long), but Leah and my dad were married for twelve years. Until I was old enough to try to understand what was going on. But I didn't try. I was too angry. And in all of these years, I've never really let myself feel any shame for my distance, indifference to Katie and acute embarrassment about their life. I was too busy blaming them for my lonely childhood.

But as much as I complain about them, I'm proud of my family. Sure, they drive me crazy, and I don't always understand them, but they love me like no one else. And I never tell them that. I should tell them, but now's not the time.

Ding dong. Shit! The door! I really do have a bit of a focus problem. Reluctantly, I uncurl myself from my comfy, blanket-covered position on the couch (they crank up the air conditioner like crazy in here) and run down the stairs to answer the door. Standing there is a young, pimply delivery guy who looks really pissed off. He's got a sack filled with what appears to be letters, and he practically throws it into my arms.

The bag weighs considerably more than the five pound dumbbells I lifted at the gym (like thirty pounds heavier) so despite my new arm muscles, it's too heavy for me to hold and it drops with a loud thump to the ground.

"Amy Carruthers?" he asks in a bored voice, checking his electronic clipboard.

"No."

"Whatever. Just sign this," he says and hands me the clipboard.

"What is it?" I ask, squinting at the clipboard. I'm not signing my name to just anything.

"For registered mail. I don't need her signature. Anyone at this address will do."

"Okay," I say, curious what's in the giant sack.

I sign the electronic machine (the kind with the weird little pen I never know how to use), drag the bag inside and close the front door. Why do they have so much mail? It's very strange to get this much mail in one day. I could find out why if I peer inside. But that would be wrong. But, if the bag falls over, a few letters might just fall out, and I'd have to look at them to get them back in.

"Oops!" I say to no one in particular as I trip over the bag. And shake it a little bit. A few business-letter sized envelopes fall out, all addressed to "Fantasia Productions." That must be Chris and Amy's web company. They work from home so I guess this is where the company mail comes in too. But that's a shitload of mail for a company run by only two people. And from the sparkling repartee I've engaged in with Chris, I assumed he was in the financial or tech field in some way.

Under the company name is a web address. Well, I'm sure it won't be a very interesting website, but it would be nice to know what they do. And Amy's been so great to me that the least I could do is ask about her job and show her that I want to know more about her. It's cool that they have their own business and manage to be together all day, every day, and not kill each other.

After dragging the bag upstairs, I turn on the computer they have in the living room (this place is such a find, what with the free digital cable and Internet) and type in the address. Hmmm. This doesn't look computer or financialish. A sky blue background covers the page, and in two opposite corners, there are silhouettes of naked women wrapped around each other. Oh, and a picture of

Amy in a hot pink string bikini. Are they in retail?

I click on Enter. I've got to see what they sell. Oh my fucking God! Holy shit! I don't believe this. In front of me, in huge detail, is the biggest penis I have ever seen in my life. Attached to a starved, bony body. I recognize those sharp collar bones. And the mouth that the penis is in looks awfully familiar as well. On the computer, sweet Amy is giving Chris what looks like a fantastic blow job. Live on film.

Rigidly, I click on each picture. Chris and Amy are porn stars! They sell, well, basically, they sell each other. I'd like to throw up, but I can't tear my eyes away from the moving images of Amy and Chris's obviously active (and very satisfying) sex life. I haven't had sex in awhile, and good sex in a very long while (well, except with my Spanish babe, but I prefer to pretend that never happened) so it's no wonder that these pictures are doing funny things to me.

But this is Amy and Chris! The guy who literally and figuratively takes up less space than my thigh. And Amy. Innocent, endearing Amy whose crotch is so close to my face that I can see the little silver ring in the folds of her pink skin. Completely hairless skin. Does she shave? Wax? This might be why Derek likes this. It does look quite, um, erotic. Oh God.

All thoughts of Lucas, Leah and my earlier guilt are replaced by hysterical laughter and nauseating disgust. What do I do now? Talk to them about it? What do I say? So, guys, I like your website? How much is a membership? Do I move? They're porn stars. In my house. That's what they're doing in the office I've never seen. "Knock before you come in." Now I see why. I see *everything.*

And I wonder why she's doing this. A bright, beautiful girl who could be doing anything with her time is having sex on camera for the whole world to see. Is it because of her childhood? Does she like it? Is Chris some sort of perverted sicko? He certainly seemed innocent enough. And boring. How can someone so socially inept have sex all day on camera?

Hanna's going to love this. They're probably her customers. In a few of the videos, Amy is wearing some spectacular lingerie for two seconds before she peels it off or Chris rips it off. What if she told Rachel? What if Rachel wants to do this? Has Chris already recruited her? No, Rachel would have told me if she knew this. I think.

I am so confused. I knew this stuff existed, but I've never known anyone who actually did it. I can't believe I misjudged them so much. And I don't even have time to think about any of this, because it's 11:30 a.m., and I'm not even dressed. Andrew will be here in half an hour.

I take a shower and try to erase the picture of Chris's dick in Amy's mouth from my mind. It's impossible. All I can see is her red mouth opened wide, and Chris's hand on her blonde head. Okay, think about something else. Lucas. Right. No, now Lucas's dick is in Amy's mouth and that just makes me angry.

Maybe I could get some pointers from her. I obviously need them because I'm a complete moron. It never once occurred to me that gritty, shady things were happening in that office. Perhaps if I'd asked a question or two instead of waiting for her to tell me about herself, I'd have known. Then again, Amy was very reticent and careful not to mention her "job." Is that why their roommate moved out? Probably. Maybe they asked her to join them. Agh!

Is that what they're planning for me? Is that why Amy wants me to go to the gym? Is she grooming me to be her apprentice? That would be a great reality show. Forget Donald Trump. You could have real porn stars mentoring the wannabees. Considering I've spent my whole life avoiding conflict, I've now got two major issues to deal with. My pornographic roommates, and the fact that in a few short days, I'll be standing in front of Lucas, trying to explain why I'm there and what I want.

Whenever we chose a movie or talked about something, he always knew what I was thinking. I never really had to explain what I meant. Once we were talking about Katie and Leah, and because I only thought about how confused by it all I was, it was hard for me to get the words out properly.

I didn't want him or anyone to think I didn't love them or that I saw anything wrong in their love. It wasn't that. It was dealing with my parents not being together and losing that dream of the perfect family and knowing what people were thinking when they sneered at Katie and Leah holding hands in the grocery store.

Lucas got it, and he helped me get it too because I certainly didn't come to these flashes of self-awareness on my own. So, maybe when he sees me, he'll just know why I'm there. Because I'm not so sure I could even explain it to myself.

Knock, knock. Shit, that's Andrew, and I'm still in my robe, hair dripping wet, surrounded by a stack of letters that must be fan mail for the fair Amy. I shove the bag to the side, whip open the door, and he's standing there in his requisite jeans and t-shirt, holding the largest coffee I've ever seen.

"For you, Madam," he says, handing me the steaming cup.

"How did you know I needed coffee?"

"Because I'm very observant, and you have a coffee cup plastered to your lips every time I see you."

"Thanks, Andrew." I smile and take the cup. "As you can see, I'm not dressed yet. I've just had some, um, interesting news, and I, uh, I didn't realize the time. Come in for a second."

If Andrew were a real guy, I wouldn't be too happy about him seeing me in my shapeless robe and no makeup. But, since it's just Andrew, I'm not uncomfortable at all. I lead him into the living room and tell him I'll be back in a moment. What I realize as I head to my bedroom is that the website is still up. Shit!

I yank on a pair of jeans and a red t-shirt (one of those tight, Lycra ones, Hanna gave it to me), drag a comb through my hair and slap on a bit of mascara and lipstick. Hopefully, he's still sitting on the couch. Maybe he's watching TV. Maybe he didn't even see the computer.

I sprint down the hall to the living room and stop dead. Yup, he found it. And his face is pressed very close to the screen so I'm going to guess that he likes what he sees. He hears me behind him and turns around.

"So, you didn't realize the time, huh?" His mouth is stretched in a huge grin, but I can see a faint red stain on his cheeks.

My own cheeks are fiery, and I just want to flush myself down the toilet.

"That's not mine," I tell him, averting my eyes from the picture of Amy with her crotch in Chris's face. "I know them."

Andrew's eyes widen.

"I mean, I didn't know they did this, but I live with them. Oh God, okay. Here's the story. I just moved in here on Saturday, and I had no idea that the people I was living with were porn stars. Who thinks that when they meet someone? So, mail came for them this morning, and I saw the website address so I thought I'd check it out. And this is where it took me to. I don't know what to do now, and since we're leaving for a week, I can't do anything."

"What do you need to do?" he asks, still smiling.

"Well, move out, I guess." I shrug.

"Why? Don't you like them?"

"No! Of course I don't like them. What kind of person do you think I am?"

He laughs. "Not in that way, Jamie. I mean are they good roommates? Because if they are, then what's the problem? This is their business, and they obviously enjoy it, so who are you to tell them what to do?"

"But they're porn stars."

Now it's Andrew's turn to shrug. "So?"

"So, they make porn in my house."

He shrugs again. "So? You don't have to do it. You don't even have to see it because you haven't since you've been here. Do you have a problem with porn?"

Okay, this conversation with my boss is getting strange. I don't want to tell him that I was the one who wanted to get some dirty movies, not Derek. I thought it might spice things up, but Derek thought it was gross to watch it with me. I don't want to tell him about the stack of videos I'd seen in Katie and Leah's room and watched them. And liked them. But, my cheeks have gone from a containable fire to a full alert blaze so I guess he has his answer.

"Can we just go?" I beg.

"Sure. But I think you should shut this down so they don't know you've seen it," he says, with mischievous laughter in his voice.

I turn off the computer, grab my bag and lock the door. I'll deal with this later. Now, the rest of my life awaits.

CHAPTER TWENTY-TWO

Andrew's car is a silver Honda Civic hatchback, and it's even messier than Eleanor. Files, bags, papers, and DVDs crowd every available space. I'm not surprised. I've seen his office. In the time he's been at the show, Andrew has managed to cram everything he owns into the small office that Sue barely used.

"Do you live in your car?" I ask, getting in and slamming the door.

"I used to. I've spent so much time travelling that I just take everything with me. I'm not used to staying in one place, and I'm always worried that I've forgotten something so I grab it all and stuff it in the car. Are you uncomfortable? Do you have enough room?"

"Luckily, I'm pretty small so I can fit anywhere," I lie, as I try to maneuver my ass between the CDs he's brought.

"I think you're sitting on the music."

"Ah, so that's what's digging into my ass." I reach around and hand him the stack of music.

"Aren't you going to look at them?"

I turn my head to look at him. "You know, it's funny. I grew up with a lot of music in my house, but I got so used to listening to whatever was on and I still do that, I guess."

Andrew shifts in his seat to face me. "I couldn't live without music. My music. When I was in Iraq, I had John Lee Hooker and Johnny Cash on my iPod all the time. With all the soldiers, tanks and absolute terror around me every day, I needed the music to work. It drowned out all of the other stuff. And even though I never got to finish that documentary, I will one day, and that's going to be the background music. So, I just can't believe you don't

210

have music, your own music that you listen to."

"Maybe because my thing is the television."

"Okay, well here's the first step to knowing what kind of music you like," he says and hands me the CDs back. "Look at them and decide."

We're on the highway, and with the cool breeze coming in from the window, the tension in my body dissipates and I relax. Derek was always so concerned that someone might nick his car that we never talked or enjoyed the scenery. Now, though the scenery from Chicago to Indianapolis leaves much to be desired (flat, barren nothingness), the ease of being with Andrew is making the long drive ahead of us seem more pleasant.

The smooth, smoky voice of Norah Jones fills the car, and as I listen to the lyrics, tears spring to my eyes.

"So I guess you like this?" Andrew asks and reaches over me to grab some Kleenex from the glove compartment. He hands me a tissue, and I quickly dab at my eyes.

"You know, I never cried until a few weeks ago, seriously. Now, even the long distance telephone commercials make me want to bawl. But, yeah, I do like this. It's, hmm, what's the word? Soulful."

"Yeah, I think so too. Kelly prefers Top 40, but I like the more eclectic stuff better. The right music just makes you think about things you might otherwise push to the back of your mind. So, what's on your mind that triggered the tears?"

I tuck a strand of hair behind my ear and smile at him. "Are you sure you're a man? You really want to know what I'm thinking about or are you making polite conversation?"

"Jamie, we've spent enough time together by now that I don't need to make polite conversation. And when a woman is crying in my car, and she'll be in my car for hours, I think I kind of need to ask or it'll be one tense ride."

I glance out the window and back at Andrew. "Well, I'm thinking about my life, me. We're going to see all these people who are willing to humiliate themselves for a small chance at love. But, I spent five years with someone who never even wanted me. I got so lost in the relationship, and the scary part is that I probably could have stayed with him for another five years if it weren't for the fact that everyone in my life hated him."

"Why did they hate him?"

"He's an asshole. He only cares about money and checking his achievements off mental lists of things he's gotta do. And nothing gets in the way of that. He's the total opposite of me. And my friends have never been ones to keep their dislikes a secret. If it weren't for Lucy wanting me to find-"

What the hell am I doing? Andrew is so bloody easy to talk to that I almost told him about Lucas.

"If it weren't for Lucy wanting you to find what?" he prods as we pull into a Starbucks for a coffee refill.

"Um, myself. I wouldn't have found myself."

I restrain myself from rolling my eyes at my hippie dippy answer. Andrew is quiet. Was that too much information?

"I don't have a lot of my own friends, I mean, independent of Kelly. We've had the same group of friends for so long that I never really needed to meet anyone else. I have a few buddies from the documentary stuff, but Kelly doesn't like them so I only get together with them without her," he says while holding open the door of the restaurant for me.

"Why not?"

"Not ambitious enough, don't dress right. I don't know. You talking about losing yourself is making me think about a few things."

"What things?" I ask as we stand in the never-ending line of caffeine junkies.

After discovering that my very own roommates are bonafide porn stars, I have decided that it's high time to ask a few personal questions.

"Well, since you just laid it out, I guess I owe you one. Okay, well, I wonder if Kelly and I are doing the right thing by staying together. We're also total opposites. Not in the beginning, but ever since she got this job, she's been at me to change. But I really don't see the need to change."

"Then don't."

"But there's a part of me that wonders if she's right. I have a Yale education, and I'm not using it. And I love working in television and film because it excites me, but once we have kids, I might need to find something a bit more lucrative. "

"You went to Yale?"

"Don't look so surprised. We both did. Kelly wanted an Ivy League education, and I didn't really care where we went as long as we were together, and I could study film. Those were some of the best years. And then her family moved here so we came here instead of moving back to Detroit."

We're finally at the cash, and we both order extra large coffees with lots of cream and sugar. We carry them out, and I ask, "You don't like Chicago?"

"It's not that. I don't really even know Chicago because I travelled so much. But, I feel like something's missing, and I don't know if it's her, me, the city." He sighs deeply and pushes his hair out of his eyes.

"Maybe you can think about it while we're gone. And I don't think you have to take a job you don't want just so you can have more money. My dad's a prof, and it's not the highest paying salary, but I had enough as a kid."

"Sure, but can you just do whatever makes you happy? Isn't there a sense of responsibility that maybe means you have to bite

213

the bullet and do things you don't like?" he asks and glances at me from the corner of his eye.

"There's responsibility and then there's misery."

Silence. There's really nothing else to say, is there? I think Andrew is in the same predicament I was, but has been for many more years. Obviously, Kelly has been his whole life, and he's just now imagining the possibility of being without her. I can hear it in his voice and in the way he talks about her.

I wonder if he's ever slept with anyone else? We walk towards the car, both of us lost in thought.

"I have been with other women, you know," he tells me after unlocking my door.

God, he's polite. And I'm so embarrassed. I blush, wondering how he knew what I was thinking. He unlocks his door and starts the car for the short drive into Indianapolis. We're both silent for awhile, with just the hum of the wheels sliding across the flat road filling the car. And then he speaks again.

"I'm not stupid. When you add up the years that Kelly and I have been together, it might seem like she's the only one. And there's nothing wrong with that, but in my case, it's not how it is. We broke up for a bit during college to see if maybe we were just staying together for comfort, and I went a bit wild. And in the end we got back together because neither of us found anyone better and thought that it meant we were supposed to be together."

Maybe he needs a Lucas too. Clearly, his relationship isn't what it should be, and he's swaying between walking out the door and sucking it up and staying. Damned if he does and damned if he doesn't. I felt the same way before it became clear to me that I would be okay without Derek. More than okay. Happy.

"Anyway, we're supposed to be working, and you don't need to hear about my problems. It's just a rough patch right now."

I hear myself laugh out loud. Too late to stop it.

"What's so funny?" he asks, irritation in his voice.

"Nothing. Sorry. It's not funny. It's just that I said the same thing for a long time. But, you're probably right. You just need some time together."

"Yeah." He visibly shuts down, and I'm not going to push it. I respect boundaries. We're at the hotel anyway, and we have a lot of work to do before tomorrow. His love life is his problem to fix.

Up at the reception desk, a perky and beautiful Japanese girl is waiting.

"Hi, we're here to check in. Andrew Harris and Jamie Ross," I tell her, tossing my bag to the floor and pushing my sunglasses up on my head.

Satoko (as it reads on her gleaming gold name tag) taps away on her computer keys, and her eyes light up when she gets to our reservation.

"Oh! You're from the television show. I love that show. Do you think there's a chance you can get me on it?" she asks, sucking in her cheekbones to look more model-like.

I raise my eyes to the ceiling, but Andrew seems enchanted by the question. I guess because he hasn't heard it every day for the last three years.

"Sure, there's always the possibility we may find something. Why don't I write down your name?"

He actually takes out a pad of paper from his bag, borrows her pen and writes down her information. I nudge him to get it over with so I can go to my room, unwind, and watch a bit of TV before our meeting.

"Your room is 613. The elevator's to your right, there's a swimming pool and workout room that's open until eleven, and the dining room closes at ten."

"There are two rooms," I correct her.

She looks at her computer again. "No, there was only a

reservation made for one room. There's a double bed, mini bar..."

"No, we should have two rooms," I tell her again. I am *not* sharing a room with my boss. I have things to plan before I see Lucas, and anyway, I've had enough sharing of space to last me for awhile.

"I'm sorry, but someone changed the reservation just yesterday. We had you for two rooms, but someone from your show called and cancelled one of them. And we're all booked up now. Summer season, you know."

"That fucking bitch!" I growl as my stomach sinks to my knees. Eva did this. I know she did. Maybe she wants me closer to Andrew so she can get her trampy hands all over Derek. Which means she's afraid that Derek still wants me. Or she just wants to see me unhappy. Why does she hate me so much?

Both Andrew and Satoko turn to look at me. "Who are you talking about?" Andrew asks.

I purse my lips and narrow my eyes. "Eva. I'm sure she changed the reservation."

"You're being paranoid. Why would she do that?"

"I have no clue, but there's no other explanation. Now what do we do? We have to get moving or we'll miss our meeting. But..."

"Is it so bad to have to share a room with me? It's only for one night. I promise you I don't snore. Do you?"

"No! It's just that, it's just, oh fine, whatever."

Bemused, Satoko smiles at Andrew, which he returns. I scowl. We take the elevator to "our" room, and I feel a smidgen better when I see there's a huge television, those white fluffy robes and a great view of Purdue University. I throw my bag on the bed and wander through the plush carpeting to the bathroom where I pocket the little bottles of free goodies. That's what they're there for.

"You haven't spent a lot of time in hotel rooms, I'm guessing?" he asks when he sees me try to stuff conditioner, body lotion and a shower cap in my jeans' pocket.

"Why do you say that?"

"Because you're practically vibrating to touch everything. Oh, awesome, there's a huge TV!"

He's already turned it on and is flicking through all of the stations to see what we get. And he stops at a raunchy scene complete with handcuffs, oil and I think, a feather. "This is what you like, right?" he asks, pointing to the screen and chuckling.

I hurl a pillow at his head, and he picks it up and whacks me back. Hard. "Hey! Stop that!" He hits me harder, and I have to run to the other side of the room to escape, which is difficult because I'm laughing so much that my sides hurt.

"You are such a child. Give me that remote."

We both get on the bed and lean back against the one pillow that's left. Comfortably, we watch a rerun of "Oprah" although he keeps trying to switch the channel to some political documentary. But, I want fluff, not intellect, and he finally gives up after I hide the remote under my ass. As I watch Oprah gush over Tom Cruise (why doesn't she just jump him already, everyone knows she wants to), and Andrew flips through the *New Yorker*, only glancing at the television when I laugh at something, I realize how nice it is to spend time with a man I'm not attracted to. I mean, Andrew's good-looking and everything, but he's no Lucas.

A while later, he brings me a glass of water from the bathroom and hands me the file for the people we need to meet. And he puts his hand on my arm. "Hey, Jamie?" he starts.

I tear my eyes away from the screen. "Yeah?"

"Thanks."

"Why? What did I do?"

"You made me laugh, and it was much needed. You're a cool chick and a good person to talk to so thanks."

"You know what? So are you. Now shut up."

217

CHAPTER TWENTY-THREE

"And why did you break up?"

We're at our first interview, and Andrew is letting me take the lead and ask all of the questions. He keeps sneaking off to dump the super-sweetened, lip-puckering iced tea into the potted plant next to the bathroom. I, on the other hand, have to sit here and drink it because I need to get some answers so we can go. Unfortunately, Bubba is less than forthcoming. And he wants to be on television?

"It just ended."

I stifle my frustration, move my jaw around and make a face at Andrew. Perceptively, he picks up on what I'm trying to say (which is, ask this very boring man some questions before I scream) and smiles at Bubba.

"It's amazing what we remember about high school. Do you have a yearbook or something you can show us? We'd love to hear some stories."

Bubba lumbers off (and I do mean lumbers, the man must be two hundred and fifty pounds of what was once muscle and is now certainly not) to get the yearbook.

"Andrew, how will we get him on the show? He can't even answer a direct question," I duck my head and whisper.

"Just be patient, okay? He might feel more comfortable talking to a man. Why don't you go and look around? Or powder your nose?"

"Powder my nose? Is it shiny?" I ask, touching the end of my nose for any grease that might be falling off.

He grins. "It's a figure of speech."

"I knew that." I get up, leaving the horrid iced tea on the table, and wander into the living room. Above the fake fireplace rests a few framed pictures. They are all of a former football player, buff and popular, linking arms with the requisite blonde cheerleader.

There are no pictures of Bubba now, and my heart sinks with pity. This man's life is his high school football career, and obviously, he's been carrying a torch for this Meghan woman for a long time. Will she want to see him like he is now? It makes me wonder if Lucas has become a balding, doughy version of his former self. Will I still want him or do I only want the boy he was when we were kids? Am I trying to recapture my youth? A bark of laughter from the kitchen startles me so I leave the living room and drift quietly back into the kitchen. I don't want to interrupt their male bonding.

"Oh, and this is Meghan after we won the championship. She's wearing the promise ring that I'd given her. Isn't she beautiful?"

Andrew is nodding and smiling in agreement, and my heart tugs, hoping that the makeover artist can do wonders for Bubba. We leave with a few yearbooks and newspaper clippings about Bubba and drive back to the hotel in silence.

"What's up? You're very quiet," Andrew says.

"I just wonder if we're doing the right thing," I tell him, nervously biting my fingernails.

By "we" I actually mean "me," but Andrew doesn't need to know that.

"What do you mean?"

"Well, you saw him. The Bubba that Meghan loved has doubled in size, lives in a small town outside Indianapolis doing welding and is nothing like the star he was back in the day."

"Maybe she's changed too. But now you're worrying me too so stop it."

"I just don't want anyone to get hurt."

I don't want to get hurt.

"I don't want to hurt anyone either, but I don't think I will. How many people responded to the teaser? A lot, right? There are a lot of people out there hoping for a second chance."

Is there anything else but hope? Back at the hotel, we go to our room where I wait while Andrew calls Kelly. I try not to eavesdrop, but it's hard not to hear her shrill voice through the phone. Even from the bathroom where he's barricaded himself for the last half hour. And even over the sound of the television which I keep making louder.

I walk over to the potted plant near the window, pretending that I'm extremely interested in the soil until Andrew's done. He comes out, despondence slackening his normally sharp features.

"You okay?" I ask.

He covers his dejection with a quick smile. "Sure. Fine. Kelly has an important business dinner that I was supposed to go to, and she's a bit upset I won't be there. But, to be honest, I really hate her business things so I guess I wasn't sounding as disappointed as I should be. It's so ridiculous to watch all these people in their suits, everyone trying to one up each other with what they have. I just can't stand it. And when they hear what I do, they give her these looks of pity, and I want to strangle them. Anyway, I'm sure I'll make the next one. I can't avoid them all."

He sits on the edge of the bed and rubs his chin while I walk over to the mini-bar on the other side of the room. Expense account! I grab two bottles of beer and toss one to Andrew. I sit cross-legged next to him on the bed and open my beer.

"I remember Derek's business dinners. All I wanted was my jeans and a cold beer, and I had to sit there for hours, listening to them ramble on about sales figures, revenue and watch the women who just knew which fork to use. No matter what I wore or how hard I tried to fit in, I always felt messy and unkempt next to them. Like I wasn't good enough to be there, you know? And every time,

Derek and I would have a huge fight after. I'll never miss that."

He twists the top off his beer and flicks it off the wall. Putting the bottle to his mouth, he nearly drains it in one swallow. I just know that he's running the conversation with Kelly through his head over and over again. Sipping my own beer, I remain silent, and we drink, both arguing with our minds instead of talking about it.

"Can I borrow your phone?" I ask. I just realized that I didn't even tell my family I'd be gone, and I know that his phone bill will be covered by the show.

"Sure. Who do you need to call?"

"My parents. They tend to worry about me."

"They're not together, right? You told me they divorced when you were twelve."

I lean back on one hand on the bed and take another sip of the beer. "You have a good memory. Yeah, my mom lives with her girlfriend, Katie, and my dad is married to Mo. It's a long story. I also have a sister, Rachel. You wouldn't believe my family history if I told you."

Andrew lifts himself up on his wrists and leaps backwards until he's comfortably settled against the wall. Spreading out his legs, he says, "You've already told me a bit. And I've unloaded my shit to you."

"You're way too easy to talk to, you know that?" I tell him.

"That's funny that you say that. Kelly thinks I'm closed and emotionally immature."

"Emotionally immature?" I shake my head in confusion and lie back on the bed at the opposite end. I'm thinking "too much therapy," but I say instead, "Andrew, can I ask you a question?"

"Yes. But not until you tell me about your family."

I roll my eyes at him, take a long swig of my beer and tell him. I tell him about my lonely childhood, my coldness to Katie, how

221

my sister was conceived. I tell him how ashamed I am at how I treated them. I tell him how amazing they all are, and how I'd never realized it until I stopped being so selfish and thoughtless. What I don't tell him is that Lucas helped me understand all this because for some reason, I just don't want him to know about Lucas. Once we're back together, sure, but until things are clearer, I'd like to keep it to myself.

And when I'm done pouring out my whole life, he says, "You're really hard on yourself, Jamie. What kid wants their parents to get divorced? I don't know anyone who came out of that unscathed. And, for your mom to tell you she's gay and then move in with her girlfriend? Fuck. I'd be in analysis for years just for that. I don't even really talk to my parents, and we just kind of went our own ways as I was growing up. You had a whole soap opera going. It was normal for you to react like you did. What's not normal is the fact that you've told me all this while picking the skin off your feet."

"Oh God, was I really doing that in front of you? That's a sure sign of true friendship," I say and look down at my ripped up feet.

"You're lucky. Your family sounds lovingly insane. Mine is just so boring. Family dinners consist of loud chewing and a few grunts of stilted conversation."

"That's better than being asked if you've had your colonic irrigation when your boyfriend's over for dinner."

Andrew laughs, his kind brown eyes lighting up again, and the dimple in his cheek deepens. Kelly's an idiot I decide as I steal a peek at his soft hair falling over the chiseled line of his cheekbone. This guy's a keeper.

"Okay, my turn. If we're playing psychiatrist here, I have a couple of questions for you," I say.

"Shoot."

"Have you really asked yourself why you stay with Kelly?

222

You've given me some obvious answers, things I said when everybody asked me about Derek. I knew that my friends hated him, my family worried about me, and still, I stayed. I defended him, made excuses for it all because it was easier than being alone. And I know that eighteen years is a lifetime, but even I can see that you're not happy."

Andrew crosses his feet and looks at me. "Because I was happy. It's been me and Kelly for so long now, and I just keep thinking that things will go back to where they were if we can get through whatever shit is going on now."

"And if you can't?"

Andrew shrugs and doesn't answer. Instead, he reaches over the side of the bed into his bag and pulls out an Eminem CD. Under the television (which I'd much prefer turning on if we're going to play avoidance) is a CD player, and Andrew gets off the bed and slides in the disc. I can see that his jaw is clenched, but there's nothing more I can say. I knew that Derek and I were over a long time before we ran into Claire Howard, but I wasn't ready to let go. Hopefully, Andrew will find the strength to walk away. Until then, he can find comfort in the lyrics of an angry rapper who is telling him to lose himself.

He hands me his phone, and I dial my dad's number. Mo answers. "Mo, it's Jamie."

"Jamie, where are you? Rachel told us you've moved, but you never gave us the number."

"I'm in Indianapolis for work. We're leaving for Wisconsin tomorrow. I'm sorry I didn't call. The move happened very quickly, but I'll be back by Friday. Maybe you and Dad can come for dinner."

And then I remember the unsavory occupation of my roommates. My family will love this. They'll all sit down with Chris and Amy and try to understand their motivations for getting naked and licking each other online, and they may even give them some suggestions.

"That sounds wonderful, sweetie. How are you doing without Derek?"

"Better than I was with him."

"I'm proud of you, Jamie. You did the right thing. Your dad wants to speak with you."

My dad gets on the phone. "Jamie? Everything okay?"

"Everything's great, Dad. I'm just in Indianapolis for a business trip, and then I'm off to Wisconsin."

"Are you alone?"

"No, I'm with Andrew, my boss. We're going to Detroit too, and then, we'll be home. What's new with you?"

"Rachel brought her new boyfriend to dinner. I swear your sister gets more beautiful every time I see her. She said that your new place is awesome, to use her words. Are you settled in okay? Leah wants to come over and do a thorough spiritual cleansing. There are ghosts that haunt the new owners or tenants of the house, and she says you need to make friends with them."

"I'm just getting to know my roommates. Maybe the ghosts can wait for a bit."

"Leah says you need to do it immediately before they feel you've taken over their space."

I bet the ghosts are pretty damn happy considering they get a live sex show every day. Unless they're Mormons.

"Okay, I'll call her now. I just wanted you to know that I'm okay."

I hang up and I'm about to call Leah and Katie, but when I peer at Andrew, who's back on the bed, I see his shoulders are shaking, and he's wiping tears from his eyes.

"What?" I snap at him.

"You have to make friends with the ghosts?" Deep rumbling

224

laughter rolls through him again.

"Don't you have anything better to do than listen to my phone conversation?"

"On a cellphone, you can hear everything. It's just so funny. Hello, ghost, why don't you come in? Would you like a martini or perhaps a dry sherry? Oh, serve yourself, you know where everything is."

He goes on in this vein for two minutes. And for once, I start laughing too. Most of the time, I can't see the humor in Leah's wacky ideas, but with Andrew falling all over the bed and laughing, and me smiling at him, I do. "She's not totally insane, you know," I tell him.

"I never said she was. I think she sounds really cool."

"Well, I have to call her too so try to contain your laughter for a few minutes."

I call Leah, and while she repeats the necessity of a ghost e-vite, Andrew pretends not to listen. But his hand is covering his mouth to smother the giggles, and I can just imagine what he's thinking.

He's my boss, and he knows way more about my family than Horace and Adrienne who have worked beside me for years. This might not be my brightest career move. And then, he makes retching noises when he hears Leah say, "Maybe your boss would like some of your fish oil pills. Driving for a long time can do terrible things to your equilibrium and liver. Or pick up a bottle of Nu Greens and give that to him for breakfast."

"Leah, stop. I can't talk about this right now." C'mon, I need to have some professional dignity.

"Oh? Can I talk to him?" she asks.

"What?! No!"

But Andrew hears that and holds out his hand for the phone. I furiously shake my head at him, but he wrestles the phone away from my grip. My stomach is churning at what Leah might say. God, she may ask him about his sex life for all I know.

"Uh huh, yes, I will, no I don't, garlic pills for Jamie? Yes, I'll remember. No, I feel good. I have a naturopath. My girlfriend doesn't go to her, but I see her regularly. Am I regular?"

"That's it! Give me the phone!" I yell.

"Bye, Mrs. Ross, Leah? Okay, bye Leah, I'll book that massage when I get back," he says and gives me the phone.

"Leah, what are you doing?"

"Sweetheart, not everyone is uptight about their health. Your boss sounds lovely. Good luck with the trip. Love you."

"Yeah, love you too. Bye, Leah." I turn off the phone and stare at it for a few moments. Hugging my knees, I say, "Well, that was sufficiently mortifying. What did she say to you?"

"Just to make sure you take your vitamins. I do have a naturopath, you know. I think it's great that your mom is in alternative medicine. It's surprising you eat so much crap."

"Can we just watch TV? I'm never telling you anything else about my family."

"I think you're lucky to have them."

"You want them?"

"At least they show you how they feel about you. My parents still shake my hand."

"Maybe we were switched at birth because I'd much prefer that."

"No you wouldn't."

"Well, it would be better than watching your mom and her girlfriend make out all the time."

He grins. "That might not actually be so bad."

I stick out my tongue in disgust. "Okay, that's gross. What is it with men and lesbians?"

"You're right. My mother in any sexual manner is not

226

appetizing in the least, but two women, it's erotic."

And now that I've started this conversation, I'd like to stop it. I'm blushing to the roots of my hair, and I want to hide under the bed.

"So, what do you want to watch?" I ask, flicking on the remote and settling myself comfortably against the pillows next to Andrew.

He licks his lips and winks at me. "Some porn?"

I smack him on the shoulder. Turning on the television, I convince him to watch a "Grey's Anatomy" re-run by telling him about all the sex they have in the hospital.

Being out of the country all the time, Andrew has never even heard of the show, and he's got a lot of catching up to do. As his friend, the least I can do is fill him in on the latest TV shows. Although he doesn't seem to like it as much as I do. Crazy.

CHAPTER TWENTY-FOUR

After ordering room service (pizza for me, some healthy salad for him, Leah had made him feel guilty about his recent eating habits), we figured out the bed thing. Andrew took the floor. I told him I would sleep there, but he was having none of it. And since it was "his" company which screwed up the reservation, he should sleep on the ground. I just couldn't share a bed with him. As much as we get along, I'd feel weird sharing blankets and a mattress with him. I mean what if we mistake each other for lovers or something? Can you imagine?

So, that means I slept very well, and Andrew slept curled in a ball only to wake up with excruciating back pain.

"Ow!" he says the next morning as he walks to the shower.

"Ow!" I hear as he's taking a shower.

"Ow!" he yells from the bathroom as he bangs around in there.

"Okay, Andrew, I get it! I'm really sorry. What can I do?" I yell from the bed, where I am snuggling under the most luxurious of sheets.

"How are you at massages?" he asks from behind the closed door.

"Considering I've only let Katie near me once in my life, not too good. Maybe we can stop at a walk-in clinic on the way to Milwaukee. Andrew?"

There's no answer from him, and I fear that he's fallen over and can't get up. Reluctantly, I throw off the downy covers, walk over to the bathroom and knock softly on the door.

"Andrew? Did you hear me?"

"Yes, I'm just in too much pain to answer. What about your stepmom?"

"That's all the way back in Chicago. What's wrong with a clinic?"

"I want someone I can trust. What if we stop in Chicago and then go to Milwaukee?"

I stare dumbfounded at the bathroom door. "That's a three and a half hour drive for nothing."

"Not for nothing. I'm dying here. I just want someone good because I have a lot of problems with my back, and if I don't go the extra mile-"

"Extra 280 miles," I interrupt.

Andrew opens the door, a towel wrapped around his waist, and hobbles out. He's been hiding a nice little six-pack under those t-shirts. Not as cut as Derek (which was way too buff for me), but just the faint outline of muscle against a smooth stomach. He rolls his eyes.

"Fine. If I don't go the extra 280 miles, it'll happen again, and it will be worse. And we have plenty of time. We don't need to be in Milwaukee until tomorrow. And Detroit's whenever we make it."

He says "Detroit," and my stomach clenches. Excitement? Fear? Slight nausea? All of those, I guess.

"Okay, I'll call her. You must love driving, though."

"I do, but I don't think I'll be able to. Can you drive?"

Ugh. I hate driving. "Is it a stick shift?" I know it's not, but I *really* don't want to drive.

"No. Automatic."

"Um, yeah, I can drive. At least, we'll get there. Can I get you anything?"

"A wheelchair?"

I snort. Men are such babies when they're in pain. I call Katie, who's delighted to help my boss, and Leah is ready with a gluten-free lunch. The last thing I expected was for me to have to introduce Andrew to my crazy family. Thank God I didn't tell them about Lucas. They'd spill that little secret so fast. Without meaning to, for sure, but they just don't have the normal filter that everyone else has. Theirs has been hijacked by Dr. Feelgood.

Not only do I have to drive all the way back to Chicago, but I also need to meet Meghan. Alone. I leave Andrew, moaning and groaning, lying flat on his back on the bed, and I take the car to Zionsville, about fifteen miles northwest of Indianapolis. And even though that's a relatively short drive, it takes about double the normal time as I'm a slightly nervous (neurotic) driver. Because Derek insisted on a stick shift, and I refused to learn how to drive it, I haven't spent much time behind the wheel of a car in the last five years.

I've forgotten how to change the mirrors and push the seat up (God, Andrew has really long legs), and I check my blind spot again and again and let every car pass me. Even the terrified kids from the "Sun School for Drivers" are going faster than me. A wreck, I finally reach Meghan's high-rise, and a little boy of about seven, with the most angelic face I've ever seen, opens the door.

It turns out that Meghan is a lovely single mother who has also packed on a few pounds over the years. Still beautiful, but the high cheekbones and slender frame adorning Bubba's pictures are now buried in layers of soft flesh. But, the happy grin and twinkling eyes that instantly appeared when I told her that someone from her past wants to meet her gives me a glimmer of hope that this may all work out. For the both of us.

Once I get back to the hotel and fill Andrew in on the meeting, he's no better and still insisting on going back to Chicago. Clutching his lower back and whining, he crawls into the passenger seat and pushes it all the way back so he can lie flat. It's too bad his mouth isn't hurt because he feels the need to continuously comment on my less than stellar driving ability.

"Don't be insulted, but you are the worst driver I've ever seen,"

Andrew tells me.

Yet again.

"Oh, shut up. At least I'm doing it, and I'm not nearly as bad as my sister."

"She goes slower than you?"

"No, she has no respect for the other cars. She zips past everyone, doesn't pay attention..."

"Do you think you could give the other drivers a little less respect? They're certainly not giving it to you," he says, as yet another trucker gives me the one finger salute.

Finally, we pull up outside Leah and Katie's, and they are both sitting on the porch waiting for us. They float (the only way to describe it as they are both wearing diaphanous and sadly, transparent, ruffled skirts) to the car and help Andrew out.

"Oh, poor you, you're all bent out of shape," Katie says.

Leah laughs at the pun and kisses me on the cheek. "Hi, Jamie, why did he sleep on the floor?"

I glare at her to shut up, but she continues. "Goodness, it's not like you were going to have sex or anything. Sharing a bed can be whatever you make it. When I lived on my own, before I married your dad, we all slept in the same bed. Well, actually, there was some fun, but-"

"Leah! At least meet Andrew before you tell him all about your experiences." I cringe in extreme embarrassment.

Andrew is looking from me to Leah, and I know that he is stunned that this beautiful and spirited creature is actually my mother. "Leah, it's a pleasure to meet you. You and Jamie seem so..."

"Different?" I say.

He smiles and follows them into the house. And there is Rachel wearing a tiny lime green halter dress and a huge smile. "Hi! So, you're Jamie's boss? Can you give her a raise?" she asks, flipping her hair and licking her lips.

"Rachel, shut up. Shouldn't you be out with J.P. or something?" I ask.

"We had a fight." She pouts.

"About what?" I ask, knowing I'll regret it.

"Oh, he thinks my skirts are too short. He liked them fine when he wasn't my boyfriend, but now he says he wants to be the only one to look at my legs. Can you believe it? What a chauvinist pig!"

"I don't much like the sound of that," Katie says.

"You should be able to wear whatever you want. If he doesn't like the way you dress, bully for him," Leah concurs.

Andrew is silently watching this exchange, moving his head back and forth like he doesn't know who to listen to.

"Do you have any brothers or sisters, Andrew?" Leah asks.

"No, I'm an only child."

"Lucky you," I say and glare at Rachel.

"Jamie's just jealous because she doesn't have a boyfriend right now. Oh, are you single?" Rachel says.

Kill me now.

"Rach! God, leave him alone. Katie, he needs a massage like right now," I say, hoping to shut Rachel up.

"But are you single?" Rachel asks again.

"Rachel, love, that's enough questions. Come and help me make lunch, and you can tell me more about J.P." Leah successfully distracts Rachel from inflicting further shame on me.

"He's such an asshole, don't you think? But he's so hot. And he has the best swimming pool in his backyard..."

Once they're in the kitchen, I turn to Andrew and say, "I am so sorry about that. She has no idea what she's saying."

"She's hilarious. It must be strange for you two being so many years apart. But, she certainly loves you to pieces."

"Yeah, she does. Most of the time, she amuses me, but

sometimes, like now, I want to throttle her."

"You look a lot alike," he tells me.

"Ha! Are you joking? Besides the fact that she's so much taller than me, we have no similar features."

"You have the same mouth, same nose, same cheekbones."

"Cheekbones? I don't have any cheekbones."

"Jamie, you have the self-esteem of a turtle. Actually, even turtles have more self-esteem. You must know that you're beautiful."

I stare at him. Beautiful? Not me.

"I'd give *you* a raise if I could right about now. Okay, go get rubbed," I say, deflecting the compliment and gently pushing him towards Katie's massage room.

While he's gone, I join Leah and Rachel in the kitchen where they're spreading unsalted butter on thick, grainy spelt bread. Rach is still yammering on about J.P., and Leah is nodding and hmming.

"Your boss is hot," Rachel tells me.

"Rach, you think everyone is hot."

"He is actually a very nice looking guy. But, goodness, is he filled with sadness. It absolutely weighs on him, and it's probably why his back went out."

"He slept on a hard floor."

"Pain is more than the physical, Jamie, you know that. No, that man is keeping a lot inside."

"Well, he is my boss so could we please try not to embarrass me anymore?" I ask, sitting at the kitchen table and wishing for a cup of coffee. Or vodka.

"But if he's single, then maybe you and him should hang out. Put on some of your tight new clothes and get out there. You're not going to meet anyone if you're working all the time. And he is a hottie," Rachel says and runs her tongue over her shiny pink lips. And then reapplies her lip gloss. "And it would be easy to have a torrid office affair because you see him every day," she continues.

I smile at Leah over Rachel's head. That would not be easy at all, actually. "He's not single. He's been with someone for twenty years."

"A woman?" Rachel asks.

"Yes. And that was your last question about him, okay?"

She defiantly crosses her arms over her chest and pouts. And reapplies her lip gloss.

"Fine. Be boring. Do you wanna hear more about J.P.?"

Rachel prattles on for the next hour, her chatter periodically punctuated by the cries of pure pleasure coming from the basement. Katie comes up, brews a pot of tea and joins us at the kitchen table. She smells like lavender and sage, and she's flexing her wrist.

"Whew. Lots of tension. My arms are killing me. Nice boss, Jamie."

I nod in agreement. "Yeah, he really is. Is he feeling better?"

"Much. He just needed to work the kinks out." She winks at me.

Katie's sessions are confidential, and it never fails to amaze me what people will tell her while she's massaging them. She doesn't name names, but she has related some pretty interesting tales told to her in that room. I remember the cross dresser who didn't know how to tell his wife. For some reason, Katie's clients take the therapist part of massage therapy a bit too seriously. So, I think Andrew's probably filled her in some on the Kelly situation. That's good. He obviously needs to talk about it, and maybe I'm too close to it to be of any help, considering I did just end my relationship.

Andrew saunters up a short while later, his lean body moving like liquid around the room.

"Ah..." he says.

And nothing else. His chocolate brown eyes are glazed over

and half-lidded, and he melts into the chair at the table, stretching out his legs and grinning. "Ah..." he says again.

We laugh. "That good, huh?" I ask.

"Better."

"Do you want some tea, Andrew?" Katie asks as she pulls five mugs down from the shelf.

"Do you have any coffee?" he asks.

Four heads swivel to look at him in shock.

"That word is blasphemy in this house. No caffeine, no sugar, no meat. But there is a vast assortment of tea," I tell him.

"Um, sure, tea would be great then. I feel so damn good. I haven't felt this loose in," and he rubs his chin, "huh, years. I haven't felt this relaxed in years."

"That's funny. David does that," Leah says to Andrew with interest.

"Dad does what?" I ask.

"Rubs his chin with one hand when he's thinking about something."

"Oh, that's just one of my little habits. I also grind my jaw like Jamie."

"Do you have a navel ring like Rachel's?" I ask.

"No. But I do have a tattoo on my hip. Katie saw it," he says and winks at Katie who flushes with pleasure.

Where did Mr. Charm come from? Jeez, he is just full to the brim with surprising character traits.

"Could I have some tea too, please?" I ask.

I don't want to sit at the kitchen table and chitchat about Andrew's tattoo because before he knows it, they'll have convinced him to take off his pants to show them.

"Of course, love. Katie, mix in a little of that mulch we bought. Jamie's color needs some perking up," Leah says and peers at my pores.

"Just plain tea, please."

I move my face back so she'll stop inspecting me. It's embarrassing.

Leah sighs. "Is she like this at work?" she asks Andrew.

"Stubborn? Yes. It's why she's so good at what she does."

Leah beams at him and puts her hand on his arm. "You are welcome here anytime."

Translation: we like you much better than Derek. I hope they're this welcoming to Lucas. The only time he met Katie and Leah was when he dropped me off one night past my curfew. Like four hours late because we'd fallen asleep at his place. His mom was out of town. And even though Leah and Katie had few restrictions on me, the time I had to be home was a hard and fast rule in my house.

They were steaming mad, ranting and raving at both of us for worrying them. Then they forced us to sit down in the living room and have a chat over tea. They kept us up for hours until we were almost begging to go to sleep. Clearly a "look what you put us through" tactic that Leah must have inadvertently picked up from her parents.

Tea and brown chewy sandwiches gone, we get ready to say our goodbyes. Andrew gives all three of the women hugs, and I kiss them on the cheek. And, of course, Leah gives Andrew a goody bag of potions and pills to take with us.

"We'll see you soon," Leah says.

"Count on it," Andrew responds.

We get back in the car; this time with Andrew at the wheel. It seems like he doesn't like my driving.

"I love your family. I've never met anyone like the three of them. They're all so quirky and amazing, and in such different ways," he says, starting the car and pulling out of the driveway.

"Yeah, they're not bad," I joke.

But inside, I am ecstatic. It's not often that I introduce my family to anyone, and even after all these years, I'm still wary of people's reactions. But Andrew just gets them. And he sees what I see. We pull out of the driveway, and Andrew looks at me thoughtfully. "Really, Leah's so warm and comforting, Katie's a bit raunchy and fiery, and Rachel, well-"

I nod. "Yeah, I know. Isn't she the most beautiful kid in the world?"

"It must be great to have someone to share all those family moments with."

"It is, but remember that we're thirteen years apart. So, it's not like we actually grew up together. I didn't have someone to play in the sandbox with either."

He laughs. "You're so dramatic sometimes, and yet, so laid back. Your entire family is a paradox."

"Is that a compliment?" I ask.

"It sure is, missy." And he winks.

"You are a complete geek, you know."

"So are you."

"Can we get some coffee, please?" I beg.

"How is it possible that your mom shuns everything chemical, and you crave it?"

"Rebellion. And now it's too late. I think giving up caffeine would be impossible and absolutely ridiculous."

"Okay, coffee it is," he says as he swerves the car to the right to get off the highway that we have just gotten on.

"I didn't mean immediately, Michael Schumacher."

"Well, you get what you ask for."

Maybe.

CHAPTER TWENTY-FIVE

After getting coffee, we climb back into the car, and as I'm putting on my seat belt, I slump my shoulders and heave a huge sigh.

"What's wrong?" Andrew asks and expertly guides the car back onto the highway.

"We have another two hours of driving in this car, and it is now my daily torment. The once soft cloth of the fantastic bucket seats is now chafing my already sore butt, and there are only so many hours I can stare at the flat grey road in front of me."

"You should have had a massage too."

I bare my teeth at him.

"Ooh, what are you going to do? Bite me?" He laughs.

I redden. Again. "No thanks, I just ate."

"Okay, cranky girl, let's play I Spy."

"I Spy? Wow, I haven't played that since I was a little girl."

"You'd be amazed what you'll resort to when you're in the middle of the desert and waiting for five hours to get a good shot."

But after twelve games and a lot of bad choices like the ladybug that just flew over the windshield (and I didn't notice) or the guy with his finger up his nose in the next car over (which I had the good luck to witness, but Andrew didn't), I'm ready for a break. We're both a little cranky from being cooped up for so long, and I think the talk with Katie really bothered him. But I'll wait until he wants to talk about it.

Anyway, I'm too busy obsessing about Detroit so I can look Lucas up at Wayne County. I need to know when he teaches so I can be waiting for him when he's finished. I probably should have done it before we left, but there wasn't any time what with the move and everything. And, okay, I was too scared. I'm still terrified and sick and excited about doing this. I've never traipsed across the Midwest to find a guy I haven't seen in ten years. Actually, I've never traipsed anywhere.

But now I am, and I'll lean against the wall outside his office (maybe I should wear one of those sexy school girl outfits, no, nix that, I don't do pleats), and when he comes out, I'll give him a long, smoldering stare. He'll be so shocked and pleased, and he'll scoop me up in his big arms (well, they weren't so big back in high school, but I'm sure we've both grown) and carry me to his office. Ooh, yes, and we'll have hot, frantic sex on his desk. After he sweeps all the papers and books off and throws me down. My body will seem so light to him, and he'll remark how easy I am to lift.

"If coffee can make you smile like that, you are very easy to please," Andrew says, breaking into my reverie.

"What? Coffee? Sorry, I was just thinking about, um, I was thinking about Bubba and Meghan meeting again."

"You really care about people, don't you?"

Yup, that's me. Only concerned about other people.

Traffic is so light on the barren highway to Milwaukee that we finally arrive an hour later. This time, the hotel has two rooms for us (Eva must have gotten bored of her little mind game), and we decide to meet for dinner at 7:00 p.m.

I practically sprint to my room and fling open the door. It's small, but there's a huge king sized bed so I toss my bag to the side, pull out my laptop, and once under the covers, I start tapping away. I find the website for Wayne County and look at the list of professors. No picture, but there is his name. Lucas Simpson has been a permanent instructor at the college for three years, and he teaches almost all of the biology classes they have. And his most recent schedule lists him as working on Fridays.

I'll tell Andrew I need to meet my "friend" and send him off to explore his old childhood haunts. Oh God, what if he wants to come with me? There's that strange squishy feeling in my stomach again. I've gotten used to feeling like an outsider, and I've never really known what people are talking about when they describe that perfect comfort of being in the right place at the right time. But, for a moment there when Andrew, Katie, Leah, Rachel and I were sitting at the kitchen table drinking our tea, a perfect equilibrium settled inside me, and my anxieties melted away.

But it's gone now, and I'm back to uncertainty. Well, I still have a couple of days to worry about seeing Lucas, and all that really matters is that I will see him. I've brought three different outfits. One is sexy, one sporty and the last is casual. I'm happily fantasizing about those first few moments of reunion sex when I hear a loud crash from the adjoining hotel room. Then I hear the yelling.

"I can't fucking take it anymore, Kelly! I am exactly who I am, and that is never, never going to change no matter how much you or my parents want it to. If you want someone else, go and find him!"

Eek. That does not sound good. I hear some more banging, but I decide to let him work this out on his own. I know that when I'm angry or upset, the last thing I want is to talk to someone. And really, as selfish as it sounds, I am on such a high about my own love life that I don't want Andrew and Kelly's problems to diminish that. So, instead, I fall into a deep and dreamless sleep.

***

Ring, ring. Ring, ring. Ring, ring. What the fuck? I open my eyes and try to focus. Where am I? I slowly turn my head to the side, afraid that I have gotten drunk and picked up another stranger. Whew, I'm alone. Ah yes, I'm in Milwaukee, in a hotel

240

room, and that must be my phone. I reach an arm out to answer it.

"Hello?" I croak.

"Hey, were you sleeping?" Andrew asks.

"Mmm, yeah, but I'm up now. Dinner, right?"

"And a lot of alcohol."

"I see. Okay, meet me in the lobby in fifteen minutes. I just want to take a quick shower."

"You can shower and change in fifteen minutes? Are you sure you're female?"

"Just your regular garden variety. But don't expect me to be wearing anything fabulous. Fifteen minutes gets you just me."

"Just you is great. See ya."

I hop in the shower and quickly let the water run through my hair and over my body. When I get out, it only takes me a few minutes to do a quick blow dry and add a touch of lipstick and some mascara. Hanna says that those are every woman's necessities if you don't have a great pair of breasts.

Andrew is waiting in the lobby, wearing the most hangdog expression on his face. His hair is sticking up everywhere, and there's a coffee stain on his shirt.

"Nice of you to dress up," I say sarcastically and point to the large brown circle on his chest.

"This is me so fucking deal with it!" he snaps.

"Ooh, sorry, I was just kidding." I take a closer look at him. "Hey, are you okay?"

"No."

Okay, not talking is better right now. So, we stride towards the front door and out into the fresh summer air. The hotel is right across from the Michigan River, and there are tons of great restaurants overlooking the water. We walk past a few that are packed until we find "Riverhouse," a quaint red brick restaurant with the mouth-watering smell of seafood wafting through the open windows. I'm about to go in when Andrew grabs my wrist.

"Jamie? I'm sorry I'm being such an ass. Kelly and I had a huge fight, and I just don't feel like talking very much."

"That's okay. I'm not one for blabbing on anyway. Let's get some food, and you'll feel better."

"I think a huge gin and tonic would help as well."

"Okay, we'll get you that too. Just don't be too hungover tomorrow. We're meeting Ray and Lisa in the morning."

"I never get hungover."

Yeah, and I also said that I don't do one night stands.

Andrew may not get hungover, but the man can certainly get drunk. The minute we sit down, Andrew orders the first of his many gin and tonics. I immediately get some food for us to absorb some of the alcohol he's throwing down his throat. But he's a man on a mission and has barely even glanced at the menu.

By his sixth drink, he's letting it all hang out. Not in a weepy drunk way, but in a bare his soul kind of way.

"Do you know what the worst part is? I've wasted so many years. Years! I could have been fucking tons of gorgeous women all over the world, I could have been living in different countries, you know? I regret so much."

I take a bite of my spicy jambalaya and swallow in pure delight. "What's the point of regret? It makes you feel awful, and you can't get the time back. The important thing is to realize your mistakes and know better."

He rolls his eyes at me and pushes at his blackened swordfish with his fork. He's only had a few bites, and I'm dying to reach over and taste some.

"C'mon, Jaim, don't you regret spending five years with that bastard?"

I grin. "Sure, of course a part of me wishes I had left sooner, but I didn't. And maybe if I had left earlier, I wouldn't feel as good as I do now. Maybe I would have regretted leaving."

"Do you at all?" he asks, tearing little lime bits from its rind with his teeth. The only problem is that he ate that particular lime about half an hour ago.

I hand him the lemon from my drink, and he puts it into his mouth and gives me a great yellow smile.

"Do I what?" I ask, laughing at his silliness.

"Regret breaking up with Derek?"

I shake my head. "Nope. Not for a second. And I never will. I feel bad about how things ended. I would have thought we could be friends or even civil after living together for so long. But what's done is done. Time to move on."

"Why did I stay with her?" he whines.

"You're the only person who can answer that question."

Andrew smiles sadly and fixes his gaze on me. It's a bit intense so I look down at my plate.

"Hey, Jaim?" he says quietly.

I look up, and he's still got an eerily serious look on his face. "Yeah?"

"You know, I've never had a female friend before, and it's really cool. But Kelly doesn't like you."

What is this? True confessions? And why was she talking about me? I scowl and ask, "Why the hell not? She doesn't even know me."

"She thinks you're too pretty for me to spend so much time with. She thinks you want me."

I am so glad that Andrew is drunk and probably won't remember any of this in the morning. It's bad enough that Kelly thinks I want to steal her boyfriend, but it would be a hell of a lot worse if Andrew thinks so too. I do, however, relish a moment of pure joy that she thinks I'm pretty. Too pretty. It's amazing what a little freedom and excitement will do for you. And a $300.00

haircut.

"I don't! Not at all!" I protest.

"Thanks. What, I'm not attractive?"

"With lemon stuck in your teeth? Not particularly. No, seriously, I also don't have any friends of the opposite sex, and this is nice. I don't find it easy to talk to that many people."

"Because you have no self-esteem, my little turtle. In your shell, all hidden away." He tucks his head into his neck in a parody of a retreating turtle.

I glare at him. "Hey! Don't do that. I do have self-esteem, thank you very much, I just don't need my ego stroked all the time."

"Everyone needs a good stroking now and then." And he waggles his eyebrows and leers at me.

Okay, time to go. I don't know where he's going with that, but he's depressed and needy, and I'm not going to be *that* girl. I get the bill, but Andrew is still aware enough to grab it away from me.

"I'm hammered, not a prick," he says as he hands the waitress a credit card.

"Thank you. It's time to go. We have a lot to do tomorrow."

"Tomorrow, tomorrow, it's only a day away," he sings in a warbling voice.

Tomorrow, he is going to be so hungover. He seems slightly less drunk once we get out into the cool summer breeze, and he walks fairly steadily back to the hotel. He's very quiet on the way there. Once we're at our rooms, he looks at me, bites his lip and says, "Did I say some very mortifying things back there?"

"A few. But I won't hold it against you. Are you going to be okay?"

"I always am," he says and gives me a crooked smile.

"Goodnight then. See you at, what, five?"

"What?!" Andrew's eyes bulge out.

"Kidding. Eight?"

"That's better. 'Night."

I wash up, slither under the soft covers and close my eyes. My last thought before I fall asleep is that I'm so happy to be rid of Derek. And I'm happier that I have someone better waiting.

CHAPTER TWENTY-SIX

"Rise and shine!" I sing loudly into Andrew's ear when he answers the phone early the next morning.

"Ow! Fuck! Aw shit, that hurts."

"What hurts? Your hangover?"

"It's *not* a hangover. It's just a very, very, very bad headache."

"Right. A hangover. Okay, you need juice, eggs, sausage, toast and a lot of butter."

"I'm going to puke," he says. And then all I hear are distant gagging noises. He's back on the line a moment later and sounding a thousand times better. "Okay, I'm ready to eat."

"You're a nut."

"Yup. Let's have a huge breakfast and then go meet our next lovely couple."

"See you in fifteen."

We meet in the lobby, and Andrew's face is ashen and stubbled.

"Looking good," I tell him, smacking him on the arm.

He runs his hand over his jaw and grimaces. "Thanks. I feel like shit. But food and a massive vat of coffee will help."

We walk through downtown until we find a greasy breakfast place with bottomless coffee. We sit in a booth at the back (it's one of those places with crayons scattered everywhere so children can draw on the place mats when they're bored), and we immediately order two specials. An omelet, sausage, bacon, buttered toast and countless coffees later, Andrew's face picks up a bit of color. I kind of like the stubble. Normally, he's completely clean-shaven (Kelly's work, no doubt), and it gives him a bit of an edge.

"I should shave before we meet Ray and Lisa," he says.

246

"Why?" I look up from the drawing I'm making of Eva sitting on the toilet.

"Because it's unprofessional."

"According to whom?"

"Good point. And I have no energy to shave. You may be asking a lot of the questions."

"Not if Ray is anything like Bubba."

"They may all be like Bubba. And is that supposed to be someone I know?" he asks, pointing to my objet d'art.

"Does it look like someone you know?"

He grins and shakes his head as if he doesn't know what to make of me. We walk back to the hotel, check out and drive to meet Ray Smith, investment banker, former geek. He lives in Franklin, a suburb in a city of suburbs. The palatial house is situated on a steep hill, and we have to meander through a gravelly and bumpy trail (not so good after ten cups of coffee) that takes about five minutes to get to the front door. Finally, we pull up to the door and are instantly greeted by a pack of what I'm hoping are not wild dogs, but their sharp fangs and thick, muscular bodies tell me otherwise.

"Um, Andrew, they're staring at me, and I'm a little scared. So, I'll just stay here, okay?" I say as the dogs howl and slowly circle the car.

"Scared of the dogs? Don't be. I'm sure they're harmless. C'mon, let's go."

I open my door, and three snarling, salivating dogs bark at me, their spit dribbling all over the door of the car.

"Muffin, Lucky, Pixie, down!" I hear a man bellow.

The dogs instantly back off, and I let out the breath I've been holding in fear of the low rumblings coming from Muffin, Lucky and Pixie.

"Sorry, I breed pitbulls, and they get a little excited

247

sometimes," a ridiculously over-tanned and immaculately dressed man (crisp pinstriped button down, black dress pants and shoes polished to within an inch of their life) explains to me.

Pitbulls? Yeah, harmless, sweet creatures. The dogs are calm, but glaring at me with what I'm sure is barely controlled fury as I slowly make my way up to the front door. Andrew has no fear and even reaches down to pet one of the nightmares.

"Are you crazy?" I practically yell and pull his hand away.

"Jamie, I've been in a prison camp. These dogs are fine." And he opens his palm for one of the pitbulls to sniff.

"Well, I haven't been in a prison camp," I say and look at him like he's crazy (which he obviously is, I mean, prison camp?!), "so keep those monsters away from me."

Ray is grinning at us. "The dogs won't hurt you. They're trained not to attack. It's nice to meet you."

"Hi, Ray," I say, keeping one focused on the dogs and the other on Ray. "I'm Jamie Ross, the associate producer and this is Andrew Harris, executive producer."

He shakes our hands and leads us into his sprawling front hall, where the gleaming floors are a deep mahogany wood, the walls, pure snow white, are decorated with oil paintings that I just know are the originals, and the gorgeous room is bathed in soft, warm light from the marble sconces. We're guided past an enormous, gourmet style galley kitchen (complete with those copper pots hanging above the island in the middle) and into the den. It looks like another house entirely. Sunken floors, granite busts of Julius Caesar, and on the mantel are countless pictures of Ray. Ray snorkeling, Ray skydiving, Ray running. Ray really likes Ray.

"Can I get you two a beverage?" he asks and presses a small button on a panel hidden in the oak wall unit.

"I'd love a coffee," Andrew says.

"Me too, please." I actually have to pee like crazy, but I'm going to guess that this will be the best coffee I've ever tasted.

"Mimi, three coffees, please," Ray says into the button.

This place is incredible. Even his wall serves food. A short time later, a maid (a feather duster, Windex and rag are all tucked into the utility belt strapped around her waist) appears with three coffees on a silver tray so sparkling I can see my reflection in it. I look disturbed.

"Thank you, Mimi," Ray murmurs and gestures for us both to sit down. And I can't help but notice that Mimi is very attractive in her fitted black skirt and clinging white blouse. This is exactly the life (and wife) that Derek wants. I hate this guy already. But I still want some of his coffee.

When Ray hands me a cup, I immediately put it to my lips. I was right—it's the smoothest and richest hit of caffeine I've ever had the pleasure of ingesting. I almost moan as my body sinks into the spongy leather couch, and Andrew nearly curls up and lays his head on the pillow. I elbow Andrew in the side, reminding him to stay awake, and before I can even open my mouth to ask a question, Ray starts talking.

"So, I'm sure you're wondering why a successful man like myself would want to go on a television show to find love."

We weren't thinking that, but we both nod in agreement anyway.

"I've never been married. This might surprise you, but I can be very, very selfish. I have lived alone for many years, made my millions, and now I realize that I need to have someone special in my life. Not just for one night or to accompany me to galas, but to be with," he explains while rearranging the diamond rings encircling three of his fingers.

Galas? And without missing a beat, he continues.

"I have shunned commitment. There have been many, many women who wanted to marry me, but none of them were good

249

enough for the Ray Man."

I stick my nose in my coffee cup so the Ray Man won't see me rolling my eyes. Unfortunately, Andrew must still be a bit drunk because I hear him snort beside me.

"Pardon?" Ray says.

"Sorry, my boss has a bit of a cold," I say and glare at Andrew, who shrugs and flashes me a contrite grin.

"Anyway, now that I'm in my mid thirties, and I may retire very soon, I need a companion."

I am dying to ask why he doesn't just place an ad, but I don't because I'm a little afraid of the answer. At least I don't have to worry about making him talk. No, this guy won't shut up.

"And that's why I want to find Lisa."

Oops. He was still talking, and I missed that part. Hopefully, Andrew is listening. I glance at Andrew to see if he's heard that last part, but his eyes are rolling back in his head like he's about to fall asleep. I've never seen this side of him. Usually, he's so focused, but in the last couple of days, he's been a bit rebellious and scattered. It's good for him, but now is just a bad time to be giving a big fuck you to convention.

"And you're going to help me, correct?" Ray asks me.

"Of course. I just need to know a bit more about your relationship with Lisa."

"I just told you about that. Weren't you listening?"

No.

"Yes, but I'd just like some more detail. For example, why did you fall in love with her?"

"Because she was beautiful and popular. Everything I wasn't."

"And?" I prod.

"And what? That's it? I was young."

"So why now? Why wait so long?"

Ray's eyes quickly flit to his lap and then back at me. Aha. I knew there was more to it.

"I saw her in a magazine a few months ago, and she was still so stunning."

"Oh, do you still have the magazine?"

It will be a great jumping off point for our interview with Lisa.

"Um, yes, but, I'm not sure if you, perhaps it would be better if he..." Ray is at a loss for words and beckons to Andrew to follow him.

I have to nudge Andrew from his slumber, and he looks at me confused.

"Ray wants you to follow him."

"I have to get up off this couch?" he whispers.

This time, I shove him on the arm, and he stands up to follow Ray. While they're gone, I race to the bathroom. After going in and out of a few rooms and a closet to find it. It is, of course, incredible with a huge spa size tub, a bidet, two gold sinks and a heated towel rack. While sitting on the most gorgeous of toilets, I fantasize about what questions Andrew would ask Lucas if he were to be on the show. I'd never let that happen, but I'd love to hear some of his answers to these questions. I don't know why he wanted me all those years, why he loved me. Or if he ever thinks about me now.

I'm back before Andrew and Ray. When they walk in the room, Andrew looks suspiciously bright-eyed and enthusiastic. He hands me the magazine.

"Oh, I don't know if she wants..." Ray starts, but Andrew interrupts him.

"Jamie has no problem with pornography. Right, Jaim?"

I glare at Andrew from the corner of my eye and shake my head. "Um no, no problem at all."

I open the magazine to the dog-eared page (hoping desperately that the pages won't stick together), showcasing a beautiful redhead draped on an air mattress in a swimming pool, her legs splayed as far as they can go (much, much farther than mine ever could), and she is buck naked, a red rose clamped between her teeth.

"So this is what made you decide you wanted Lisa back?" I ask, barely masking the scorn in my voice.

"Yes. Look at her. She would fit perfectly into my life. She's the only thing I don't have."

A trophy wife?

"And I want her."

"Well, we'll certainly do what we can to make that happen." I swallow the bark of laughter that's trying to escape from my mouth. "Luckily for you, she's single, or so the article says, but why do you need us to contact her?" I ask.

"Well..." Ray hesitates.

"You've already gotten in touch with her, haven't you?" I ask.

"Um, yes I did. You see, we broke up because I sort of slept with her sister."

How do you sort of sleep with someone? Just let your penis in a bit?

"And she's still angry about it?" Andrew finally pipes in.

Welcome back, boss.

"Yes. But I think if she saw me again and realized I'm a changed man, she'll come back to me. I mean, look at me, look at my home. Who wouldn't want this?"

Me.

We chat for another hour, I drink as much of the delicious coffee as I can without suffering a caffeine overdose, and finally, we have enough information to leave.

"Well, we'll get her on the show, and from then on, it's up to you. Thank you for your time, Ray, and we'll contact you with the details later," I say as I reluctantly leave the delicious comfort of the luxurious couch and happily end the discussion with a man even more self-important than Derek.

He stands up and leads us back through the maze of his house, past the darling pitbulls (just that would be enough to keep me away) and waves goodbye.

"There's no way," I say as we're pulling out of the infinite driveway.

"I know. But you have to give him some credit for trying."

"No. He just wants her because she's a centerfold to add to his collection."

"Yes, but maybe that's what she wants. You never know what people will do."

"No, you're right." I turn my head to look at him. "But I know that you need to wake up. You were falling asleep back there."

He looks repentant and nods. "I'm sorry. I'm never like this. I just can't seem to function today," he says and narrowly avoids running over a cat that has just jumped in front of the car.

"Yes, that's what happens when you drink the entire shelf of a bar. And we're lucky you didn't just hit that cat."

"What cat? Anyway, it's not because of the alcohol. I really think that things with Kelly and me are so bad, and this might be the end. I, I don't think I love her anymore." He pushes his hair out of his eyes and sighs. "There's another problem. I'm not feeling upset, per se, and I should be. I know I should be a wreck, and all I feel is relief. Is this how you felt?"

"Before we broke up, yes. Five years is nothing compared to how long you were with Kelly, but he was a huge part of my life. But, I was so sick and tired of always defending him and so sick of the fighting, and it hit me that I really didn't have to live like that. I had a choice. And, whoosh, just like that, I felt free."

"Kelly moved out," he tells me quietly.

My heart sinks. Poor Andrew. "Why didn't you tell me?"

"I just did."

"I'm sorry," I say. "So, you've broken up?"

"Yeah, I think so."

"Well..." I don't know what to say.

"Yes, well."

His dimple appears, and I get a glimmer of a smile resting somewhere in him. He'll be okay. I squeeze his elbow, my heart hurting for him, but not knowing what to do.

"Let's go meet the centerfold."

***

Lisa is as gorgeous as her picture suggests. And certainly nowhere near as wealthy and successful as Ray. Her home is one step up from a trailer in the seediest section of Milwaukee. The paint is peeling off her walls, and the unmistakable odor of unhappiness wafts out from the ashtrays scattered around her living room. But, she is charming, and the kind of woman I hate on sight.

A master flirt like Eva. She sidles up to Andrew, and while she's shaking his hand, she also gives his shoulder a friendly squeeze. I get a quick, dead fish handshake. No squeeze.

"So, Andrew, what would you like me to do?" she asks, her pink glossy mouth pouty and inviting.

"Um, we'd like to, um," Andrew stammers.

I can't really fault him for it. He just saw her entire body sprawled out on shimmering blue water, and I'm sure he's picturing it as he looks at her.

So I take over and say, "There's someone from your past who wants to see you again, and we'd like to know a bit about you, and if you'd be open to coming to Chicago for the taping."

Her green eyes coolly assess me, but she turns to Andrew to answer the question. "Who wants to see me?" she purrs and puts her hand on his arm.

Andrew looks at her hand and visibly swallows. "We can't tell you that because it's supposed to be a surprise." He's squeaking so he clears his throat and tries again. Men. "But, you would get a free flight, a makeover, a two night hotel stay and a date with the person who is dying to see you."

"A man?" Lisa asks.

"I'm sorry, but we can't say. Now, we just have a few questions to ask. Do you mind?" I ask.

I'm afraid if I let Andrew talk, he'll tell her everything she wants to know. Lisa leads us to the broken, beige couch, and I carefully position myself on it to avoid the sharp springs that are poking through the cushions. She doesn't offer us anything to drink. Instead, she joins us on the couch and sits dangerously close to Andrew. I see her press her leg against his suggestively, and I know that we have to get out of here soon. I also know that she will have no problem coming on our show if there's a man who wants to see her.

"So, Lisa, tell us a little about yourself. Like your job, your hobbies, what your life has been like," I ask.

"I'd rather speak to the executive and not the assistant if you don't mind. There are some private things in my life that I am not comfortable sharing with many people," she tells me, and her eyes go cold.

A hot flash of irritation sparks in my chest, but I have no choice but to agree. "Fine. Lisa, it was nice to meet you. Andrew, I'll meet you outside."

Before I leave, Andrew gives me a quick apologetic smile. I head back outside to the sweltering heat and sit on the front steps of her house/shack. This gives me the perfect excuse to call Hanna so I stand up again and walk away from the house to call her.

"Hi, Han, it's me."

"Hey, Jaim! Have you seen him yet?" she asks excitedly.

"No, I think we're heading to Detroit tomorrow. Right now, I've been banished by the second porn star I've seen in a few days."

"Porn star? What the hell are you talking about? You're not doing something crazy, are you?"

"Yes, Hanna. I've decided to leave my job and start making porn films. Please. I can barely stand to see myself naked. No, it's my roommates, and this girl we're interviewing."

"Your roommates? You're not making any sense."

"You know Amy and Chris, my new roommates? And how sweet and innocent they seemed? I mean, good God, Chris can't even string a sentence together. But, mail came for them the other day before I was leaving-"

"You read their mail? That's a federal offence."

"I didn't exactly read their mail and stop interrupting me. They got this huge bag of letters, and one fell out. Well, okay, I sort of kind of tripped over the bag and allowed the letters to fall out and there was a website address written on one of the envelopes. I went to the site, and holy fuck, there was Amy with Chris's dick in her mouth."

Silence. "Han, are you there?" I ask.

Then I hear the laughter.

"Oh, Jaim, ow, my stomach, that hurts, that's so, ha ha, so funny. How do you get yourself in these situations? Ever since you broke up with Derek, your life has been crazy."

"I know. First whatshisface, um, Mathias, then Lucas, now this. But I have to say that the excitement is a lot more interesting than staring at the television all the time."

"I've been trying to tell you that for years. So, where's hot Andrew?"

"He's inside with the centerfold from the trailer park. She didn't want me to be around when they talked. Just to get some male attention. But Andrew and Kelly broke up, and I'm a bit afraid of what he's doing in there."

"He wants you," she says for the umpteenth time.

"No, Han. He doesn't. We're friends. He's had many opportunities considering Eva the bitch cancelled one of our rooms, and we had to share. Stop saying that already. It's getting annoying. I just want to find Lucas and get him back."

"You must be so nervous."

I clutch the phone tighter in my hand. "So nervous that I'm almost sick. I've put so much energy into wanting him that I'm afraid I'll be disappointed. And what if he sees me and doesn't want me? What if he doesn't even remember me?"

"Jaim, you had a thing with this guy for years. Of course he'll remember you. And you aren't that shy, pissed off, insecure girl you used to be in high school. You're beautiful and smart and pissed off, and the minute he sees you, he's going to be so overtaken by lust that he'll drag you into a closet, rip off your clothes and teach you a bit of biology."

"I don't think so. We'll probably go for a chaste cup of coffee or something. People change a lot in ten years, though. And what if we have nothing to talk about?"

"Do you still have the list Jack gave you?"

"Yes, but it's not like I can pull it out and start checking off answers. Should I memorize it?"

"Jaim, relax. Don't let Lucy's perfect vision of destiny get you all worked up. Just be yourself, and it will all flow from there."

"If he doesn't want her, he's an idiot," I hear Jack yell from somewhere in Han's apartment.

"Tell Jack thanks. You know, I can't believe you're having this kind of relationship."

"Hmmm. Neither can I," she says, her voice wistful.

"Han, don't you dare run away from him. I can hear it in your voice. Jack is amazing, and if you let him go, I swear I'll give his number to Eva."

She laughs, but there's a hollow sound to it. "I know, Jaim, it's just that-"

"It's just that you're scared out of your mind to really love someone. Don't do this."

She sighs, and I know that Jack has a lot of work ahead of him. But he doesn't seem to be running anywhere.

"We'll talk about it when I get home, okay?"

"Yeah. By the way, you won't like this, but I saw Eva and Derek together at 'Le Passage' last night."

I wait for the expected anger to dig into my chest. Nothing.

"That's nice."

"You don't care?"

"God no, they deserve each other. I should have set them up a long time ago, and I could have found Lucas ages ago. Did he talk to you?"

"He nodded in my general direction, and the second she got a look at me, she looked like she was going to spit nails."

"Excellent. I'd better go. I see Andrew coming out of the centerfold's house."

"Say hello for me," she says, lowering her voice seductively.

"Yeah, whatever. See ya."

"See ya."

I hang up and walk back over to Andrew.

"I'm really sorry about that. But I think she and Ray are perfect for each other. If they can stop talking about themselves long enough," he says.

"I don't think either of them is looking for ever-lasting love. But it will get us great ratings."

"Yeah," he says, eyes downcast.

"How are you doing?" I ask.

He rubs his left cheek thoughtfully and sighs.

"I'll be okay. It just feels surreal right now. When I go home, and she's not there, I'm sure it's going to hurt like hell, but right now, I feel this strange freedom. It's like having an empty Sunday. One of those days when you should be tying up loose ends or running around, and you don't have to do any of it, and you're sort of lost about what to do because you're so used to not having free time and then the pure joy of knowing the day is yours and you can do anything you want."

"You've been thinking about that one for awhile, haven't you?" I grin.

"The entire time Lisa was talking about herself."

"That's great you're so focused on the job."

"I got it done, didn't I?"

And I know he's not just talking about the show.

CHAPTER TWENTY-SEVEN

"So, what are your deal breakers?" I ask Andrew, blowing out a puff of smoke from the joint he's handed me.

Instead of watching television, we're sitting on the balcony of our hotel room after Andrew disappeared for awhile to procure some of the best pot I've ever had. I don't smoke that much, probably because Leah and Katie grew it themselves and smoked it all the time. They gave me nothing but vices to rebel against so instead of terrifying my parents by smoking weed, staying out late and getting arrested, I studied and came home early. They'd be so proud if they could see me right now.

"What do you mean 'deal breakers?'" he asks, looking confused.

Although that might be the drugs.

"What things would make you not want to be with someone? For example, anyone who has a problem with homosexuality would never get a second date. It's a mindset. Anyone with that attitude towards life wouldn't be someone I could be with."

He stretches his legs out and takes another toke. "Do you have a list of questions or something that you ask when you go on a date?"

"Well, I haven't been on many dates so I don't know. But after Derek, there are so many things I'd find out beforehand so I don't waste my time again."

"You've never been on a date?"

"I didn't say never. But, no, I haven't been on that many. I met Derek in a bar, I know so cliche, and we kind of just, um, started pretty quickly. And before Derek, there were guys I was seeing, but I haven't really had many guys come pick me up, take me out for dinner, that kind of thing."

"Yeah, I haven't had a real date either. Obviously, Kelly and I met before people even dated, I think we just hooked up at a party or something. Now, I'm going to have to go on dates? And get dressed up and pick women up and make small talk? That doesn't sound so appealing."

"Right now, you don't have to do anything."

"I think I've wasted my years." His heavy-lidded eyes are sad, but the spark is still twinkling somewhere in there. "I still can't believe it's over. You know, I tried to leave so many times, but she always begged me to stay. And I don't know why I did. Every time I knew that we were better off apart, but I couldn't imagine living without her. We never talked anymore, we didn't connect, and the sex, well, that was sporadic at best."

I blush, not knowing if I want to hear about his sex life or lack thereof. Actually, I know I don't.

"So, let's say you meet a girl now, what things would you not tolerate?" I smoothly change the subject.

"You first."

"Okay," I say, sipping from my cold beer. "So, first, anyone who's not cool with homosexuality. Second, a man who won't have sex with a girl when she has her period."

He spits out the mouthful of beer he's just drunk and starts laughing. I realize what I've just said and curse the truth serum I've smoked for making my mouth so loose.

"Are you serious? Oh, you're blushing! C'mon, it's so funny. But I don't understand why that's a deal breaker."

My face burns, and I try to deflect the conversation back to him to alleviate my total mortification. "So, now you."

"No way, Jaim. You have to explain that."

"Oh God, fine. If a guy has a problem with a menstrual cycle, imagine what he'll be like when she's pregnant. And, it's a natural part of life, it's just blood, and I want to be with someone who's completely comfortable."

"This sounds like something your mom has said."

"Oh, the way Leah would explain it would be a lot more detailed and informative. Okay, I'm done."

"Kelly didn't like to have sex when she had her period. I'm not sure she loved it at any other time, though."

"That's nice. I don't want to know. So what are your deal breakers?"

He takes a slow sip of his beer, swallows and bites his lip. "Okay, a woman who cares more about success and money and image than what's really important. And what I think is important is knowing what you want to do and doing it no matter how much money you make. A woman who wants to change me because I don't care if my hair's too long or my jeans are ripped or my shoes aren't the latest style. A woman who's just too damn perfect because I'm not perfect and I never will be. I don't want to be perfect because what's the point of living if you have nothing to learn?"

"Wow. You hate her."

"Right now, yes, I hate her. I hate her for making me feel like all the problems in our relationship were my fault. But I'm sure eventually I'll remember the good times, because there were a lot of good times. I just can't think of any at the moment."

"Are you scared?"

"Scared? What do you mean?"

I tuck my hair behind my ear. "I mean now that you're single again and your life begins. Because your life with Kelly is over, right? Eighteen years of being a couple and now you're on your own."

Andrew pushes his hair out of his face and rubs his chin. "Sure, I'm scared. I've stepped over land mines, touched leprosy victims and met with the heads of state, but I've never not known what happens next."

"I was more scared of being on my own, but I love it. I think it's because I have something to look forward to."

Shit! Damn pot. This is why I don't smoke the stuff.

"What is it you're looking forward to?" he asks, looking directly into my eyes and holding the gaze.

"Freedom. Let's drink to that."

We clink our beers, and I press my lips tightly together before I reveal tomorrow's plans. Oh my God! Tomorrow, I'm going to see Lucas.

"What are you smiling about?" he asks, grinning at me.

"I'm really happy for you that you finally ended it. I knew you were so unhappy, and, well, good for you, Andrew."

The wave of affection that crosses his face makes me feel guilty. I *am* happy for him, but it wasn't the reason I was smiling. We sit in comfortable silence, listening to the roar of the traffic on the street below us, and I turn my face towards the sun. Andrew's eyes are closed; a small smile is playing at the corner of his mouth.

"What?" I ask him.

He opens his eyes and looks directly into mine. "I'm actually happy. And I-" He pauses for a moment and looks away.

"You what?" I prod.

"Nothing. You're pretty amazing, Jamie."

I swallow the tears that suddenly spring to my eyes. I wonder if the best friendships are the ones you least expect.

"Jamie?"

"Mmm?"

"What are you doing with your life?"

And out of nowhere, the tears that sprang up before now roll down my face, and I don't know why I'm crying. And I can't stop. Water splashes from my face onto the concrete, and I put my head on my knees so he won't see it.

"Jamie? Jaim, what's wrong? What did I say? Why are you crying?" His arm is around my shoulders, and he's stroking lazy circles on my back. Instead of comforting me, it makes me cry harder.

"I don't know! Your question, it, hiccup, it, just, fuck, I never cry like this in front of people."

"Just cry. Come here," he says and folds me in his arms while my face soaks his t-shirt.

In all my years with Derek, he never saw me cry. Besides the bawling fest that Leah and Katie witnessed, the last person to see me cry like this was Lucas, and I don't understand why Andrew's question prompted this torrent of tears.

But the question remains: what am I doing with my life?

CHAPTER TWENTY-EIGHT

The next day, it takes us six hours to drive to Detroit. I know he wants to bring up my humiliating breakdown the evening before, but I'm pretending it never happened, and we barely talk the entire ride there. Instead, I've gone through every alternative, rap and hip hop CD in his collection, avoiding anything softer, because if I hear melancholic lyrics, I just might turn into one of those weeping women whose drama is always everyone else's problem.

"So, we'll check in at the hotel, and you're seeing your friend tomorrow?" he says as we pull up to the hotel at about 3:00 p.m.

"Yup."

He glances at me, and I look out the window to avoid his stare.

"Jaim? Listen, I-"

"It was the pot."

"Jamie-"

"I don't want to talk about it."

I cannot believe that I sobbed in front of Andrew. I can't believe I sobbed at all. But I know why. Even though I know that something good is about to happen to me with Lucas, what happens after that? This is why anticipation and planning can make your life such hell. Every time you wait for something to happen, after it does, there's that anti-climactic sadness that hovers over you until you find the next big thing you want. But beyond Lucas, I don't know what I want, and it sucks the air out of me.

We both get out of the car and grab our bags from the trunk. I know I should talk to him because he took me here just to be nice, and he is paying for it until I can afford to pay him back, but right now, I am so uncomfortable with how much of myself I revealed to him. And I want it back.

He holds open the door of the hotel, but before we get to the reception desk, he stops me. "Jamie, stop. We're friends, right?"

I look down at the bright red hotel carpet. "Yes."

"If we're really friends, you can tell me anything, and you can be yourself. You don't have to be so protective of yourself with me."

"If you mention the turtle analogy again, I *will* kill you," I say and continue walking.

"I unloaded all of my shit on you, and I don't do that so much. You know way more about my problems with Kelly than some of my closest friends. It's okay to be vulnerable."

"It's not that."

It's exactly that.

"I'm just really tired. In fact, I think I'll go to my room and take a nap after we check in."

I see his jaw tighten, but I want to be alone. All of this intimacy is too much for me. And I have Lucas to think about. We get the keys to our rooms, and before we part at the elevator, he says, "What time do you want to meet for dinner?"

"Well, I actually wouldn't mind having a few hours to myself after I see my friend. I need to do a couple of things."

"Fine."

"Is that okay?" I ask, knowing that he's pissed off, but not wanting to fix it right now. I just want to get away.

"Sure. Considering everything, I could do with some down time."

He seems cool about it. And why shouldn't he be? We only met a short time ago, and we owe each other nothing. But why do I feel so torn?

"Are you going to see your parents?"

"No."

"Don't they live here?"

"Yes."

"And?"

"And what? I can be as evasive as you. See you tomorrow."

Andrew walks away, and I'm left thinking that we're fighting. And for an instant, standing by myself in the lobby, all the people milling about and buzzing with frantic energy, I feel slightly lonely. That's probably because we've spent almost every waking moment together for days. But, this is it. Lucas—the One. And that's where my head should be right now.

I pick up my bag and walk alone to my room. As soon as I slide in the key card and open the door, I realize that I had promised to buy Andrew dinner for bringing me here. No wonder he hates me right now. I'll make it up to him. Later.

***

Once I'm in my hotel room, I go directly to the shower, but I'm shaking so hard from nerves and nausea that I nick myself in all sorts of painful places. Why is it that shaving cuts bleed forever? I've sliced both legs, bikini line, and that hard to reach area in the back. I sincerely doubt that I'll be naked tonight, but you never know.

I've laid out the three outfits I need to choose from. A wispy chiffon skirt and spaghetti strap tank top? Too glam for a college visit. And too dressy for a guy who had his shirt off most of the time I was with him. And his pants. No, can't go there. I need to choose and get over there. A pair of denim cut offs and a t-shirt? Even though I've been getting some exercise, the puckery flesh of my thighs does not make me want to choose those. Low-rise jeans and a plain black tank top? I think that's it. Simple, understated and me.

267

I spent too many years trying to be someone I'm not for Derek. I can't do that again. Lucas will have to take me as I am. And take me I hope he will. With a trembling hand, I try to apply my makeup, paying close attention to Hanna's voice in my head. Just a smidgen of base, some mascara, eyeshadow, blush and lip gloss. If he kisses me, the lip gloss will smear everywhere. Plain lipstick is better.

Is this what women have to do every time they go on a date? I'm exhausted already, and I haven't even done my hair. Luckily, the tremendously expensive haircut is still easy to recreate, and in minutes, it's falling in soft layers to my chin. It's amazing that one haircut has changed my self-perspective.

And, yes, the expensive style is partly the reason, but it's also because for the first time in ages, I feel pretty. For once, when I catch my image in a reflective surface (and trust me, I've noticed that I'm surrounded by them—car windows, rearview mirrors, lacquer table tops), I smile and don't cringe like I used to.

Not only did I have the guts to leave Derek, but I'm actually on the way to see Lucas of my own initiative. Okay, and Lucy and Hanna's. But I'm the one doing it. I close the door to my hotel room as quietly as I can and practically dance to the elevator, running soundlessly past Andrew's room, because I don't want him to see me all jittery and wonder where I'm going.

And I feel awful because I know he thinks I'm using him, and I'm not. I really like spending time with Andrew, and he offered to do this, but he just got a little too much into my head. And that's kind of reserved for Lucas. Otherwise why am I here at all?

The slamming of my heart against my ribcage is getting progressively louder as the elevator reaches the ground floor. Should I call the college first so he knows I'm coming? No, I want the element of surprise. I can't take the car, and I don't know if we'll be drinking later (I'm pretty damn certain I'll need a drink, actually, I need a drink right now) so I ask the doorman to hail me a cab.

Once I'm nestled on the cracked leather backseat, I take a deep, steadying breath and hold it. Exhaling, I feel slightly calmer, but no less terrified. This is the craziest thing I've ever done. Who goes back to find the guy they slept with ten years ago? Me obviously.

Movies of memories play in my mind from the time my red bra got caught in the car door, and he drove away with it whipping in the wind to the sadness in his eyes when he talked about his dad. Lucas and I were drawn together by loss, I think. For me, it was the loss of my parents' marriage and for him, it was his dad. Lucas kept all of his dad's letters even though he wrote him maybe once a year. I wonder where his dad is now. Even though he was a raging alcoholic, Lucas mostly just talked about his dad's brief flashes of functional fatherhood because all he wanted was for his father to love him.

My mind is a jumble of conflicting thoughts, and I'm so lost in the noises in my head that I don't realize we've pulled up to Wayne County until the driver turns around and asks me to pay him. As I hand him the money, he squints at me. "Are you okay, miss? You look a bit pale."

Great. Even the cab driver notices how scared I am.

I smile at him and answer, "Oh, I'm fine, thanks. Hot day."

He hands me my change, and I'm standing on the driveway leading to the front doors of the college. I whip out my compact (a present from Hanna) and check my nose and teeth for any danglies. All good. There's a slight pink flush in my cheeks, and the skin under my left eye is twitching.

I walk up the concrete steps and open the glass doors. Inside, there are only a few young students milling around because it's summer, and I spin my head around in a frenzy to see if Lucas is somewhere among them. But I can only picture him in his twenties, and he is definitely not going to be one of the kids flirting, shoving someone or running outside for a smoke.

Okay, I need to go to the reception desk or something. My leaden legs take me to a small office just off the student center. With her hands flying over a keyboard, a pinched brunette is sitting at the reception desk and making angry faces at her computer screen. She reminds me of Jeanette, and that is exactly what I need to get the courage to ask her where Lucas is. Lucas's mom loved me. She used to sit on the porch, smoking cigarettes and chatting with me as if I was part of the family. I'd love to see her again too. Maybe I will if this all works out.

"Um, excuse me?" I whisper.

She ignores me.

"Um, excuse me?" A decibel louder this time. It appears I've lost my voice.

"I can't hear you. Speak up!" she barks, still glaring at her screen.

"Um, hi, um, I'm looking for Lucas Simpson." When I say his name, a wave of dizziness overtakes me, and I have to clutch the corner of her desk to stop myself from keeling over.

"Are you okay? You're not going to throw up on my desk, are you?" she asks, while moving away from me.

"No, no, sorry, I'm fine, it's a hot day, and I haven't had enough water." God, I sound like Rachel with this incessant babbling.

"How can I help you?" Miss Pinched asks rudely.

I find my voice and the dash of confidence I need. "I'm looking for Lucas Simpson. He teaches biology here. Can you tell me where his office is?"

She examines me, her eyes resting on the pulsating skin below my left eye. The twitch has spread, and her stare is making it worse. Finally, she tears her eyes away from my alien-abducted face and taps away again on her keyboard, presumably to find the answer to my question.

I know only a few seconds have passed, but it feels like days while she locates his name.

"Oh, I'm sorry, but he's on vacation for the next month. Are you interested in one of his September classes?" she asks me.

I slump despondently, more disappointed than I've ever been. I came all this way, lied to Andrew, and for what? For nothing. Why the hell didn't I call first to find out if he'd be here? Fuck, I'm so upset. I must see him. I can't take the waiting anymore.

"Miss, would you like to take one of his biology classes?" she repeats, annoyed with me for wasting her precious typing time.

Yes, I want one of his biology classes. Sex 101. "No, no thanks. I'm an old friend of his."

"Do you want his email address?"

"No thank you. I'll just come back in a month."

A month is forever. I drag myself outside and back to the hotel where I lie in a sad heap on my bed. I turn on the television (back to my old ways), and for the next while, I stare at the people moving across the screen. I'm not even watching it. I'm just so sad. Don't I deserve a break? Lucy would say that this is a sign. Of what, I don't know, but maybe it's a sign for me to stop. Stop being an idiot and looking for love in a place I'll never find it. Maybe I should put out a personal ad. Lumpy Lonely Lady Looking for Love. And then the phone rings.

"Hello?" I answer flatly.

"Hi. I heard you come back a while ago."

It's Andrew. He would be the perfect person to talk to about this, but of course, I can't. I can't deal with how exposed I feel after crying all over his t-shirt. I want him to think I'm strong.

"Oh yeah, I just went to see my friend. How are you doing?"

"I'm alright. It comes and goes in waves. One minute I feel free and so happy, and the next minute, I feel like shit and depressed."

271

"Yeah, that's how it goes." I dig my nail into the sole of my foot and start pulling.

"So how's your friend?"

"Um, he's good. We went for a, uh, coffee. I know him from college."

God, lying to him hurts. It actually hurts, but I have no choice.

"Are you busy now?"

I look at my foot. "Now? No."

"So you got your stuff done?"

"Um, yeah."

"Are you up for grabbing some dinner and a drink?"

No. I want to wallow in self-pity and stupidity all night. But, he's my boss, he's my friend, and I owe him.

"Sure, but can you give me an hour? I need to call a friend first."

"Sure, I'll come and knock on your door at eight."

I hang up, hold my forehead in my hands and sigh hugely. Only Hanna can make me feel better.

"I just feel so stupid," I tell her after phoning the store and filling her in on the most useless day in my life.

"Yeah, you should have called to check, but think of it this way. Now you have more gym time, and you'll look even more gorgeous when you do see him."

"But a month? I can't wait for another month. God, I am now one of those people I hate." I slap the comforter with my hand. "The people who plan for all the good things to happen and then bide their time until they do. I won't enjoy anything else until the month is over."

"Aren't you being a touch dramatic?"

"No! I want to see him now!" I wail.

"I know, Jaim, but unless you find him on vacation, you won't. So, work, live and you'll see him eventually."

272

I make a face at the phone. "You're not helping."

"I don't know what to tell you. You can't change the fact that he's not there, can you?"

"No. But I also can't keep doing this. And I feel so bad for lying to Andrew when I could only have gotten here because of him."

"Lied about what?"

"I told him I came here to see a friend, and it's not true."

"Sure it's true. Andrew doesn't need to know everything about you. Unless you want him to know. Unless you like him."

"I think he's a great friend, and he makes me feel like I can tell him anything, but when I do tell him stuff, I cry."

"You cry? You? Cry? Are you serious?"

Hanna knows me so well, and I know she's so surprised that anyone can make me cry.

"Totally. I'm so different with him, and I know I've only known him a short time, but his friendship is so important to me. But that's not really the issue. The issue is that I'll never see Lucas, I'll wonder forever what could have been, and I'll just keep going on like this, single and miserable, probably living with a roomful of stuffed cats, rocking in my chair and holding pictures from my past."

"No. You'll probably be sitting in front of the television in a roomful of stuffed cats," Hanna says, laughing.

"You're so good at making me feel better," I say sarcastically.

"I'm just teasing you. What are you doing tonight?"

"Going out for dinner with Andrew."

"Hmmm..." she intones.

"Oh, give it up already. I gotta go."

"Jaim, everything's going to work out, okay? You just have to be patient."

"Yeah, that's my best quality."

She laughs. "Just think about the fact that Eva has to have sex with Derek, and you can do it with hot Spanish men."

"Is that supposed to be comforting?"

"It's just supposed to show you that you can do anything you want, and you're finally free."

I hang up and lean back on the bed, existentialist dilemmas making part of me wish that I could be back with Derek, letting him make all of the decisions so I wouldn't have to think. With freedom comes choice and responsibility, and I have no idea which is the best direction for me. Stop looking for Lucas and wonder forever or find him and potentially destroy any self-confidence that I have gained in the last few weeks? Maybe I'll become a relationship communist and let everyone else do my thinking for me. Then, there's no question of being happy or not; there's no questioning at all.

CHAPTER TWENTY-NINE

At dinner, Andrew alternates between staring morosely into his beer and talking my ear off. The gist of his rambling is that Kelly is a total bitch and treated him like her pet project for a long time. She even lined up his clothes the night before he went to work so she could approve what he wore. I can't believe there is someone worse than Derek. And, wait for this little juicy tidbit, she won't have sex doggie style because it's disrespectful to women. All of this lovely information that I don't want to know. I can't even imagine what Derek is telling Eva about me. My cellulite has probably been an enthralling topic of conversation.

"And," he continues on with yet another Kelly story, "she threw out all my stuff that she hated every time I was away. My favorite ratty chair, old Yale t-shirts because they had holes, souvenirs I'd brought back from other countries. I'd give her such shit, and she'd promise not to do it again, but she couldn't resist having total control. Like when I visited an orphanage in South Africa with children whose parents had died of AIDS, and one little girl gave me this bracelet she had made. It wasn't high quality or anything like that, but it meant a lot to me. Kelly thought it was disgusting and was worried that it was disease ridden so she tossed it. Can you believe it?"

Yes.

"Andrew, enough. You have a whole slew of reasons why it's better that it's over so now you need to enjoy the freedom. She won't be throwing out your stuff anymore or telling you what to do. I think you're scared because now you'll have to make your decisions on your own."

"Pot? Kettle?" he retorts.

"Yes, it's true that I was a bit freaked out after I left Derek because I hadn't lived alone or paid for everything by myself. But, I'm trying. You're just stewing."

He takes a bite of his veggie burger (damn Leah), and I chew on my so rare it's still alive steak. He puts his pseudo-burger down, pushes the hair out of his eyes, and smiles.

"Okay."

"Okay what?"

"I'm done stewing. I really appreciate all of this, Jamie. I probably couldn't have gotten through the last few days without you. You've listened to me blabber on about Kelly, and I haven't asked you a damn thing. I'm sorry. I know you're worried about your roommates and money and all of that."

With the whole Lucas thing, I'd actually forgotten that when we head home tomorrow, I'm going to have to face Slutty and Sluttier. I cut another piece of bloody steak and shove it in my mouth.

"Thanks for reminding me. I think I'll just let it go and pretend I don't know. I really hate conflict, and what they do isn't my business. They do it in the office with the door closed, and it's not like other people come over and get involved. And I grew up with enough sex in the house to be able to deal with everything."

"You had a lot of sex in the house?" he asks, eyes widening, forkful of salad poised in mid-air.

"No! Katie and Leah. Anyway, I have too much work to do before the show airs to think about anything else."

"Are you thinking of dating again?" he asks, shoving the oily greens in his mouth. His jaw looks very defined when he chews, and I find myself watching him instead of answering the question.

He catches me looking and stops chewing. "Jamie?

"Yeah?"

"Are you thinking of dating again?"

276

I go hot and drink my beer to cover the red spots that have inevitably rushed to my cheeks. "Um, sure, I mean, yeah, I'll date when, uh, when I'm ready."

"Well, it won't be a problem for you."

"What do you mean?"

"You're gorgeous. I'm sure men hit on you all the time."

"Ha ha. That's funny."

He looks at me very seriously. "I'm totally serious, Jamie. Not only are you beautiful, but you're so much fun to hang out with. Life is never boring when you're around."

I don't think Derek ever told me I was gorgeous. He told me how to become it, but I don't think he saw me that way. And I don't know what to say. This is the second time Andrew's said that to me. I always hate when I get a compliment, because I'm not sure if I should say thank you, compliment him back or ignore it. I choose the last option.

"Do you think you'll stay in your apartment?" I ask, changing the subject back to him.

Either he notices or he doesn't, but he doesn't say anything about his last comment. We talk for another hour and then head back to the hotel. It's been a long, disappointing day, more than he knows, and I need to sleep. And think.

When we get to our rooms, Andrew pulls me towards him in a tight hug, and it's just what I needed. Because I don't often touch people, I'm usually extremely stiff when someone hugs me. But in his arms, my head smushed against his warm chest, I feel safe. And I hug him back.

To mask my vulnerability, I reach up and ruffle his hair. "You really need a haircut, you know."

He grins. "Yeah, I know."

I watch him open his door and go inside. As his door quietly closes and I stand for a moment on the scarlet hall carpet, I miss him. I open my own door and fall straight into bed without washing my face or brushing my teeth. I go to sleep to the sound of the humming air conditioner and dreams of Lucas teaching naked.

***

I'm back at work, and I'm just about to sit down at my desk when I see a flash of black from the corner of my eye.

"Jaim!"

It's Lucy and the flash of black is her hair, the only thing I can see clearly because she's dressed in white on white and blends into the wall behind me.

"God, Luce, you scared me."

I sit down and try to find my computer mouse, but it's buried under the clutter of crap on my desk.

"What happened? Did you see him? Did you sleep with him? When can I meet him?"

I glance over at Eva's desk and sigh with relief that she's not here. "No, I didn't see him, talk to him or sleep with him. Andrew was nice enough to take me there, and Lucas is on fucking vacation. There was no point in going at all."

Lucy leans against my desk, her own disappointment clear from her turned down mouth and slumping shoulders. "Oh crap, that sucks." Then she smiles. "Well, don't despair. It just means that that's not how you're going to get him. What's your next step?"

"What makes you so sure I have a next step?" I ask and put the ends of my hair in my mouth. It's just long enough to do that, and I'm stressed. Nothing's working out like I thought it would.

"Because this is how it's supposed to be. Don't worry. I *know* you'll see him. Just because it's later rather than sooner means you'll be even more excited."

"Do I look excited to you?" I ask.

278

She brings her face close to mine and says, "Jaim, you look better than you have in years. Why don't you just call him and leave a message?"

I move my face back and grimace. "Because every time I go to pick up the phone, I start having seizures and can't hold it in my hand."

"Just do it."

I move my finger around the dust that's collected on my desk in the last week (even the cleaners were scared off by my mess), wondering if the answer is there somehow.

"I should just give up. But he's all I think about. I constantly run through all these memories. Like he used to stroke my hair when we watched a movie, and it felt so good. You know I've never liked people touching me, but I just melted when he did it."

"So what do you have to lose if you call him?"

"My pride?"

"Didn't Derek take that years ago?" She laughs.

I smack her arm and glare at her. "Ha, ha." Then my face falls. "Please don't tell anyone, Luce. This whole thing is becoming pathetic."

"Of course I won't say anything. But it's only pathetic if you do nothing about it."

"I'm so sick of talking about this. What's up with you?"

"Do you remember Leticia?"

"From the bar? The hot little waitress in the kilt?"

"Yeah," she says and grins. "I think we're seeing each other. She took me out for dinner last night."

Lucy always has mini-relationships. For about three months, she'll be gaga over someone, ready to pick out china patterns, and then, boom, it'll be over.

"Is she girlfriend material?" I ask.

"I'm not bored yet if that means anything. She's hot, we can

279

talk about everything, and she's wicked in bed."

I hold up my hand. "Enough. I don't need to hear the details."

"But the details are the best part. Can I tell you about her tongue? It's-"

"Luce, I'm not getting any sex these days so be nice. But that's great. Really. When are you seeing her again?"

"She's coming to my place for dinner. I think I'll eat it off her."

I wrinkle my nose at her, but I laugh. Opposites really do attract. I could never be as open as Lucy. She flicks her tongue at me, walks back to her desk, and I consider picking up the phone and just doing it.

Luckily, I'd memorized all of Lucas's numbers because the papers (the home and work numbers and short bio Hanna had given me) are also lost somewhere in the disorganized mess I call my desk. I should find them because I don't want that information out there for anyone to see (especially Eva), but after searching through each page again and again, I still can't find them. But I did find the mouse so I'm sure they're here somewhere.

But Lucas isn't my only problem at the moment. When Andrew and I got back last night, Chris and Amy weren't home, but they left me a note telling me they went on a trip. Probably a porn festival. So, we didn't have the uncomfortable conversation that I know we need to. I'd be perfectly willing to pretend I don't know, but Andrew pointed out that it would be a lot easier to live with them if I'm honest. I guess I'll just have to do it when they get back.

By lunchtime, I still haven't called Lucas. Instead, I get to watch Derek bring Eva back after taking her out for lunch. A long lunch, obviously, because she's been gone for hours, and I haven't had the pleasure of seeing her today. Now I get to see her *and* Derek. That's always nice for a Monday. And I'd be lying if I said it doesn't hurt at all.

Only a few times in our entire relationship did he come get me and take me out for lunch. My job was ridiculous for him, but he's so clearly smitten with Eva's great desire to fit into his "Crate and Barrel" lifestyle that what she does is unimportant.Or maybe it's because she's so gorgeous. What was he with me for if that was who he wanted? I truly think he never left me because once Derek had decided what his entire life's plan would be, and because we were already together, he just assumed that I was the woman he would spend the rest of his life with. And maybe he thought it'd be easy to mold me into his vision of the perfect wife, but it wasn't ever *me* that he wanted.

After about five surreptitious (or so he thinks) glances in my direction, Derek swaggers over to my desk. I expect him to take a roll of bills out of his pocket and start handing them out like flyers. He walks around my desk and leans over me from behind my chair.

"Hello, Jamie," he says.

"Hiya. Hope you enjoyed your little lunch."

"Still as snide as ever I see."

"Still as anal as always I see."

He is the only person who makes me this nasty. I don't even like myself when he's around. And it's not until right this second that the full force of that makes sense to me. He made me dislike myself. No, no one can make you do anything. I disliked myself by staying with someone I didn't love anymore. And for becoming a person I didn't recognize.

"You know, don't you, that Eva is much more suited to my lifestyle. My mother adores her. The three of us just went for lunch at the nicest restaurant."

I glance up from my keyboard (where I'm inputting the data for the show—questions to ask, such as "And where did you see Lisa again?" "What, Ray Man, was your fatal mistake in high school?")

281

and stare at him. And the corners of my mouth turn up in a smile.

"You know, Derek, you're amazing," I say, turning around to face him.

It'd be a lot easier if he didn't look so good. Because even though I have almost zero attraction left for him, he is still an indisputably good-looking man. His full lips, that razor sharp jaw and cunning brown eyes are the features of a model in a GQ photo shoot of the "Well-Dressed Man at Lunch." And that was the problem all along. Derek acts as if he's just stepped out of a magazine and into a life. I don't know who the real man is.

"I am?" he says, and his chest puffs out a bit.

"Amazingly obvious. I don't care who you fuck although I'd be a bit wary of that one."

"I'm not fucking her, as you so eloquently put it. We're dating. She has too much respect for herself to have a tawdry one night stand." He smirks.

I peer at him carefully to see if that was an insult. It's not really a one night stand, is it, if it turns into a five year relationship?

"She said no, huh?" I sneer right back at him and pretend to calmly go back to my typing. Like I don't give a shit. In reality, there is a deafening roar in my ears, and I feel queasy. But there is noway I want him to see that.

"And I see that not much else has changed," he says, examining my plain black dress pants (although they are from Marshall Field's and have a stylish red belt looped through the belt holes) and wrinkled white button down.

"What do you want?!" I snap.

Enough of this banter. Not only do I have to organize the show, but I have to get up the balls to call Lucas without throwing up in the garbage can under my desk, and I don't need Derek around during any of that.

"I just want to know when you're going to start paying me the money," he says, feeling his bicep. And checking his reflection out in my computer screen.

"Oh, it'll be in your account post haste. Are you fucking kidding me? Just leave me alone. Just the sight of you depresses me because I start to think about how miserable I was. I can't believe you turned out to be such an asshole."

His jaw clenches, and he spits out at me, "When we met, I liked your spirit and freedom. But you never tried to make me reach for better things. You never backed me up, never supported my career. You wanted me to be a loser so I could fit into your deranged, dysfunctional life."

I know he's just insulted my family and has thrown a huge dagger in my general direction, but I focus on the other things he said. Is it true that I never supported him? Did I not try to make his life more enjoyable? I guess not. He wants the car, house, big man job and luxuries. I never wanted anything to do with it. Yes, part of our downfall is my fault, and I can accept that. But now, I want him to snuggle up with the ice princess so I can go back to Lucas.

"Whatever. I don't have time for this. Derek, it's better if we don't see each other. I don't want to see you, and I know you want to, but you can't hurt me. It's too late for that. And I really don't see why I have to be reminded of everything that you think is wrong with me or with my family. Got it?"

Derek looks directly into my eyes with that very sexy, smoldering stare he's perfected over the years. Found in an article entitled "10 Surefire Ways to Make Her Pant" in "Details." And bloody hell, it still has the power to make my heart jump a little.

"Jamie, never think I didn't love you. I did."

And he walks away. What was that?! He treats me like garbage for ten minutes and then leaves me with that sentence floating around in my head? He is one total mindfuck.

Derek finally struts out of the office (after sticking his tongue down Eva's throat, and I'm sure it's just to do some tongue exercises), and I feel someone watching me. I look up from my computer and make eye contact with Eva. Uh oh. Why is she staring at me with a smile as wide as my ass?

I sweep my eyes across my desk. Oh my God, the papers! How could I have been so stupid to leave a copy here while Andrew and I were gone? Shit, shit, shit! But how would she know? Lucas could just be another guest, right?

For the rest of the day, my jaw is being ground into little bits (and it hurts so much because I haven't done it in weeks) because I'm trying to act like everything's normal, and I can't even look for the missing papers because every time I glance up, she's still staring, a malicious glint in her eyes. And I'm just waiting for something to happen, but by six o'clock, nothing has. But that might just be part of Eva's plan to make me suffer. I grab my bag and get up to leave. I don't even make it two steps before she's standing dangerously close to me.

She looks at my stomach, laughs, and tells me, "You really have let yourself go. Derek's right."

Breathe. Don't make her any madder than she already is. Information is power, and I have no idea what she knows. Relax, Jamie, or she'll notice that I'm sweating.

"Yes, Derek likes his women loose and slutty."

Damn, I can't help myself.

"You fucked with the wrong person, Jamie. If you thought it was bad before, you have no idea what I can do to you. I was in a sorority, and you were what? In band? I know how to make women suffer, and you, oh you are going to pay big time for everything you've done to make everyone here hate me. Everyone thinks you're so nice and easy and sweet. They don't know what a fucking twat you are."

And suddenly, the truth dawns on me like a bright shining

strobe light. I take a step towards her and bring my head so close to hers that I can see where she missed a spot with her foundation.

"Are you jealous of me, Eva?"

She snorts. "Jealous of you? Of what?" she spits at me.

I mean, really, she just spit on me. I actually don't think it was intentional, but it's pretty gross nonetheless.

"Jealous of all the people I have in my life, of being liked at this show, of being with Derek first. *I* am not the reason that everyone here hates you. You did that to yourself. I think you just want everything I have. But, Eva, don't you know that all of it will always be out of your reach?"

I'm strangely calm, and the only sound I can hear is her spluttering.

"Really, Fart and Fall?" she says and stretches her lips into a diabolical grin.

That asshole! I can't believe he told her. Once when Derek and I were having sex (in the early years), I was laughing so hard that I fell off the bed, and, oh God, well, I farted as I hit the floor. And the fact that he told Eva is just the cruelest thing he's ever done. But as mortified as I am, I'm also giddy with relief because I know that I'm right. She's jealous of me, and it kills her.

"Very clever. Say what you want, Eva. Now that I know why you've been such a bitch to me all these months, I'm going home." And I can't resist a final jab. Fart and Fall strikes again. "You know, you should really see someone about that paranoia. Oh, and you might want to get a bit of Botox if you're going to be with Derek. Wrinkles do nothing for him."

As coolly as I can, I walk to the elevator and repeatedly press the button to make it come faster. I can hear her behind me, and there is no way I want to be cooped up in a small space with her for any length of time. The elevator comes, and I get in. She's right behind me, but instead of getting in with me, she smiles slowly, narrows her eyes and just stares at me until the door closes.

I breathe for the first time in hours. My stomach hurts, and sweat is plastering my shirt to my back. And the air conditioner's on high. Now for the next fun part of this perfect day. I need to go home and face Amy and Chris. I can't even remember the easy and carefree life I had before the Lucas thing. And right now, I'd go back to being miserable with Derek over any of this.

CHAPTER THIRTY

"J! I missed you so much!"

When I unlock the door, Amy is racing towards me (today wearing a red tank top with a pony on the front, God, I hope they're not into bestiality) and crushes me in a smothering hug. I stiffen, but I try to hug her back. As her spectacular breasts press against my bony chest, I feel incredibly uncomfortable.

"Hi, Amy, how are you?" I ask, untangling myself from her arms.

"Awesome! Chris and I went to New York for a few days. How was your business trip?"

Amy would probably be a great person to get some advice from about this whole Eva thing, but I need to tell her I know her secret before we talk about anything else. I would never have expected to become friends with a girl like Amy, but friends we are.

"Good, good. Were you in New York for business or pleasure?" The word 'pleasure' gets stuck in my throat, and I squeak it out. Amy blushes and ignores the question.

"Do you want to go out and get a drink or something? Do you want to go to the gym?" she chirps.

"Um, Amy, there's, uh, there's something I need to talk to you about."

Her face drains of color, and I'm sure she knows what's coming. Instead of looking ashamed, she sets her mouth in a hard line and frowns. Sweet Amy is not always so sweet.

"So you know."

"Yes, I know."

She looks me straight in the eye and says nothing. I finally see what years of abuse have done to her. All of a sudden, Amy's face has morphed into a much older, harder version, and I'm slightly intimidated.

She waves a finger in my face. "Don't you dare judge me. This is what I do. This is what I've always done. And I like it."

"Amy, I don't care what you do for a job, I just wanted you to know that I know so there are no secrets between us."

She crosses her arms over her chest. "So how did you find out?"

And here I lie.

"I was surfing the web, and I ended up there somehow. How I know doesn't matter. I really am fine with it."

She shoves my shoulder and barks, "You don't need to be anything about it! This is my life, and my house, and you don't need to live here."

I rub my shoulder where she's just smacked me. She's stronger than she looks.

"Amy, aren't you listening? I'm not like your other roommates. Look, my mom's a lesbian, my sister was conceived through an injection of my dad's sperm, I have some interesting life experience myself. I'll be honest that at first, I was shocked. And, Chris, well, Chris seemed so-"

"Shy? He is shy. This is the only way he can come out of his shell. And we are totally there for each other. It's not like it's just me up there, and God, my stepfather took enough pictures of me anyway so this isn't any different."

I take her small hand in mine and try to draw her close to me, but she's stiff and unwieldy to my advances.

"Amy, honestly, you've been so good to me and for no reason. You were there when I needed a friend, and we are friends. Don't feel you have to defend yourself to me. Ever. Okay?"

Amy wrinkles up her nose, and with no warning, fat tears spill from her eyes and down her face. She drops her defensive stance and whispers, "Really? You don't think I'm a whore?"

"I won't pretend to understand why you do it, but God, no. Of course not. I think you're beautiful and kind and wonderful."

She wipes her cheeks. "I don't have any girlfriends, you know. Once people know what I do, they distance themselves. And I have no family. All I have is Chris, and this," she says, gesturing to her body.

"Oh, Amy, you have so much more than that. And I *am* your friend. I don't have many friends either because I'm so damn self-protective all the time. We're good for each other, hey?"

She sniffs, smiles through her tears and pulls me in for a hug. "Your mom is a lesbian? That's like really cool."

I relax into the hug, and you know what? It feels kind of nice. But, as she's resting her head on my shoulder, I remember the predicament I'm in, and I heave a deep sigh.

"What's wrong?" she asks, noticing the tension in my body.

"Oh God, Amy, I've screwed up big time. I can't believe how badly. I'm in so much trouble, I don't know what to do."

"Are you pregnant?" she lifts her head from my shoulder and glances down at my belly.

"It might look that way, but no. I'd need to have sex to get pregnant. I don't even know where to start."

"At the beginning," says Amy and leads me into the living room.

I tell her everything from the years with Lucas, the letter, Derek, going to Detroit and not finding Lucas, and my epiphany about Eva. When I'm finished, her mouth is a big O.

"You have a lot more pent up than I originally thought. Wow. This is like quite the mess. But, no worries. It's easily fixed."

"How?" I snivel and throw my hands in the air.

"Well, first, you've got to get in touch with Lucas immediately because you'll regret it if you don't. That's like total destiny. You guys had something special as kids so imagine how it could be now. Yeah, you've like got to call him now. Next, you must keep an eye on that bitch Eva at all times. She's already dating Derek, and for sure, she'll find something to destroy you. And, it's like pretty cool that you're trying to find your fuck buddy. It's also kinda deranged, but it's nice to know we all have our secrets."

"That's what I feel the worst about. Andrew, my boss, and I have become pretty good friends, and he has no idea why we really went to Detroit. It's not a big deal, but, still."

"He'll never know. And even if he does find out, if you guys are like really friends, he should be happy for you."

"I guess, yeah, but I didn't exactly tell him the whole truth."

"And you didn't exactly lie. We'll just do what we have to do. Did you find the papers and bring them home?"

"The papers?" I ask, confused.

"With Lucas's information. Did you bring them home?"

My stomach plummets to my feet, and my blood runs icy cold. I slowly shake my head.

"You didn't? Jamie, how could you leave them there? You need to go back now and get them!"

"But they were gone!"

"Eva sounds like a total bitch, but not stupid. She wouldn't just take the papers. She probably copied them and put them somewhere else so you would know that she's seen them."

"I looked, but I was so scared that she knew something that I probably didn't look hard enough. But, anyway, the office is closed now, and I can't get in."

"Can you call Andrew and tell him you left your wallet there or something? You need to get those back tonight before she gets to them."

"I'll go in early tomorrow. No, I won't sleep if I wait. Will you

290

come with me?"

"Of course. Go call Andrew, and I'll just change."

"Can I ask a stupid question?"

"Sure."

"What's with all the animals?"

Her eyes light up, and she gives me a huge silvery smile.

"I want to be a vet. I don't want to be in porn forever, and once I hit thirty, I won't be able to anyway. The money's amazing, and when I have enough to go to veterinary school, I'll stop."

And off she goes to change while I think of a reason to need Andrew to open the office for me. Not my wallet, because I won't be able to plant it and retrieve it while he's there. Why not work stuff? I'll just tell him I have to get work finished before tomorrow.

"Andrew?" I say after calling his cell. "I need a favor."

CHAPTER THIRTY-ONE

"This reminds me of that scene from 'My Best Friend's Wedding,'" Amy says, giggling, as Andrew is unlocking the door and turning off the alarm.

I glare at her eye, narrowing my eyes in warning, but I think the excitement of our little mission is making her ramble, and she doesn't realize what she's saying.

"Remember when Juliana tried to get Michael fired and sent the email off by mistake and had to get back to the office before it was too late?"

"Oh yeah, that was funny."

So not funny.

"I loved that movie!" Amy exclaims.

I know she's trying her damnedest to distract Andrew, hoping to keep his attention long enough for me to grab the papers without him seeing anything on them, but I wish she'd shut up.

"I never saw that movie. Who's in it?" Andrew smiles at her.

I'm sure he's picturing her naked on top of Chris, but at least his attention isn't on me.

"Julia Roberts. Have you seen all of her movies? Now that she has like kids and everything, I wonder if she's going to keep acting. She's hasn't like been in many movies. Oh, Andrew, is this your office? Can you show me your office?"

Amy jumps up and down and claps her hands, making her perfect breasts land right at eye level with Andrew's head. I'm starting to realize that the innocent and bouncy airhead I thought I'd moved in with is a clever and manipulative woman of many talents. I even admire her.

He beams at her, thrilled by the attention (and the curvy

292

sweetness of her, I'm sure) and leads her into his office. While they're there, I run to my desk and search for the papers, but they're definitely gone. The papers are fucking gone!

I tear open drawers, my heart crushing my breastbone, get on my knees to look under the desk, but nothing. Nothing!

"Jamie? What are you doing?"

I can see Andrew's sandals from my crawling position. If I lick his feet, will he forgive me? Hmm, he has very nice feet. Not buffed and pedicured like Derek's, but tidy and soft-looking. I raise my head to say something and bang the top of my head against my desk.

"Ow! Fuck!" I scream.

"Are you okay? Get up. What are you looking for on the floor?" he asks.

I stand up slowly and let the blood rush back to my head. That really hurt.

"I'm fine," I tell him, rubbing the top of my head. "I was looking for some of my materials, but I must have already finished them and put them away. Huh, not thinking today," I say with a sickly smile.

He looks puzzled at my ineptness and slightly pissed off that I brought him here for nothing. Nothing but my impending demise.

"I'm so sorry I dragged you here. I don't know what's wrong with me."

"Don't worry. Take me out for dinner, and you're forgiven."

"Oh, Andrew, I can't. I, um, I promised Amy that I'd help her with something."

His eyes flit to the ground, and when he looks up, they're half lowered in what I think is disappointment.

"Oh, okay then, I guess I'll just lock up."

"I'm sorry. How about another time?"

I just want to get home and crawl into bed, but Andrew did me a big favor. And I'd be happy to go, just not now.

"It's not a big deal, Jamie. Whatever."

He's pretty quiet in the elevator on the way down and doesn't say anything when he walks to his car parked in front of the building. "Can I give you a lift?" he asks, tight-lipped.

He's angry, and I'm not sure why. Probably because I dragged him out at night for nothing.

"It's okay. I don't want to put you out anymore than I have. I'm really sorry about this."

"Just get in the car, okay?"

I nod, and Amy and I get in the car. She's trying to keep up the talking, but neither Andrew nor I are responding much. We pull up in front of our house, and I touch his shoulder to thank him. He stiffens.

"I'll see you tomorrow," he says flatly and speeds off in a cloud of dust and screeching brakes.

"What was that about?" Amy asks.

"I have no idea, but that's not my problem right now. What the hell am I going to do? She took them. I know she did. Oh my God, what if she calls him? What if she sleeps with him? What if he wants to marry her?"

I'm acting like a lunatic now, I do realize that, but I'm sure Eva will do whatever she possibly can to make me suffer.

"There's nothing you can do until tomorrow. We need to do something to take our mind off things. Do you like dancing?"

"No dancing. How about we watch television? That's what I usually do when I'm like this. And 'American Idol' is on."

"I love that show!"

We settle ourselves on the couch, both sprawled at opposite ends, eating chips and watching television until Chris gets home. He grunts at me, and they disappear into the office to "work." I stay up all night, grinding my jaw, sucking my hair and biting my nails.

***

In the morning, I ache from my self-mutilation, and I can't even choke down a cup of coffee. That's how bad I feel. I know that when I get to the office today, something horrible will happen, and Eva will have some excruciating torture planned for me. I'm glad we're on the third floor otherwise I might just toss myself from the window and end my misery now. Or maybe I'll throw her headfirst into traffic. Do they have televisions in prison?

I have no idea what I'm wearing, and I decide to walk to work to calm myself down and think of all the different scenarios that might await me. I actually have to stop and throw up in a garbage can on the way, which doesn't make me smell or look any better than when I left the house. It's not until I'm in a gas station bathroom that I realize my shirt is on inside out, and I'm wearing two different shoes.

Thumping wildly, my heart is in my throat when I walk into the office. Eva's not here. Stacey's not here. What's going on? Pretend like everything is normal. That's what criminals do, right? Innocent until proven guilty? And I've done nothing wrong, have I? I sit at my desk, boot up my computer and stuff a wad of gum in my mouth to cover the smell of fear and puke. I pretend to be working intently on something while I peer around my computer trying to see inside Andrew's office. The bile rises in my throat again when I see Stacey, Andrew, and Eva having a big old meeting in there.

Oh my God, oh fuck me, this is so bad. I am so dead. I should just grab my stuff and run. I can leave Chicago. I'll work somewhere else. I can move to a kibbutz and pick oranges. I'll do something without people so I don't get myself into trouble. The door opens, and Andrew walks slowly and heavily over to me.

"Hi," I whisper.

He looks so angry. Fiery eyes, frantic jaw grinding, and his hands are clenched into shaking fists.

"Come to my office now." And he stalks away.

I don't move. I can see Eva draping her body over the chair and crossing her legs in such a way that her skirt rides up very high. No cellulite. Oh, I hate her even more now.

Suddenly, she turns her head to the side, looks at me and shouts, "Jamie, we don't have all day! Surf for sex later!"

That clinches it. I catapult out of my chair, put my finger in my mouth and chew while I take the endless walk to hell. I walk into Andrew's office, and Eva, who is still stretched languidly across the chair as if she doesn't have a care in the world, runs her forked little tongue across her lips and winks at me.

If your heart stops, are you dead?

I slowly lower my ass in the chair next to Eva and then Lucy struts in, glances at me out of the corner of her eye, and she looks as perplexed as I do.

"Eva, would you like to tell Lucy and Jamie what you just told us?" Stacey says.

I try to read her expression, but it's completely impassive, and I still have no clue what's going on. I just know it's bad. Andrew's expression, however, is easy. He is furious.

I swallow the spit swirling in my mouth and breathe through my nose to stop myself from being sick all over Andrew's desk.

Eva grins, winks at me again and starts speaking.

"Well, as you all know, Jamie has been going through a difficult time lately and-"

I whip my head to the side to look at her and widen my eyes. What the hell is she talking about?

"What?!" I bark.

"Let me finish, okay? Jamie, I know that it has been so hard for you that Derek broke up with you and that I'm seeing him. It wasn't our fault, and we never meant to hurt you, but it just happened-"

"I broke up with him, you fucking bitch!"

Andrew and Stacey look at me in shock. "Now, now, there's no call for that language, Jamie," Stacey says gently, and I am seconds from wrapping my hands around Eva's self-tanned throat and squeezing on her windpipe until her tongue turns blue.

I bite my lip because I can't lose control here, not at work, and I look helplessly at Lucy, who still seems baffled by what's going on.

"Okay, forget me and Derek."

I'd love to, but you keep bringing it up, you twisted bitch.

"But, you've been scattered lately, more than usual, and I knew how important this segment was to Andrew and the show. It might be our biggest ratings this year, and we couldn't afford to screw it up in any way. So, I finished my segment on sexy elderly strippers pretty quickly and thought I'd see if I could help you out at all. I guess I felt guilty for what happened with me and Derek."

Eva looks down at the floor, in supposed self-hatred for fucking my ex. I don't know where she's going with this little speech, but it's in no direction I want to take, I'm sure.

"Eva, can we move this along, here? I'm already upset with you for cancelling the other room in Indianapolis, and we all have work to do. So, just tell Jamie want you want to say," Andrew tells her, still not looking at me.

And Eva, angry at losing center stage and for being called to task for cancelling the hotel room, turns a slightly putrid shade of green and her eyes bug out of her head. For a split second, she looks like an extra from "Finding Nemo," but she composes herself quickly and like a cat, stretches her back muscles and continues.

297

"That's what I'm trying to tell you. I was trying to take the initiative and cut costs by cancelling the room. When Sue worked here, the associate producers did all of the travelling on their own, and I thought we needed to be more cost-efficient. I'm sorry if you disagree, and it won't happen again. And again, in the hopes of being efficient, while you and Jamie were on the road, I decided to help out, collaborate if you will, and I discovered some crucial material that Jamie had forgotten before she left."

And now Lucy knows what's going on. She looks at me and mouths, "Oh no."

I put my hand on my leg to stop its frantic jerking vibrations and wish I had the talent to teleport myself to anywhere but here.

"So," Eva licks her lips, tosses her perfect hair in my face and kills me. "Jamie had another guest for the show that we knew nothing about. This guest didn't find her. She found him."

"What do you mean 'She found him?' Eva, you're making no sense, and I'm getting tired of this little game. This is ridiculous," Lucy snarls, and I know she's trying to help, but it's too late.

"What I mean is that Jamie had a proposal and expenses requisition ready for a guest from Detroit, and she never told us. I guess she was planning to surprise us all when on the day of the show, she'll bring on her ex-boyfriend and be reunited with him. Lucas Simpson lives in Detroit, and since Jamie completely forgot to do it, I handed in the proposal and requisition for the hotel and meal expenses and called him. I'm just waiting to hear back."

Shooting stars explode in my brain, and I breathe in and out to stop myself from fainting. There is no way that what I just heard is true. Eva called Lucas? *She* called Lucas? And what proposal is she talking about? To do that, she would have had to forge my signature. And to find out that Lucas was my ex and that Andrew and I were going to Detroit, she would have needed to do a hell of a lot of research.

298

She hates me even more than I thought, and even though I like the fact that this gorgeous woman is so jealous of me, she has just ruined my life. Oh God, oh no, I'm going to puke.

"Jamie, you look a little pale. Do you want some water?" Eva asks in a saccharine sweet voice, and I'm speechless. I can't get my head around what she's done because nobody could be that vindictive. No, I'm wrong, Eva is toxic.

"So, let me get this straight now that we're all here," Stacey says.

I look at Andrew with pleading eyes, but he's too busy mashing his teeth together to notice. If only he could understand what really happened, but right now, he just thinks I lied. And lied big time.

"Jamie had planned for her ex-boyfriend to be the third guest, organized it, went to see him in Detroit-"

"No, she just went to get some information in Detroit because of course, she couldn't see him before the show or it would ruin the element of surprise," Eva explains.

I want to defend myself, but I don't even know where to begin. I'll wait until this is over and talk to Andrew. He'll understand.

"Right. Fine. Then, while Jamie and Andrew were on the road, you found the requisition and materials on this Lucas guy and took it upon yourself to do Jamie's job," Stacey finishes and looks questioningly at Eva to make sure it's all clear.

"I didn't do Jamie's job. I was helping her. I just wanted to make sure that everything was organized, and really, I was surprised that she didn't tell anyone that she was planning to be on the show. That's a bit manipulative if you want my opinion. But once I figured out what she was doing, I decided to help out because of, well, Derek, and because she was right about this being a fantastic idea. I have to give credit where it's due. The other shows always have three guests on for these reunion segments, and we only had two, so I wanted to make sure it was a fait accompli."

299

Because Eva's obviously had a lot more time to think this scheme of hers through, I only have a few seconds to come up with a defense, and right now, my brain can't possibly work fast enough because the synapses stopped snapping after I heard, "Planning to be on the show."

I start shaking, my teeth are chattering, and finally, my brain clicks into gear. "I-"

But before I can even get to the next word, Lucy holds up a finger and jumps in.

"Okay, Jamie, I think it's time we told them about our plan," she says, smiling at me.

Our plan? What plan? "No, Luce, not-"

"Oh, Jamie, we have to ruin the surprise. We have no choice."

And she grins at Stacey and Andrew, bypassing Eva completely, who now looks a bit confused herself.

I look at Lucy and shake my head slightly in warning. I know Lucy, and whatever she's about to say is going to get me in huge trouble.

"I'll tell you. Stacey, Andrew, I'm sorry this turned into such a mess when it was meant to be a huge ratings booster. You see, Jamie has a high school crush she'd like to meet again, right Eva? Since you stole the papers from Jamie's desk and all, which is pretty underhanded, if you ask me. Anyway, Jamie and I thought it'd be a great coup if the associate producer and her high school crush could be part of the show."

"But she didn't tell me," Andrew says, looking straight at me.

The disappointment in his eyes is enough to make me wish the chair would swallow me whole and spit me out on the other side of the world.

"No, no she didn't, and we're sorry for that. But, think about it. This is an incredible way to increase our viewers! Having the associate producer on? Think of what we'll do for this show."

"I'm thinking that this doesn't make sense, Lucy. I am the executive producer of this show, and I should know *everything* that's happening. It didn't need to be a surprise from me. And Jamie, we spent hours together! How could you not tell me what was going on?!" Andrew is almost yelling now.

I shiver and take a big gulp. "Andrew, I-"

Again, Lucy interrupts before I can slap my hand over her mouth. What is she doing? She's ruining my life here, and she just keeps going.

"I told her not to tell you. I thought it would be great television to get your reaction to Jamie being the last guest. I may have miscalculated, and for that, I do apologize. But, if we forget all the other stuff and just focus on the programming, which is our job, I'm sure you'll see how creative this is."

Lucy has her hands firmly planted on her hips, displaying an air of confidence. I, however, am dumbfounded.

Stacey looks at all of us and smiles. "Lucy, I can see your point. I also would have preferred you had talked to me first before making this decision, but I do admire the initiative both you and Jamie have taken. Really, Jamie, it's quite brilliant. I always knew you had it in you. Sue always told me how good you are at getting things done, and now, you've gone above and beyond."

Crash! My heart just smashed to the floor. I widen my eyes and try to get Lucy's attention to stop this right now. But she's ignoring me and is instead looking at Andrew, whose eyes are narrowed in deep concentration as if he's trying to figure out what's wrong with this scenario. He knows full well I'd never go on television, but he's too angry right now to realize that.

"Fine. What's done is done. It just doesn't make any sense to me. Eva and Jamie, I have had enough of your bickering and childish arguing. You two have got to learn to work together because we are a team here, and if you can't do that, then we will have to discuss letting both of you go before you damage the integrity of this show."

I nearly choke when he says "integrity" because really, what integrity is there in humiliating people for ratings? But I can't lose my job. And it seems like I've already lost Andrew's friendship. I just can't take anymore. I swallow hard.

"You're right. Andrew, I'm so sorry if you think I lied to you. I hope-"

"Meeting's over," he snaps, not letting me finish, and opens the door.

I'm not leaving until I talk to him. Stacey, Lucy and Eva walk out (Eva, with a triumphant strut, and I lift my leg to kick her in her aerobicized ass, but she's too fast for me), but I stay in the chair.

"Aren't you leaving?" he asks, glaring at me.

I take a deep breath, but I swallow so much air that I start choking. Alarmed, he whacks me on the back. A little too enthusiastically.

"What is it, Jamie? I'm very busy now that I need to add you and your friend," he says "friend" in a whiny, patronizing voice, "to the roster of guests."

I try to speak, but my mouth is so dry that no sound comes out.

"Spit it out!" he snaps impatiently.

"Andrew, you don't understand!"

"What don't I understand, Jamie? That you lied? That I paid for you to go to Detroit? All those times we talked, you were lying. I told you everything, Jamie. About Kelly, my family, my dreams. The whole time you didn't give a shit about me. You used me!"

"Used you? I don't understand what finding Lucas has to do with our friendship. I told you stuff too. You met my crazy family," I argue.

Maybe I'm stupid, but I'm confused about why exactly he is so

302

angry with me.

"I, Andrew, I, look, I'm so sorry. I never meant to lie to you. Eva stole my stuff! Lucy's lying. There was never any proposal or requisition. Eva forged my signature and planned all of this! This isn't what I wanted. I *do* care about you. You *are* my friend."

"Friendship?" he spits. "Friends are honest with each other. And really, Jamie, you expect me to believe that everyone is lying, and you're the only one telling the truth? Do you think I'm completely stupid?"

"No, of course not. I know how it looks, but you have to believe me."

"I don't have to do anything."

"Look, yes, I wanted to find the guy I was with in high school, but I didn't really tell anyone about Lucas. You know how private I am. And you know exactly how I feel about being rejected. I didn't want anyone to know until I knew what would happen."

"And what did you want to happen?"

I'm quiet for a moment. "I wanted someone to love me."

As I say it, I realize that it's true. I just want someone to love me. The Jamie with the stringy hair, big bum and serious addiction to television.

His expression softens slightly, but his voice is stone cold.

"Well, I wish you the best of luck with that."

And then I notice his hair. "Hey, you cut your hair," I say, trying to smile and lighten the mood.

"Yes. This morning. Someone I care about told me I had to get it cut."

Is he back together with Kelly? God, I hope not. He deserves better than that. But, I'm sure that now is not the time to discuss it when he'll barely look at me.

"It looks great."

"I have to work, Jamie." And he turns his back on me.

303

"I know, but if you'd just let me explain-"

"There's nothing to explain. Again, I've completely misjudged someone. And I have nothing to say to you. I'm your boss, and I want you to go back to work."

The fury in his eyes is just too much to bear. And all for nothing. I don't know how any of this happened, but none of it was worth the agony I'm feeling now.

CHAPTER THIRTY-TWO

The phone rings, and I'm afraid to answer it because who knows what other surprises await me?

"Jamie Ross," I say listlessly.

"So, you're going on television, huh? How sad are you?"

Thunk. I didn't think my depression could sink any lower, but oh, it can. It's Derek.

"Your girlfriend just can't stop talking about me?" I retort.

"You are so jealous of her, Jamie, and it's not attractive."

"Jealous? Of what? Of the two of you? Don't make me laugh." And I emit a deep chuckle to show him just how funny I think that is.

"You are the epitome of white trash. I can't believe I didn't see it earlier. But, what really bothers me is that you lied to me for five years."

"I lied to you? About what?"

"Who is this Lucas guy, Jamie? Why didn't I know about him?"

Oh my God, Derek is jealous. Why can't he just leave me alone? I think it's because for the first time, he can't control everything, and it makes him crazy.

"If you had ever listened to me, Derek, you would have known exactly who Lucas is. It doesn't matter because you and I are long over. Why don't you just focus on your relationship with the gold digging slut and leave me alone?"

"I should have left you long before I did."

"I left you, you fucking idiot!"

Slam! Oh, this is just perfect. Jeanette will probably call me next. I have to get out of here. The walls are closing in on me, I can't breathe, and only a triple espresso will dull the stabbing ache in my stomach. And a swift kick to Lucy's head. I get up, look around for Lucy, and when I don't see her, I know where I can find her.

"Do you have any idea how much you've just screwed me, Lucy?" I yell after I've found her at Starbucks.

"I-"

"No, no smart ass remarks. I can't believe what you've done. Now I have to go on television, and what's worse, what's way worse is that Lucas will think I'm a crazed stalker!"

"What was the alternative, Jamie? Making it look like Eva needed to do your job for you?" she argues, flipping her hair back defiantly.

"Yes, that would have been preferable. And I could have explained! Jesus, Luce, what the hell were you thinking?"

"I was thinking that since your mouth was opening and closing like a fish, and you weren't defending yourself, I had to do something. And I had to make you look good and find a way to stop Eva from winning. At that point, I thought that her story was a hell of a lot more plausible than yours."

"But mine was the truth!"

"You know as well as I do that people hear and see what they want to, and at that point, both Andrew and Stacey were convinced that you did this. I had to make you come out on top. And anyway, we don't exactly have a huge viewership. Who's going to see it?"

"Who?! Everyone! Claire, Derek, Eva, Andrew, everyone in my childhood who thought I was already fucked up! And this is not how I wanted to get Lucas back!"

I'm screaming at her so loudly that everyone in the coffee shop is staring open-mouthed at us, but I don't care.

"Maybe he'll be flattered."

"Flattered?! Would you be fucking flattered, Lucy? No, you'd be terrified. And humiliated. You have to get me out of this."

"I can't."

"Oh yes, you can. You started this whole thing. If it weren't for you, I might still be with Derek."

"Oh, yeah, that'd be much better. I just brought up the subject of Lucas, you did the rest. Don't you dare blame me," she says, waving a finger in my face.

"Don't blame you? Who should I blame then? I don't even want to speak to you!" I scream and stalk out of the coffee shop.

My face is boiling hot, and I'm sure unattractively fuschia, but the rest of me is shivering. I race over to the alley beside the studio building and lean against the dirt-streaked bricks. If I could imagine my worst nightmare, this wouldn't even compare. I can't go on our show. I can't bring Lucas here. But thanks to my good pal Lucy, I have no choice. Why can't anything in my life be easy and normal? How do other people get regular families, normal friends and meet someone in the normal way? What is it about me that invites ridiculous drama into my life when I never ask for it?

I push myself away from the wall and hail a taxi. You know, as much as being with Derek made me unhappy most of the time, it's certainly better than this.

***

"Oh shit."

Hanna's reaction says it all. I'm at her place, watching Jack rub her perfectly scarlet toes while I down as many G&T's as I can without throwing up.

I hold out my glass and say, "More, pleashe."

"Is that a good idea, Jaim? You've already had four."

Jack pulls his attention away from Hanna's feet to shoot me a concerned and fatherly glance.

I take another cigarette from the half-finished pack (I bought

307

these two hours ago) and light the wrong end.

"Ish a good idea," I slur. "I never wanna be shober again. Fucking Lushy, fucking Lucash, fucking Eva."

Hanna and Jack have been listening to me re-tell the story for two hours now, and I think they might be losing patience. I don't care. Besides my parents' divorce, this is the worst thing that's ever happened to me. No, this is way worse.

"The camera adds fifteen pounds. My ash ish going to look like a truck backing up."

And that sobering thought eats up all the alcohol I've just drunk. Damn it.

"You have a great ass," Jack says and leers appreciatively.

"Good try, Jacko. But if my lithe friend here is the love of your life, my mushy butt would never pass muster."

"Jamie, you're beautiful. Don't even worry about that. I think you need to see the positive side to all of this," he says.

"The positive side?!" I scream as the gin and tonic splashes on Hanna's pristine couch.

She stands up, plucks the drink out of my hand and exchanges it for a glass of water. I pout at her, but drink the water.

"How could Lucy do this to me?"

"I know you're going to slap me for saying this, but it's not really Lucy's fault," Hanna says, moving far enough away so I can't reach out and whack her.

"You're right. Come here so I can slap you. It was her psychotic plan. 'Find Lucas, he's your destiny,'" I mimic in a high and childish voice.

"But you did it. She never told you to go to Detroit and see him. And she never told you to leave your papers on the desk. You did that. And Eva is the total bitch who got you into this, not Lucy. She stole those papers, she set you up, and she called Lucas. But don't worry. That girl will get her own."

"But how could I just sit there and let her get away with it? It happened so fast, and I just couldn't believe that even she would stoop so low. So low!"

"I think you guys are focusing on the wrong things here," Jack interrupts.

"Which wrong thing? My total and utter humiliation that will happen in a few days or my hating Eva? Or Lucy getting in on Fuck With Jamie Day? Or my big butt?" I ask sarcastically.

"All of it. Since I met you, you've been complaining about how complacent you've been. Staying with Derek, not taking a risk, not going after what you want. Well, here's your chance. So you're going on TV? So what? You love TV. You'll get a makeover and look fantastic. And you'll finally see Lucas again because nothing else is working, is it?" Jack holds my gaze.

"Oh, please. I'm not stupid. Did you and Hanna take the same fruity therapy course?"

Jack grins and comes to sit beside me.

"You're in dangerous territory there, hon," Hanna warns him.

"Jamie's bark is much worse than her bite," he says and pinches my cheek.

I try to slap his hand away, but I like him too much.

"Jack's right, you know. You'll have professional hair and makeup, and Derek, Claire and Eva will be sick with jealousy. Derek'll be devastated he lost you, and Eva'll wish she took the show for herself. And Lucas? Well, honestly, Jaim, the whole idea of finding your fuck buddy is ridiculous as it is so how is this worse?"

"It just is," I argue. "I've spent my entire life avoiding being the center of attention, and now, I'm throwing myself right in it."

Jack drapes an arm over the back of the couch and says, "You know, this may turn out to be a lot better than you think it will."

"Or it won't."

"Well, either way, it's a hell of a lot better than disappearing into the television or your head. And if you don't do it, you'll never know what could have been," Hanna agrees.

I ignore them by curling myself up in a ball at the end of the couch and closing my eyes.

Sleeping is the only thing I'm doing right these days.

CHAPTER THIRTY-THREE

Where am I? My head aches, my lips burn, and I don't recognize the bed I'm in. I hear the door creak open.

"Jaim, are you up?"

Right, I'm at Hanna's.

"Go away."

"Amy's on the phone. She was worried when you didn't come home last night."

I hold out my hand for the cordless phone she's brought in. She leaves, and I burrow further under the covers to talk to Amy.

"Hey, Amy," I say miserably.

"J! I was so worried about you! Why didn't you call me? I was dying to know what happened at work."

And that was just the reminder I didn't need.

"Amy, it's all fucked up. You have no idea how bad it is."

"Did you lose your job?!" she screeches.

I pull the phone away from my ear. "Ow! Hangover head! No. Worse."

"Does Andrew hate you?"

"Yes, it appears so. But that's not the problem."

I tell her the whole awful story as briefly as possible, and I hear nothing on the other end except girlish giggling.

"It's not funny."

"Not to you, no. J, you have no worries. Not only will you look, like, totally fab on camera, but this is something you and Lucas can tell your children about."

"Sure. Like he's going to want anything to do with me after this."

"You never know. And it's time you did something out of the

311

ordinary, you know? Aren't you tired of being safe all the time?"

"Safe is easy."

"Yeah and like totally boring. I'm the best person for this, J. I'm a media whiz. I know exactly how you should be on camera."

"I'm not in a porn movie, Amy, it's a mortifying talk show."

"All an audience wants is drama. You'll be famous!" she squeals, and I can practically see her hopping up and down with the thrill and adventure of it all.

"Oh goody, that's all I ever wanted. To be noticed."

"Do you always just want to blend in with the crowd? You're like worth way more than that."

So are you, I want to say. But I don't.

"I'll see you at home tonight, okay?"

I can't seem to convince anyone that this is the worst thing that could ever happen. I won't even bother calling my family because they'll probably want to play "This is Your Life" with me. I hang up and toss the phone to the floor. I need to go to work. I can't lose my job on top of everything else. And I can't let Eva know how much she's hurt me.

I take a long, hot shower, but it does nothing to alleviate the stabbing pain in my jaw or the gurgling in my stomach. I dress in the same clothes I wore yesterday, and when I get to work, Lucy is there, but she won't even look at me. Great, now I've lost two of my closest friends and for nothing. As I sit heavily in my chair and turn on my computer, I'm hit with a brainstorm. There's no way they'll get Lucas here in two days! He's on vacation. He might be in India or Afghanistan or somewhere equally across the world. It's Tuesday already, and he'd have to fly twenty-four hours to get here.

And the Lucas I knew would never go on a daytime talk show. That's it then. I'm okay. I breathe a huge sigh of relief, and for the first time in days, I feel okay. I should repair this fight with Lucy. I know she was just trying to help, and it wasn't really her fault how messed up it all got. She was just trying to make me happy.

Walking over to Lucy's desk, I pass Eva, who is buffing her nails and admiring a ring on her finger. When she sees me, she flicks her hand so the jewel catches the light and blocks my vision.

"I didn't know a cubic zirconia could be so bright and showy," I say.

"It's a gift from Derek. I don't think he ever gave you one, did he?" she purrs.

"Did he give you gonorrhea too? That's what I got."

Her eyes widen in fear, and reflexively, her hand shoots for her groin and she twitches uncomfortably.

"I thought so." I smile.

I tap Lucy lightly on the shoulder. "Luce, can we talk?" I ask gently.

"What? To yell at me for ruining your life? No thanks, I get that enough from my father."

"I want to apologize."

She faces me; her mouth set in a hard line. "I'm listening."

I lean on the edge of her desk and wring my hands.

"Look, I know this wasn't your fault, and I'm sorry I reacted so quickly. I would be terrified to be on television, and I just got so scared, and you were the closest person to blame. I wanted to find Lucas, granted it was your idea, but I went to Detroit, I went to Wayne County, and I was the idiot who left the papers on my desk, not you."

"Well, now I've been yelled at, lied to my boss and only to save your ass. But, Jamie, yes, I just wanted you to be happy because I love you."

"I know."

We smile at each other, and she says, "Drink after work?"

"Sure."

Everything's back to normal.

***

Or so I thought. Because after we sit in Leticia's section and order our drinks (vodka tonic for her, and an apple martini for me), Lucy tells me the plan for Thursday. The very plan I had just quashed in my mind.

"So," she continues, sipping in a very ladylike manner from a very unladylike drink, "we got in touch with Lucas."

The glass freezes at my mouth, and I stare at her.

"He's on vacation. In Zimbabwe."

"Um, no, he's at home. I told Cindy that if he called to transfer it to me and not Eva. And, well, he did call."

"And you spoke to him?"

I still haven't taken the sip because I can't move.

"Yup. He's coming in on Wednesday night, we're putting him up at the Holiday Inn, and on Thursday, your life will change."

I take a huge gulp of the martini and relish the way it makes my head spin. Maybe if I can stay drunk from now until Thursday night, I'll survive this.

"He's going on the show?" I ask incredulously.

"He sounded very intrigued. He asked a million times who wants to see him, but I didn't tell him."

"Did he mention my name?"

Lucy looks down and starts ripping the corner of her napkin.

"He didn't even say my name, did he? Oh, God, Lucy, what if he doesn't remember me, and I'm forced to explain how we had sex in the backseat of his car, and how I gave him my first blow job. What else did he say? How did he sound?"

"I shouldn't tell you this, but he did ask if the person who wants

314

to see him is Claire."

I crumple, and tears threaten to spill out of my eyes. After all these years, Claire is still the woman he wants. Well, he can fucking have her. I want no part of this anymore.

"Why would you tell me that?" I whine and drain the rest of my martini in one swallow. "What if we bring Claire on the show instead?"

"And then how will we explain that to Andrew and Stacey?"

"You can tell them I've checked into a mental hospital for a nervous breakdown because I'm certainly on the verge of one."

"Of course he remembers you, Jamie. But he knew how private you were. I'm sure he'd never guess that you would be the one to go on national television."

"What happened to nobody really watches the show? Now it's national?" I slam the glass down on the table.

She jumps from the noise and sighs. "Look, it's only the next two days of your life, and then, it's over."

"And re-runs?"

"Maybe you'll be off on your honeymoon by then."

"There's nothing I can do, is there?" I bury my head in my hands and close my eyes to try and block everything out.

"You can stop worrying about it and just let it happen. Isn't that the Jamie Ross motto?"

I lift my head slightly and say flatly, "I don't know what happened to Jamie Ross, but I've become a planner and a worrier. All because of Lucas. This guy is ruining my life, and he won't even recognize me."

"We'll make you so stunning that every man in there will want you." And she brings her head closer to me. "Like Andrew does."

"Andrew? Why does everyone keep saying that? Andrew and I are friends. In fact, he is one of the only friends I have, and now, he won't even speak to me. There is nothing Andrew wants from me but honesty, and I couldn't even do that. He's still in love with his ex, I'm sure. Trust me, I'm not his type."

"What's his type?" she asks, reaching for a cigarette and re-adjusting her tube top.

"Tall, skinny, and pushy."

"You've got the pushy part down pat."

"I am not pushy."

"You're not as laid back as you think you are either. Jaim, I really am sorry that I didn't talk to you about this first. It just came to me in the meeting, and I was so angry at Eva that I didn't think about how it might affect you. But I promise it will all work out."

"And if it doesn't?"

"You can leave the country."

"That's helpful, Luce. Thanks."

CHAPTER THIRTY-FOUR

A few hours later, I'm snug in Chris and Amy's "office." Incredibly uncomfortable because of the video camera, bed, whip, and assorted scraps of lingerie scattered around, this is where Amy is giving me some much needed media training. She's spun my head around so many times to get the perfect angle that I'm dizzy and disoriented. At this point, if she asked me to star in one of her videos, I'd probably say yes.

"Okay, that's it! That's the angle your face should be. No, don't move! Okay, I'm like going to ask you the questions again and remember to smile. You look like you're lined up for the guillotine."

"That's how I feel. I can't sit like this. It's not comfortable," I complain.

"It's like only for about twenty minutes. You know Eva is writing the questions so you have to be prepared for everything."

Oh yes, another tidbit that is making me even sicker. Because Lucas is *my* guest, Stacey thought I would have an unfair advantage if I wrote the questions. So, to help build "team morale," Eva gets to write all of the questions, and I'm not even allowed to preview them. She's going to make me look like the biggest loser, and there's not a damn thing I can do about it.

"What if I suddenly get sick? That might work. Let me take my clothes off, and we'll crank the air conditioner up really high." I turn to Amy and start lifting my shirt up from my waist.

"Put that down. They'll bring you on anyway. J, we'll get through this, and when it's all over, who knows what will happen? This is like everything that you wanted, and he's who you want."

"But what if he doesn't want me?" I ask in a small voice.

317

She stops fiddling with the knobs on the video camera and looks at me. "How can he not want you? You read me that letter. Those feelings were genuine, and of course, he's thought about you."

"Then why did he ask if Claire was the person who was looking for him?"

"Because just like you never thought he'd go on the show, I'm sure he thinks you would never do it either. Stop stressing. It's giving you like little lines in your forehead."

I touch my hand to my forehead and try to smooth out the worry lines.

"Um, by the way, I did something, and I hope you're not going to kill me, but I thought you needed some support."

I narrow my eyes and ask in a warning voice, "What did you do?"

"I called your family."

"You what?!" I bolt out of the chair and knock the video camera over. Sort of by accident.

Amy picks up the camera, dusts it off, and unconcerned with my outburst, says, "Well, I called Rachel, and I think she told your mom. So, they're all coming over tonight."

"Amy! How could you do that? God, why is everyone trying to sabotage me?" I cry, rubbing my temples where a ferocious headache has just begun.

Obviously, she thinks I'm joking because she starts giggling; the little turtle on today's shirt, jiggling. When I see the turtle, I think of Andrew, and my heart squeezes. I miss his friendship.

"I'm serious. What have I done that's so bad to deserve this?"

"Oh, puleeze. Would you, like, chill?" She holds the camera up to her eye and swings it in my direction.

"Sorry about the camera. Is it okay?"

"Yeah, yeah. It's taken worse knocks than that. I remember this one time-"

"Amy!" I interrupt. "Could we please focus on me here?"

She puts the camera down and faces me. "Jesus, whine, whine whine, it's all about you. What's like so bad about your family knowing, anyway? From what you've told me, they sound really cool."

"That's the problem. They're too cool. If Eva can get to them, I'm sure they'll be on the show too. And nothing for them is private. Look, it's just that my family's so different from me. I like my privacy."

"No kidding. Well, I think they'll help you. You're lucky you have a family."

I roll my eyes at her obvious attempt to make me feel guilty, but it works, and Amy's right. Of course she's right. But it doesn't mean that I want the world to know about my "unique" upbringing.

"I'm sorry, Amy. You're right, yet again. What's the worst that can happen?"

***

"And, Jaim, we'll be right there in the audience cheering you on," Leah says, while sitting on the couch in the living room and flicking through Amy's porn catalogue of photos and sex acts. Only $29.99 plus delivery.

Katie's next to her, with her legs draped over Leah's lap. She grabs one of the magazines, and without looking at me, announces, "That's what she's afraid of."

Rachel strolls back into the room with a Diet Coke for herself and a beer for me. Handing me my drink, she says, "Well, I think it's awesome. You get to be on television, back together with Lucas. I just can't believe you never told me. Nobody ever tells me anything."

A familiar refrain.

I take a sip of my drink. "I didn't know about this until a few days ago, Rach. And of course I was going to tell you about Lucas, but I wanted to check things out myself first."

"I would have told you immediately."

Katie looks over at her affectionately. "We know you would have, sweetheart. But you and Jamie are so different."

"I wish I could go on television." Rachel pouts.

I sit up straighter on the floor and look up at her.

"So why don't you? You could pretend you're me."

Maybe *that's* the way out of this.

"Good try, J. But, I think you're forgetting that Rachel is eighteen and you're, well, you're not," Amy reminds me and hands Leah her newest DVD to take home.

"Can I please see that?" Rachel asks for the tenth time.

"No!" we all yell in unison.

"So, what should she wear?" Amy asks, sitting next to Rachel on the other couch. Most likely to deflect her attention from the porn. Although we all know that the minute Leah and Katie leave the house, Rachel will rummage through their drawers until she finds the video.

I know why I don't want her to see it. I'm afraid she'll want to do it. But, Leah and Katie are much more protective of Rachel than they were of me. Either because I'm nowhere near as pretty (and this is more probable), I wasn't much to worry about or they've learned their lessons from my mistakes.

Amy purses her lips in deep thought. "Hmmm, something sexy, but not too much. She doesn't have any time to go shopping, though."

"Do you own anything sexy, Jaim?" Rachel asks me.

"My version of sexy and yours are completely different," I tell her, taking in the tea towel of a black skirt and belly-baring yellow tank top she's wearing today. "I'm sure I have something just fine."

"Oh honey, you need something more than fine for your debut," Katie says.

I wish they understood how devastated I am. Instead, they seem to be enjoying this as if it's some Ross family adventure.

"I don't understand how you're all so calm about this. Can't you at least pretend to be worried about me?" I ask and pick off the remaining bit of skin left on my feet.

"You're not going to do that on camera, are you? It's so gross." Rachel grimaces and makes gagging noises.

"No, I only do it for you."

"I think you're making a much bigger deal out of this than you have to. What is meant to happen will happen. You can't control the universe," Leah tells me, smiling beatifically and rubbing Katie's feet with chamomile massage oil, and the smell is making me even sicker than I already was.

"Oh really? I'm so glad you think so. It's great that the almighty universe made Andrew hate me, Lucas doesn't even remember me, and I'm about to humiliate myself on national television."

"First of all, love, Andrew could never hate you. In fact, I think he's a bit in love with you," Katie says and moans as Leah's fingers dig into the arch of her left foot.

I roll my eyes. "Really, dear sage?"

"Oh, that's so good. Really, oh naysayer. And this might be your big break. Your chance to do something different."

"I'm already different."

They all burst out laughing at this.

I fold my arms over my chest and sneer. "What's so fucking funny? I'm not different?"

Katie gets up and sits beside me on the floor. She reaches over and brushes the hair out of my eyes. "Jamie, sweetheart, you've tried so hard to be like everyone else that I don't think even you know who you really are."

"And this will tell me?" I retort, moving away from her.

"It's a start. Hey, how about a massage? That might relax you."

After one incredible massage and a few more hours of mirthful entertainment at my expense, they're gone. I crawl into bed and try to stop the screaming in my head. I have twelve hours left to either leave the country or show up at work tomorrow. And because I can't sleep, add huge bags under my eyes to the pasty skin, flat chest, flabby butt and cellulite, and I'm every man's dream.

I move from one side of the bed to the other, trying to find a comfortable position. But every time I close my eyes, I'm confronted with the image of an audience laughing in my face and Eva clapping her hands in joy. And the worst thing is that I'm on last tomorrow. Eva made sure of that knowing full well that I'll be gnawing off my arm in fear the whole time.

With images of Andrew's hurt eyes and Lucas's confused stare (when he doesn't remember me) in my mind, I finally fall into a jerky, restless sleep.

CHAPTER THIRTY-FIVE

I hear bells clanging, and the irritating sound wakes me up from the worst nightmare I've ever had. I dreamt that everything got all screwed up, and I was actually going to be a guest on the show and have to face Lucas. I close my eyes, hoping that I can go back to sleep and forget what I just imagined.

"J! There's a call for you!" Amy shrieks from the living room.

Groaning, I open my eyes and reach out a hand and pick up the phone.

"Hello?" I answer groggily.

"Jaim, it's Lucy. How are you feeling?"

"I'm fine. Why wouldn't I be?"

"Um, because today's the show," she says hesitantly.

All good feelings disappear into a sinkhole of dread. "The show? You mean it wasn't a horrible nightmare?"

"A nightmare? No. Are you okay?"

"No, Luce. Of course I'm not okay, hold on."

I toss the phone aside, race to the bathroom and heave out last night's ravioli. "I'm back."

"What were you doing?"

"Puking."

"Oh, Jaim, this can't possibly be as bad as you think it's going to be. Just get here." She consoles me by ordering me around.

"Yeah, whatever."

I hang up and plod, dizzy and still nauseous, to the shower. All I need to do is wash my useless hair because the stylists will do the rest. An emergency phone call to Lucy late last night (which I now remember) ensured they'd have some great clothes waiting for me too. Yippee. I stand in the shower and do everything by rote. I see myself pick up the shampoo and rub it into my scalp, slide the razor along my pale legs, but I don't feel any of it.

In all of this craziness, the actual idea of seeing Lucas again got lost. But now today is the day that after ten years, I'll be with him again. Mind you, not in the setting I imagined, but he'll be here. Maybe he *will* be flattered. Maybe he's always loved me and was too shy to call after so long.

Bolstered by this new found (and probably short-lived) confidence and excitement, I quickly get dressed in a pair of navy blue sweats and a white tank top with coffee stains on it and leave without saying goodbye to Amy and Chris. They'll see me at the show anyway. Lucy got tickets for my whole family, including my dad, Mo, Hanna and Jack, as well. How very sweet of her.

When I get to the studio, Eva is already there organizing my execution. She's running around in an aqua micro-mini and a white band-aid across her chest, jiggling and bouncing, making sure the lighting and sound checks are done. Carl is waving at me from across the studio, and I wander over to him.

"Hey, Carl," I drawl.

He's turning the knobs on his camera to make sure the Zoom is working properly.

"Hey, you big star. You didn't tell us that you were going on the show."

"It wasn't exactly how I wanted it to work out," I say, pulling on the ends of my hair nervously and trying to find a way to break his camera without his noticing.

"Good luck, Jamie. You deserve it."

I'm not sure if he means I deserve to find love or total humiliation.

"Carl, is there any way you could maybe not turn on the camera today?" I ask, winking at him in what I hope is flirtatiousness.

He winks back and smiles. "Nope."

Well, I tried. I step through the television studio I know so well. Three hundred seats are organized on stacked raisers, with a long wide aisle in the middle for Mitzy to prance through, and a rectangular stage at the front is set up today with one chair for Mitzy and two chairs for the couples. They'll bring the couples on separately and then add more chairs during each commercial break until we're all on the stage together, like one big happily dysfunctional family.

The floor is made of trampoline-like material in case a guest loses his or her temper and decides to throw someone to the floor, and there are two exits to the backstage for the guests who run out screaming and crying during taping. There are cameras everywhere: on the stage, in the audience and at the exits to capture the most natural of human reactions. There is nowhere for me to escape.

Eva is taking extreme delight in my anguish. Her face is glowing, hair flipping perfectly and catching the light in her auburn highlights, and these devilish giggles keep escaping from her mouth every time she does something. She sees me from the corner of her eye and struts over.

Practically standing on my head, she squeezes my shoulder much too hard, digging her long manicured fingernails into my flesh. "Good morning, Jamie. You must be so sick with nervousness."

I wave my hand around in an attempt at cool indifference to her. "Oh no, I'm so excited. Thanks to you Eva, I'm getting everything I ever wanted."

She narrows her eyes as if she's not sure whether to believe me or not. "Well, it's exactly what *I* wanted. Oh, and I have another surprise for you, but you'll just have to wait. And you might want to spend a little extra time in hair and makeup. You don't want to look dowdy next to the other women. Oh, by the way, Derek and Jeanette will both be here."

And she flies away on her broom.

This can't get any worse than it already is. If she invited my entire high school, I wouldn't be surprised. I run backstage to check on my other guests, because yes, I *am* still working here. We've separated everyone into the different rooms we have so our guests won't see each other before they surprise, appal or ruin each other, and they all seem to be doing okay. Except Bubba who's ensconced in the one at the end of hall.

I rap lightly on the door, and when Bubba opens it, I see that he's drenched his shirt with sweat. Two other soaking wet shirts are already lying on the floor. I grab him a cold bottle of water from the cooler at the back of the room and hand it to him.

"I know how you feel," I tell him.

He gulps down the water in one swig, and I'm dying to advise him to take small sips. But I don't.

"No, you don't, Miss Ross."

"It's Jamie, and yes, I do. You see, I'm on this show today too."

He turns to look at me and a puddle of sweat from his forehead lands in my lap.

"What do you mean?"

"I mean, my lost love is here today, and I'm terrified that he won't want me."

"But you're so pretty, and I'm a big fat nothing. Who's going to want me the way I am now?"

"Anyone looking for a good, honest man will want you. And if Meghan doesn't, she's not the woman for you."

He puts his soaking wet hand on mine and says, "Maybe you should take some of your own advice."

I smile at him (dying to wipe my hand, but I can't do that to him) so I grip his dripping palm with my own.

"Good luck, Bubba."

"You too, Miss Ross. Jamie."

I let myself out and start walking towards the stage, when Lucy and Stacey come tearing around the corner, their headsets on and clipboards in hand. "There you are! We need you in hair and makeup now!" Stacey commands and pushes me towards the makeup room.

"Okay, but what about setting up? I'm not done, and I haven't checked in with all of the guests yet."

"Stop procrastinating. Eva will do it. You know, Jamie, when Eva brought this clever little scheme of yours to me, I thought it was fantastic. But, it's even better than I could have hoped. We've filled the house today and all because of you! There's a huge line-up outside because of all the promos Eva put together. I'm so glad the two of you have put aside your differences," Stacey says, scrambling to keep up with Lucy.

Lucy catches the look of terror and hate in my eyes and pulls me away from Stacey.

"I'll tell you where I'd like to put our differences," I hiss at her.

"Not now, Jaim. This is all going to work out, and Eva will wish it were her. Anyway, your best revenge is that she has to have sex with Derek," Lucy says as she hands me the clothes I'm supposed to wear today.

I grin at that. True, he has a great body, but it's been a long time since he's known what to do with it. I can just see the two of them having sex in front of the mirror and judging how their bodies look in each position. Mind you, he only knew a few positions when I was with him—ones that wouldn't muss up his hair. One last grin and a friendly shove from Lucy, and I'm inside the makeup room.

"Jamie, welcome! It's such a pleasure to have you here," gushes Rhonda, our hair and makeup woman.

Her short, blunt pink bob is only outdone by her thick purple eyeshadow and candy floss lipstick. I'm going to look like Barbie on crack after this.

"It's not exactly a pleasure to be here," I say and plunk myself down in the chair.

"I think you're so brave. I could never do what you're doing. Oh, stop scrunching up your face, please. I can't apply your makeup evenly."

"Sorry. I'm really nervous. Would you mind stabbing me in the eye with that pencil?"

She either doesn't hear me or she's ignoring me because she continues drawing on my face. "What lovely skin you have! Okay, Jamie, just a bit of base here, mmm, and some lipstick. Okay, I'm done, and you're beautiful. Are you ready to look?"

Nope. But I do anyway. And despite Rhonda's own eclectic style, she's kept it pretty natural for me. I look pretty damn good, except for the greenish tinge highlighting my skin.

"I hope you get what you want, Jamie," she says.

I don't even know what I want anymore.

I stand up, try unsuccessfully to stop my knees from buckling and go to the dressing room to change into my outfit. At least they chose all black so I can mourn the loss of my dignity. I pull on the skintight black dress pants and v-neck, lycra t-shirt and look in the full-length mirror next to the sinks. This stuff actually makes me look slim and curvy, but it isn't nearly enough to change how ill I feel. After one last look, I open the door and drag myself to the green room.

I take a seat next to Ray and Bubba on one of the brown couches facing the little televisions they have mounted on the wall so the "surprisers" can watch what's happening on stage. Time seems to have stopped. My breathing, as well. I can't even make niceties with the guests that I brought here, but both men seem fine with it. Ray's too busy stroking his chest hair, and Bubba looks as ill as I feel. And I know that I've been sitting here for thirty minutes, but it feels like seconds until I notice that both Ray and Bubba are gone, and all I'm left with is just my churning stomach for company.

Before they bring on Lisa, Meghan and Lucas, Ray, Bubba and I are subjected to invasive questions about why we're here. It never fails to surprise me that our guests seem oblivious to the cameras pointed at their heads as they reveal long buried secrets to an audience of complete strangers. I'll get the same humiliating interview, but I will *not* use this as a therapeutic opportunity. No matter how much Eva has tried to destroy what little self-confidence I have, she is not going to win.

Somehow, she's taken over my whole segment, and the promos she'd put together promised the audience an exciting day with "One of Our Own." I'm sure they'd prefer new cars a la Oprah, but all they'll get is me. My hands are trembling uncontrollably, and I sit on them to stop them from flinching. I can hear the audience laughing and cheering at something, and at least, I feel a smidgen of pride in that. This is my show, my baby (or it was until Eva got her sweaty little paws on it), but I can't even concentrate on what's happening.

I run my fingers through my hair and shoot a quick glance at the television. I can barely take in the fact that Meghan and Bubba are making out like drunken teenagers on the stage, and Lisa has just walloped Ray in the gut. I do notice that Mitzy is giving the Ray Man a lot more TLC than he deserves. I look away from the monitor again. And then it happens.

I dart my eyes left and right to find a possible escape hatch, but it's too late because Mitzy says, "Well, everyone, as you know, we have an extra special surprise today. Our own associate producer is coming on our show to surprise the man she hasn't seen or talked

329

to in ten years. And she is one of our favorite people, so let's give Jamie a big round of applause so she can hear it in the green room."

In my ear, where the tiny speaker is hidden, I hear Lucy bark, "Jamie, go!"

I breathe in and out to slow my racing heart and take the short walk down the hall from the green room to the studio. Once I'm at the edge of the stage, I peek my head around the corner and sweep my eyes across the huge audience. Stacey was right. We're full to capacity, and I can feel the energy and tension mounting. I glance at Andrew, who's sitting in the front row keeping tabs on everything, but his head is down, his hair falling into his eyes (no matter how much he cuts it, it keeps flopping around his face), and he won't look at me. Why won't he even look at me?

But I can't think about it now because I'm about to go on national television. One foot on the stage, and the audience starts screaming. I see the cameras and the crowd, but as I stroll towards Mitzy, whose spaghetti arms are reaching toward me for a hug, I don't feel nervous anymore. I feel...comfortable. There's a thrilling surge of power coursing through me as I realize the audience is rapt, gawking at me like I'm somebody special. And, now I get it. Fame is a heady thing, and I want more than fifteen minutes of it.

Mitzy pulls me in and hugs me, and I think my face is bruised from her pushing it against her jutting collarbone. "Welcome, Jamie! You look beautiful! Doesn't she look beautiful, people?" she asks the audience, and they clap in agreement.

What are they going to do? Say no?

Mitzy leads me to the one waiting chair, and I smile at Bubba and Meghan (Bubba winks at me and grins), and I nod my head at Ray and Lisa. Ray nods back, but Lisa looks at me as if she has no clue who I am. I cross my legs, push my hair back and take a deep breath.

330

"Hi."

"Jamie, it is wonderful to have you here on this stage and not working behind it. And what a fantastic makeup job you've had."

I narrow my eyes at Mitzy, but really, I know that whatever she's saying isn't her fault. She's just Eva's mouthpiece at the moment. Eva wrote everything, and Brian, the sound guy, is reading it all into Mitzy's ear.

"Jamie, since we have all worked with you for many years, we know that it has been a difficult time for you recently, and we applaud your courage at risking rejection. And on national television! Your boyfriend broke up with you, you had to move out, and you haven't been on many dates. So, is that why you decided to find Lucas? Were you too scared to find a man you didn't know?"

Inside I'm cringing, but outwardly, I smile at Mitzy.

"Oh no, Mitzy, you've got it all wrong. Derek, my ex, and I were in a passionless, dull relationship, and I am a very passionate person. *I* broke up with *him* actually, because well, no, I shouldn't be telling you this."

Mitzy looks out at the audience and says, "We all want to hear what Jamie has to say, don't we?"

"Yes!" they cry in shameful excitement at hearing about someone else's weaknesses just to feel better about their own. Really, this should be the "Shaudenfraude Show."

I pause as if it pains me to tell them. "I left Derek because he didn't give me what I needed, if you know what I mean," and I smirk at the audience (who is this little actress inhabiting my body?), "but luckily, he found a woman who just doesn't need that kind of pleasure. For her I guess, love and fun just aren't as important as a fat bank account. In fact, I want to thank his new girlfriend for getting the noose off my neck."

I locate Eva in the audience and give her my best shit-eating grin. She, however, is not smiling.

"Anyway, I started this as a lark, finding Lucas, my old love. I've met a few other men since Derek and I broke up, but really, I loved Lucas when we were younger, and we lost touch, and I thought that if the other people on this stage could take a chance at finding love, then I should do it too because we all have that question in our minds. What if?"

"And you had a terrible childhood, Jamie. You were unpopular, your mother and father-"

"Oh no, Mitzy, I don't know where you heard that. I have the most incredible, loving and supportive family, and they are all here today."

Carl swings the camera in my family's direction, and they stand up to wave at the audience. Rachel, in her tight skinny jeans and black tube top, flips her hair back and purses her lips together in a kiss for the camera.

"My mother and father are divorced, yes, but I am so lucky to have two amazing step-mothers and one gorgeous sister. If I had listened to them, I wouldn't have been miserable with Derek all of those years."

The camera now moves in Derek's direction, and the audience, my audience, bless their hearts, boo and hiss at him. Eva is clutching his hand in a death grip, her mouth tight and her eyes wild. I have *never* had this much fun.

Mitzy looks at me and for the first time ever, she focuses on what's really happening. Smiling sweetly and shaking her head as if she's ignoring what's coming out of her ear, she says, "Well, Jamie, we all hope that you get what you want today because you are a great person, and you deserve it. So, why don't you go back to the green room and wait while we get your Lucas out here?"

And I'm done. I leave the stage to thunderous applause, and it's not until I'm back in the corridor on my way to the green room that

I realize what's just happened. I was on television! And I liked it! I wish I could remember what I've said because at the moment, it's all a blur, but I think I trumped Eva. I hope so. Back on the couch, I face the monitor again.

Mitzy's brief flash of intelligence is gone, and she's blinking blankly at the camera (as she does when nobody is telling her exactly what to do) until she gets the direction to smile and say, "And here's the man we've all been waiting for! Lucas!"

And there he is. My Lucas. In fitted dark jeans, an extremely tight white tank top (what a silly shirt), and a much less sullen expression than he had ten years ago. His body has definitely become more muscular over the years, I realize as I drink in the tanned biceps, sinewy shoulders and smooth neck. I wait for the free fall of my stomach. I wait for the pounding of my heart and the warm rush of blood to my head, but, strangely, there's nothing. I feel...nothing. Oh my God, I don't feel anything!

I grab one of the chairs and put it under the television. Standing on it, I try to press my face to the screen to get a closer look at him. The same black hair, now instead of messy and in his face, has been cut into a neatly cropped and spiky style, only achieved with massive quantities of gel. The Lucas I knew would never wear gel. Or a tank top. His face is lightly tanned and unwrinkled, and though he is still gorgeous, I feel not a flutter, a twinge or tingle. Nothing. What's going on? This is my destiny. The man of my dreams is out there waiting for me. And I don't want him.

Lucas takes a seat, looking around frantically, I think, for the reason he's on this ridiculous show, and he seems awfully confused.

"Lucas, welcome! You are an extremely good-looking man."

He crosses his legs, squints and mumbles, "Um, thanks."

"You must be wondering why we brought you here." Mitzy beams at him.

"The question did enter my mind, yes."

Mitzy giggles and stares at him. One second, two, three, four. Jesus Mitzy, get with it!

"Before we bring out the person who wanted to see you again, your lost love, is there anything you want to tell us? Any secret we should know about you?"

Lucas's face falls, and for a moment, he looks downright scared. He covers it pretty quickly with a dazzling smile, but I know that look of fear and anger in his eyes. The last time I saw that look was when we walked into his kitchen and found his mom's boyfriend pushing Wanda, his mom, up against the fridge with a crazed look in his eyes and a raised fist. When the boyfriend saw Lucas rushing for him, he fled and never came back. Like me, Lucas always pretended to be tougher than he was.

And I realize that Eva knows something about him, and it's big. And bad. But Lucas is too smart and wary to reveal whatever it is.

"Nope," he says.

"But aren't you-"

"I'm so excited to see whoever this person is, and I don't think I can wait any longer!" Lucas sits up straighter and looks directly at the audience, hoping, I guess, to get them on his side and to deflect their attention from whatever secret he's hiding.

"But-"

Suddenly, Lucy, dressed in head to toe combat gear, jumps up from the front row and clomps onto the stage. She grabs the blindfold from Mitzy's hand and smiles at Lucas. Mitzy tries to snatch the blindfold back and steps in front of Lucy. "Lucy! What are you-"

"I think we've made this patient audience wait long enough." She turns to face them. "Hello, everyone. I'm Lucy, the assistant director here, and I know that you are dying to see Lucas and our special guest reunite, aren't you?"

The audience screams in delight at the total chaos and unexpected turn of events, and Lucy elbows Mitzy out of the way, nearly knocking her onto the floor because she only weighs about fifty pounds, and forces her to fall onto Ray Man's lap. The Ray Man leers at Mitzy, and she grins at him. With Mitzy's attention diverted, Lucy walks over to Lucas, stands behind him and gently ties the black silk blindfold over his eyes. But I catch the look of total confusion in his sea green eyes before Lucy covers them. Enough is enough. I have to get out there.

I tear out of the green room and run down the hall to the stage door. But before I get on the stage, I look at Andrew, and this time, he looks back at me. And the strangest thing happens. The flutter, twinge and tingle that I'd expected to feel seeing Lucas is finally here. My heart is thrumming, my palms are sweaty, and my mouth is dry. Oh no. I'm a complete and utter idiot! Why do all of my hard hitting realizations always come at the worst times?

Lucas may very well have been the impetus to end things with Derek, but he is not the man I want. But I was so determined to find him and make him that man that I didn't see that the man I truly wanted was there the whole time. Andrew, who's been so good to me, who I have so much fun with, who's so good-looking and wonderful that I couldn't believe Kelly would let him go, is the one who's making me all hot and excited. Now what do I do?

What I do is walk confidently across the stage, barely registering the roar of applause and screaming from the audience. I quickly glance at the people hooting for me like they're at the Super Bowl and the ones who are saying nothing: Derek and Jeanette. Eva is slumped in her seat, obviously devastated that none of this has worked out like she had hoped. And since *none* of this is what I would have hoped for, especially the complete lack of attraction I feel for Lucas, all I can do is stare at Andrew, who looks crushed.

Was everyone right? Does he like me? There's only one way to find out. But I can't do it now. Now, I have to fake it because I am way too private to tell Andrew how I feel in front of a shrieking audience. I make my way over to Lucas and smile at the audience. They laugh in response and a huge rush of adrenalin makes me wink at them. I put a finger to my lips to quiet them, stand in front of Lucas, slowly untie the blindfold and stare at him. Right into those incredible eyes that used to drive me crazy, but now, do absolutely nothing for me.

He shakes his head as if not believing it's me and his mouth breaks out into a huge grin.

"Jamie! Is that really you?" he says, getting out of the seat.

"It's me, Lucas."

And he picks me up in a tight, crushing hug and twirls me around. The audience is going wild, screaming and cat calling, and Mitzy is trying to calm them down so she can hear what her next question is supposed to be.

"So, Lucas, are you shocked? Tell us how you meal," Mitzy says.

Meal? Really, this lady's gotta go.

"I'm stunned. The Jamie I knew would never go on TV unless she could watch it at the same time."

Another burst of hysterical laughter from the audience. I don't know why they find that so funny because you can only get the joke if you know me.

"It's been ten years since you saw each other. Jamie, here's your chance to tell Lucas why you brought him here."

I quickly run through my usual signs of stress. Hair? Not rolling around my tongue. Pinkie? Dangling comfortably near my hip and not clamped between my teeth. Jaw? Loose. I reach over and take Lucas's hand, which is cool and soft, but the touch doesn't send shivers up my spine or moisten any parts that he used to. I give him a sickly smile.

"Lucas, I recently ended a horrible relationship," and I look directly at Derek, which makes the audience swivel their heads to look at him too. When they do, they all boo at him again, and Derek flushes, while Eva is looking everywhere but at him. I guess it doesn't feel too good to be with the guy who's the biggest loser in the room. "And I, I thought that if I found you again, I'd be happy. I remembered how good you made me feel, how good we were together, I kept that beautiful letter you wrote-"

"Jamie, I think I should tell you something," he interrupts, worry and pain suddenly darkening the crystal clear green of his eyes.

I hold up a hand to stop him because I won't let him humiliate me on television. I am done looking like a fool. And I won't let him tell me what Eva knows about him. No, I'm going to give this screaming audience what they want. But the only way I can do that is to avoid Andrew's eyes which even from across the stage, I can see are filled with sadness.

"Lucas, you were always there for me, and I couldn't have gotten through the things I did without you. I don't know why we lost touch-"

"We lost touch because I told you I loved you, and you just drove away without a backwards glance. But, Jamie-"

"Ever since I decided to find you, I can't stop thinking about everything you meant to me, and I don't want to lose you again."

I swallow hard because although what I'm saying is true, I really don't want to say what I'm about to because it will be the biggest lie of all. The whole audience by this point is leaning forward, desperate to catch my every word, and even though there's a camera trained at my head and a microphone taped to my bra, I, like everyone else who's been in my exact same spot, have somehow forgotten that I'm on television.

337

I look out into the audience and the whole lot of them are open-mouthed. Except Derek and Jeanette, who are tight-lipped and tense, which gives me the kick in the ass I need. And so, I say it.

"Lucas, I want a second chance."

Lucas looks shocked, and before he can say anything (and I have no idea what he's going to say because he certainly doesn't look happy right now), a roar erupts, and it's not from me. No, the audience is on its feet, screaming, "Kiss her! Kiss her!"

Whatever Lucas is feeling, he masks it by grinning, his beautiful pouty lips coming close to mine. He turns his head slightly to face the hyper audience and asks, "Should I?"

"Yes! Yes! Yes!" the unruly crowd screams, now banging their hands on the backs of the chairs in front of them and stomping their feet so hard that the stage vibrates. I sneak a glance at Andrew, whose jaw muscle is jumping out of his skin.

"No, wait, I-"

I don't get to finish. Lucas awkwardly cradles my face in his hands (and this is odd because there was never any awkwardness between us when it came to our sex drives) and whispers, "We really need to talk after this," in my ear and presses his lips to mine.

Not one part of my body is zinging. I feel like I'm kissing my brother and it's actually a bit nauseating. But for the sake of the show and for Eva, who so desperately wanted me to be utterly degraded and belittled, I put my hands in his thick gelled hair and pull him closer. Counting to five in my head, we kiss long enough to give the audience what they want and for me to know that I have never been so wrong in my life.

You can't go back.

CHAPTER THIRTY-SIX

Two hours later, Lucas, Lucy, Hanna, Jack, Amy, Chris and my entire family are having lunch (paid for by the show, of course, since Lucas and I are here together) outside at a restaurant overlooking Lake Michigan. We didn't invite Derek and Jeanette. Oddly, they disappeared with Eva very quickly after the show ended. After that uncomfortable and platonic kiss, I know that Lucas and I have to talk, and I was going to invite him out for lunch with us anyway, but Rachel got to him first. I'm surprised that Carl and his rolling dolly haven't followed us here, but I guess the novelty wore off after we left the stage. Well, there goes my foray into fame. And my chance with Andrew is long gone, too. He took off right after the show, and I never got a chance to talk to him.

I should be focusing on Lucas considering the last few weeks of my life have been entirely devoted to this moment, but I can only stare morosely at the tablecloth. I don't have much time to wallow, however, because Katie, Leah, my dad and Mo just keep staring at me in wonderment.

"She gets her stage presence from you, David," Mo is saying.

My stage presence?

"What stage presence?" I ask.

All heads swivel to look at me, and everyone starts talking at the same time.

"You were incredible up there."

"Gorgeous."

"A natural."

"I can't believe we didn't know this before."

What are they all talking about? I'm sure I was stiff as a board

339

up there. But, I have to admit that it felt so good having everyone's attention on me and manipulating the situation to make the most of it. Me. The person who never likes being looked at was addicted to the adrenalin and rush.

"So, Lucas, now that you're back with Jamie, are you going to move back to Chicago?" Rachel yells at him from across the table.

I purposely sat us as far away as possible from her because I knew she would ask him embarrassing questions the minute she could. Apparently, she can still do it.

"Rach!"

"No, that's okay. Actually, Jamie, can we go somewhere and talk? This is kind of overwhelming, and, well, we really need to talk."

Yes, we do. We push our chairs back from the table, and as we pass Leah, she smiles at me. She knows something. I go to reach for his hand, but something stops me so instead, I point to a bench near the water that's far enough away so my family can't hear us, and we sit down. I stare straight ahead and take a deep breath. "So."

"So."

I watch the water lap against the rocks on the shore for a moment. The slapping sound lulls me, and I take another big gulp of oxygen, but before I can say anything, Lucas starts talking. "God, Jamie, it's good to see you again. You look great. Really great."

"So do you. Different, but good."

He puts his hand on mine and turns to face me. "Jamie, I don't know why I'm here. When I got the call, I thought it was some crazy joke and so I played along. I still thought it was a joke until a courier dropped off my plane ticket, and-"

"Lucas, I am so sorry. I never wanted it to turn out like this. I wanted to find you, because, uh, well because I broke up with my asshole boyfriend after five years, and I was a mess. I was so scared to be alone and so scared that I'd never meet anyone again."

I've said all of this while looking at the water, and now, I turn to look at him. Something in his eyes makes it okay for me to be honest, and it's that feeling of total ease that I missed. Not the sex, not the love, but the friendship. I just wish I'd realized it before now.

"Oh, Jaim, I'm so sorry. I wish I'd been there for you when you were going through all of that." He holds my hand and squeezes. "I wish I hadn't been such a coward."

"A coward? What do you mean?"

"Okay, look, Jamie, I don't want to hurt you. You are the last person I would ever want to hurt because you were so important to me. And even though we haven't talked in so long, I have never forgotten you. I would never have found the clarity in my life that I did without you and without knowing who your family was."

"Clarity? I don't understand."

"Oh God. Jamie, I'm gay."

My mouth opens and hits the ground. Hard.

"What?!"

"I am so sorry. I know that you were hoping that we could get back together, and I really did love you, and you are an amazing woman. I always knew you would be, but-"

"Hold on. You're gay? Gay as in Leah and Katie gay? Liking men gay?"

"Yes. I didn't know when we were together, I swear, but you were the last woman I was with. After you drove away that night, I spent a good long time looking at myself and after a few months, well, I couldn't deny it anymore."

And now I understand what secret Eva had discovered.

"That bitch! She knew! That's why she did all this. She wanted me to sit there and tell the world that I lost my virginity to a gay guy. And that the love of my life didn't even like women!"

341

Lucas wrinkles his forehead. "What are you talking about? Who's a bitch?"

"Okay, oh God, here's the story. Yes, I wanted to find you, but God, I would never have wanted to bring you on the show! I would never do that to you. All I wanted was to find you and see you again. So, I went to Detroit, and you were on fucking vacation, and I was about to give up when Eva, one of the other associate producers, found out what I was doing and sabotaged me. She made it look like I'd planned for you to be on the whole time, that underhanded bitch! She's with my ex, Derek, but noooo, that wasn't enough for her. She wanted to see me fall and so she got you here, somehow found out you were gay and was just waiting for you to announce it so everyone would know what a loser I am."

"Looks like she's the loser now, doesn't it?"

I grin. "Karma's a bitch."

After a few seconds, I calm down from my tirade, move the sand beneath my feet around with my toes and chew on the inside of my lip.

"Lucas, did I make you gay?"

Lucas smiles and gently strokes my cheek. "Jamie, c'mon, you know better than anyone that you can't make someone gay. It had nothing to do with you. Well, it did, but only in the sense that you helped me be myself. And knowing Leah and Katie and how you grew up helped. My mom wasn't like yours, you know that. She wasn't educated like Katie and Leah, and she worked so hard to raise me on her own. I don't think she could see beyond the food she had to put on the table to look at life's bigger questions. And I think she always hoped you and I would end up together. Jamie, you were my best friend."

"And Lucas, you were mine. I'm happy for you. Really. I would only want you to be happy. I'm just shocked because, well, because in the last few weeks as I was looking for you, most of the memories I had, were, um, were of-"

"Sex."

I blush, but I nod.

"Jamie, the sex with you was amazing. Not because you were a woman, but because you were you. But if I had known that it was you who wanted to see me, well, I would have called first."

I laugh. "Who did you think it was?"

"Honestly? Claire. That girl constantly called me until I changed numbers after college."

"Well, she's married, rich as sin and living like a queen now. Hey, didn't you sleep with her before we got, um, got together again?"

Now it's his turn to blush. "I tried, but she's the kind of girl you've got to give a big old rock to before you can get her pants off."

"And what? I was easy?"

"No, you were perfect."

"Stupid question, but what's been going on in your life for the last ten years? How's your dad?"

"Dead."

My stomach drops."Oh, Lucas, I'm sorry. When?"

"About eight years ago. He died alone in his apartment, and it was three days before anyone found him. He never got help, he never came back to see me, and he died alone."

"And how are you? How were you?"

"It took a lot of therapy to deal with it. I guess like kids always hope their parents will get back together after a divorce, I always hoped he'd get better, go to AA, come back and live with us. But, I'm good. Really. My mom was always both of my parents."

"How is your mom? When I started thinking about us, I always thought about her."

"She's married now to a really nice man who adores her."

I smile. "That's so great. You have to say hello to her for me."

"I can do better than that. Since we're going to stay in touch, you'll just have to see her."

I wrap my arms around myself. "I would love that. Does she know, um, know that you're gay?"

"Yes. She was pretty stunned at first, and I guess a bit confused by it all, but when I was with Mark, my ex, she treated him like family."

"And you and Mark had a bad break up?"

"If you call finding him in bed with a friend of his bad, yeah, you could say that."

"God, our lives haven't been easy, have they?"

"No, but they've been good, I think. And we were good for each other. You look sad, though, Jamie, and I don't want it to be because of me."

I shake my head. "It's not. I swear. Sure, I'm shocked you're gay, but even though I'd built up seeing you again so much in my mind, when I actually saw you, I didn't feel anything like I'd expected to. When we were younger, every time I saw you, I was more attracted to you. And now, well, even though you're even better looking now, I just don't feel that way anymore. In some ways, I'm glad that you're gay because then I don't feel horrible for bringing you here for nothing."

"Not for nothing. But I knew when I kissed you on that ridiculous stage that something wasn't right." He laughs. "What a surreal day. So, if it's not me, then who?"

"How do you know it's a who and not a what?"

"Because I know you. So, what's the problem?"

I tell him. From Andrew's friendship, sexy rumbling laugh, eyes that crinkle in the corners, his one dimple, all our talks and the fact that he now hates me.

"Come here, Jaim. Andrew will come around. You're too good

to let go of."

Lucas pulls me towards him in a close, comfortable and completely tingle free hug, and I hold him tight. His strong arms wrap around me, and I feel safe. The way I always felt when I was with him. My nose is buried in his lovely scented shoulder (gay men really do smell better) when I hear someone cough.

"Well, I wish you guys the best of luck. Lucas, you've got a good one here so treat her right."

Andrew is standing behind us, watching us hug, and I'm sure, totally misunderstanding what's going on because he speedwalks away as soon as he sees us holding each other. Before I can react, he's gone.

"Andrew, wait!"

I jump off the bench and race after him. Lucas runs beside me, and we pant to catch up with Andrew's long legs. I spot him heading back to the table (where I'm sure my family and friends are watching all of this with bated breath), and I run up behind him, grabbing his arm. "Andrew, please, listen to me."

"I'm done, Jamie. Leah asked me to meet her at the restaurant, and I thought that maybe, well, whatever, I was wrong. Again."

"Leah asked you to come? When?"

"After the show, she came up to me and said that if I met her here, I would understand what's been going on. And I really like your mom, but I don't think she has any idea what's going on."

"Oh, she probably does. She sees things." And I know that Leah's figured it all out. Lucas being gay, my wanting Andrew, all of it.

Lucas catches up to us, and he puts his hand on Andrew's shoulder. "Hey, man, just wait a minute."

Andrew shakes off Lucas's hand and continues walking, saying over his shoulder, "I just wanted to tell Jamie she did a good job. Obviously. She got what she wanted."

"No, she didn't. Not yet. Look, man, you need to know that I-"

"I don't need to hear it. Really. Lucas, you seem like a good guy, but I don't need *you* to tell me anything."

"Andrew, I'm gay."

Andrew stops in his tracks and slowly turns around. "Pardon?"

"He's gay, Andrew. Lucas is gay. But it doesn't matter. I thought all this time that I would be happy if I could find him. I thought that everything would be okay if I could just get back what we had when we were younger. But I was wrong. I am happy that I've found him, but not because I want him back, but because I don't want to lose a great friend again. It's not, he's not, I don't want him, not like that."

"No?" Still curt. Still angry.

"Leah was right. I have something I need to say to you. And you know how hard it is for me to talk about how I feel so don't say anything until I'm finished, okay?"

He nods slowly, still wary of me, but at least he's willing to listen. I take a deep, steadying breath and look into his warm brown eyes. "It's been you I've wanted all this time."

"Are you fucking joking?" he spits at me.

"No, I'm not joking," I retort and cross my arms over my chest. "I was so busy looking for Lucas that I didn't realize that the guy I really wanted was right in front of me. I'm a bit unfocused sometimes."

"Sometimes?"

And just as I'm about to shoot one back, I see his dimple deepen, and he's smiling. "And it's been you I've wanted all this time, Jamie, but you knew that."

"What?! Every time we were together, it was Kelly this and Kelly that. How was I supposed to know? Am I a mind reader now?"

"I told you that you're beautiful, I told you that I love being

346

with you, I told you I love your family. What else do I have to do? Kiss you?"

"No! I mean, no, not here with my family watching. Later. Oh God."

Andrew laughs and runs his finger over my eyebrows, eyelids and cheeks. "Jamie, just shut up, okay?"

I nod as Andrew's arms reach out towards me, and instinctively, I fall into his chest and stay there. It's warm, firm, and totally the right place to be. Then he does it. He tucks a finger under my chin and lifts my mouth to meet his. And there's a moment of magic, not too fast or slow when our mouths meet, and suddenly, we're in that sacred space between being distant and intimately close.

Andrew puts one hand in my hair and presses his other fingers into the nape of my neck and draws me in closer. Deeper. Of course, like everything in my life, all of this is happening at the wrong time. In front of my crazy family. And Lucas, who's walked back to the table, is enough of a voyeur to join the ever watchful eyes of my family. But all I can think about are Andrew's soft lips pressed against mine and how his scorching kiss is making me lightheaded and dizzy.

Finally, he unclamps his mouth from mine, leans back and says, "Wow."

I swallow. "Yeah, wow."

"Woo hoo! Good one, Andrew!" I hear Katie yell from across the grassy field.

Everyone at the table is giving us a standing ovation, and sure, I'm embarrassed, but I'll just have to learn to take my family as they are. Lovable freaks. Andrew and I smile at each other.

"Should we join them?" he asks, tangling his fingers in my hair.

I shiver at his touch and nod. We sit down, and everyone

resumes eating and drinking as if today were completely normal. I guess in the recent life of Jamie Ross, it is.

"Finally! Jamie, I thought you'd never clue in. I was planning to stage an intervention," Katie says and grins at us. "But, Leah was right. Let nature take its course, she said, and it would only be a matter of time before this happened."

"You knew?" I ask, not surprised at all and turning to look at her.

"What do you think we talked about the day he came for a massage? Poor guy was such a mess over you. Did you really think he drove all the way back to Chicago for a massage from me?"

I turn my head the other way to gape at Andrew.

"You said you needed expert help."

Andrew laughs. "In Chicago? No, Jamie, I wanted to meet your family."

"But I thought you were upset about Kelly."

"I was. Because you made me see how wrong she was for me. How scared I was to leave. The minute I met you, I knew there was something so special about you."

Now it's my turn to blush. No man, besides my dad, has ever called me special.

"Oh, gag. Can you guys stop? I'm trying to eat here," Rachel pipes in and shoves more burger into her mouth while changing seats with Lucy so she can get closer to the action.

I look around the table at all of the people I love and sigh happily. "Thank you so much guys for being there for me. All of you. It's funny. I thought this would be the worst day of my life, and it's turned out to be one of the best."

"And I'm so happy we found each other again, Jamie. Or I'm happy that you found me," Lucas tells me and reaches out to hold my hand.

"Hey, Lucas, you're single, right?" Lucy asks.

He nods. "Unfortunately, yes. I also just ended a bad relationship. It's hard for me to meet people, and I'm so busy teaching that I don't have the time to get out there."

"But you're hot," Rachel argues and tries to take a sip of my beer. I snatch it out of her hand and raise it to my mouth instead.

Lucas smiles at Rachel. "And shy. Like your sister here. That's why we always got along so well."

Lucy smiles wryly. "Well, being shy is not a trait I possess. Why don't we hit some of the gay bars tonight before you go back to Detroit?"

"You don't mind?"

"Mind? She'd be delighted," I say.

"Can we come?" Leah asks, eyes shiny with excitement.

Lucy leans over and kisses her on the cheek. "We'll all go."

"Actually, Jamie and I have other plans," Andrew says mysteriously.

"We do?" I ask him.

"Yup. First, we have to go back to the office because Stacey wants to see you, and then, tonight, it's just you and me."

A bubble of delicious anticipation bobs in my chest, and I'm grinning like a fool. I nod at Andrew, and he takes my hand in his, stroking my fingers with the most erotic light touches. If this is how I feel when he touches my fingers, just imagine what will happen when he gets to the rest of me.

"Jamie, you're bright red!" Rachel kindly points out.

"She's imagining having sex with Andrew," Amy pipes in.

The red turns to fuchsia, but instead of closing up and getting quiet, I laugh and say, "You betcha."

CHAPTER THIRTY-SEVEN

Walking beside Andrew, my hand in his, neither of us can keep the stupid smiles off our faces. But there is something else I need to talk about.

"Andrew, can we sit for a minute?" I ask, indicating the curb outside our office building.

After today, I think I'll be chock full of heart to hearts. He locks eyes with me and tightens his grip on my hand. We sit down, and I put my hand on his thigh. Oh, and what a thigh it is! Rock hard with lean muscle, it fits perfectly under my wandering hand.

"Okay, here's my problem. You and Kelly were together for so many years, and I do not want to be your rebound girl. I want to be the girl after your rebound girl. What if you realize that after being with her for so long that you really want to be single? I'm, hmm, I'm-"

"Scared?"

I nod. "Okay, yes."

"And you think I'm not? I didn't plan on meeting someone so soon after Kelly. If I hadn't met you, I might still be with Kelly and miserable. But, I'm in love with you, Jamie, and I have been since the day I saw you in that meeting arguing with Eva. I was in love with you when I was still with Kelly. And I know that that's not the most moral thing to say, but it's true."

I take my hand off his knee and squint at him. "Really? Why didn't you tell me? We were alone for days, and shit, we even shared a hotel room."

"C'mon, you weren't exactly open to it. And I tried. Every time I tried, you shied away. Every time I made some comment or told you you're beautiful, you changed the subject. And now I know

350

why. I'm worried that because Lucas is gay, I'm the runner up here. It was pretty crushing to know that you worked so hard to see him and to know that he was the one you were thinking about the entire time you were with me. And all I could think about was kissing you."

"It was the idea of Lucas I wanted. Derek really hurt me. I always felt that I was never good enough for him, and I got it into my head that the only man who might want me is the one who had already had me. But, I promise you, Andrew, the second I saw him, I realized what a fool I'd been. I felt nothing for him, and we were both just pretending on that stage."

"That worries me too. Jamie, you lied about Detroit and the requisition, and you manipulated it so he could get on the show."

I drop his hand and bolt up. "You really think I brought Lucas here? After all this time, you still don't believe me? You still don't know me?"

I stand up, furious that he still doesn't get that it was Eva all along.

"Jamie, wait."

I turn around. "No, you wait! I'm so tired of being misunderstood and not being taken for who I am. It was Eva, you idiot. I told you that! *She* stole Lucas's information off my desk, *she* wrote a fake proposal, and *she* forged my signature! Lucy only said it was us in a misguided attempt at saving my ass. And I don't know what I can do to make you believe that. But, I'm so fucking tired of trying. I *never* wanted to be on the show. Ever! And if you don't believe that, then we have nothing more to say."

I stomp heavily towards the revolving front doors of the building and push my way through only to realize that he's gotten in with me. He stops the door from turning with his foot and presses his body against mine.

"Fuck off, Andrew."

351

"No. Not this time."

His full lips rub against mine, and his tongue delicately strokes and twirls around the tip of my own; he pushes his tongue deeper inside my mouth and nips at my bottom lip, tugging on it with delicious little bites. My head spins, and my anger melts into giddiness as the kiss gets more frenzied and his hand strokes my lower back, encircles my waist, and he draws me even closer to him.

"So, you believe me?"

"I believe you. Can we stop fighting?"

"I've never heard better words."

There's more kissing while his fingers lightly trace the outside of my breasts, and I just want to tear his clothes off right here. I don't give a damn that Julius the security guard is watching us, his tongue hanging out; eyes, the size of dinner plates.

"I don't want to stop, but Stacey has," he says and kisses me again. And again. And again.

I stroke my hands along his probably very stressed out jaw, smile and say, "Stacey has what?"

"What?"

"You said Stacey has, and then you stopped. What does she have?"

He grins, showing off his bright teeth, the bottom front one a little crooked. "I don't remember. Oh God, what have you done to me, girl? Right, right. Listen, Stacey has something she wants to talk to you about."

"Do you know what?"

"Yes." His tone is teasing.

"Tell me."

"Nope."

"I can make you tell me," I say and tickle him under the armpits.

352

"Stop, stop! I can't. C'mon, we'll go talk to her," he says, pushing on the door so we both spill out into the lobby.

"It's always 'we' with you, isn't it?"

Andrew pulls me close and kisses the tip of my nose. "Only with you, Jamie. Did you honestly think that I really go with all the associate producers on business trips? How would I get any work done if I did that?"

I'm such a moron.

Back in the studio (after I catch Julius eyeing my ass appreciatively after seeing it pushed up against the glass of the revolving door), it's a buzz of electricity, and Eva is nowhere in sight. Andrew goes to his office, and seconds later, Adrienne, Horace, and Jennifer come rushing over.

"Oh my God, Jamie! You little vixen! I never knew you were so good on camera. And looking for that Lucas guy? Julius just called up and told us to watch the security camera so we saw you and Andrew! One guy's not enough for you, hey?" Horace says.

"You certainly don't take the boring road, that's for sure. Here we are thinking you're this shy, innocent girl, and all this time, you were sleeping with the boss!" Jennifer shrieks.

I open my mouth in shock. "Oh God, is that what everyone thinks? We weren't. We haven't, I mean, it wasn't until today that we even talked about it."

"Sure, sure, you lucky girl," Adrienne tells me and smacks me on the ass.

"Jamie," Stacey wanders over and interrupts the little gossip session. "Can I speak with you for a minute?"

"Uh oh," Horace sings. "Somebody's in trouble."

But when I'm in Stacey's office, I discover that I'm in no trouble at all. In fact, she wants to change my life.

"Jamie, the phone has been ringing off the hook. We have never received so many calls after a show."

"Well, like Andrew said when he suggested the idea, these shows always do well."

"No, you don't understand. It wasn't the topic, it was you."

I squint in confusion and point at my chest. "Me? What do you mean?"

"We've had hundreds of requests, by phone and email, to have you back on the air. Here, look," she says and hands me a thick stack of papers.

I quickly read through them, seeing many with the words, "You must get that Jamie woman on air again. She should be the host." And there are pages like that. Adjectives like "bubbly," "clever," "charming," even "beautiful" come flying at me, and I don't know what to say.

I hand the papers back to her. "I don't know what to say."

"Don't say anything, just listen. You are a fantastic associate producer because you get things done. And as I'm sure you're aware, Mitzy isn't exactly working out like we had hoped. I will admit that I wouldn't have expected you to be so effervescent and magnetic on air, but you are. Almost every person who's contacted us today has told us that you should be the host of the show."

I'm frozen. I see Stacey's mouth opening and closing, and I think she's still talking, but the last thing I heard was "you should be the host."

"Are you out of your mind? I could never do that! Today was a one off. I never even wanted to do this. I'm a behind the scenes kind of person, Stacey."

She shakes her head. "Not anymore. Just think about it, okay? I've already talked to Andrew about it, and he thinks it's a great idea."

"He does?"

She examines me for a moment. "Jamie, there's a lot more to you than you give yourself credit for."

"Yeah, I'm beginning to realize that," I say and start walking out of her office.

"Oh, Jamie? One more thing."

I turn around.

"Eva quit."

A huge grin spreads across my face until it hurts. "Are you serious?"

"Completely. She came in with Derek and some angry woman and dropped her resignation on my desk. Apparently, he doesn't want her working for this show anymore."

"I won't see her again?"

"No. And neither will we. I will say that she is very determined, but I wasn't blind to how she treated you, and I know what she did to you. Lucy explained everything. I was about to fire her when she quit."

"So you know everything?"

Stacey nods and nervously wrings her hands. "You're not going to do anything about it, are you?"

I cock my head to the side in confusion. "About what?"

"It's illegal to forge someone's signature. Some kind of fraud, I think. But, Jamie, if the papers found out how Eva stabbed one of our own staff in the back, it could be disastrous for us, but if you want to, we'll stand behind you."

I hadn't even thought about that. But as much as I'd love to see Eva brought to her knees, I won't do anything about it. I'm not her, I'm not cruel, and in the end, I did get what I wanted.

"No, Stacey, I won't do anything. It might actually give us some great exposure in the press, but I think it's time for this show to focus on other people and not the people who work here. I hate what Eva did to me, but I just want it to be over. I want to move on."

Stacey breathes an obvious sigh of relief. "Thank you, Jamie.

You know, Eva is a manipulative and shrewd woman, but I always knew you could hold your own."

"Yes, I can."

CHAPTER THIRTY-EIGHT

"It wasn't me!" I scream happily for the fifth time, bouncing my butt up and down on my bed.

"Will you stop saying that!" Andrew bellows at me. But he's smiling.

"No, no, no! I am the best in bed! Ha, ha, it was Derek all along."

"Now that we've got that taken care of, come here and let's do it again."

I jump on top of Andrew (I've just jumped off a minute ago after having sex for the third time in about an hour and a half) and cover his chest with tiny kisses. This is unbelievable. He's unbelievable. And I, well yes, I am also quite unbelievable.

"Jamie," he says in between kissing my little breasts. "What about the job?"

"I don't know," I sigh.

I roll off him and back on my side of the bed. We've been in here all evening, and I don't even know if Chris and Amy are home. I don't care. All I care about is this. Andrew and me, and the best sex I've ever had. After being with the same woman for almost twenty years, he certainly knows his way around a woman's body and is so happy to learn a few things about mine. He keeps squeezing my ass and sighing with pleasure.

Now he does it again and says, "Never lose this. It is so goddamn sexy."

"Really?"

"Really," he assures me and flips me over so he can bite it.

"Ow!" I yell.

But, it feels so good.

357

"I would love to see you on television. But all the men would come and see you, and I'll have to chase them away with my manly muscles."

Andrew is definitely in good shape, lean and sinewy, but I wouldn't exactly call him hugely muscular. More trim and taut, except where it counts. Derek can't hold a candle to him in that area. I laugh and stroke his cheek. "I doubt that. Anyway, you're the only one I want."

"Took you long enough to figure that out."

"I'm a little slow sometimes."

"And blind."

"And blind."

"And stupid."

"Alright, I get it."

Ring, ring. There's the phone again. It's been ringing off the hook since we got here, but I haven't picked it up. But, this time, it's Hanna's special ring (call once, hang up, and call right back), and since we had no time to really talk after the show, I answer it.

"Hello?" I chirp.

"Hello back. Are you getting laid?"

"That's so romantic, Han. But, yeah, I am. Oh my God, I can't believe how it all turned out."

"I told you he liked you."

"I know. I wasn't listening."

"Always trust me. Anyway, Jack and I just wanted to tell you how incredible you are."

"Without you and Jack, I couldn't have done it."

"As much as I'd like to take credit for it all, it was all you, Jaim. I honestly never would have thought you'd be so good on stage. You had that audience eating out of your hand."

"I know. And guess what?"

"After today, I couldn't possibly guess. What's up?"

"Stacey called me into the office, and, Andrew, stop it," I tell him as he's licking my toe from under the covers.

Instead of coming up for air, he slithers up my body with his tongue, and the phone drops to the floor.

"Hello? Jamie?" I hear Hanna yell.

I grab Andrew's chin in my hand. "Wait!" And I reach an arm out to get the phone. "Sorry, Andrew's here, and it's kind of hard to concentrate."

"Just tell me what you were going to tell me, and he can fuck you in a second."

"Does that sweet talk work with Jack?"

She laughs. "Oh my God, just tell me!"

"Right, sorry. Stacey asked me if I would be the host of the show and replace Mitzy. Can you believe it?!"

"Last week, I would have said no. But after seeing how you glowed up on that stage and how you just came alive, I think you'd be amazing at it. But do you want to do it?"

"Part of me thinks it would be awful to be on camera all the time, at the center of everything. But then the other side of me thinks that's exactly why I should do it."

"What does Andrew think?" she asks.

"He thinks she's amazing," Andrew says into the mouthpiece.

"Let me talk to him for a second," Hanna tells me.

"Why?"

"I just want to talk to him. Don't worry."

Andrew has now since moved and is on his back, stroking my leg. I put my hand on his chest and tangle my fingers in his silky brown hair and hand him the phone. "Hanna wants to talk to you."

He takes the phone from me, kisses my hand and listens to what she has to say. He's smiling and nodding, looking at me with those beautiful brown eyes that once looked so sad and now have the sparkle back. And I love that I helped bring it back.

"I will," he says and hangs up.

"What did she say?" I ask, curious and slightly nervous.

"She told me that I'd better treat you the way you deserve to be treated, and if I break your heart, she'll kill me."

"She would too, you know."

"With her boobs or her nails?" he asks.

I laugh, but then I get serious. "Andrew, I'll be so good to you. You're the best thing that's ever happened to me, and I-"

"I love you too, Jamie."

So this is what it feels like. Actually being accepted for all of my quirks, all of my idiosyncrasies, and not in spite of them. I prop myself on one elbow and gaze adoringly at Andrew.

"Thank you," I say quietly.

He kisses me and asks, "For what?"

"For giving me a chance. For forgiving me. For coming to work at the show. What would have happened if I had never met you?"

"We'll never know. But with you, I feel like I can do anything. Without your family, you wouldn't be the nut you are. This is meant to be."

I smile and shake my head at him. "Nothing is meant to be, Andrew. Life doesn't work that way. If it did, there wouldn't be a point in trying anything because you'd know exactly how your life is supposed to turn out."

"How about we try something new?" he says and flips me over on my stomach again.

He trails his tongue down my back, holds my arms over my head and thrusts inside me until I'm yelling, "Ah, oh God, oh, I'm going to come!"

It may not be destiny, but, oh my, it's exactly where I want to be.

CHAPTER THIRTY-NINE

So, I didn't take the job. Not because I was scared or because I thought I couldn't do it. But because there are things that I've never done that I've always wanted to and now seems like the perfect time. So, I've sublet my room (to Rachel, who somehow convinced everyone that this would be good for both me and her) for the next six months because I am going travelling. Well, I'm not exactly travelling, and I'm not going alone.

Both Andrew and I have left "Tell It Like It Is" because working there hasn't exactly been what dreams are made of. I stayed because I didn't see the possibility of anything better, and Andrew only took the job because Kelly wanted to be in Chicago. Andrew's last documentary on the lingering effects of the Cold War was nominated for a Hot Docs award, and he's been offered the chance to write and direct a documentary on AIDS in Africa. He wants me to go with him to produce and narrate it. In front of the camera. And I jumped at the chance.

Not just the chance to finally leave North America, which I have never done, but to be with him. All Andrew's ever wanted was to do good, and I've spent most of my life only doing things for myself. So, in one week, after all of the goodbye parties thrown by my family (who have now adopted him as their own) and his parents (who are having a bit of trouble getting used to Katie and Leah, but they'll come around, everyone does), we'll be ready to go.

It's a gorgeous end of summer morning when the air is fresh and cool, and the delicious smell of the freshly cut grass being watered under sprinklers permeates the air. Today, we're taking a picnic to the Lakefront Trail (by car) and spending the day just

361

together. With all of the fanfare, we haven't had that much time to be alone. And that's all I want when I see him. To kiss him, lick him, bite him and yes, love him now that I know what being in love really feels like. And with someone who likes me just the way I am. Because of the way I am.

I open the front door, flooded by the warm sunshine, and see a cream-colored envelope sticking out of the mailbox. Curious, I pick it up and rip it open. Tell me this is not a wedding invitation. They did *not* send me a wedding invitation.

Mrs. Jeanette Leeds

&

Dr. and Mrs. Robert Goldentool
request the honor of your presence
at the marriage of their children
Derek Harold Leeds the Third

to

Eva Martha Goldentool
October 25th at the Beverly Country Club
Black Tie Required

Well, that's one wedding I'm not going to. They probably invited me just to gloat in my face. But, they should know that this is the only revenge I can imagine. I never knew that Derek's middle name was Harold, and I certainly didn't know that "Goldentool" was Eva's last name. That prompts me to put the invitation on the fridge. Maybe Amy and Chris can do something raunchy and seedy with that name.

Anyway, Andrew and I have another wedding to attend. Yes, Hanna and Jack are getting married. My stunning, perpetually single friend is getting married to a great man, and I couldn't be happier for her. Jack took her to New York for the weekend, filled a hotel room with orchids and did the whole on one knee thing. And he waited until she said yes to let her know that the reason it's so easy for him to leave the law and follow his dreams is because he's a trust fund baby and has way more money than Hanna ever could. Smart guy. I am her maid of honor (we wouldn't have it any other way), and Andrew and I will be back right before the wedding. I'm sure Lucas and Lucy will go together since they've become close texting friends who constantly message each other with their romantic woes.

I couldn't have planned for my life to be better. And that part of me hasn't changed. I still believe that you have to live life in each second it gives you, and you can't really search for happiness because God, look what happened to me when I did that. But, what I do know now is that you have to reach out and seize it when it's staring you right in the face or you'll never know what you're missing.

Or what you will find.

ACKNOWLEDGEMENTS

Writing and publishing *Finding Lucas* could not have been accomplished without the support and love of all of the wonderful people in my life. I have so many to thank.

First, I must thank my parents, Celia and Michael Stroh, who have always taught me to go after my dreams. They have always believed that I could do great things, and without them, I wouldn't have had the courage to publish *Finding Lucas*. They support me in everything I do and are there for me in every way I need. My mom, who was a fantastic publicist, and one of my incredible editors, gave her insight and intelligence which helped shape the book into what it is.

To my brother Jonah, talented, clever and ambitious, watching all of your success over the years has motivated me to fulfill my potential. Your support, love and friendship mean the world to me.

To my Bubbie, Zaide and Grandma, you might be gone from this world, but you will always be in my heart.

To my in-laws, Ron and Eileen Bailey, who love me for who I am and read everything I write. I love you so much, and you are more than in-laws, you are my second mom and dad.

To Scott Bailey, Todd Bailey and Lori Henderson, my brothers-in–law and sister-in-law who complete my family and inspire me all of the time.

To Miko Dubiansky, my very best friend and sister of my heart. We met in a bathroom at McGill University eons ago, and ever since, she has been my soul mate. I might never have written any of my novels if we hadn't decided to write one together. With a pen in one hand and a drink in the other, we sat down to co-write a novel that never came to be. Instead, a lifelong passion to write became a reality as I took that idea and wrote my first novel. Not only has Miko read and edited everything I have ever written, but she has always believed in me. I love you, Miko.

To my sisters-in-law, Perlita Stroh and Lindsay Reid, for also editing my novels and laughing out loud at the funny parts. Their brilliance, wit and guidance helped make my words sparkle and my characters come alive.

To my gorgeous and brilliant nieces and nephews: Hannah, Mikey, Felix, Brynna, Owen and Sebastien. I love you so much.

To my godchildren, Zackary and Zoe, you are so special to me.

To Jessica Hayton, a wonderful editor, teacher and friend, whose honesty and sharp eyes caught my every mistake.

To everyone who helped in some way make this book a reality: Tim Moffat (who designed my original ebook cover), Allison Signer, (whether near or far, I am always thinking about you), Jenny Zucker, Carlo Carosi (my brilliant tech guy and paperback designer), Briar Young, Lesley Swartz, Rebecca Eckler, Catherine Moore, Michael Dubiansky and Brigitte Waisberg.

To my PLI family, thank you for all your love and support on my publishing journey. You mean so much to me.

To all of my readers, without you, *Finding Lucas* would still be but a dream.

But most importantly, the three people I have to thank are the ones who I live for: my husband, Brent, and my two incredible kids, Spencer and Chloe. Brent, you are my rock, my love and my everything. Thank you for giving me the time and space to work, for reading everything I write and always being right about the things I needed to change in the book—even though you would never read a romantic comedy.

Spencer and Chloe, you are the kids I have always dreamed of having and you are everything I have ever wanted, just as you are.

www.ingramcontent.com/pod-product-compliance
Lightning Source LLC
Chambersburg PA
CBHW020822180626
46814CB00001B/65